THE GILDED BOY

THE GILDED BOY

CONNOR MACHARG

MacHarg

Copyright © 2023 Connor MacHarg
All rights reserved.
ISBN: 9798218258351

DEDICATION

To my loving family and my wonderful girlfriend, whose love for reading prompted me to write. I love all of you and thank you for everything you have done for me.

Special Thanks

Thank you to all my high school senior teachers who may or may not have known that I was writing this instead of paying attention in class.

(This is sarcasm. I did pay attention, sometimes)

Table of Contents

1	The Boy and the City	1
2	Gladiator's Breakfast	18
3	To Find What's Lost	30
4	Eighty-Seven	41
5	The Legacy of a Father	53
6	Royal Memories	67
7	Earned Respect	77
8	Mission One	86
9	Brothers	95

10	Drunken Misplacing	120
11	The Trap	145
12	A Plot Against Hell	167
13	Revenge of a Son	201
14	New Roles	229
15	Recovery	246
16	The Passion of Sons	269
17	Chapter 17	292
18	A War for Peace	313
19	Handling the Dead	331
20	The Final Funeral	346
21	Discovery and Reconciliation	356
22	The Gilded Boy	376

1

THE BOY AND THE CITY

A city is a place of bustle and noise, but for a young mother, it was torment. The constant noise pounded in her head as she felt pain like no other. Her ragged clothes covered her distressed body as she prepared to have a child. She let out muffled screams but nothing too loud because it would attract people who could cause more pain than childbirth. Only a flower pod was hanging from its chains in the distance; it glowed blue-green through a glass case. No one was around her as she continued to contort in pain. It had now been 8 hours, and her body was getting weaker. Her energy was drained, but the child was nearly born. She sat in anguish for another hour before it was time for a new life to be introduced to the city. Then, as her child was born, she heaved one last breath of pain. She had given birth to a son, but her memory would be forever black as her body gave out once the child was born. Through her death, the city received a new life. Her body lay on the cold metal of a bustling city with nothing but soft flower pods to comfort a wailing child.

The city, Uguria, was on the planet of Carenth—the only world in its star's orbit. Carenth itself was a small planet with two small moons that orbited it. Uguria, or "the great city," was built in 87 different levels (with level 87 being the lowest), all in concentric rings stacked on one another. Each level was smaller than the one below it, with the bottom being larger than one could comprehend and the top being the size of a small town. Levels 1-10 were called the high city and possessed much of the city's wealth. Levels 11-35 were called the upper city. Levels 36-70 were called the central city. Levels 71-80 were called the dark city, and at the bottom, levels 81-87 were called the deep city.

On the edge of level 87, a massive wall around the whole city was erected to touch the sky. The roofs of every level's buildings were built into the foundations of the level above them. Most levels had simple homes or apartments for citizens. Some were industrial plants that processed metals or other resources, and some were made for pleasure and entertainment.

Within the levels, eight giant support beams ran through the entire city. They were built in an octagonal pattern with two beams in each cardinal direction. They were also close to the hollow center, so walking to them was easy if someone wanted to find them.

On every level, except for level 87, silver metal paths branched from the inside the level to the center of every level's circular shape, and they connected to a small circular walkway that went around the levitation platforms. These levitation platforms moved up and down the hollow center of the city, the only part that could bathe in starlight. The platforms themselves were silver metal with red and blue lights on its side. They never entirely stopped but would slow down as they approached different levels so people could get on or off. They had railings to guard against falling, but now and then, a drunkard would fall over them. And the walkway around them allowed citizens to walk to either side of their path. The flower pods hung from the bottom of these walkways and held various artificial plant life ranging from vines to flowers.

These flower pods were the only real nature Uguria had, and their light was brighter than the dim light from Carenth's star, Ades6-Beta, in many areas. Ades6-Beta's light never reached the bottom levels because of clouds, the layers above, and the wall around the city that reached the sky. Around level 40, the light started to fade. Any remaining light was swallowed by black clouds on level 71 and made everything below dark. But, once one went far enough toward the city's top, enough light poured from Ades6-Beta to light the levitation platforms.

However, there were places the platforms didn't reach-the deep city. The deep city had been abandoned because Uguria was losing its population, and it no longer needed the space. Because of this, no one cared for the levels' condition, and they turned into damp, dark areas that weren't appealing to anyone.

There were also giant loading docks every four levels (beginning at level 5) numbered 1-15, with 15 being the lowest. They were massive flat areas that replaced one branch of the path to the circular walkway. They were used for trade and the movement of other oversized items that may not fit into the bustle of the city. They were still close to the hollowed-out levitation platform's area, so the sides had a lethal drop.

In all of its beautiful infrastructure, the city looked orderly, but once one went far enough down, one would find it was anything but orderly. Crime and malice ran rampant. Every day was a struggle for those who lived in the lower levels. They had to fight for anything as simple as electricity, which was spread by level 9 to the entire city; however, the infrastructure carrying the electricity to the dark and deep city had collapsed. Because of this, any electricity on the lower levels came from personal generators. The levels all had, or used to have, essential lights built into the bottom side of the foundation above them, but these hardly lit their respective level's floors. But as the levels descended, the upkeep of the lights decreased drastically. However, the upper parts of the central city had installed stronger lights or actual streetlights to brighten the cold nights.

Water was another city-wide resource provided by the high city. A machine created it on level 7, and it pumped its artificial water throughout the city. The pipes it flowed from were in 3 of 8 support beams and ran water through the foundation of each level. Because it was such an important resource for the city's survival, these pipes were maintained from level 1 to level 87.

Food was just as vital, but it was individually generated. In most places, a food generator was programmed to make artificial meals or just ingredients if one wanted to cook. In the end, these machines made cooking not the obvious choice, so nearly every citizen depended on a machine. It would also wash all of its dishes.

The weather was also interesting in the city. During the day, the light would warm the city, but at nightfall, the city would become nearly freezing. Rain was also relatively common, but only during the night.

The city ran on its own unique currency, Ugurns, symbolized with Ʉ. Ugurns were all minted on metal coins by mints on level 6. The thicker coins were worth more, with the highest being worth 500 Ugurns. That coin had a picture of the city on one side, while the other had a massive 500. The remaining coins were all valued at either 1, 10, 15, 25, 50, or 100 Ugurns. They had the same picture of the city on one side and their value on the other. Those coins drove the city and made everyone move from their day-to-day tasks. Unfortunately, it also motivated crime and evil in the city, like the Berserker clan.

They lived on level 42, with their compound right off the platform walkway. There were alleys on either side of their compound, and a metal floor allowed regular people to walk around their compound; however, people tried to avoid it as much as possible. They were an aggressive group with warriors that would steal Ugurns from any target they saw fit. With arms like trees and legs like the mast of warships, they trampled anyone that dared stand against them.

The sword their leader possessed was, unbeknownst to them, sacred and powerful, and it was also said to be connected to the soul of its wielder. The blade itself was moderately short and slim with a slight curve and razor-sharp edges. The blade itself was draped in a beautiful flowing cover of thin, liquid gold. The hilt was enveloped in black leather with openings where more gold shone through.

It was believed its possessor carried great power, and the king and leader of the Berserkers, Helpar Caddel, had just that. He had stolen it from another group known as the Devil's Hand. Stories said he murdered a great warrior to steal his blade. The battle was one of the legends in the Berserker compound, and it had raised Helpar to the highest ranks of warriors. And it eventually led him to become a commanding king.

His voice boomed like the loudest thunder, and his command was unchallenged. But somehow, he found a soft spot for a crying baby on the floor. He had been out doing a weapons deal when he found a wailing child next to a dead mother. The umbilical cord was still attached, so he cut it. And as he did, a drop of the golden sword went into the newborn's blood, and a tint of red went into the blade. The child's vein shone gold for only a second, and it went unnoticed by Helpar and his crew, who was attending to the mother's body.

Helpar reached down and wiped the baby's forehead. He tried to rock the child and lull it to sleep but to no avail. "Should we name it?" a man from behind asked. Helpar turned to face the man who spoke and indifferently said, "I suppose." He looked the child up and down, saw it was a boy, and thought about an appropriate name.

"Magnus Aureum."

The man looked back, intrigued, and said with a question, "Aureum?" "Yes, Aureum," Helpar said confidently. The man shrugged it off, and the group went on their way. It was a strange choice for a last name, but Helpar had created it, and he wasn't a man to go back on his choices.

They left the mother and took the child to their compound, a massive, curved building that ran through level 42. It began with the king's room and a door that opened to the entire city. After one opened the massive double doors from the king's room, a large hallway with bedrooms and other storage places revealed itself. It was lit by faux candles that were just soft light bulbs. Finally, when one got near the end of the hallway, there was a massive doorway: the training room. It had massive wooden double doors with carvings of wildlife and trees. And when they were opened, they revealed an octagonal room made of wooden walls etched with the names of every fallen Berserker. Just on the left, another door led to the dining area, where a machine made artificial food for all the Berserkers to eat.

After Helpar returned, he took Magnus to be raised with the youths. This was a brutal process for the youths because once they got taken into the children's area, which was behind a door in the main training room, they rarely got to see their parents again. So, they never really developed relationships with their parents once they were taken. They all lived together until the age of sixteen.

In his time, Magnus learned to be a brutal warrior, but something never felt right; he was different. His hair was jet black, his skin darker than the other children, and his eyes were a deep green no other Berserker had, but he continued to train with the Berserkers, nonetheless. He has always hated being separated and wished he could be like the others.

So, one day, he asked Medya Lauriur, an elder in charge of leading the children's program, "Medya, why am I different from the rest of the children? I have trained and lived just like them and still feel different." She replied with a shallow, unfulfilling answer, "You are unique, Magnus; you could be something no one else could ever be for us." He scoffed at the answer and left her presence. As he did, he thought, *I want to be free from the talk of changing things within the Berserker walls and go out and actually change the city.*

This changing of the city is what he was taught the Berserkers did. He was taught that they were forces of good blessed to heal Uguria. They were some saviors that wanted to bring the dystopian city back to glory. Even though they were meant to help the city, he never felt like he actually wanted to be a Berserker. So, he continued to train with no real goal but to be the most potent warrior. He wanted to prove he was worth something to everyone around him.

While all the other children mastered the ax or the long sword, Magnus took after a blade similar to Helpar's, with a curved edge and a fine hilt, katana like. He had trouble with the weapons the others used, like Rechnal Caddel, Frory Kitry, and Treni Lauriur.

These three were the most prominent of the Berserker children, whose numbers were becoming increasingly thin due to Helpar. He had decided to make a new law after his son's birth that limited the number of children each couple could have; everyone could only have one child. He did this because he felt the clan was getting too large and that someone would try to overthrow him. He also thought a large clan would be too difficult for him to maintain control over if they didn't try to harm him. And though many tried to get him to change his mind, he never did. So, in the end, these three became the figureheads of what it meant to be a Berserker youth.

Rcchnal Caddel was Helpar's son and had the potential to be another great warrior like his father. He had dirty blonde hair, piercing blue eyes, and a stocky build like his father's.

Frory Kitry was a light-hearted boy, always trying to find the positive and make a joke in any situation. He had brown hair, brown eyes, and a similar stocky build.

Treni Lauriur, the daughter of Medya, was a beautiful young girl with light skin, perfect gray eyes, and dirty blonde hair that looked the slightest bit red in the right light. Her mother was once the greatest woman in the clan, so that legacy motivated Treni to become the most powerful woman she could be.

Magnus had always thought Treni was beautiful, but she was tangled up with Frory nowadays. Magnus was shy and a bit strange, so he didn't stand a chance anyway. However, it hadn't always been this way. She was best friends with him in her younger years before differences, and her mother's legacy pushed her into becoming a new person.

As kids, these two would run around with fake swords, mimicking the warriors they watched daily. They listened to stories and giggled at the jokes; all while being awed by the plot twists. They would even eat together at mealtime and share smiling faces. Many thought they would grow to become a great couple together, and even their childish brains believed it. They went as far as to say that they loved each other in their youthful bliss. But as they grew, they started to interact less and less simply because of their growing personality differences and motivations. Then day by day, their training began to look different. She was being trained to be a caretaker as much as a warrior while he was learning every piece of combat.

Because of time and the distance that drove the two apart, plenty changed as they both grew into teenagers. They were both 17 when they began seeing each other in more training sessions. Magnus tried to start a conversation with her on a couple of occasions; however, she didn't see him as she once did. Now she saw him as the odd boy that everyone else saw. She usually brushed him off and avoided him, but she wasn't able to avoid him forever.

Then, one day while she was training with a sword, he walked up to talk to her. His hands nervously fidgeted by his side as he approached her. She didn't give him a second glance and trained relentlessly. He finally reached her and said in a pleading tone, "Treni, we could still be friends; you know you don't have to forget about me completely."

She stopped swinging the blade at the target dummy and stepped towards him. She looked annoyed, put her sword away, and spoke without any care for him. She simply and bluntly spoke her mind.

"Magnus, you're different, and I wish I could have seen that as a kid. Not to mention I've gotten close with Frory, and I think he's a decent person.

He's funny too."

Her eyes turned dreamy, and she would have wandered into a daydream if she hadn't snapped herself out of it. She knew what Magnus really wanted, so she looked at him without a dreamy look and said, "But in your case, I don't think we're meant to be good friends anymore. It was good while it lasted, but we were just kids." He tried to keep his composure, "I get it, have fun with the rest of your training."

He couldn't look at her without hurting anymore, so he turned to go to his room. With his face dropped as he turned, he reached to push the training room door open, and his hand was shaking. He was devastated. He got into the hallway, and time felt as if it was frozen. The one person he thought actually cared about him in the whole compound didn't. The hallway felt longer than ever as he slowly returned to his room. He held back tears, but he was able to keep his form until he got to his room.

His shaking hand opened the door, and as it shut behind him, he lost it. He ran to his bed with an ornately carved frame and buried his face into the pillow. It muffled his sobbing, but it still faintly echoed through the room. Through heavy tears, he yelled, "You ruined the only thing you had!" He bashed his hands into the bedding, and his sobbing increased. His emotions were shocked, and the weight of everything broke him. He had hoped he could salvage the relationship he had because her beauty was still staggering to him. He wished he could hold on to some bit of happiness in his life, but he let it slip away.

He knew she meant what she said as he slowly, over the weeks, recovered, but he still needed to prove himself. His main motivator was to be as cold-hearted and powerful as possible. He also knew that people like Rechnal and Frory would always have the advantage, and he didn't really care about Rechnal, for he stood no chance against him. However, Frory was the only thing between him and Treni. Many nights he would sit alone in his bed wondering what he could do better, but deep down, he knew he would never beat Frory either.

So, he trained daily for a year, perfecting his abilities to impress anyone that saw him and, if he was lucky, another girl. But unfortunately, there weren't too many girls besides Treni. There weren't many children at all. It was always puzzling to him, but he never really thought of it. There were only 12 others and only one other girl besides Treni. She was the strange type anyway, and he never even knew her name. So, he was left alone to train with the boys around him.

Over time, he learned all the Berserker combat, but his strength was not enough. He was the agile type with quickness and little strength. But with the Berserkers relying on heavy blows and high power, it wasn't exactly a perfect match. On top of that, the others were always better than him. He was bested time after time and was becoming more and more frustrated with himself.

Then one day, after his 18th birthday, he was sparring with Rechnal, and Rechnal was taunting relentlessly. He hid his face behind a mask that resembled a bear. Magnus thought it would be annoying to fight with and that it looked stupid, but it wasn't his choice to make. And because of the taunting, Magnus snapped and tried to charge, but Rechnal used a simple yet effective Berserker combat move. He used what he called the whirlwind, spinning through the air and using his foot's blunt force to disarm his foe. He perfectly placed his kick, disarming Magnus and pushing him to the ground. He thudded down, dropped his sword, and crawled backward, but Rechnal walked to him, stood above him, and yelled, "That's another time I beat your sorry ass! You don't have what it takes to be one of us; just look at you! You don't even train with us anyway." "It's so I can improve, Rechnal," Magnus said as he turned to stand up. Mockingly, Rechnal snickered, "It's so I can improve." Then he lowered his tone, "Well, try improving more."

He spat on Magnus's face and left laughing with the others. Magnus was devastated and left the room, holding in tears. He had always had thoughts of running away, but this was the final straw. He wanted to leave but had nowhere to run. So, he started down the hallway, trying to reach his room as fast as he could. As he walked, his eyes started pouring tears, and he picked up his pace in hopes of avoiding anyone. It wasn't long before he reached what he thought was his own room, but because the watered eyes blurred his sight, he wandered into somewhere far different. He busted through the door expecting his room to be there, but instead, he found Helpar, sword in hand, executing a trespasser.

As the gilded blade glided through its victim, Helpar turned and saw him, and with a yell like that of the mightiest thunder, he yelled, "Get out, now!" His voice rumbled through the halls and Magnus's head as he turned to sprint away. Luckily, Helpar wasn't able to see who he was. But as Magnus turned to run, he got a glimpse of a pile of bodies strewn across the ground. All of them were mangled in some way, and it was terrifying to see. A good portion of them also belonged to the Ugurian police force. He then felt the chills of an evil he never knew existed in the place he called home. The people he was taught by and who helped raise him were not the people he thought.

He sprinted in pure fear back to his room. Lit by the faux torchlight, his shadow danced across the hallways. He finally reached his room and collapsed onto his sheets, and he tried to catch his breath. What he found haunted him as he tried to remember the details and prayed that he hadn't been identified. His mind was racing, but he was also tired from a long day. He figured Helpar would have found him by now if he had been recognized. So, he went to lie down with the presumption that he was safe for now. As he lay his weary head down, a final thought shot across his mind. *Why would they kill the ones they are trying to help?* He eventually shrugged the question off and slowly drifted to sleep.

He dreamt as he slept. And in the dream, he saw the gilded sword slice through a man's neck repeatedly, almost as if the sword was calling to him, begging to be used. In the dream, he also heard a voice he couldn't identify saying, "Run, run, run!" He shot up from his sleep, doused in sweat, and realized it was time to make a move. It was nearly morning when a surge of bravery he had never seen shot through him. He knew the building's layout, a simple right, down the long hallway, and he was out. But there was always one issue with ever trying to leave; he wasn't sure where he would go, but something told him it was time.

Another problem was that the only exit was through the king's room, where Helpar rested. Still, Magnus figured he could slip out quietly, so he put on his clothes and quietly left his room. He was ready to leave, but because of that dream, something about that sword was calling to him–an echo in his mind that he couldn't get rid of. And after seeing the horrors committed by its owner, he realized he needed to take the blade before he left.

He walked silently down the large hallway and heard the levitating platforms rising and lowering, the sound of freedom. He continued walking while looking at the eerie paintings as decor. Some portrayed battles, others sacrifice, and many other things. He finally reached the door to Helpar's room. It was made of pure oak with ivory handles, both materials nearly impossible to find in the city. Delicate carvings lined it, but he had no interest. He snuck into the room and saw Helpar asleep on his bed. But he also saw the blade, the gilded blade that was mounted on display above the bed. But that was not enough to stop him. He saw the magnificent nightstand and figured it was his way up. He used it to climb up to the bedside.

He lifted himself and stood up carefully. He reached out a hand to grab the sword, only to freeze as Helpar rolled in his slumber. His massive arm swung onto the nightstand and knocked into Magnus's legs as he was about to grab the hilt. Magnus's hand hit the sword as he fell, and he thudded onto the ground. The sword clattered across the floor with him. The loud jolt had woken the giant. Helpar sat up, confused, but he soon saw Magnus crawling across the floor to reach the sword. Enraged, he jumped from his bed and swung with hands that were like the paws of bears; luckily, the first blow missed by a finger-length. His swing had offset his groggy body, and he took time to reel back his arm. As he did this, Magnus finally grabbed the hilt. He felt a rush of boldness in his veins. It felt as if a missing piece of him had returned. He now stood facing Helpar, the only thing between him and his freedom. There was a metal door that could lock in between the room and the outside world, but Helpar slept with only a small ornate wooden door closed. He enjoyed the sound of the city outside at night because it helped lull him to sleep. So, Magnus knew all he had to do was get to it, and then he was out.

He looked toward the exit and spun the sword in his hand. The blade fit perfectly, and its movements felt like the wind. Helpar laughed at him, who looked like a child comparatively. He watched Magnus twirling the sword and cracked his battle-worn knuckles. Magnus stared him down until Helpar charged.

Each step shook the boards beneath them and, with it, Magnus's entire frame. Then with a movement swifter than Magnus knew he possessed, he dodged the first swing and swung the blade upwards. His aim was clinical, and the blade's edge streaked straight across Helpar's face—a gash from his left cheek to his right temple, nearly missing his eyes. It knocked Helpar back, and his hands shot to cover the wound. He roared in bitter rage, and Magnus knew this was his only window to escape.

He dashed for the door. He ripped it open to see the descending levels beneath him and the platform walkway in front of him. Through a blood-stained hand, Helpar yelled, "You, you scum!" Magnus had been frozen in fear and awe at the city until the screaming awoke him. And when he turned around, a bloody giant was running at him. Blood gushed from his face, and his eyes burned with hatred as Magnus leaped from the door. As he jumped, he heard Helpar cry, "Magnus!!"

He stumbled onto the walkway, and Helpar was close behind. He chased Magnus down the metal walkway. Magnus ran as fast as he could toward the center, where the platforms moved normally. Helpar tried to reach him and was hand-length away. But when he nearly grabbed him, Magnus jumped over a slowed descending platform and caught himself with one hand on an ascending platform's railing. He hung above the black drop to the bottom of the city. Helpar stopped on the walkway's edge and watched him fly through the air. He tried to run around the walkway to jump onto the slowed ascending platform Magnus hung from, but before he could get close, the platform sped up and left level 42.

"You won't survive! Not for long!" he roared into the night. He thought about continuing the chase, but the blood and pains from his face stopped him. He turned, enraged, and made his way back to the compound. He would find Magnus again and bring the force of the Berserkers.

Magnus tossed the sword onto the platform and pulled himself over the railing. He knew he would collide with the Berserkers again, but he was free for now. He was shocked to look around and see all the different lights and sounds the Berserkers had hidden him from. The cold metal of the levitators was a different sensation to him, and the rising showed other people with their doors and windows looking out onto the levitator pathway. He saw the flower pods and heard a distant conversation. And as he turned his gaze upward, hope overcame him for the new life he could now live.

2

GLADIATOR'S BREAKFAST

As Magnus rose on the levitators, he saw all sorts of different people: tall, short, big, and skinny. He saw different skin colors for the first time and realized he was right when he believed he belonged somewhere else. Children were playing on the edge, their bodies distorted by the flower pods he looked through. But the flower pods dimmed as Ades6-Beta's light began to shine brighter. He felt warmth from the light and nearly fainted in pure ecstasy. He knew no ordinary citizen went into the high city where the affluent bathed in starlight and drank by the gallon, so he hopped off the levitator at level 14 and walked into the upper level. Its light wasn't like the lower levels; it wasn't dull and lit by street signs advertising fortune tellers and mediocre food. Instead, he heard revelry as if these people had time to do other things besides survive. After the novelty wore off, he realized he was famished. He didn't have any Ugurns to pay for food, but he looked for something anyway.

He saw houses and people walking the streets carefree. He saw a sign with glowing lights pointing to a place named Hero's. It was a local spot that had did great business with local upper city Ugurians. He saw the building, which was shiny chrome with bright lights on the sides. He saw the line outside already forming for the morning rush. The smell coming from it was fantastic, and he would kill for a bite. He hoped he could get free food by sweet-talking the cashier. So, he hopped in line and started waiting. He waited for what felt like forever until he finally got to the counter, where a tall, burly man exclaimed, "Welcome to Hero's! What can I get you today?!"

Magnus stood flabbergasted at the man's excitement but quickly realized he had to choose. He scanned the menu boards for anything that looked good until he finally saw it. He put his hands on the counter confidently, "Can I have the Gladiator's Breakfast?" (Five eggs, three pancakes, six slices of bacon, four hashbrowns, and a large drink) "Sure thing," the man said. The man typed on some sort of calculator, "That'll be 18 Ugurns." The man waited for a payment and was surprised when Magnus started talking. His tone changed from confident to desperate, "I'm just a poor boy who needs food. I don't have any money, but I can pay you back. Please, can I have the food?" The cashier started to chuckle, "You're joking." Magnus nodded his head and hoped he could get lucky.

"Sorry, kid, but if you can't pay, I can't give you food," the cashier said.

"Come on," Magnus pleaded.

"I'm serious. If you can't pay, then get out of here."

Magnus could feel the glare from the people waiting behind him, but he needed food. He didn't know what to do, so he foolishly drew his sword. The people behind him flinched back, and the man put his hand on his hip. Then, he saw Magnus's arm shaking and the blade wobbling in his grip. He moved his hands back onto the counter and bellowed through laughter, "What are you gonna do with that, poke me?" All the customers laughed from their green diner seats as Magnus tried to look strong.

But one man in line didn't laugh, for he saw the weapon Magnus had drawn. He was tall, tan-skinned, and brown-cloaked, and he started making his way to the front of the line.

"I'll use it. I will," Magnus said while waving the sword around. All the people laughed again. "Sure, you will, kid," the waiter mocked. Magnus wasn't joking and went to swing the sword. The cashier ducked behind the counter and pulled out a knife from his side. However, as he swung, the tall, tan figure grabbed his hand and disarmed him. He then grabbed the blade from the counter and admired it. "Let me go!" Magnus said as he squirmed for freedom. The man tightened his grip and pulled him to the counter. He spoke in a low tone, "Excuse my friend here." He dropped a 15U and a 5U coin on the counter and walked away. The cashier stood shocked, but he had been paid, so he put his knife back, took the money, and put in the order.

Magnus still squirmed around, but the man held him tight. "Go back to your things," the man told the line behind him. The rest of the customers listened and returned to their normal day cautiously.

The man's cloak covered all but his scarred arms. They had slashes and brandings all across them, and Magnus asked shakily, "Who are you?"

"A man who's seen some things," he answered.

His tone was cold and emotionless. He sat Magnus down at a back table and brought out the blade. He held it in front of him and asked, "Where did you find this?" Magnus still sat shocked, and again the man demanded in a fierce whisper, "Where did you find this?!" Magnus stuttered and said in the most intimidating voice he could muster, "I found it." The man scoffed, "Sure, kid, sure, you just found one of the greatest weapons known." Magnus tried to hold his intimidating voice, but he couldn't and said shakily, "The gr-greatest weapon, what do you mean?"

The man looked around the room to make sure no one was eavesdropping on the conversation and whispered, "That blade is more than you could ever imagine. It has served powerful masters and led each to glory. It is said to have been crafted with the finest touch and that can cut any man to pieces. Its gold runs molten on the edges, and it's as old as the core that used to power all of Carenth." Magnus looked confused about what the man was talking about, but the man carried on, "Before the explosion that turned this world into a wasteland, gold was a rare and powerful metal. Now, it's even more so." The man noticed Magnus's confused look and attempted to explain, "The core powered the whole planet and gave us the energy to run the whole planet." Magnus now looked intrigued, "What happened to the core?"

The man looked with his cloak-covered face and said, "A worker in the core tried to warn all that it was doomed to fail. Very few listened, but he knew better than to give in, so he built a bunker to hide in; that bunker became the place this whole city was built on. He took his family and a few friends that believed him. They repopulated the planet and gave life anew, but that day seven hundred years ago ruined this whole planet. It's why we have this city, no nature, no mountains, no animals, only these metal sheets and blinding streetlights." His tone became more annoyed, "Not to mention those flower pods that try to make you feel like there's some life here besides our decrepit race."

Magnus tried to think of all the things the man was describing, but the Berserkers had held so much of the city back that he couldn't think of much. So, he let out a smirk in disbelief, "That's a bit harsh, isn't it? I mean, I was saved as a child. There has to be a little good out there." The man didn't raise his voice, but he raised his tone.

"No, boy, they only wanted to use you; look at these scars on my arms; look at these brands. They're all things this life gets you. Especially with that sword." Magnus was the slightest bit intimidated, but he still had more questions.

"You still haven't told me where the gold itself came from if the core blew up," he said, intrigued.

"Where the gold came from is uncertain, but it is more powerful than you know. Yet you use it like it's a measly dagger." Magnus was slightly offended and went on the defensive.

"I had no idea, but the sword used to belong to the Berserkers before I stole it. I felt connected to it once I saw it and stole it as I ran away."

"You were a Berserker?! They had the blade this whole time? How did they steal it from the Devil's Hand?!" the man yelled.

"Who is the Devil's Hand?" Magnus said with perked ears. The man knew he had said too much and tried to cover it up.

"No one, just a deep city group. Still, no one had heard of them since the sword was lost," he said nonchalantly.

"Who are they? What do they look like?" Magnus prodded.

"It's not important," the man said as he got up and swiftly left the diner.

Magnus sat shocked in his booth at the man's quick exit, but the waiter brought out his food. He devoured the meal while wondering who this "Devil's Hand" really was. But it didn't really bother him because of how great the food was. And once he finished his meal, he wiped his face and swiftly stood up to leave.

As he stood, he looked outside the diner's window, saw the bustling upper city life, and wondered what life up here meant. But he knew there was more information he had to find about the Devil Hand, and there wasn't time to appreciate the view. Then, he saw an ad for a new Ugurian history museum on a sign and knew it was an excellent place to start. He left the diner and walked to the museum. It was a long walk, and he saw the big houses and the extravagant living of the people on the upper level. He envied this lifestyle, but he knew this wasn't what he was called for. He was 18, and he knew he was a fighter.

When he finally got to the museum, he realized he was lucky enough to find out it was its grand opening, and it was accessible to all guests for free. He walked straight in and began to look for any sign of the city's criminal history. The building was massive, with huge rooms dedicated to each monumental event. It started with the core explosion, which told of the planet's devastation. He walked in and saw that it was a vague explanation that gave fewer answers than the cloaked man did. He moved on to other areas of the museum, and he saw pictures of animals that used to roam the planet, like the Truntoin, a massive mammal with four furry legs and an enormous body. Its skin was like the finest silk. Its face was the mix of a feline and reptile, with a cat's piercing eyes and a lizard's curiosity.

He kept moving into the deeper parts of the museum, looking for anything about the Devil's Hand. He then turned into a small room after seeing the Berserker crest, a bear's head severed by two crossed longswords. He walked in and saw another crest; one he had never seen. A red hand clenched over a curved and crooked horn. He looked under the crest and saw a small plaque that read *The Devil's Hand*. He looked at the description underneath that said the group used to reside on the lowest levels of the city in its early days, but years ago, they were lost after a great battle. The text ended there, and there were more questions than answers. He then went to ask a gentleman dressed in a white suit, who looked like an employee, about the exhibit he had just left.

"Sir is there anything more about the Devil's Hand?" he asked. The man looked down at him.

"The Devil's Hand is an extinct group that only zealots portrayed a false image of power. But the Hand used to reside in the deeper parts of the city. That is all I know, and a kid like you shouldn't be worried about extinct cults."

Magnus was disappointed, but he brushed the response off and went to leave. As he was leaving, he saw another room that caught his eye. It was near the museum's entrance, and he had run past it initially. It had a blue and green planet with the name written in blue cursive above that read Carenth. He went inside to look at all the other things around. He read about the vast planet that the Berserkers never even mentioned. Carenth used to be more beautiful than he had ever imagined. It was luscious with life besides just the human race. It was perfect, and the humans had ruined it. He saw pictures of massive and magnificent trees that reached the sky, but now all that reached the sky was the city's metal.

The next part showed the city's construction and the planet's nature, and it ratified the cloaked man's explanation. The original survivors of the core explosion survived because of a massive bunker. They had had a feeling something was wrong with the core from the start. They were called crazy by Carenthians and were laughed at for their beliefs. But in the end, they survived. The description said that the bunker possessed all the materials and goods they used to build the first levels of the city. The survivors ate authentic food stored in the bunker before artificial nutrition was invented. The city's scientists eventually made synthetic food, nature, and materials that were always different and could only attempt to mirror its origins.

At the same time, materials to make any sort of firearm were lost. The people in the bunker stocked most resources lost in the core explosion, but none saved the materials needed for firearms. The material was called ragupt, an already rare plant on Carenth that couldn't be replicated successfully. The potency of its explosion was lost in the synthetic version, so the city eventually turned to melee weapons as their defense source.

This bunker was the founding point of Uguria, but it had been lost with time. No one knew where the bunker was now, and most people didn't even know it ever existed.

He continued to read and learned initially that the people in the bunker tried burrowing down into the ground. However, the land wouldn't break to the human hand. Unlike many planets, Carenth was alive and felt the devastation the humans caused. It would not let the humans break her surface. So, the survivors decided to use what resources they had to build up to the sky.

His reading only taught him more about the planet's history. He learned that it was extremely dark until the builders broke the first cloud layer. These were the clouds that would permanently rest above level 71 and block all the light to the levels below.

Rain was the only thing that remained natural on the planet of Carenth. When the explosion occurred, most water evaporated. This left plenty of water in the sky to come down as rain. The water would then fill back up old rivers and lakes, and the rain cycle would continue. But the rest of the land was so damaged even the rain couldn't heal it.

Regardless, the city continued expanding upward, with the wealthy trying to move further from the slums forming on the lower levels. Once the people reached a layer of white clouds, they reached their limit, and they stopped building due to the other cloud layer. As soon as the people touched these seemingly harmless white clouds, they would instantly asphyxiate. There were chemicals in the clouds from the explosion, so these chemicals and the high altitude would lead to a lack of breathable air.

So limited on both sides by the ground and clouds, the city rested at 87 levels. The plaque also said that expansion to the side was nearly impossible as winds outside the city walls were unbearable. These winds had worsened over time since the explosion and caused the walls to be built higher. With all the issues cared for, the size of the city was set, and every problem the people had happened within its 87 levels.

After seeing all there was to see in the exhibit, he left the museum and realized the day was waning. He had never slept outside his old home, and fear and loneliness crept over him. He had nowhere to go, but he saw an old bench in an alley and decided it would be his bed for the rest of the night. He heard the quieter bustle of the nightlife and the buzz of neon signs drawing in customers. He sat awake while his mind raced and his body tried to get comfortable. He tried to drown the feelings of loneliness, and finally, his eyes began to close as his restlessness finally wore off. He dozed off and had another dream. This dream again had an unknown voice, and it repeatedly said the number 87.

Over and over, he heard 87, and when he finally woke, it was etched into his brain. He tried to think of what it meant until it struck him. *There are eighty-seven levels, and I know the deep city is dangerous. But what if that's what the dream is telling me?*

He sat for a moment to think of his options. He knew the Berserkers would be hunting for him, and it was a miracle that they hadn't already found him. So, his options were to stay and wait to be discovered or to find answers to his questions by descending into the city. He wasn't sure what he would find, but the dream assured him that level 87 had something waiting for him. He also knew it was the lowest level and that it was supposedly abandoned, but he was willing to go there to find what he needed.

So, he stood up, walked off his stiffness from the night before, and started his walk back to the levitation platforms. People never went as far down as he now intended, and he knew it had to be for a reason. For the certainty of uncertainty was guaranteed to anybody who dared venture down the city. He knew this and knew the future was uncertain, but he pressed on.

He walked toward the platforms with a facade of confidence until he stumbled into two lowly thieves. It was a typical crime for the upper levels; it was nothing as organized as the lower levels, but still enough to get one killed. "A boy ripe for robbin'," the first and bigger man said. The second, scrawny man lurked behind like a vulture.

Quickly, the first man drew his dagger, a cheap blade made of weak material. Magnus drew his blade in response, and as he did, he felt a sense of confidence and peace while holding it, but he still was afraid. He pointed it at the two to try to intimidate them. He tried to speak but couldn't get any words out because of the fear bounding through his veins. The two thieves backed away but soon charged confidently. The burly one swung his dagger, but Magnus swung the gilded blade as hard as he could, a bit ungracefully, and intercepted it.

The dagger flew from the man's hand and clattered across the ground. With the dagger out of reach, both the thieves saw the power of Magnus's swing and cowered in fear, thinking they had encountered a truly great warrior. Finally, the big man backed up with his hands in the air and said, "We're sorry; we never meant to challenge you." They both turned around and fled into an alleyway. Magnus's hand shook from the fight, but he was proud of his actions.

He stood silent and let the men run away before sheathing his weapon. He then picked up the dagger and saw the damage done by his gilded blade. His swing was so hard he almost cut the dagger in two. People stared for a stint until the mundane nature of their lives brought them back to their tasks. Street life continued as usual, and Magnus felt a new sense of power now that he had wielded the blade effectively.

He continued to walk until he saw the edge of the level before the walkway. The starlight shone in through the city's open top, and it was peaceful. The windows of various houses and buildings glimmered down at him in the daylight. He craved the peace from the upper city and wished he could stay to enjoy it, but then he looked down and saw the flower pods and the neon lights and knew that's where he was bound to go. He exhaled and walked onto the walkway. As he got to the circular part, a platform began to slow down, and multiple people were getting on and off.

He stood and watched it until an older man pushed through and said, "C'mon, move!" He jumped a little and shook himself from his trance. He stepped onto the platform, and it began to go down slowly. The light from the city turned from bright, welcoming daylight to a solemn blue-green as the flower pods became the only light. Signs flickered, and people chatted about various things. Each level was becoming darker than the one before it. Most people were off the platform by level 35, the upper city's official end. And after level 35, crime became a more nagging and ongoing issue. The lights continued to dim as less and less light shone down on the cold metal buildings. He knew nothing of what lay ahead of him and the journey he was embarking on, but he knew one thing, 87.

3

TO FIND WHAT'S LOST

Helpar watched as Magnus rose, and he felt the gash on his face. His hand was stained red, and he wiped it on his pants. He was wearing a green silk pajama set now stained with blood. He stormed back to the compound and said, "You piece of-!" But the door shut behind him as he finished yelling. He punched his bed frame and left a hole in the footboard. Medya, who was wandering around the hallway, heard the noise and quickly entered the room.

He was faced away from the doorway as she entered. "What's going on?" "He got away," he said furiously. She looked lost, "Who?" His voice shook with rage, "That little rat, Magnus. He slipped through my fingers with my sword." He turned to face her, and her face was shocked at the blood dripping from the gash. "Helpar, what is that?" she asked. He covered it back with his hand, "He gave it to me on his way out. It's nothing." "Are you sure?" she asked as she looked at the wound with great concern. He was impatient and yelled, "It's nothing! Call everyone to a council meeting! Now!"

The council was made of the finest warriors and a few of the wisest elders. He stormed from his room to head to the council room, and she followed close behind. "Helpar, you're dripping blood," she said, concerned. "I told you it was nothing. Now, wake everyone up!" he screamed.

She went room by room, waking up council members like Helpar's closest warriors, Gret Nilsin and Darian Hourt. Both were decorated in combat and were Helpar's right-hand men. They were as tall as Helpar, but unlike Helpar's red, Gret had long blonde hair that was pulled neatly into a bun. His beard also grew to great lengths, long enough to have little braids coiled inside of it. Darian had shorter brown hair and a well-kept beard. He kept it shorter because he believed long hair was a disadvantage in combat.

They all slowly rose from their beds and went towards the council room. Their groggy eyes shot alert when they saw Helpar's blood-stained face. Gret was the first to voice himself, "Helpar, what happened to you?" His voice was full of concern, and he walked over to help; Darian wasn't far behind. Helpar saw his friends approaching and soon shunned them away, "It is nothing! Both of you take your seats!" The two immediately listened and went to their place at the council table. The rest of the council sat down at their seats and started to yell out, questioning the new wound. As the noise of talking and asking peaked, Helpar raised his hand to silence them. They all fell quiet and gave him their attention. He looked over the council and said, "As all of you can see, I was wounded. Not by a worthy foe but by a defective child who had the audacity to attack me in my sleep. That little rat of a boy, Magnus. We took him in, and he betrayed us!"

Berserkers were many things, but loyalty was held in their highest respect. Their bodies shifted uncomfortably at the thought of a defector. Helpar continued, "He moved in while I slept to take my sword and used it to leave this mark on my face. By the time I could react, he had already jumped to a platform. Though he escaped my hand, he will not escape again!" Mumbling rumbled over the group but was soon silenced as he continued, "We will send out people to find him; if you find him, bring him back alive. Now I ask for volunteers to go find the defect."

He ended his speech and quickly sat down. As he sat, he motioned his hand, and a doctor came in to tend his wounds. "Sit still while I clean you up," the doctor said. He grunted in pain. The doctor finished looking at the wound and whispered, "It doesn't seem too deep, so you won't need any stitching. But it will leave a mark." The rest of the room sat and watched quietly until the doctor finished the bandage. It wrapped around his head and nose but left one eye and the mouth uncovered. The doctor finished his work and said, "You need rest, Helpar, so don't go out there."

As the doctor packed his bags, Helpar glared at him but nodded. He wanted to go out and find Magnus, but he could tell the gash was severe enough to hold him back. He went to speak again to break the silence. He addressed the group, "So, who of you will go and find Magnus?" Gret and Darian raised their hands quickly while the rest of the room stayed quiet. He smirked a bit, "Well, I know who is loyal to me." Four others raised their hands out of guilt. He looked around and believed he had enough manpower to track Magnus. "The rest of you may leave," he told the council. They all left, and the door shut behind them.

He addressed the remaining group, "Magnus went on an ascending platform, so you four go to levels one through twenty-one and thirty-one through forty-two, and you two get twenty-two through thirty. I won't be joining you, but I wish you the best of luck." The instructions were clear and concise. They all shot up from their seats and went for the door. Helpar was the last to leave the room, and he shut the door behind him.

Gret walked to the edge of the circular walkway and looked up and down at the massive city. The rest of the crew was standing behind him, waiting to get on their platform. He said, "Well, go find him. It's only a kid. The worst he can do is slip away from us and die somewhere else in this place." The others all chuckled in agreement. The group jumped onto the platform, and it accelerated shortly after. Darian and Gret got off at level 22. "See you, boys, later. Meet back at the compound at dusk. Good luck," Gret said. The other men nodded, and the platform carried the next four up to their respective levels.

"Should we split up and cover more ground?" Darian asked as he walked. Gret pondered for a moment and then said, "Well, that does sound smart. I'll go down one. If something happens, just run back here. At the end of the day, it's only a kid." Darian smirked and walked into level 22. "I'll meet you on level twenty-three," he said as he walked off. Gret walked to the other side of the circular walkway and descended to level 23. Level 22 was a regular level like the ten above it. Floors 12-22 were all higher-class residential areas with large houses and a well-kept environment.

Level 23, however, was full of bars, shops, restaurants, and casinos for people in the upper class to enjoy. The level's streets were lit with street signs trying to attract customers. All types of people would come here, and it was one of the happiest levels in the entire city. There were places like Higurn's, the best place to get a craft drink and a good bite, or Frothy's, the best place to get a milkshake. All the food items were artificially crafted, but the people didn't know any better. There was also the famous Itwit's casino. Many men and women made or lost their money in its walls. Gret even walked in to play a hand. He walked to the counter and said, "I feel good; give me 50 Ugurns worth." He put a 50U coin on the table. The dealer gave out the chips, and he sat in the casino playing cards. Eventually, he ran out of money and cursed as he exited.

Defeated, he kept walking around the level. He thought a young boy would love the level's entertainment, so he was confident he would find Magnus. He quickly skimmed the level, asking for a black-haired boy in clothes like his—a pair of trousers and a tunic with a heavy fur overcoat. None of the people gave him any hints, and the flashing signs and sounds of level 23 left him empty-handed. *You think a kid would come here, wouldn't you?* he thought as he reached the end of the entertainment strip.

Darian's search was just the same. He walked in between large houses with multiple stories and large windows. All of them were painted off-white with blue window frames, and they were all two stories. They had black rooftops, which didn't do much since the level above already covered them. He went down the street, usually lit by bulbs that would imitate daylight, but now, they were faded to represent the night. No one was out on the road, so he turned around to look for someone to ask. There was no one to be found, so he decided there was nothing and turned to go back to meet with Gret. The two met back on level 23 and did more searching. They worked all night tirelessly, but in the end, found nothing about the runaway.

As they searched, the others moved towards the even more luxurious upper levels. One man said, "Well, none of us have to go to levels one through ten. The boy wouldn't go there anyway. So, I'll go to level eleven, and you all can divide the rest." He walked into level 11 as the other men went to the different levels. Levels 11-19 were also all residential but had grocery stores and everyday commodities. In addition, there were public pools and gyms for everyone to use. The houses were all massive, with three stories and arched front doors. They were painted a light gray with white window shutters. All the front doors were ornate glass pieces protected by metal bars. They were all quiet except one with the lights turned on, located on level 14. The Berserker walked up to the door and knocked. It cracked open with a well-dressed man behind it. "What do you want?" the homeowner said. The Berserker asked, "Have you seen a young boy with black hair in similar clothes?" The homeowner looked confused at the question, "No, I haven't, but good luck."

He shut the door and turned off the light inside. The Berserker walked away from the house disappointed. He turned his head and saw a chrome diner filled with people and a sign above that read Hero's. There was a line to get in, and he figured a runaway wouldn't stop to wait that long. He shrugged and returned to the platforms to begin the rest of his day of searching.

* * *

As his men left, Helpar went to where his son, Rechnal, slept to tell him about the evening's events. Rechnal was becoming of the age where he was curious about his father's doings, and Helpar wanted to teach his son about running the clan that would one day be his. He knocked and opened the door to Rechnal's room. "Son?" he asked. Rechnal shifted in his bed and opened his eyes slowly. He was annoyed until he looked at the bandage in his dad's eyes and immediately became interested. "What happened to you?" he asked. Helpar sat down at the foot of the bed and said, "I was coming in here to talk to you, actually." The bed creaked under his weight. He asked, "You know that Magnus boy, right?" Rechnal responded nonchalantly, obviously focused on why his father's face was wrapped in a bandage, "Well yeah, I trained with him sometimes. He is kinda weird, though. He wasn't good at fighting, either. He was so fun to pick on too. What about him?"

Helpar pointed to his face, "He's the one that did this." Rechnal looked at his father in disbelief, "Him? How'd he ever get to you?" He seemed to doubt his father's skill, and a look of questioning concern entered his eyes. Helpar noticed and felt the need to explain himself.

"It was while I was sleeping. He came in, stole my sword, did this, then left."

"Did you at least make it a challenge for him?" Rechnal asked.

"I was asleep, son; by the time I was fully awake, I was already wounded," he answered.

"Well, you're okay right?" Rechnal worriedly said.

Helpar responded, "Yeah, I'll be fine. I came here to talk to you about how I handled the situation since you're coming of age to know these things."

Helpar ended in a serious tone, and Rechnal sat up to sit with his father. His clothing was a cool blue made of silk-like his father's. He sat attentively and looked directly to hear his idol. Helpar had always been a role model to him, and now that he was nearing 18, he wanted to be just as bold as he was. Helpar took a deep breath and started, "Well, the first thing I did was call a council meeting because I never do anything rash without advice." Rechnal nodded in understanding. He continued, "Then, with the council, we decided it best to try to find Magnus. So, I sent six, including Darian and Gret, to find him. If they don't, we don't want to punish them harshly. Why is that?" "Because the task you're asking them to do is nearly impossible?" Rechnal answered.

"Well done, my boy," Helpar smiled and patted him on the back. He looked at his son, who was smiling up at him, and said, "Well, I'll let you know if they bring him back, and you can have the honor of punishing him if you'd like." Betrayal earned the death penalty for Berserkers and was usually done by decapitation. Rechnal smirked, "I'd love to. He always annoyed me anyway. Why does he not train or talk with us? He said it was to improve, but I beat him anyway. If he returns, I'd love to finally put him in his place." Helpar smiled again at his son, "That's the attitude a true Berserker leader needs, no mercy. I'm returning to the medical bay to ensure this bandage is on correctly because it feels like it's slipping. See you later." He walked from the room and shut the door.

He got to the medical area and walked into the doctor, who was asleep in his chair. "Hey!" he clapped, and the doctor shot awake, "Is this thing right?" Dazed, the doctor said, "Um, let me check." He straightened himself and went to check the bandage. He felt the wrapping move slightly, "Well, it's a bit loose, so I'll change it." He took his bag and pulled out more wrap. The old one was stained with blood and came off to reveal the wound. The doctor saw it and analyzed it. "Well, the bleeding has stopped, so you're already headed in the right direction," he said. "Great to hear, but just patch me up," Helpar commanded. "Yessir." The doctor carefully wrapped Helpar up. It took a while, but when the doctor finished, he said, "You're all good." "Thank you," Helpar said as he got up and left to head back to his room for some rest.

* * *

Rechnal got up after the conversation and changed into more casual clothes. He was going to tell Frory about the events of that early morning. He walked to the training room where Frory always was. "Frory, Frory!" he yelled. Frory looked annoyed, "What?" Rechnal answered with a jeering smile, "You know Magnus?" Frory looked disgusted, "That interesting kid?" He spun a sword in his hand and cut through a wooden target. Rechnal was still smiling.

"He's gone."

"Did he just leave or something? What do you mean gone?" Frory questioned.

"He left. He ran away, and we don't have to deal with him again," Rechnal said with his eyes growing wider.

"You're serious?" Frory said as a smile started to form on his face. Rechnal's smile was fading, but he was still quite happy.

"Yeah, he's gone."

"Took him long enough," Frory said coldly. He finally lowered his sword and smiled. He had another idea come to his mind.

"You know what that means, right?"

"What?" Rechnal wondered.

"Treni is mine now. You know Magnus was close to her when we were kids, and I think he still had something for her. Too bad I'm just better." He jokingly flexed his arms. "She's all mine now," he said again. Both smiled at each other.

Rechnal joked, "Alright, I just figured you should know that your love interest is safe now."

The two laughed with each other for a while. Then Rechnal slowly stopped laughing and said, "Well, I have to do some things. I'll be back." He started walking back to his room to fully prepare for the day. As he turned his back to wave goodbye, Frory spoke across the room, "As if it was in danger anyway." Rechnal shook his head, smiled at his friend, and walked from the training room.

* * *

The day passed as usual, with training sessions and other daily activities. It wasn't until that evening when the men sent out to find Magnus returned. Gret and Darian arrived first, with the second group not far behind. Once they all got there, they opened the main door with their key, but this time, Helpar had shut the metal door between the king's chamber and the city. So, after using their keys to open the main entrance, they knocked on the metal door. The clatter woke Helpar up. He had a throbbing headache from the wound but stood up slowly to get to the door. "Gret, Darian, that you?" he bellowed. "Yes, it is," Darian said. The door muffled their voices, but Helpar recognized his friend's voice.

He unlocked the latch on the door and pulled it open. "Welcome back." His voice was drained, and his body weak, but he continued, "Did you find Magnus?" The group was initially timid, but after a moment, Gret said, "We didn't find him, Helpar." Helpar's one eye glared at the men in the doorway. Gret defended their case, saying, "He'll probably die out there anyway. This city isn't going to help a kid like him. He's too scared to do anything. I think we're okay." Helpar raised his left arm to Gret's right shoulder and rested it there. He looked into Gret's eyes with his one uncovered eye and said, "I appreciate the honesty, but I do have to do something to punish you all." "What are you-"

Gret was cut off as Helpar used his left hand to punch through the chest of one of the others. The man grunted and fell over before being caught by another. The men's faces were shocked by the rash hit, but, as Berserkers, they respected the actions of their king. Helpar looked at Gret and said, "You had a hard job, and I didn't want to punish you harshly, but people need to know what happens if things can't get done. Go back to your rooms and get rest. Thank you for your effort." The men returned to their rooms without a word, and Helpar locked the metal door behind them.

After all the men had left, Helpar talked to himself before laying his head back down, "I do know one thing though, if Magnus ever steps foot near a Berserker again, that boy will die." Even his whisper was chilling, and the anger stirring inside him over a mere boy was more than he could have imagined.

4

EIGHTY-SEVEN

Magnus was dropping down, and then he realized a familiarity with the levels. As he passed level 42, he saw the very door he leaped from one long day ago. The door had a warning written in an ancient language that he had never seen before, but he knew what it meant: *TO DEATH*. It was a sign for anyone who walked through those doors. His bones ran cold as he passed further down.

As he reached level 65, the flower pods began to look more and more derelict. They hadn't been cared for; most were shattered glass domes with dead plants inside. The starlight fully abandoned him as he passed through the clouds on level 71. Now left with dim neon signs and the warmth of a few other bodies on the platform, he descended.

As the platform continued its descent, more and more people got off and walked into the dark. It stopped at level 80, for no one ever desired to go deeper, nor did anyone sane live there. The only light from down this low was the light of strip clubs and bars, both ways for the people of the dark city to numb their pain. He saw the dilapidated nature of the levels and raised his hood to protect his face. He turned down an alley on his left to explore. It was also much colder without natural light to warm the inhabitants of the lowest levels, so he shivered as he walked. Then a shriveled, old lady in dark clothing with a crazy sparkle in her eyes approached him, saying, "My magic will tell all. My price is not too tall." Her wrinkled fingers and frail frame scared him, and he quickly moved past her.

He kept his head down and kept looking for a way down to level 87. He walked steadily with the intoxicating smell of sweat crowding his nostrils. The air was thick and felt as heavy as the guilt on the people's souls that were there. For their actions must have been atrocious for them to allow themselves to live here. As he turned to another alley, he ran into an average-looking man, but when the man removed his hood, he saw a face with no eyes to look into. Where the eyes should have been, botched flesh waited. Magnus screamed and took off in a sprint as far as he could from the man who had never even said a word. *You're gonna get yourself killed if you keep going that way*, he thought through harsh breaths.

But with a stroke of luck, he ran toward what looked like an elevator. It was rough, to say the least, but he knew it could be a way down, so he walked over. The elevator was an old one used by the people of Uguria before the city built itself up to the massive height it was now. There was a figure sitting on a stool in front of it with a small light dangling from the ceiling above him.

Only four others were there, but none tried to get on the elevator. As he got closer, he saw the man's skin was bronze, and his frame was stoic. He approached the man until he stood up and froze Magnus in fear. The man said nothing and stepped toward him. Magnus stepped back and, in a false-calm voice, said, "Eighty-seven." The man stared at him for a minute before chuckling. The man sneered as he opened the creaky door. The other people looked at him strangely, as if his request was taboo. He stepped into the elevator, pressed a faded button that said 87, and the doors closed. It slowly started moving down until he felt it smack into the ground.

The door opened with a creak, and he saw nothing but black ahead of him. Cautiously, he stepped into the dark, heard the door shut, and the elevator left him behind. He pulled from his waist a portable torch all the Berserkers were given and struck it alight on the ground. As the fire brightened, he realized the absolute quiet he was in. Fear began to creep its way into his body, and he wondered if any life existed this far down. He wandered around while the torch lit the walls, and faint inscriptions could be made out. Then his torch lit the floor around him, and he stood frozen as he saw stains. He looked further down and saw no circular walkway on this level like the rest. Where the platform would be, the metal floor he was standing on extended. He thought he saw a massive hole in the center of the ground, but it was too far for him to make it out. He figured it wasn't important and turned back to the structures around him.

He held the torch up and saw marks on the walls and realized the patterns on the wall weren't writing but sword slashes. He turned back to face the elevator before he heard movement from the darkness in what seemed like all directions. Something was wrong here, and he felt his heart drop. He screamed, "Help, Help, Help me, please! I don't want to be here; I want to go home!" He turned in desperate fear to see men clad in black with their eyes sharp enough to pierce the soul focused on him. "Who are you?" they demanded. Magnus was shaking and forgot to even draw his sword.

"I-I am Magnus. I mean no trouble," he said shakily.

"We have no interest in what you want; if you came this far, you know something, and either you're our blood or more blood to be spilled," one said.

"What do you mean blood to be spi-."

Before he finished, Magnus was knocked out by the hilt of a blade. The warriors in black carried his limp body through a small red door and disappeared. He woke without his clothes and his weapon confiscated. Black straps strapped his wrists and ankles to a chair where medical supplies lay around him. He shook his arms and asked frantically, "Where am I?! Who are you?! Where are my things?!"

Then a man, who appeared to be a doctor, said from behind him, "None of that matters now. What you should concern yourself with is if you live after I'm through with you. If your blood does not align with ours, then you will be tossed back into the black as prey for our finest warrior to hunt." Magnus shook his bonds in vain. "Sit still, boy!" the doctor yelled before slapping him across the face. The doctor forced a needle through Magnus's skin and into his arm. A bag attached to the syringe filled with his blood, and it was a scarlet red with an ever-slight gold taint. The doctor removed the needle and grabbed the bag. "Pray you are one of us," he said ominously as he walked out. Magnus was stunned at how quickly everything had happened, and his mind started to race. *Blood to be spilled? I'm going to die here,* he thought. His only option was to try and free himself.

He tried to loosen his bonds, only for more of the men to come into the room and take him from the chair. They brought him into a brightly lit interrogation room where a man sat stoically. Once Magnus got close enough to see the man clearer, he realized it was the same person he had met in that diner. "You, how did you? You were with them the whole time?" Magnus asked as his escort shoved him down into a chair. The man's tone was monotone and commanding as he said, "Yes, I am. Now, have a seat."

The man looked up, and Magnus saw his eyes for the first time, gold and shocking. He needed to know more about what was happening.

"How did you find me in the upper city? Why didn't you bring me here all along?" He asked desperately. The man adjusted his posture.

"I am the watchman of the sword. I cannot take it, nor can I truly wield it, but its power is strong enough for me to sense when a new owner has picked it up. I tried to talk you into giving me the sword until I made a mistake in my words and mentioned the Devil's Hand."

"How did you become the watchman?" Magnus asked. The other man straightened himself again.

"It was a long time ago. I was a young boy like yourself, and I saw the sword in the main training area. I was interested and picked it up. I felt a strange feeling and, suddenly, became aware of its presence. Then, the king at the time yelled at me and took his weapon back. I don't know why the sword chose me to do this, but here I am."

He paused for a moment and asked, "Now, tell me about your mother." Magnus was quick to respond.

"I never knew her; the stories I was told let me know she died while giving birth to me. But I don't even know her name."

The man figured he was telling the truth and relented his questioning. Then, the doctor came back into the room and whispered something into the man's ear. He nodded and turned back to Magnus. He extended his hand and said, "Welcome, fallen angel." Magnus was taken aback and wasn't sure what the best thing to do was. The man extended his hand further until Magnus finally reached to meet it. As the two shook hands, the man said, "I'm Ghuri, and I'm proud to say that you are now one of us, Magnus. Welcome to the Devil's Hand." Magnus still wasn't sure what to make of it all, and he didn't have any extra time before the doctor said, "Follow me; I'll escort you to your room." Magnus looked up, confused, "My room? I have a room?" The doctor ushered him forward and escorted him out. They turned right, and he saw giant red doors with torches on either side. They were shut, so the doctor opened them carefully and quietly.

"Do not speak or look at him."

"Who?" Magnus asked.

"Quiet!" the doctor snapped.

Magnus shut his lips and followed close behind the doctor. Once the doors opened, he saw a giant room that seemed to be vacant. There were guards inside, but they didn't seem to protect anything.

He didn't realize he was staring until the doctor grabbed his hand. "Move," he said, grabbing Magnus's arm and taking him to the left. There were halls on each side that were draped in red. He got glimpses through doorways of warriors training. Their bodies moved like birds, and their strikes were like meteors. He watched in awe at these fine warriors, but the doctor ushered him on. He finally arrived at his room, and the doctor bowed as he entered.

The room was lavish, with a full bathroom and all other possible accommodations. He walked over to his king-size bed and saw his new clothes freshly folded. They were a crisp white set of ninja armor, complete with a mask. It had a note that read *for the finest*. He was overwhelmed as he had never had all these things before. But his revelry was cut short when, immediately, someone told him to put on his clothes and to be ready for combat. He scrambled to get his clothes on, but then a gold glare caught his eye. He knew what it was and rushed to grab it. He sheathed his sword and continued changing.

After he finished, he walked into the hallway, with dark oak walls and floors draped in red carpets. Lightbulbs were used in most of the compound except for in the main entrance hall to prevent fires. The lights still gave off the appearance of a flame without the real threat a flame brings. He followed the trainer into a large training room. The equipment was excellent, with dummies and dull blades to protect the students. The students leaped about, spinning through the air, and their movement was smoother than silk. He saw methods the Berserkers never used. Because the Berserkers were brutal and taught the young that only power and strength prevailed, not technical ability. Once he entered the room, all the students stopped and turned to face another warrior dressed in purple.

They were dressed in all colors according to their mastery. White was the lowest, followed by green, yellow, orange, and black. He spoke to Magnus in a short and harsh tone, "Welcome to the training room. May your skills be heightened here." The teacher then turned around and walked back to his students to begin their training. "Get in line," the teacher yelled. So, in fear, Magnus fell in line and began training with the others.

With his blade in hand, he felt more confident and was able to complete basic-level training. He continued training, and the other students encouraged him instead of the bullying he was used to. They lifted him up, and slowly his combat improved.

After a week of his initial training, he was following the doctor around the compound. He led him to a sauna that, according to legend, cleaned the souls of the clan's members once they devoted themselves. That's at least what the writings on the stone outside it read. The doctor stopped in front of the sauna door and said, "When you're ready, you will spend a minimum of thirty minutes in this chamber, and any time after that is up to you. Also, if you lose consciousness at any point before the half-hour, you would be tossed back to the elevator and spared. But if you were to tell the location of the compound, you would be killed."

The threat echoed in Magnus's mind until the doctor's voice woke him from his trance.

"But if you remain awake through it all, you will be considered worthy enough to meet the leader and become a fine warrior."

Magnus was excited at the chance to prove himself, so he reached for the handle to go inside. However, the doctor struck his hand and said, "You are not ready to enter that room; only the strongest of us go in there." He ushered Magnus to continue, and the two walked away. He intended to deliver Magnus to the weapons room and turned to face him, only to find he was gone. Magnus was sprinting through the hallway towards the room he was shunned from. He craved to belong like he never could with the Berserkers, so he was going to prove he belonged here. He ran past others, who looked confused, but finally, he got to the door and pulled it open. The room was not hot yet, and he stepped inside curiously. As the door slammed shut behind him and made a locking sound. Then, the light turned off, and he felt the heat. At this point, any regret would be in vain.

There was a clock inside the room to tell whomever how much longer they had to endure. A switch near it could be pulled after half an hour, and the room would cool down. But flipping the switch was voluntary, and the subject could pull when they wanted. He also saw an arm wrap connected to wires dangling from the ceiling. He assumed he should put it on, and when he did, it started beating with his heart. This device monitored his heart rate and would stop the heat if it noticed the heart rate decreasing too much.

After some frantic searching, the doctor walked to the room, saw the door shut, pulled on it, and felt it was locked. "Magnus! Magnus!" he pounded on the door to find no response. Magnus was already enveloped in steam and heat and didn't want to waste his energy answering the doctor.

The doctor's pounding echoed through the room, but he sat calmly, breathing breaths of pure heat. He was going to prove that he was significant and that he could become greater than even he thought he could.

The room was miserably hot, but he fought and fought. He felt his eyes close multiple times but would not give in. On top of the heat, the room was also pitch black, so he could only feel how blistering it was. He felt his lungs get heavy, and his body wanted to give up, but he persisted. After a while, the steam in the room made it impossible to see the clock anymore, and he could not last any longer. Finally, he dragged his sweaty body to the switch and pulled it, hoping he had lasted long enough. The door popped open, and he crawled out of the chamber and fell onto the ground. The doctor looked shocked, but there wasn't enough time for Magnus to notice his expression before he passed out.

He awoke to the smell of fine spices and heard, "Magnus, you lasted more than two hours inside the room that has killed men in far less than that. You have something extraordinary. It's time for you to meet the king. Stay here." The doctor ran down the hallway. Magnus was wondering where the doctor went when he heard footsteps. He saw the doctor, followed by a group of large men. He was scared and tried to back up. "Don't be scared, Magnus!" the doctor yelled down the hallway. He still tried to back up. "They're your escort to the king," the doctor said. He finally stopped retreating. It was time for him to meet the king.

The guards, all wearing blue robes with the crest embroidered into the right arms, escorted him. They all carried glaives and didn't speak. They walked to the same massive double doors Magnus was ordered to quietly pass through earlier. They pulled them open, and they all walked in a wedge in front of Magnus, blocking his view. They walked into a massive chamber with luscious paintings and fine wooden floors. They continued to walk in front of Magnus, but the room continued to impress. A giant tapestry hanging from the ceiling depicted a great battle with warriors like the ones in front of him protecting a man in red. Then, the guard fanned out to reveal a throne on top of an obsidian stairway that was glistening spectacularly. Made of stone, the throne rose above everyone. It was carved with ancient writings that Magnus couldn't make out, and its armrests were the size of his entire body.

The chair emitted power and brilliance across the room, and he stood in shock. The guards then, in unison, pounded the glaives into the floor and said, "Your majesty." The room fell silent, and Magnus stood in the center of it. Then the largest of the guards pounded his weapon into the ground again and yelled, "Kneel!" In fear, Magnus obeyed. The king spoke without raising his head, "Welcome, your blood has led you here, and now I must know, who are your parents?" Still frozen, Magnus sat silent until the guard hit the ground again and yelled, "Speak!"

"She died in childbirth. I never got to know her. I never knew my father," Magnus stuttered.

"Then how are you one of us? Have you fooled us and snuck into our ranks? Who are you, boy?" the king drilled.

In a quick, fearful tone, he answered, "I am Magnus Aureum, your excellency, and I am honored to be in your presence." At this moment, the king noticed the blade hanging from Magnus's side. Its golden hue shone faintly through its sheath, and his voice dropped.

"Where did you find that blade?" he asked.

"I stole it from the Berserker king, your majesty. I have no idea where he stole it from," Magnus replied. The king's tone changed to indicate he was impressed at the boy sitting in front of him.

"Well, young Magnus, that sword looks like the one that belonged to my father and to me before I foolishly lost it. But that is nothing new, as clearly, you have earned it."

"It belonged to you? Let me return it," Magnus said eagerly.

"No, Magnus, that sword belongs to you now. Its power doesn't belong with me anymore," the king said with a tint of pain in his voice. There was silence until the king used a lighter yet still authoritative tone.

"Now, to introduce myself, I am King Patri Tecorian, and I'm in charge of the Devil's Hand. Now raise your head so I can see my newest warrior."

They both raised their heads, and as Patri removed his royal hood from his head, Magnus saw a miracle. He looked upon the king's face, and though he saw the years of stress and turmoil in the king's face, a pair of astounding green eyes met his own. He saw the eyes he had only seen in himself now staring back at him.

5

LEGACY OF A FATHER

Magnus was in shock, but Patri was unfazed. He then ushered the doctor and whispered something incoherent to him. The doctor shuffled off, and Patri rose from his elevated seat. He stood with a slight hunch that told of wear on a once young body. His hair flowed gray, and his face was worn, but wrinkles had not fully overcome it. The guards immediately went down to their knees and bowed to their king. He looked down at Magnus and said, "Come, sit with me."

Next, he looked at his guards and said, "You can leave now. I'd rather be by myself." He had never liked having guards around him all the time, so most of the time, he was alone in his massive chamber.

He led Magnus towards an elegant table engulfed by foods of all sorts. It was on the room's right side and surrounded by portraits from the past. There were foods Magnus had never seen or dreamed of sitting on the table. Fruits from exotic trees that he never got from the machine at the Berserker compound. Meats that smelled of heaven and were cooked to perfection. He was awestruck while he looked at more food than he had ever seen in his life. Patri sat down at the head of the table and told him, "Please join me; I can't eat all this alone." Magnus shook off his glossy gaze at the table and said, "Yes sir, I'm sorry your majesty." "No need to apologize. Please enjoy," Patri reassured. "As much as I want?" Magnus asked in disbelief. As a Berserker, he was provided his portion, no more or less, so seeing all the food on the table shocked him. He still couldn't believe he could eat as much of this as he pleased.

Patri smiled back at him, "Yes, as much as you want." Magnus took his plate and filled it with every morsel he could fit.

Patri scoffed before he took his first bite and said, "Don't be too excited. The food comes from a machine just like everywhere else in the city, but ours is a bit older, so it has recipes newer models don't. But some of these fruits you see are grown in my garden." Magnus looked up with food in his mouth.

"There's a garden? Where is it?"

Patri chuckled again, "That's information for those with more training and reputation than you, so please eat."

"But I thought all the food in the city was artificial?" Magnus asked.

Patri laughed and said, "It is, but this fruit is something special only we get to experience, so enjoy."

Magnus finally listened and stuffed his mouth with as much as he could. And at the same time, the doctor whispered something to Patri. His eyes widened, but he continued to let Magnus eat to his heart's delight. He scoffed down berries and foins, a fruit from the old age that tasted sweet with a tart finish, and the artificial trug, a boar-like creature with tender meat. He ate until his stomach nearly exploded.

Then, Patri asked, "Have you had your fill, my son?"

"Son? You called me son?" Magnus said, confused.

Patri looked back confidently, "Yes, I did, Magnus. After I saw your eyes, I knew something was connected between us, and the results Doctor Shew brought me told me just that. You are my son. I do not know of your mother because I hopped from place to place years ago, but I am happy that you have found us. I pray you stay and join us. We have lived here since the explosion and founding of the city." Magnus interrupted, "I-I thought you were dead. I was told stories that the Hand had fallen right after my birth." Patri froze for a moment until he said, "I was dead."

He lifted his shirt to reveal a scar from a wound so large Magnus could barely fathom. It was like an ox had been hurled through his chest. Yet, he still stood. "Who did this to you?" Magnus asked. Patri cleared his throat, "It was a dark night, as most in this city. I was completing a mission on the forty-second level. Of who it was that hit me, he was a man with a fiery orange beard and a horse's build. His strength was immeasurable. He wielded a hammer with blue liquid flowing between its engravings. Engravings like vines growing from the hammer's base. I was never able to see the handle. Still, it looked brown or black." Magnus's face immediately turned to fear because he knew the man who fought his father, Helpar Caddel.

Patri continued, "I was able to disarm him with that very sword that now latches to you, but I could not defeat him. He threw his comrades' battle ax straight at me with lightning speed. I could not move, and I was struck. It shattered my bones and threw me from the ledge I was defending into the darker parts of the lower city. That blade you hold was thrown from my hands and landed at his feet. All I heard from him was a maniacal laugh like he enjoyed it. As I fell, I hit the descending platforms. The ax was dislodged from me, and I continued to fall. But by strict luck, I landed in a garbage pit that had just been filled with fresh food. It was enough to cushion my landing, but I was still only clinging to life."

His tone changed to a softer one as he continued, "The next thing I remember was being in the back room with a woman with the beauty of an angel, but the clothes of a street rat, caring for my wound. She told me I had been unconscious for over a week and was lucky to be alive. I continued living with her for over a year while I healed and grew fond of her. Until one day, when her care was nearing its end, she left, and I never laid eyes on that beautiful face again. I long to see her again or at least know why she left, but I've moved on. After she left, I came back here to find out that my entire crew was killed. I was distraught to hear they were dead, but those monsters thankfully never found our oasis." There was a grimace of sadness that he quickly wiped from his face. Magnus let Patri gather himself and said, "That warrior that hit you, I know him; his name is Helpar Caddel, and he is the leader of the Berserkers. They raised me, and now I wish nothing more than to escape them. They made me feel worthless, like I was nothing, but here feels, it feels, different."

Patri stood up violently, "You were one of them?! Have you been sent here to finish what this Helpar could not?!" Magnus threw his hands up, "No! I ran from and scarred Helpar. I took the blade from him. I am the one who chose to be set free from him." Patri looked skeptical, but he sat back down. Then, after a moment's silence, he said, "I do believe you, my son, but don't think for a second that if you try to harm anyone here that we will let you live." His green eyes stared into Magnus's very heart, and he felt the weight of the threat. "I understand," he said seriously. They both finished their meals and no longer had a purpose in sitting at the table. Patri noticed and said, "Head back to your room to rest now." They locked eyes again, and Magnus bowed as he was escorted out of the room.

Patri returned to his throne and wondered if this boy was why that woman had run away. She was afraid of intertwining with a crime lord and ran to protect herself. *Was she the mother? Could she be the mother?* He knew his past was filled with holes and sins, but surely Magnus wasn't the result of one. He sat with his hand on his chin, pondering for the next hour. A few others came in to see or talk with him, but he dismissed them all.

Magnus returned to his room, and he nodded at the unfamiliar faces that walked by him. Once he got back, he laid down on the red bedding, wondering about everything he missed out on by being "saved" by the Berserkers. They had taken away his family and his entire life, and it infuriated him. He festered in his fury and sat up. His legs started to shake, and his hands gripped the bedding. His breathing got heavier, and he started to shake with anger. A single teardrop fell from his eye, and he looked up angrily. He told himself, "Helpar, I will not rest until your body lies dead at my feet." Then, he let his anger subside and went to the shower, where he would wash off the long day. And after the shower, he quickly went to sleep.

He walked in the next day for training only to find Patri awaiting him. Patri wasted no time and told him, "Come here, my son. We have work to do."

Magnus walked over and saw a few training dummies laid out with battle axes instead of the usual katana-like blades the other dummies had. Patri walked him over to a dummy and said, "I want to know everything the Berserkers taught you. I want to know their fighting style, their strengths, and their weaknesses." Magnus replied, "I don't know much, but I will show you as much as I remember from their lessons."

He approached the dummy, drew his sword, and said, "Their favorite tactics involve wide swings like this." He swung his blade directly into the dummy's head with both hands clasped onto the sword's hilt. His strike split the dummy's head into splinters.

Then, he did the next set of moves the Berserkers taught him. "This is what they call the flying eagle," he said. He leaped into the air and swung upwards through the dummy's chest. As he landed, he said, "They also love to throw their weapons and use enemies' weapons as their own." He took an ax from a dummy and put his sword in its place. He threw the ax into its chest, which dislodged his sword. He grabbed it midair and used the flying eagle to cut another dummy. He landed with a stroke of grace and looked to his father for approval. Patri stood with a face of stone, looking at his son perform the moves he was attacked with years ago.

"Now, son, how do they defend themselves?" he prodded.

"That's just the thing, they don't. They believe a real warrior attacks until he is killed. Then and only then can they be considered worthy of death."

"They don't defend themselves well. Interesting. As dangerous and uncivilized as that is, it can be effective. Their tactic relies heavily on powerful strikes, but our gracefulness can surely overcome that."

"How can we try the same tactics you failed with before?" Magnus asked innocently.

Patri's eyes shot with anger. He was enraged and screamed, "I did not fail! My tactics showed no failure; my men were lazy and underestimated our foes. That is why we lost, not because we were lesser. If you do not want your fate to be the same as my men, I recommend you listen!" As he shook angrily, he burst again, saying, "I gave it all, and my punishment was to be left alive! I wish I would have died with the rest of my men so I wouldn't have to feel the shame of leading a poor battalion to their deaths. I wish I didn't have to live with my failings. I wish I could take the Berserkers by the neck and slit every throat until they plead for mercy. I wish I could, but my body fails me!" He threw his hands to the side and continued, "I am not the man I used to be. My power left me with that ax. I have become a faded copy of myself. Look at me! I am nothing but a failure to my people." He dropped his head and looked to the ground. Magnus even thought he saw a glimmer of a tear.

He was stunned but quickly understood his father's anger. The Berserkers had ruined his life too, but he knew he had the chance for revenge Patri didn't. He looked to Patri and said, "I will continue what you started; I will end this in your name, Father. Just show me how."

Patri picked up his head, "If that is your wish, I shall give it to you. I will teach you our ways. Pick up your blade, and let's begin." Magnus eagerly picked up his sword and followed his father's instructions. Then, he quickly asked, "I can call you Father, right?" Patri turned back and said, "Of course, I didn't even notice you did." He grabbed a spare sword from a bin close to him and said, "This is Devil's combat, and it is much different than what those Berserkers taught you." He started doing smooth slides through the air and told Magnus when he would jump or evade. He moved slowly, yet the grace of his movements was beautiful.

Overall, the style consisted of smooth and elegant movements. Flips and agile moves were at the core of the movement—a stark contrast to the aggressive and blunt tactics of the Berserkers. The main attacking points were slashes of the sword and quick and precise jabs. But unlike the Berserkers, defense was pivotal.

Another cornerstone of Devil's combat was counterattacking, using another's strengths as their own weaknesses. Taunting was also taught as an effective way to draw opponents in so that a counterattack could be landed, but it had to be done correctly. After a while of demonstration, Patri said, "I want to see you use these tactics on this dummy now."

Magnus did as he was told, and he was clumsy; however, he showed great ability and potential.

He had a gift; he was able to combine Berserker and Devil's Hand combat styles to create his own unique style. It consisted of the agility of Devil's combat and the heavy attacks of the Berserker's combat–thus, allowing him to be almost unstoppable in every way. His swings would be born from flips and rolls, allowing him to land blows in clinical areas. Defensively, he was also powerful. He would use the strong parries taught by the Hand to avoid attacks.

Additionally, the quickness of the Berserker style played a role in his defense, as almost every defensive maneuver was quickly followed by a strong offensive one.

After watching Magnus train, Patri grew impressed, but there was still more to be done. He addressed Magnus, "Son, your natural-born ability for combat is impressive, and with time you will become a great warrior. I want you to write the moves you have adapted from both styles and give them names so that I and others of us can learn." Magnus was breathing heavily as he said, "Yes, sir" He went to take up his sword until Patri stopped him. "Return to your room. You have done enough here," he commanded. "Of course." Magnus said.

He crept back to his quarters, wondering what he would name his newly created style. He sat down at his desk and began to sketch the different movements. One he titled the *Rising Phoenix*. Like the Flying Eagle, it had a strong upwards strike, but this strike was born out of a roll instead of a much more vulnerable flip. He created many other moves of similar caliber as he stayed up into the night focused on his new fighting style. In the end, he finally named it. He named it *The Way of the Phoenix*. He was inspired by the legends surrounding a phoenix and its ability to be reborn, and he saw this new period of his life as his rebirth.

Later that night, he went to show his father his drawings, hoping he would still be awake. "Ah, Magnus," Patri said as he entered the room. He was surprised to see Patri sitting on his throne at this hour. It felt like he was waiting for someone or something. Regardless, he eagerly said,

"Come look at these." Patri stood and walked over to the table. Magnus set the first drawing down, which depicted the rising phoenix. Patri picked it up and began analyzing it. "Wow, this is impressive," he said while flipping the paper in his hand. He continued to study the pictures and instructions carefully and quietly. Magnus stood close to the table with his hands behind his back, hoping Patri would be as proud as he was of his work. Patri made his way through the sketches and set them back down. "Are they good?" Magnus asked. Patri nodded, and before he could say anything, Magnus said, "You wanna see some of them in person?" "Why not," Patri nodded.

Magnus drew his sword and walked to one of the dummies on the other side of the room; Patri followed. "Here's the rising phoenix," Magnus said as he showed the move. Patri looked quite impressed and applauded him, "Well done, well done." He continued to show off different moves he created until the throne room doors burst open.

A young man dressed in black stood ominously at the door. He wore a mask that resembled something of a smiling devil. It had red outlines and horns. He held a large bag of what sounded like Ugurns. He spoke in a charismatic and somewhat irritated tone, "I have finished your bidding, Father." He took a knee as Patri walked up to him. He went to the man and laid a hand on his shoulder, "Good work." He said other things that Magnus couldn't hear. Magnus was flabbergasted and wondered if it were true. The man had called Patri father. *Could he be my brother?* he thought. If this was his brother, he wanted to look as intimidating as possible. So, he stood up straight and puffed up his chest. Patri lifted the man from his knee, and the two started to walk over. He signaled for a guard to come to take the bag, so one did and walked away with it.

As the two kept walking, the man walked into the light and removed his mask to reveal a face like Magnus's and hair as black as night. It flowed from the middle of his head and ran over his ears. He shook his head to remove the hair dangling in front of his eyes. His eyes were a blue that told of great power. His clothes were cut, and tender wounds were underneath. His face was young yet mature, and his mannerisms were charming. His jawline was sharp with a little stubble growth. He didn't see Magnus until the king ushered them toward each other. "Who is this?" Magnus questioned. "Magnus, this is your brother." Magnus and the new man stood in shocked confusion as they looked at each other. "Brother?" Magnus said. Patri took a deep breath.

"Yes, this is your brother. Magnus, I want you to meet a long-time member of the Hand, a decorated warrior, and a descendant of my line, Rain Tecorian."

Magnus stood stunned as Rain extended his hand to shake his, and they locked hands. They introduced themselves, and then Rain asked Patri, "I never knew I had a brother. Why wasn't he here with me all these years?" Magnus sat stunned at the new person before him, and he couldn't get a word out. Patri then spoke to break the silence, "I'll let him tell you that story over a nice meal." He snapped his fingers, and people with plates came flying in to put food on the table. He grabbed both their shoulders and walked with them to the seats. They sat down and began filling their plates without saying a word. But before anyone took a bite, the questioning began. Magnus was the first to speak.

"Why didn't you tell me about Rain?" He had turned toward Patri as he asked the question, and Patri seemed defensive.

"Well, I didn't want you to have anything else on your mind while adjusting to a new home."

"But I feel like knowing I have a brother is pretty important to know," Magnus said, sounding a bit upset.

"It is, but I wanted to wait until you felt safe here until you found out news like that," Patri reassured.

Magnus was still unsatisfied with the answer but ate on in silence. Rain swallowed his bite and spoke, "So, Father, how has the compound been while I've been out doing your dirty work?" He had been gone for multiple days completing his task. Patri smiled dryly, "It's been good, and the trainees have been performing well, and your brother here created a whole new combat style. I want to teach it to you because it could effectively take down Berserkers." Rain looked to Magnus and back to Patri confidently as he said, "Berserkers, they don't fall without a hell of a fight? So, how's some new kid's tactics gonna be any different?" Patri's glare was excited, and he said, "Cause he used to be one of them, Rain; he's the one that's seen inside. He can give us what we need to finally win. He even has the sword."

Rain's eyes became envious and skeptical, "Let me see it because I don't believe some boy is finding what you lost." Patri gestured to Magnus, "Show him." Magnus nodded and stood from his chair. He drew the sword with its golden edges glistening in the light, and Rain was quickly silenced. "Impossible," he said under his breath, "Let me see it." He reached across the table and tried grabbing the sword. Magnus reeled his hand back and put the sword back into its sheath. He commanded his brother, "It stays with me." So, Rain, disappointed, withdrew to his seat.

He kept his gaze on Magnus and asked, "So, how did you get out of being a Berserker? Because that's a story I've never heard before." He ate another bite of his trug as he waited for an answer. Magnus swallowed his bite and tried to keep a neutral face, "Well, my mother died in childbirth, and I never really knew who she was, but the Berserkers took me in and tried to raise me like their own. I trained with them and learned to be like them, but I hated it there. All the others were big and burly with pale skin and eyes as blue as yours, and I sat there with this tan skin and green eyes." He pointed at his chest, "I hated being different, so I ran away and found my way here." Rain wanted more information, so he continued to prod.

"I don't believe you could just run away," he said.

"You're looking at me, aren't you?" Magnus said, holding his arms out wide.

"Even if that is true, how did my long-lost brother find the most secluded compound in Uguria?" Rain asked skeptically.

"Well, to be honest, I had a dream of floor number 87 and came down and was taken inside and found to be related," Magnus answered.

"A dream? That's what brought you here? Sure," Rain said, irritated.

His tone had started to elevate, so Patri said, "Rain, please, we need to get along. So put this question down and enjoy a meal." "Yes, Father," he replied as he began to eat more. He still stared through Magnus, but he didn't say a word. The three ate silently until Rain sat up, ready to question Magnus again.

"What is this new combat style father mentioned?" he asked.

"I named it the way of the phoenix because it represents me rising from adversity faced by the Berserkers. A lot of Berserker tactics involve the

word eagle, so I kept the bird theme," Magnus answered.

"What combat are we talking about? Cause I have my ways too," Rain said questioningly.

"It combines the movement of the Devil's combat with the aggressive tactics of the Berserkers. I think it'll be great against everyone," Magnus said.

His tone dropped in anger at the thought of his old home, "Especially Berserkers." Rain still seemed impartial, and he continued to eat normally. After his last bite, he spoke stone-cold and concisely, "In the morning, we will head to the training room and begin to learn each other's tactics. In the meantime, let's go to our rooms. I'm not trying to sit here exhausted for the rest of the night." "Agreed," Patri chimed in. They stood from the table and walked from the chamber to Patri's personal room. Magnus wasn't sure what was inside the room, but when the door opened, he saw a massive bed and a window that looked into what must have been the gardens. As the two walked, they said nothing to each other.

Magnus went to the end of the room, where the double doors stood, and went to the right. He thought to himself while he walked. *For a father and son, something seems off*. He also wondered why Rain didn't have his own room, but that didn't seem too important anyway.

6

ROYAL MEMORIES

Patri's personal room was behind a small wooden door. When they opened, they would reveal a secluded bathing pool with a massive curtain around it in one corner, a giant bed in the next, and a small window looking into the garden. Patri never went or cared for the garden; instead, he let others take care of it. He just enjoyed the view. There was also another small door that led to Rain's room. It was much smaller, with a twin bed and a small bathroom off to the side.

Patri approached his bath and began to get undressed for his nightly wash. As he was doing so, he heard the door bang open. Rain was infuriated, "How could you let some kid we've never met sit at our table like he's been here all along?!" Patri stood half naked, scars exposed, "Rain, my boy, he needed a home, and he is family. How can I turn him down? How can I not do to him what I did to you? You would still be living out there if I hadn't got you from your mother. You would have been some shop boy mopping floors if I wasn't there for you. Realize there's more than you!" He stepped toward Rain, nearly touching his face, and they both stared in gridlock. Rain looked longingly and angrily into his father's eyes, "You never gave me what you're giving him?! I have lived here my whole life, and still, I don't get the care he does?!"

With Rain's tone escalated, Patri backed away and said, "Rain, be careful." Then, suddenly, his face went soft, and his eyes became gentle. He raised his hand to hold his son's face, "I have trained you since you were a little boy. I will fight for what is mine, and you are mine, along with Magnus. Now go get some rest and leave me to wash." Rain mockingly bowed, "As you wish." He walked into his room, unsatisfied with his father's answer. It seemed too nice, and he assumed, per usual, Patri was just trying to diffuse the situation instead of fixing it.

Patri closed the curtain behind Rain and let out a deep sigh. Bringing up Rain's mother had opened the doors to memories he hoped to forget. He had hurt many people before, and regardless of his efforts, he couldn't escape it. He was living out his guilt every time he saw Rain. He got into the bath, and thoughts of the past emerged as he settled in.

He was born into the clan like his father before him. His father, Valc Tecorian, was the warrior king of the Devil's Hand, and he ruled scrupulously. Every failure was a major offense to him, and he never allowed Patri to forget his mistakes. His father often beat him for his shortcomings. Patri repeatedly tried to plead with him to stop, but he never did. He was scared of his own family, and he hated it. He saw other families within the clan get along, but he never felt the same because his father was a king. Valc was rarely around in the first place, and when he was, it was only to tear Patri down.

His mother, Bri, was kind-hearted, but her kind heart was always stopped by Valc. He kept her silent by threatening to have her killed, so she never dared try to stop him. This threat drove her to act similarly to Valc and only hurt Patri. However, there would be times when her eyes would go from strict to caring, but it often stopped at either the sight of Valc or the thought of him. But the memories of her were faint in Patri's mind because she died shortly after he turned eight. He never got to know his mother, though he desperately wished he could have. In the end, he was used as a tool by his father and felt as if he was useless.

As he aged, he was undoubtedly a great warrior but didn't feel any progress. His father still broke him to nothing, and he reached the point where he was waiting for his father to die. He eventually got his wish. When he turned 20, Valc died in combat and thrust him into becoming king. He was overwhelmed by the freedom and power he now possessed. He went crazy ordering heists and building wealth at absurd rates. He was with women nearly every night, but he tried to be careful because children were the last thing he wanted to worry about. One night when he was in his early forties, he forgot his morals. He slept with a young girl who would eventually become Rain's mother. And as he thought, the one night she found out she was pregnant flashed back to his mind.

* * *

Rain's mother, Zurin, had allowed Patri to stay with her while he completed an extended mission. It had been nearly two months, and she noticed she wasn't feeling the same. She went to get a pregnancy test, and when she got home, she took it. The test showed she was pregnant, so she went to find Patri to tell him the news.

"Patri! Patri!" she yelled as she burst into the room Patri was staying in. It was a smaller room with a small bed and a nightstand. "Yes?" he answered. He was lying on the bed reading something. "I'm pregnant," she said in a weary tone. She took out the test and held it in front of her. He stood up enraged. He snatched the test from her and saw she was telling the truth. He started breathing faster and was getting angrier. Finally, he threw the test to the ground, "You're what?! How could you be pregnant?! I can't raise a kid! I'm a king, not some father!" He backed her into the corner and yelled down at her. She sat against the wall and slowly slid to the floor. She was now cowering, unable to stop a raging Patri. He screamed, "It won't be my fault! This is on you, and you will be responsible for this kid!" He steamed out of the room faster than she had entered, and he descended back to level 87.

She was still sitting in the corner, and she started to cry. She didn't know how else to feel. She was scared, and now, she was alone. She hoped he would've stayed to help, but that hope was long gone. She cried into the night until a new feeling of resentment overtook her. She spoke to her stomach with her left hand over her womb, "He won't find you. He won't."

She promised herself she would keep the baby hidden until she decided someone could keep it safe. She kept her house doors locked until she finally heard about the Berserkers. They sounded like they could care for a new child, and she could forget about it. So, shortly after Rain was born, she arranged a meeting with the Berserkers to give him to them. However, Patri found out about the exchange and wanted his son back. He didn't really care about Rain, but he wanted to ensure the Berserkers didn't get another member.

* * *

One cold night on level 42, Zurin went to take Rain to the Berserkers. She had arranged the meeting in an alleyway on the opposite side of the Berserker compound. She stepped off the platform and started walking toward her designated location, but Patri was waiting as she turned a corner. "Help!" she yelled. But she wasn't close enough for anyone to hear, so her screams were in vain. She kept backing away with Rain tucked safely in her arms. Patri said nothing but continued to push her back until her back hit a wall. He pinned her to the wall, and she knew she was helpless. She had no option but to try and talk him out of the situation.

"Patri, I thought you would never come back," she said.

"I wasn't going to until I heard you would give my boy to the Berserkers. He is something special, and you will not take him for me," Patri said boldly.

"Your boy! You ran away; how dare you call him yours!" Zurin screamed.

She tucked Rain behind her to protect him.

"You left me to birth him, and you dare to call him yours!" she yelled. She was enraged at him, but there wasn't much else she could do to him. Patri kept a calm and monotone voice.

"He's mine, Zurin, and you won't stop me. So, either give him to me, or I will take him." She knew he was serious, but she still wouldn't hand Rain over.

"I'll die before I give him to you," she said.

"So be it," he said as he rushed her.

He didn't draw a weapon but instead used his hands. She only had one free hand, so he grabbed it and threw her to the ground. She screamed in pain as she clutched onto Rain. "Please, Patri! Please!" she yelled as he stood over her. He said nothing and gave her a cold glare. He reached down and grabbed Rain. "No!" she yelled. But she was no match for his strength, and he ripped Rain from her. She made one last desperate reach for his legs. She missed, and her hands slammed into the ground. He turned back to look at her. He glared at her, pulled up his hood, he ran off into the night, and disappeared with Rain.

She started to cry while lying on the ground. Then she remembered that the Berserkers were waiting on her, and it was past their meeting time. She also knew the Berserkers were not the people to be late with, so she sniffled, got up, and ran back to her house. She never tried to find Rain again and was forever crushed by what Patri had done that night.

* * *

Patri ran Rain to the platform and leaped onto a descending one. Once he reached level 41, he got off and ran to an elevator in one of the eight support beams. The Devil's Hand secretly built the elevator into the support beam ages ago. The beam was strong enough to handle the elevator inside without becoming compromised, and the seven other beams were more than enough to support the rest of the city. Because of this, no one but the Devil's Hand knew of the elevator's existence.

When he finally returned with Rain, he immediately put him into the children's program. For Rain, it was the beginning of a very rough childhood. At the same time, the Berserkers found out about Patri's daring robbery and wanted their revenge. They left men in any areas they thought he would return to, and about three months later, he did. He was with nine others on a routine arms deal. The deal was on level 42, and it would change his life forever. He knew there could be trouble, but he doubted the Berserkers cared about a missing child.

So, he carried on as usual as he got off the elevator. But a party awaited him; the Berserkers were ready to fight a king. The fight went down the alley, with Berserkers pushing Patri and his crew back. He and his team were able to hurt the Berserkers, but they couldn't kill them. Two of his crew were already killed, and the rest wouldn't last much longer. The fight had made its way to the walkway's edge, and Patri knew he couldn't fight his way out. He was one-on-one with Helpar, and he knew he couldn't win. But he wouldn't let himself die a coward. He tightened the grip on his sword and charged. Helpar drew his arm back and released an ax with a grunt. It flew end over end until it hit Patri square in the chest. He dropped the sword, and it clattered to Helpar's feet. His body kept flying through the air. He hit the walkway's edge and plummeted to what Helpar presumed to be his death. But little did both know that the apparent deal of death would bring a new life into the city. When he fell, he fell into the care of who would become Magnus's mother, Rebecca.

* * *

While being in Rebecca's care, he began to feel for her. And after some time, they started sleeping with each other. He never told her who he was, and she innocently believed that he had nothing to hide. But, He felt something special for her and wanted to be honest with her. He was lying in bed one night after the two had finished when he said, "Rebecca, I want to tell you something. I haven't been honest about who I am, and I want you to know if we're getting this close." She looked at him, ready to hear what he had to say. He paused to gather the strength so he could tell the truth. He took another breath.

"I'm actually involved in all this crime in the city." She sat up from the bed in disbelief.

"You're what?! You told me you would keep me safe, and now you say you're involved in the crime I hate the most?!" She scoffed in anger, and he tried to calm her down.

"I'm sorry, but I thought we could get past this," he said. She stood up and started putting her clothes on.

"Patri, you lied to me; how will I forgive that?! What role do you play anyway?" He scratched the back of his neck.

"If it's honesty what you want, then I'll give it to you. I'm the head of one of the deep city crime groups." She began to have a panic attack as she realized who she had intertwined with. She finished throwing her shirt back on.

"No, no, you can't be. I don't wanna get brought into that. You knew that and ignored me anyway! How could you!" She pushed him down on the bed. He sat back up and tried to apologize.

"I'm sorry, Rebecca."

"Sorry isn't enough! I don't want to see you, hear you, feel you, or know you anymore! Stay away from me!" she screamed.

She burst out of the room and left him shocked. When the door slammed, he sat in the bed and tried to process what had just happened.

After she left the room, she returned to her little shack on level 46. She could barely afford the thing, and now, unbeknownst to her, she was pregnant with the child of a king.

Shortly after the outburst, he went back down to level 87 and was met with shocked faces from the people who believed he was dead. The lead guard ran to him, "My king, you have returned." He was immediately crowded. It overwhelmed him, and he said, "I'm fine. Get away from me and let me have my peace!" He retreated to his room and collapsed on the bed. He had ruined two women, and the guilt was building. The only thing he knew was Rain, and he would make him the best the clan had ever seen, regardless of the cost.

For years Rain was treated the same as Patri was as a kid. He was scorned and beaten for never being good enough. He wasn't allowed with the others and was kept isolated, with only his father to keep him company. His bed was in the room that branched from Patri's. It was a plain room with a twin bed in the corner and a small bathroom on the side. He was allowed there and in the main chamber. Patri would bring him meals and drinks, but he could never go by himself. Patri would enable him to join him on a mission if he were lucky, but it was rare. Every day was the same. He would wake up, be told his purpose, and train until it was time to sleep again. Patri always told him it was to better him as a warrior and turn him into the best warrior he could be. And like the child Rain was, he believed it.

One day stood out as a breaking point in their relationship, as Patri had felt Rain grow away from him ever since. It was after an abysmal training session, and Patri unleashed onto Rain, saying, "Rain, get your act together! You are my son, and you are no better than the children just picking up their swords! I was better than you, and this whole place is better than you! You dishonor me, and if this stays this way, I will gladly disown you, my failure of a son!"

After that, Rain ran away in tears back to his room, and every training session after that was bleak and silent. Patri would command, and Rain would follow. Patri was upset with himself and didn't know how to fix it with Rain. Magnus was a new chance, and he wanted to make the most of it, but the wounds he had with Rain were deeper than Magnus could fix.

* * *

Suddenly, Patri awoke from his thoughts and remembered being in the bath. He wasn't sure how long he had been in the water, and he figured it was long enough. He jumped out and dried himself. He put on his silk clothing, moved the covers of his bed, climbed into it, and carefully pulled the blanket over himself. He reached the nightstand and turned off the lamp by his side. The window to the garden let in a weak light because some light was needed for a few of the plant species to grow. It gave a comfortable night light. He settled in, and his brain still fired with thoughts and memories. But finally, He rolled his way to sleep full of stress and regret as he did almost every night.

7

EARNED RESPECT

Magnus returned to his room after meeting Rain, removed his combat clothes, and showered in his bathroom. Then, he stepped out, brushed his teeth, and put on his nightwear. Everyone in the compound had a black robe with an embroidered golden H on the left breast. He was thinking of his new brother and what that meant for his training with Patri. *If my brother could be a warrior that impressive, surely I could do the same?* He imagined himself saving the compound or even his father in dramatic battles. It excited him to think about what he could become.

He went to his bed, and as he went to turn out his lamp on his bedside, he saw his sword and thought about his past days. He went from jumping from the Berserker compound to spending the night on a bench to finding the Hand's compound to starting his training and to finding his lost family. It was overwhelming, but he was also grateful for it. He couldn't think for too long before his body started to give in to the comfort of the mattress. He yawned and whispered, "Thank you," as he rolled over. He turned off his lamp and fell asleep shortly after.

The following day the compound woke up and began their training lessons. But Magnus and Rain were called into the king's chamber yet again. They passed the other training rooms, and Rain nodded at some of the others walking by. But when they got to Patri's chamber, they found him standing alone, surrounded by dummies. "My sons, welcome to training," he greeted them. Rain scoffed, "What type of training? Have I not spent my entire life training?" Patri grinned, "You have, but like Magnus, we are all learners and will learn how to fight again. Now draw your weapons. Time is not an ally."

Rain reluctantly drew his beautiful blue sword with a dragon head carved into the hilt, and Magnus followed his lead. The blue shine from the blade was dim but beautiful. It had white streaks that ran from the base to the tip, and it made the lightest hum as it cut through the air.

Rain wasn't happy with Patri's apparent favoritism, but he now had the chance to show that he was better. "Watch this," he said to Magnus. He leaped from his position corkscrewing through the air, cutting the dummy in half from the right shoulder to the left hip in one fluid motion. The broken half skid across the floor and landed at Patri's feet. Patri's face showed nothing. He gestured to Rain and said, "Magnus, let Rain introduce his style, Pure Motion." Rain stood from his majestic landing and shook his hair from his eyes. "It's all about, as he said, constant motion. It has flips and leaps to keep one as light and an impossible-to-catch target," he said. It intrigued Magnus, and he wanted to learn more, so he continued to listen. Rain continued, "Then you take the opponent, wait for their strike, and pounce. It's pretty simple, really. You can do a flip, can't you?" He finished with a cocky tone. Magnus looked at him and smiled. Then, he jumped into the air and did a double backflip. "Yes, yes, I can," he said with confidence. "Not bad," Rain said plainly.

Magnus could still hear the cocky tone and knew he had to prove his skill again, so he ran at the other dummy and rolled right in front of it. As he exited the roll, he sliced through one leg and jumped back as he sliced the opposite arm. Then, in one last attack, he jabbed his sword through. He turned back at Rain, who had put his sword back into its sheath, and said, "That's the rising phoenix, strong attacks strung together with a quick movement. Very similar to your style, but this is always on the attack and only using defense if absolutely necessary." Rain was impressed but not yet convinced of his brother's prowess.

"Let's see how good you are without that blade," he snickered. Magnus tossed it to the ground and replied, "Gladly." He flipped over Rain and punched one of the dummies over before turning around and jumping back. As he landed, he took Rain's blade from its sheath and pointed it at his neck. Rain casually pushed it away. Magnus spun the blade to face the ground and handed it back. Rain was quite impressed and turned to his brother to offer him a handshake. He put his sword away with the other hand, "I'll learn to fight with you because, with skill like that, I would be a fool not to."

Patri clapped his hands, "Well done, boys; it only took a show of your combative ability to tolerate each other." The boys took their swords and began to teach each other moves, each like performers in a two-way dance leading to destruction. They sparred for hours, each winning some and losing others until they grew fond of each other's company. Though it had only been a day, their chemistry was undeniable, and they had a subliminal sense of trust building. They didn't even have personal conversations, but they were personally connected. It was a different feeling for them, and neither wanted to end it nor did they know what it meant. They felt a little more at home knowing they had a partner.

* * *

A couple of days later, Magnus was showing Rain more of his ideas, and Rain was even more impressed with his brother's ability. Then, Rain began to demonstrate another one of his abilities. He took his sword out and said, "The Spider, as I call it, is a move where you use the walls around you to your advantage and leap from one wall to the next in rapid succession. Then you simply attack the target's confusion and strike them down. I don't really have any walls to demonstrate, but you get the picture." Magnus understood the concept and nodded along. This was one of many things the two taught each other over their few days together.

* * *

Two weeks later, after Patri had bathed, he stood in pride above his sparring boys and retreated to his chamber. He sat in his room, grateful that his past mistakes could be fixed. His life had done nothing but divide people, but now with his new sons, he could start over. Before he got into bed, his mind conjured a pledge. *Swear to yourself you will be here for these boys. You have done some terrible things, but this is your second chance. Your past and what happened to you doesn't mean you have to be the same.* The future was open to him and his sons, and he would make the absolute most of it.

He carefully tucked himself into bed and turned off the lamp. For once, his mind wasn't racing with regrets and pain. He rolled around for only a few moments before he drifted off to sleep. It was rare for him to fall asleep so effortlessly, but now, he was at peace. It was a new feeling, but he was glad it overcame him.

Over the two weeks, the boys had grown better and better by teaching and learning from each other in their time together. After Patri left, they spared each other into the night, and they were utterly exhausted. They were bent over, trying to catch their breaths. "Rain," Magnus took a deep breath, "I haven't had to fight like this against anyone I ever met, and because of that, I'm proud to call you my brother." Rain took a deep breath, "You have earned that title and my respect." He gave the slightest of grins through his breaths. Magnus straightened himself, "Thank you, and I feel just the same. Now I need to rest because fighting you is exhausting." Rain hunched over again, "Agreed." They smiled and gathered their things. As they did, Rain said, "Means a lot to have a training partner." "I appreciate it, Rain, I do," Magnus responded fondly. They turned away and began to walk their separate ways.

Magnus walked with his head down and began to think if asking Rain personal questions was the right thing. Rain was always reserved about his past and anything too personal. But, after the moment they just had, Magnus figured it was a good time and that he had the right to know.

He whipped himself around and yelled, "Rain!" Rain turned back to look at him, "Yes?" Magnus walked back toward him and lowered his voice, "I never did ask you about your past or age or really anything about you, so I'll start by asking how old you actually are." Rain was caught off-guard by the question.

"Not much older than you, it seems. I'm 19," he said blankly.

"Younger than you look," Magnus remarked.

"You see some things when you do this long enough," Rain said solemnly.

"What all have you seen?" Magnus asked curiously.

Rain quickly said, "I'd rather not."

"You know my story, Rain; at least give me a taste of yours," Magnus begged.

Rain was still hesitant, but he had grown close enough to Magnus to feel that telling the truth wouldn't hurt him. He looked around the room to protect his now soft voice.

"Magnus, my past is riddled with horror that started with my mother, who tried to take me away. She knew who Patri was, so she hid me away so I couldn't be found and could keep me to herself like the greedy woman she was. She claimed it was to protect me from Father, and maybe she was right, but it was so she could hand me over at the right time to the Berserkers." Magnus strained at the word but kept listening. "Anyway, she bid me to the Berserkers, but the Hand figured out the trade details. So, they met my mother there and took me back. They brought me here." He gestured towards the tapestry ceiling, "They brought me to my new home where I was trained to become the best soldier in generations. I trained under the iron fist of our father. None of his lessons came easy, but I learned. Now I'm a killer who does the dirty work for this place. I bring in the money that gives us beds, and soon enough, Father will have me do it again. I sometimes feel like a tool here, but it's all I have, so I serve until I die honorably." Magnus processed it all and still wanted more.

"There's got to be more than that," he prodded.

"Well, there is, but I don't really want to tell you cause it hurts me too, but let's just say I had it rough," Rain said dismissively.

"But you're okay with Father, right?" Magnus said, trying to get more while not directly questioning.

"Okay, that's a little too nice of a word. It's more like we just tolerate each other. He lashed out at me once, and honestly, I haven't been the same with him since," Rain replied. He stopped on his own, but Magnus needed to hear the rest of the story.

"What did he do?" Magnus asked. Rain tried to stall.

"Well, I can't exactly blame him. He's just taking after his father."

"What did he do?" Magnus repeated.

"I told you. He lashed out at me!" Rain said, nearing a yell.

"Okay, okay. I'm sorry for asking, then," Magnus said.

Rain calmed himself and said, "It's fine." He cleared his throat and said, "If you want to know, Father told me, 'Rain, get your act together! You are my son, and you are no better than the children just picking up their swords! I was better than you, and this whole place is better than you! You dishonor me, and if this stays this way, I will gladly disown you, my son!'" He paused and said dryly, "So that's why I just tolerate him."

Magnus was shocked by hearing that his seemingly benign father would say that. Rain saw his concerned expression and comforted him, "But don't worry. I think he's learned from me and won't treat you the same. I think it hurt him to see me like that. I hope it did, at least." Magnus nodded and remained hopeful about his father's relationship with him. He still felt awful for Rain, so he tried to console him.

"Well, I'm sorry, Rain, but maybe you guys can change."

"I don't think we can, Magnus. It's been too long," Rain said.

"It's never too late. You could fix it," Magnus urged.

Rain shrugged it off and stood silently. Bringing up his past stung, but he was glad Magnus knew it now. It made him feel like he was heard. However, this didn't stop him from sitting in silence. Magnus saw he wasn't taking his advice, so he tried changing the subject.

"What do you do exactly to bring in this type of wealth? Cause this place is drowning in money I've never seen," he said.

"I give back to people what's rightfully theirs. The police sirens you hear up there don't even matter. They haven't done a thing to stop the cruelty of this place, so we took it into our own hands. We steal from other wealthy groups like the Berserkers, for example, and give it back to the people of this city. There aren't too many of us now, so I do a lot of the work. But I manage. Then, when it's all done, we take our fair share, but this city needs us, and we're here for it." Magnus wondered if Rain meant that or if it was like the Berserker lies he was told, but he trusted his brother.

"That's amazing, Rain, and I wanna help. When can I help?" he said with eager eyes.

"You can, but not tonight. Rest, and I'll begin more specific training in the morning. I'll work on getting a mission together," Rain said optimistically.

"Just tell me when," Magnus smiled.

Rain finally lowered the tone of the conversation and said, "It's really time we go to rest." "You're right," Magnus agreed. They gave each other a quick hug and walked to their rooms. Rain smirked as he walked. He was happy to have someone who really did care about him. Magnus smirked, for he finally found a home.

8

MISSION ONE

    The next night, Rain woke Magnus and told him to put his clothes on. He put his hand over Magnus's mouth before he could ask any questions. He whispered to a groggy Magnus, "You said you wanted in. Now you're in. We have our first assignment." He paused and said, "And you're gonna need this. I think you earned it." He pulled out another mask from his pockets, which was better than Magnus would have imagined. It had the same exaggerated features of a smiling devil but with gold around the eyes and mouth, and it had new golden horns. Magnus grinned as he put his mask over his black hair. Rain was looking the other way and said, "There's a small package of weapons being delivered to the police, and they're paying 15,000 Ugurns. All the money will be in a crate, so it'll be easy to carry. It should be on level twenty-nine, and it'll be easy enough." He looked at Magnus and smiled as he removed the mask. "You don't need that yet. I'll tell you when to put it on," he said. "Oh," Magnus said while putting the mask away.

    They started to walk down the hallway quietly so they wouldn't wake anyone else up. They didn't see anyone awake as they arrived at the massive doors, and Rain opened the one on the left. "Go on," he urged Magnus. Magnus walked through, and Rain carefully shut the door behind them. They left quietly and walked toward the actual exit. They opened the door and walked into the cold night before them. They walked for a second until a voice from beside them said, "Who are you? And where are you headed?" Magnus jumped back, and Rain grabbed his shoulder and told him, "It's just the guards. They're messing with you." He then looked back up and said into the dark, "Rain and Magnus, to take this one on his first assignment." The guard again responded, "First? You're in for a good time. Have fun." Rain nodded the guards off, and the two went on their way.

The two walked to the small elevator Magnus had initially ridden in. Its doors squeaked open, and the two stepped inside. The elevator brought them up to the top, and the guard sat on his stool. Rain nodded, and the man nodded back without a word. The two left the earshot of the man down a dark alleyway, and Magnus looked at Rain, "Who is that guy anyway?" Rain scratched his head and said, "I don't know. He's been there as long as I remember, but I've never even heard his name." Magnus seemed confused but shrugged it off.

The alleyway was getting dark, and Magnus wondered if Rain was just taking him to the platforms. But, as he thought, Rain checked over both shoulders and grabbed him. He pulled him into a smaller dark hallway on the left. "Where are we?" Magnus asked. He could hardly see and was really wondering where Rain was taking him. "We're at the elevator," Rain said as he typed on a pin pad. Though it was dark, Magnus's face was full of curiosity. "Elevator?" he asked. Just then, the doors opened, and Rain invited Magnus inside.

"The Devil's Hand built this long before we were here. Come on," Rain said. He hit the button that read 29, and the doors shut behind them. The elevator rose upwards and let out into a dark alley where they got off. "Follow me," Rain said, pulling his mask over his face. Magnus did the same and watched for Rain's next move. He started to run, and Magnus struggled to stay with him. They sprinted down dark alleyways quieter than the night itself. He was outrunning Magnus, and Magnus was about to lose sight of him when he stopped. Magnus was out of breath, "Why'd you stop?" He put a finger over Magnus's mask and pointed to the wall. A ladder was there, and he started to climb.

"Why are we going up there?" Magnus asked before he started climbing. Rain looked around carefully and answered, "There's a ladder near the elevator on every level, and it's so we don't have to look for things from the ground. It gives us a massive advantage." "Makes sense,"

Magnus said as he climbed. They reached the top of level 29 and looked down to find their weapons deal. "It should be somewhere over there from what I know," Rain said as he pointed vaguely to the right. They had to be careful not to hit their heads on the foundation of level 28, but they had enough space to run and jump around. The two looked around and hopped on top of a few buildings until Magnus saw something in the distance. "There," he pointed at a group huddled in the left corner of his vision. Rain nodded, "Well done for your first time. That's them."

The two leaped from building to building under cover of darkness. Magnus was joyful as he saw his brother jump from roof to roof, and he ran after him. His smile was from ear to ear. Rain looked back to see Magnus following his lead. He realized how much he loved seeing his brother learn and saw his potential, and he, too, was smiling from ear to ear.

When they reached the weapons deal, it was near its end. It took place on the corner of two residential streets, and a streetlight on the ground combined with the lights on the ceiling of the level barely lit the area. Only four men were guarding the money. Two of them were police, and the other two were regular civilians. The civilians were trying to sell the weapons to the police for reasons the brothers were unsure of. "On my signal, we jump down and land on those other two, and we'll beat the police after that," Rain whispered. Magnus nodded and continued to look at the deal in progress. "Why don't we just kill the police too?" Magnus asked. Rain looked back at him, "Father said they were always after him before I was born, and he doesn't want that pressure again."

Magnus nodded affirmingly. And as the police turned their backs and loaded the money, Rain whispered, "Now." The two flew from the ceiling and landed straight on their targets. Those two were gone as soon as they landed on top of them.

The police pulled out their electric knives after hearing the loud thud. They hummed in the cold night and gave off the faintest blue light. They were both wearing armored suits with blue-striped helmets. They had large badges on their sleeves which stuck out in the night air.

(Recently, the police force in the city was being replaced by robots built in the high city. It was rare to see these robots because of how little existed. It was rumored the police in the high city were all robotics, but no one really knew. Regardless, these two weren't robots and belonged to the living sector of the Ugurian police force.)

"Who are you?!" they yelled. Their knives hummed with electric power, but they did little to stop the brothers. Rain and Magnus flew through the air and clashed their weapons with the knives. Sparks flew everywhere. Rain was easily blocking every swing from his opponent and yelled, "Lot easier with someone else!" He was smiling during the fight from the joy of finally having a partner. Magnus was having an equally easy fight. They kept sparring with the police until they both got the chance to strike.

The two police swung at their targets and missed. Rain used his spider move, and Magnus, his phoenix. Rain bounced from wall to wall and smashed down onto the first with massive force, and the blow cracked through his helmet. The policeman was knocked out, and he fell to the ground. At the same time, Magnus sprung from the ground and put his hilt through the man's chin. His helmet also flew off, and his body landed with a bang. It slid across the ground and stopped when it hit the other officer's body.

He looked up to see Rain take off his mask. He had his sword in one hand and his mask in the other, throwing them both in the air. He was smiling wide as he yelled, "Wooooo!" He ran to hug Magnus. He lifted his brother in the air, and the two felt connected entirely at that moment. Magnus looked into Rain's eyes and finally saw the approval no one else had ever given him. "Woooo!" he yelled into the night.

After the celebration, they collected the loot with smiles on their faces. Magnus ran his hand through the mass pile of Ugurns and nearly lost his mind. "That's a taste of what I do," Rain told him. Magnus looked back up and closed the crate. They both picked it up, and Rain turned toward the elevator.

The two walked back, and before they got there, Rain said, "I haven't enjoyed a mission like this in a long time, a long time, so thanks, Magnus, you made this fun again. And with how easy that was, we're not done doing this either." Magnus smiled and said, "I can get behind that."

They kept walking until they reached the alley with the elevator. They reached what would be a dark wall, but Rain dropped the crate and popped open a hidden keypad from the wall. He typed in 6 digits, and the elevator returned to them. He picked the crate back up, and the two entered. The doors quietly shut, and he hit the button labeled 80. The elevator rocked as it went down, and when it hit bottom, the door opened. The two walked out onto the cold metal of level 80, and Rain guided them back to the little elevator with the guard in front. The guard recognized the two and opened the door without either of them saying a word. They both just nodded, and the elevator took them to level 87.

They walked into the dark, and the same guard from when they left spoke, "They're back, and look at that; they got the money!" The other guards laughed, and Rain said, "Don't worry, you're gonna get your fill soon enough." The guards cheered as he opened the compound door.

Before they snuck quietly back into their rooms, they put the crate of Ugurns in the back corner of the hallway between the exit and the double doors. They were standing right outside the double doors, and before they went their separate ways, Magnus gave Rain another hug, and as they let go, Rain said, "Good job tonight. I'm proud." Magnus smiled, "Let's do it again." Rain smirked, "We will." They both turned and walked to their rooms, happy. When each returned, they washed off and got into bed.

They woke up shortly after and went to training. It was already too late for them to get any breakfast, so they went hungry. Patri loved to sit on his throne and watch his boys train, so he was sitting there when the two walked in. He asked, "How was your sleep?" Magnus was the first to respond, "Nothing out of the ordinary. Little sore for some reason, though." Rain smirked and replied, "Me too. We can work it off, though." Patri saw the boys smiling and thought nothing of it. Then he said, "Well, you boys get to it."

They shook off their sleepy bodies and took their swords out. Rain looked at Magnus and saw the weariness in his eyes. "I've done this overnight stuff before, so I'll beat you today," he taunted. Magnus taunted back, "Be quiet, Rain. I'm tired, but I'm perfectly able to beat you. So, come get me."

He put his sword in the air and pointed it at Rain. Both smiled and started to fight. They hit and sparred with each other. Each was able to use effective moves and impress the other through their tired dazes.

* * *

It had been a few hours when Magnus jumped through the air, disarmed Rain, and knocked him over. He jumped on top of Rain to pin him to the ground. He grinned victoriously, "So, who's got who now?" Rain looked up at him and smiled, "I do." He shoved Magnus and threw him onto his back. Magnus's sword flung across the floor, and Rain pinned him to the ground. "Told you," he said as he looked down at Magnus. Magnus tried to shift from under Rain to no avail. "You can get off of me now," he said, frustrated. Rain wanted to make the moment last. "Tell me I win first," he said haughtily. "Fine, you win," Magnus said reluctantly.

He crawled off of Magnus and went to collect his sword. Patri had seen the whole thing and finally spoke. He said, "Well done, boys. Magnus, be careful not to get too cocky next time. Rain, well done to pin him, but you shouldn't have let him pin you in the first place."

They went to get back into sparring positions when Patri stopped them. It was already halfway through the day, and he had no reason to exhaust the two. He said, "Anyway, you two can have the rest of the day. Go get some lunch and rest." Both were surprised but didn't want to complain. In unison, they said, "Thank you." After putting away their things, they walked from the king's chamber together to get food.

They both went to the machine in the dining area and ate trug and rice with foin juice to drink. They sat at a table across from each other and started eating. There was some mumbling from around them, but they were focused on the food. They were famished since they slept in and missed breakfast. They each went back for another plate without exchanging a word. After Rain finished his second plate and Magnus was almost finished with his second, he looked at Rain and raised a toast. "To Brotherhood," he said, putting his cup in the air. "To brotherhood," Rain responded, hitting his cup against Magnus's. The two finished and went to bed early to get the much-needed sleep. They were growing closer every day, and for the first time, they each had a family to call their own.

9

BROTHERS

It was over a year into their work when they got an assignment for a regular drug bust. Both didn't know that this mission would be one they would remember for a long time to come.

It was the end of the afternoon, and Rain walked into Magnus's room to deliver some news. Magnus slept late that day, so he was in his bathroom when Rain entered his room.

"Magnus!" he yelled.

"What, Rain? I'm busy," Magnus said through his bathroom door.

"We have another drug bust we gotta do. It's on level nineteen," Rain said.

"Another one? I thought we would get a break here and there. I'm kinda getting tired of these missions all the time. When do we get to do fun stuff?" Magnus asked with a curious tone.

"That's the life. Just eat, sleep, and do stuff for Patri. It gets monotonous after a while," Rain said plainly.

Then, Magnus walked from the bathroom and seemed disappointed that his life seemed to become the same story over and over again. He shook his hands dry and asked, "What if we did something different for once?"

Rain shrugged, "What would we do? There's nothing that interesting in this city." Magnus responded, "I don't know. We're going a bit higher tonight; maybe there's something up there." Rain had seen almost every level beneath level 10 and knew about the entertainment options on the 23rd level. He lowered his voice, "I know a few places on level twenty-three we could go if we get the time. But it's not like we will anyway." He seemed saddened as if something had happened with the 23rd level in his past. Magnus smiled reassuringly.

"We will, Rain, don't worry about it. It's good not to kill and fight people all the time."

"Yeah, yeah, just come on to the main chamber. I want to show you a new move I've perfected," Rain said.

"I'll be there in a second," Magnus responded.

His voice trailed behind Rain as he left the room. He was distraught about level twenty-three because it was where Patri promised he would take him if he did well in training. But after Patri scolded him, he never got to go there again. Bringing it up made him think of all the other families he'd seen, especially on that level, in his time in the city. All of them looked happy together, something he had never had. A vivid memory of a boy sitting on his father's shoulders in front of Itwit's burned in his brain. It reminded him of the relationship he never had but craved so dearly.

He walked down the hallway, deep in thought, until he reached the main chamber. "Father!" he yelled from across the room. Patri was cleaning off the table from his breakfast and adding a polish to the wooden frame. He ate simply, with usually some bread and fruit of sorts for his meal. "Yes!?" he answered as he lifted his head from the table to face Rain.

Rain was now walking toward his father. He said, "Magnus and I are going to train." Patri smiled and said, "Ah, Magnus, he's got some potential, that boy." "He really does, doesn't he," Rain whispered under his breath. He knew his father preferred his stepbrother, but he didn't want to accept it. He loved his new brother, but the favoritism made him upset with his father. Nevertheless, he didn't blame Magnus for any of it.

He turned to face the door, hoping to see Magnus because being alone with his father made him feel uneasy. Magnus was fixing his hair as he walked in and waved at Patri.

"Father."

"Magnus, good to see you. You coming to train?" Patri asked positively.

"Yes, Rain wanted to show me something new," Magnus answered.

"Well, enjoy yourself. I'm gonna finish with this table."

He continued to clean the table and put some polish on it. "Come on, Magnus, let's go," Rain said. He gestured toward the training dummies to show off his new skill. "So, what is it you want to show me?" Magnus asked. Rain scratched his left elbow and looked back.

"I don't really have a name for it yet. I figured you could help me out with that," he said while gripping his sword's hilt.

"Well, I'd love to see it so I can name it for you," Magnus said excitedly.

"Then just watch," Rain said.

He took his blade from its sheath and pointed it at the training dummy. He stood for a while before Magnus spoke again, "Are you going to do something or?" As he spoke, Rain tossed his sword into the air. It spun end over end until he hurled himself into the air after it. He caught it mid-air. It flew perfectly from his hand and landed directly in the dummy's head. The wood splintered as he hit the target. He landed gracefully and walked over to pull the sword from the dummy. He confidently sheathed his sword and said, "There you go, Magnus." Magnus's eyes were glazed over in awe. He said, "W-wow, not bad at all." He continued with a bit of questioning in his voice, "I don't see how well it could be used in combat because no one will give you the time to throw your sword in the air." Rain responded, "Oh yeah, I don't really plan on using that in a real fight, but it could be a cool trick to use one day." Magnus was still impressed, but he smirked. Then, he said, "I don't know when you'll need a bar trick, but I'm impressed, to say the least."

Rain stood momentarily before asking, "So, what should I name it?" Magnus paused to think about a possible name. Finally, he answered, "Something to do with air would be fitting," They both sat puzzled for a moment before Rain's eyes perked up.

"Falcon! That's what we should call it."

"Seems a little bland, though," Magnus replied.

"Okay then, what do you want to call it?" Rain asked.

"I don't know. I just thought it was a little boring."

"Well, I'm going to stick with it anyway. Falcon it is," Rain said decisively.

"Falcon it is," Magnus repeated.

He paused until he said, "What else do you want to do today before we do our thing and go fight more people?" Rain answered, "Honestly, I don't know. I want to save my energy, so something light." They sat and thought before Magnus suggested, "We could work on throwing for a bit. You know I could use some work on throwing." Rain chuckled, "You do need work, so let's do it." It was afternoon, and lunch was still being served, but they went to train anyway.

They both turned toward the dummies. There was an area where all the daggers went in for training, and Magnus grabbed one and twirled it in his fingers. He said, "First one to hit the head gets in line for food first." He threw his first dagger and missed entirely. Rain laughed and grabbed his dagger. "This is how you actually throw," he taunted. The blade flew from his hand and perfectly hit the dummy's head. He smirked proudly, and Magnus waved him off. "So, I guess I'm getting food first," he teased. Magnus smirked and said, "Yeah, yeah, whatever. It'll probably suck anyway. And you know I never learned how to throw." Rain frowned and mockingly said, "Excuses, excuses." Magnus walked back with the dagger he had thrown and gestured at Rain, "So how do you throw?" Rain smirked again and said, "You just throw it." And without looking, he drilled the dummy's head again.

Magnus was irritated with how good his brother was. He didn't want to deal with the mocking anymore, so he said with an annoyed tone, "Just go get your stuff and let's go eat." Rain smirked again and went to pull his daggers from the dummy. They both put their daggers back in their place and started to walk to the hallway.

Before the boys got to the hallway, Patri caught a glimpse of them from his throne. He lifted his head and said, "Where are you going?" Rain quickly responded, "To get something to eat." Patri nodded his head and wished them a good time. They left the chamber and went to the right to head toward the dining hall. They heard the sound of people talking in the distance, but they couldn't make any of it out.

Then, Magnus asked, "You seemed upset when I asked about doing something more fun. Were you?" As he walked, Rain looked at the ground and answered, "It's just a hard topic, having fun and all." Magnus scoffed and said, "That's vital to your life." Rain smiled sarcastically, "It has never been to me. I've always just been a worker. I go out and kill for Patri to earn his respect. The whole idea of free time or fun just doesn't exist." Magnus seemed distraught at his brother's statement and put his hand on Rain's shoulder. He said, "Well, we can fix that when we're done tonight." Rain shrugged and walked the rest of the way in silence. Since, they had trained later into the afternoon, most of the compound had already eaten, so there weren't any others on in the hallway.

He remembered all the pain his father had brought him and wondered if Magnus was as good as he seemed or was pretending to be kind like Patri did. He wasn't sure if people could be good at all. He was always trained to kill and be a heartless warrior, but Magnus showed him something different. He also noticed that Patri was lightening up ever since Magnus came into the picture, and he hoped it stayed that way. He had more freedom in adulthood, like missions and getting his own food, but his father was still tight with him. Magnus was changing everything.

The two got to the dining hall, and it was, for the most part, empty. There was an older couple, two young women, and an older man sitting on the far side, and they all gave the two a quick wave. They waved back, and they walked to the machine and were lucky enough to get two pre-made plates of roasted yut legs, a type of old-world bird with tender meat and a true delicacy before artificial food ran rampant.

This machine wasn't as new as the one Magnus was used to in the Berserker compound. Most of the city ran on more recent models that could make food much quicker, but this model took a ridiculous amount of time to produce one meal. So, they usually gambled for who went first since the machine took so long.

Magnus smiled and said, "Neither of us has to wait. It didn't matter that you were so good with the daggers." Rain smiled and shrugged, "I guess you're right." They walked to a table and sat to eat.

Magnus dug into the meal and tore the meat from the bone while Rain carefully used utensils to get the meat from the bone. Magnus talked through a stuffed mouth, "Weren't you starving?" Rain looked up from his plate and said, "I'm just taking my time, is all." "Your loss," Magnus said as he dug his face back into his plate. They continued to eat, and Magnus finished first. He ran his plate to the return area so the machine could wash it. After, he sat back down and quietly waited for Rain to finish.

Rain usually liked to eat alone or in silence because it was the only time he got away from Patri as a child. He finally finished his plate and stood up to put his plate in the tray. He returned to the table and sat down with a quiet grunt. Magnus quickly asked, "So, what are we gonna do the rest of the day?" Rain sat silent for a moment, "Well, we could go back and work on that pathetic throwing of yours." He chortled at his comment, and Magnus gave him an upset yet playful look.

"Might as well. I could use a bit of work, couldn't I?" he agreed.

"Yeah, you do," Rain jeered.

"You're not supposed to affirm that. You're supposed to say something nice," Magnus poked.

"The truth isn't always nice, is it?" Rain said dramatically.

"Oh, shut up," Magnus retorted playfully. He waved Rain off.

They were about to stand up when the old man from earlier tapped Rain on the shoulder. "Training with your brother going well? Everyone loves the two of you, and it's a shame you don't come out of the king's chamber that often," he said. Rain looked up and answered, "Everything is going well, and you know how Patri can be. It always just training when he's around." He man chuckled and responded, "It's always been that way, even when he was closer to your age." Magnus smiled and little, and so did Rain. The older man patted Rain again and said, "I should go. Have a good rest of your day." Rain smiled, "You too."

As he left, Magnus leaned in and asked, "Who was that?" Rain smirked and said, "That's an old friend named Indoe. I dunno much about him, but he was around a lot when I was younger." "Ah," Magnus nodded. He continued, "Let's get back to training." Rain nodded and said, "Agreed."

They got up and walked for the hallway. When they were there, they saw the women from earlier ahead of them.

"She's cute. Isn't she?" Rain said abruptly. Magnus turned his head quickly.

"What?"

"The one on the right," Rain added.

"I mean, she's fine," Magnus said nonchalantly. Rain looked offended.

"Fine? I think she looks gorgeous."

"Well, good for you. Can we focus on training please," Magnus said joking. Rain waved his hands in the air.

"Fine, fine. You're the one who needs the work anyway. Besides, looking at girls is fun. I never knew that when I was stuck with Patri."

"It is. But right now, I want to learn, and you're the one who can teach me," Magnus said.

"Okay. Okay," Rain responded as they turned the corner for Patri's chamber.

Patri himself must have retreated to his room because he was nowhere to be seen. The two got back to the training area, and both picked up a dagger. "Bet you can't do it again," Magnus said, challenging his brother's prowess. "Watch me," Rain taunted. He threw the dagger from his hand, and it hummed through the air. It landed directly on the dummy's head and almost went through the wooden surface. "You were saying?" he said as he smirked at Magnus. "Fair enough then. So, you want to teach me?" Magnus asked. He gave playful eyes, and Rain couldn't help but smile, "Sure, Magnus, I'll teach you."

"Grab a dagger," he commanded. Magnus grabbed one and pointed it at him. "Put it down, Magnus," Rain teased. He laughed a bit and lowered it down. He said, "Alright, Rain, what do I have to learn?" Rain walked over and grabbed himself a dagger. He stepped back to face the dummy. He stood in a throwing stance and taught, "So you have to plant your feet and look through where you want your throw to hit. Hold it tight and let go at the peak of your arm's motion. Like this." He moved slower than normal and threw the dagger across the room. The blade flew into the dummy's head. He looked back and said, "Just like that. Give it a go." Magnus stepped forward and held the dagger in his right hand. "So how do I hold it?" he asked. "Don't hold it too tight, but you also have to have enough grip to control the blade," Rain said as he put his hand on Magnus's.

Magnus shook his head and stared through the dummy. He took a deep breath and let go. His foot raised off the ground, and the dagger flew into the dummy's torso. Rain looked mildly impressed but still corrected, "Magnus, you can't lift your foot like that, or your dagger will fly low. Keep your feet balanced." Magnus grabbed another dagger and responded, "Got it, got it." He took another deep breath and threw the dagger. His feet shifted slightly, and the dagger landed on the dummy's shoulder. Rain smiled and said, "Not bad, not bad at all." Magnus turned with his hands held up in celebration. "That was pretty good, huh?" he said excitedly. "You still have plenty of work left to do, so don't get too excited," Rain said calmly. But there was a hint of pride bleeding into his voice.

They trained for hours until Patri finally returned and saw them on the other side. He asked the two, "How's it going over here?" Both were getting bored with the throwing, and Rain said, "We're just finishing up." Patri nodded and said, "From what I saw walking over here, you guys put in some good work, but Rain, you might want to watch your throwing speed. A good fighter will see right through that." "Of course, of course," Rain said reluctantly.

Patri moved quickly to Magnus, "Magnus, you're coming along beautifully. Keep up the good work, my son." He nodded and walked back to his room as it was nearly time for him to sleep that night. After he left, Rain stayed silent, but Magnus said, "Should we get ready to leave then?" Rain still stared at the ground in reaction to Patri's words, but he shook it off and said, "Yeah, yeah, I guess we should. Meet back at the doors in an hour." The two collected all the daggers and put them back where they belonged. "I'll see you then," Magnus said as he returned to his room to get ready.

Rain sat for a moment processing the reason why Magnus received so much praise while he was put down. He thought about all the issues with his father and figured it was too late to save his relationship with Patri. He had always wanted a strong relationship, but it always eluded him. He stepped back to Patri's room, hoping his father was asleep so he wouldn't have to talk with him.

Though his past hurt him, he was happy Magnus could have what he never did. His hand extended to open the door, and he saw his father had just finished changing into his sleeping clothes. They were smooth red wool with the Devil's Hand's crest on the right side of the chest. Rain said nothing and quickly disappeared into his room and shut the door behind him. He despised his father for keeping him so close, but he couldn't disobey the orders of a king or a father. He plopped onto the bed and sat briefly just to rest his legs.

Then, shortly after, he stood up and went to change into some new battle clothes. They were black and tight-fitting, with the crest on the right side of the chest. He slipped them on, took his elegant sword, and attached the sheathed weapon to his waist. He went back and sat on his bed to kill time and make sure Patri was asleep before he went back through to the main chamber.

Magnus did similarly and changed into his clothes. He also packed a bag of extra clothes to change into for him and Rain and put it on his back. Next, he took his sword and attached it to his waist. Finally, he went to the bathroom in his room, took his sword out, and sat admiring it in the mirror to kill some time. The gold that ran the edge shimmered, and the ornate nature of the blade still awed him. He still wasn't sure where it came from but was glad it was in his hands. He sat for a bit longer before getting up to go back to the main chamber. And when he got to the main doors, he didn't see Rain, so he waited patiently.

Rain quietly opened his door and saw his father asleep, so he slipped across the room and left for the main chamber. He quietly shut the door behind him and saw Magnus standing at the other end of the room. "There you are," Magnus said. Rain sarcastically remarked, "I'm here, aren't I? And what's that on your back?" Magnus responded, "The bag is for later, don't worry about it." Rain gave a look but decided not to pursue the idea.

The two went from the main doors and walked to the compound's exit. The guards were close enough so that the light from the doorway illuminated them all. Magnus smiled and pointed at the head guard, "Can't scare me this time." The man laughed back, "I'll get you again. I'm not worried about it." Magnus smiled and shook his head, "You're probably right." Rain remained quiet throughout the process and walked toward the first elevator. Once the elevator came down, they got on and were carried up to level 80. The doors opened, and they nodded at the guard as they headed toward the main elevator.

They got in and made their way to level 19. Both sat in silence as the elevator raised itself. They both pulled their masks over their faces, and the elevator slammed to a halt. The two exited and climbed to the nearest rooftop. As always, it was a cold night, but the two had a simple task ahead of them. They moved across the rooftops and eventually got to the drug deal. Rain looked closely and said, "It only looks like two of them. It'll be easy enough." Magnus looked over and nodded in affirmation. They found their way off the rooftop and hid around the corner.

One of the dealers was a bigger man, and one was an average-looking woman. They were handing each other the Ugurns until the brothers pounced behind them. Rain kicked the man down before he could even draw his weapon. Magnus took a bit longer, but eventually, he knocked the woman to the ground. The man drew his weapon while still on the ground, a small cutlass, and raised it at Rain. "Who are you?" he asked.

The woman soon tried to do the same, but as she drew her knife, Magnus kicked it from her hand. "Ah!" she yelled as she shook her hand off from the hit. Simultaneously, Rain looked calmly into the man's eyes and said, "We're here for the money. Give it to us, and no one will die." The woman had given the man the money for him to count and knew fighting wouldn't be her best option. She didn't like losing profit, but she got up and ran away. She picked up her knife as she ran, and she soon disappeared into the dark.

The man tried to crawl backward, but Rain calmly walked toward him. Magnus turned to see him standing over the man. The man looked around frantically for an option. "I won't give it to you!" he yelled. Rain tilted his head menacingly.

Suddenly, the man yelled, "Raah!" and swung at Rain's legs. Rain was too far for him to hit, but he still cautiously jumped back. He swung his sword at the ground, and it made sparks fly through the air. But the man managed to evade and scramble to his feet. Then, he started trying to run away. Rain had to regain his composure before chasing him. But before he could do anything, Magnus reached to his side and grabbed a dagger. In one fluid motion, he threw the blade and hit the man in the square of his back. The man let out a quick grunt before skidding to a halt and falling to the ground, dead.

Rain looked over proudly and said, "Someone learned something today." Magnus smiled wide and walked over to collect the money from the man's body. He turned it over and rummaged through the pockets until he found the sack of Ugurns. It was 2,455 Ʉ, and he loved what he saw. He raised the money in the air and said proudly, "Jackpot." Rain smiled back and put his sword away. He said with a proud undertone, "Good work. Let's go back to the compound and get some rest."

He turned around and went to find a way back up to the rooftops of the level when Magnus grabbed him, smirked, and said, "There is still definitely time for us to go have some fun." Rain looked at him like he didn't want to, but Magnus's eager eyes were hard to resist.

"It's really not that special, you know?" Rain said in a last effort to convince Magnus not to go.

"Anything is gonna be a bit more entertaining than killing people," Magnus poked. He pulled Rain back to him. Rain was still trying to stop the idea, so he made another excuse.

"Magnus, we don't have a change of clothes. We can't just wear our stuff to another level."

"Remember the bag you were so curious about?" Magnus said with a small smile crawling over his face.

He took the bag off his back and opened it to reveal the clothes inside. He had grabbed two pairs of cargo shorts with two black t-shirts for both of them to change into. Rain looked stunned, "You did not bring a change of clothes. I thought that bag would have something useful to fight with." Magnus laughed again, "Nope. It's time for some fun." He reached his hand in and pulled out Rain's outfit. He tossed it onto the floor, and Rain looked at it confused. "You want me to change here?" he asked. Magnus looked up from the bag and reassured, "They were doing a drug deal here. I don't think anyone's watching."

He took out his outfit and put it on the ground. He took off his clothes down to his undergarments and stuffed them into the bag. Rain watched him stupidly. Magnus chuckled, "Come on, Rain, don't make me the only one standing here in my underwear." Rain smiled weakly and finally started to take off his clothes.

They finished changing and shoved their old clothes back into the bag. "I'm not used to short sleeves," Rain said as he moved his shoulders around. Magnus put the bag on his back and ushered Rain toward where the platforms would be, "Let's go have some fun."

They walked their way through the residential area until they arrived at the walkway. They got on an empty platform and rode it to level 23. As they stepped off, Rain looked overwhelmed by the surplus of options, so he asked, "Where do you want to go?" Magnus looked back, "As if I'd know. I've never even seen this place. But if I had to choose, that Higurn's place looks pretty good, and we have the Ugurns to pay." He shook the bag of coins in the air with a smile. Rain pushed him and said, "You know that's for the clan." Magnus turned, "And how would anyone know?" Rain looked flabbergasted at the response but had no time to process it before Magnus took off in a sprint toward Higurn's. He chased after his brother and felt a thrill he never got while isolated in his room back home.

Magnus opened the doors to Higurn's and saw it wasn't too busy. The restaurant had an open area with plenty of seating. It had soft lighting with decorations that made the restaurant feel like a wooded cabin. There was a bar where a bartender mixed up drinks, along with plenty of booths for people to sit and eat a good meal. They were made of faded blue leather and dark wood.

He walked through the door to the hostess stand. Behind the stand stood a larger woman with a blue uniform with black pants. Her hair was tied in a messy bun, and her skin was glossed with a light sweat. He placed his name with her and waited on a bench inside. Rain burst into the doors soon after. He looked around the room frantically and saw Magnus. He sighed in relief and sat next to him.

"How long do we have to wait?" he asked.

"The hostess said not too long," Magnus reassured.

"No, how long," Rain pressured.

"She literally said that, so I'm not sure," Magnus said back.

He shook his head with a smile. The two sat for a bit longer until the hostess came back and said, "Table for Magnus?" He stood up, "That's me."

She motioned the two to follow and led them to a corner booth. She put two menus on the table and said, "Here you guys go. Your server will be with you soon, and don't forget tonight is karaoke night." Magnus removed his bag and placed it next to him in the booth. They both looked at the menu for a bit until they decided what they wanted to drink. The drinking age in the city was 19, but no one cared, and a restaurant like Higurn's wouldn't bother as long as they made a profit.

They sat just a second before a waiter came to talk to them. He was an average man who looked to be in his twenties. He also wore a blue uniform shirt with black pants. He had a pleasant smile and said, "Hello, my name is Cody. What can I get you to drink?" Magnus answered, "Can I have a nice fragerita?" The menu said it was a chilled berry drink with an explosive taste. Cody nodded and pulled out a notepad while turning to Rain. He asked, "And what for you, sir?" Rain paused, "Um, I'll just have what he's having." Cody nodded, "Okay, two frageritas. Anything else?" Magnus spoke next, "Can we also get those bread rolls?" "Of course," Cody said. He still wore his pleasant smile and asked, "Is that all for now?" Magnus smiled back and said, "Yes." Cody clicked his pen and put his notepad away. Then, he said, "That'll all be to you shortly." He then walked off to place the orders in the kitchen.

Magnus looked at Rain and wondered why his brother looked so lost. "Rain, you okay?" he asked. Rain tried to shake off his glazed appearance, "Oh yeah, I'm fine. It's just this is kinda new. Living a whole normal city life is something I never had, and I've never really drunk either." Magnus nodded and said, "To be fair, I haven't drunk much either. The Berserkers would give me drinks from time to time, but it was a rare thing. We can have a good time tonight though." Rain finally smiled, "To that, we can."

They sat for a bit until Cody returned with the drinks and bread. "Thank you," both said. He pulled his notebook back out and asked, "Are we ready to order?" They both nodded, and he looked at Magnus first. Magnus said, "I'll have the grilled trug with the steamed vegetables." He scribbled it down quickly and turned to Rain, who said, "Um, I'll have the yut wings with the extra side of the Higurn's sauce." He wrote it down and asked, "Is that everything?" Magnus looked at Rain, who nodded and said, "Yeah, that's everything." Cody smiled again and said, "Okay, I'll put that in for you, and it should be here soon." Then, he walked back to the kitchen to place the order.

"Wanna try these drinks?" Magnus asked. Rain shrugged, "I see no reason why not." Magnus raised the glass, "To fun." Rain raised his drink to collide with Magnus's, "To fun." They took the first sips of their glasses and realized the drinks were better and stronger than they thought. "Wow, that's actually really good," Magnus said through a scrunched face. Rain nodded to agree as he swallowed. Next, they tore into the bread and didn't even wait to talk to each other as Rain got a half-loaf and Magnus got the other half. They scoffed it down and washed it down with more to drink.

Shortly after the bread was demolished, Cody brought out the food and water to wash down the drinks. He put the plates down and smiled wide. He said, "Hope you enjoy it. Anything else for you guys?" Magnus looked at Rain's glass and saw it was nearly empty like his. "Two more frageritas," he said cheerfully. Cody pulled out the notebook again and wrote down the order. "Two more coming up," he responded happily. He returned to the kitchen, and the two dug into their meals.

Rain ate with a determination he didn't have back at the compound due to the drink. Each bite tasted like heaven, and the Higurn's sauce was a creamy, savory sauce that accompanied his yut wings perfectly. Magnus's mouth was half-full, and he asked playfully, "You like that throw I had tonight, didn't you?" He smiled and put the next bite of trug in his mouth. Rain swallowed his yut and said, "It was a pretty good throw, but I'll have to see you do it again to prove it." He smiled and ripped into his next wing. Cody returned with the two drinks and set them on the table, "Enjoy." He then walked off and went to serve another table.

Both the brothers were starting to feel the effect of the drinks, and they weren't stopping now. "This food was sooo good," Magnus said in a dragged-out voice. "It really was," Rain said slowly as he took another sip of the drink. Both had finished their meals and were finishing the last of their drinks. Magnus took the last sip and slammed his glass down dramatically.

"I have an idea," he said boldly.

"What is it?" Rain asked.

"What if we go sing on that karaoke night the hostess mentioned?" Magnus suggested.

Even though Rain was drunk, he was still reluctant to get up on a stage and sing. He said worriedly, "I don't know. What if we sound bad?" Magnus laughed again, "That's the beauty of it; no one cares." Rain was still hesitant, but then the drink did the talking, "I guess you're right. No one does care." Magnus smiled again, "Now that's what I love to hear. Let's leave our swords here." Rain backed up, offended by the idea, "My sword stays with me." Magnus looked at his brother and said, "Have it your way. I'm leaving mine right here."

As they went to stand up to go to karaoke, Cody returned with the check. He said, "Here you two go. Enjoy the rest of your time." He walked back off and went to take an order across the restaurant. Magnus opened the check, and his eyes shot open. His voice was sluggish and loud, "65 Ugurns. I didn't know living up here was so expensive!" He pulled his bag over and looked for the sack of Ugurns he stole earlier that night. He reached inside and grabbed a handful. "That'll do," he said as he threw the coins down on the table. He had actually placed down 220 Ugurns on the check. "Let's go sing," he said, putting his sword next to his bag.

They got up and walked toward the back of the restaurant, where a microphone and speaker waited for them. Rain still seemed somewhat nervous, but Magnus's peer pressure pushed him onto the stage. Magnus pointed at the DJ sitting behind a table with a set of records to play. They were all songs from the old world that had been circulating since the explosion. The DJ lowered the needle to the record player, and a classic came on. It was titled "Play With Fire." It was a heavy metal song that blended its words together into one harsh sound, perfect for a drunk mind.

Magnus sang along to the best of his ability, but Rain had no idea what was happening. He hadn't heard much music and had no idea what this song was saying. Magnus saw his brother standing awkwardly and signaled the DJ to cut off the music. He reached to Rain's shoulder and shook it.

"What's wrong, Rain? Come sing with me."

"Magnus, I don't know much music. I have no idea what that last song was," Rain answered weakly.

"Well, what songs do you know?" Magnus asked.

"I do know one. It's called Legend. Patri used to play it for me all the time," Rain said.

"I love that song! I always heard it growing up," Magnus said excitedly.

He smiled, pointed at the DJ, and mouthed Legend. The DJ nodded and pulled out a new record. He set it on the machine, and the song started to play.

It was an upbeat song with a strong base that echoed through the restaurant. Rain stepped onto the stage and grabbed the microphone Magnus wasn't using. The two started slow, but soon their energy was endless. They belted their lungs out until the line, *So I made myself a legend.* They both sang so intensely to this one line that they almost stopped momentarily. They were both smiling and dancing around the stage. The rest of the restaurant looked at them like they were crazy, but they didn't care. They sang their hearts out and enjoyed every second. "Woooooo!" Rain yelled as he jumped close to Magnus. He yelled, "This is awesome!" Magnus smiled back, "I know!"

"I love you," Rain blurted out under the harsh sound.

"You what?" Magnus asked, confused.

"I love you, Magnus," Rain said again. Magnus froze, and for the moment, it was silent.

"Did you just tell me you loved me?" he asked.

"Yes, I did. It hasn't even been too long, and I already realize how special of a brother you are. You have taken me out of my shell and shown me more than I would ever see. I thank you for that, and I'm glad you can be by my side."

Magnus almost began to tear up, but he quickly stopped himself, "Thank you. I love you too. I don't know everything about you, but I know I'm here for you even when no one else is."

Rain nearly broke down, but he kept his composure and went to hug his brother. He leaned in and whispered, "I think it's time we go back home." Magnus was a bit disappointed, but he knew he was right. "Yeah, I guess it is. This was a really fun time, and I'm glad we're getting as close as we are." Rain agreed, "I am too. I am too. Let's get out of here." They walked to the DJ and placed the microphones on the table.

They hopped off the stage and walked back to the table. Their walking wasn't exactly straight, but they managed. "Man, I'm exhausted," Magnus said as they neared the table. "Oh, I am too, and we're going to have to train tomorrow, too," Rain said as they got to the table. Magnus looked back to hear what his brother said and grabbed his stuff from the seat. He kept looking at Rain as he threw the bag over his shoulder and chuckled, "Training is going to suck tomorrow. But we got a good night in, and I think it was worth it." Rain looked down and smiled, "It definitely was." They walked from Higurn's back into the main street on level 23, but Magnus forgot a vital piece in that booth, his weapon.

The cold wind struck them in their clothing, and Magnus turned toward the platforms. He started walking before Rain grabbed his shoulder and said, "We're using the elevator." Magnus looked surprised and said, "Oh, right." He guided Magnus back to the elevator as fast as he could. And once they arrived, He hit the keypad, and the elevator picked them up. They both got in and tried to keep their balance as it started to head down. In silence, they took the long trip back down to level 80. Once they reached level 80, they went to the other elevator and nodded their way past the guard. They stepped into the elevator, lowering them to level 87. When it hit bottom, the doors creaked open, and the two stepped out. "It's me, Magnus!" he yelled so that the guards at the bottom wouldn't arrest or try to murder him. The head guard spoke from the darkness, "There you two are. Where have you two been all night?" Magnus stayed quiet for a moment but realized he needed to answer.

"We busted a drug deal and then went to Higurn's for dinner."

"Oh, Higurn's, it's been quite a while since I've eaten there. Was it any good?" the guard asked.

"It was amazing, and it felt really nice in there, too," Rain said stupidly.

"Well, you two better get inside and rest up. You're probably going to have some form of training tomorrow," the guard said.

"We most definitely will," Magnus assured.

The two walked into the smaller entrance and saw the massive double doors standing tall before them. They cracked open the right door and slipped inside before shutting it quietly. "So, I guess it's time for us to go to our rooms then?" Rain said. Magnus yawned, "It is. I'm exhausted, and my bed sounds fantastic right now." "Agreed," Rain said while fighting off a yawn. It was quiet for a bit until he extended his arms. "What do you need?" Magnus asked. Rain gestured for him to come closer to him and said, "Just a simple hug." They held each other for a long moment until Magnus heard sniffling. "Are you okay?" he asked as he buried his head in Rain's shoulder. Rain struggled to get the words out, but he said through sniffles, "Thank you." "For what?" Magnus asked in a surprised tone.

Rain paused again to get adequate air and said, "For being the brother I always needed." Magnus started to sniffle from such a heartfelt comment. He fought off tears and said, "I'm here for you, Rain, and I'm proud to call you my brother." Finally, a single tear ran down both their cheeks as they embraced tighter. They stood longer than they probably should have in silence, just holding each other. Magnus sniffed and said, "It is definitely time for us to go to bed." Rain wiped the tear in his eye and nodded, "It is for sure." The two both saw each other crying and laughed a bit before giving each other another embrace. "I'll see you tomorrow," Magnus said as they pulled apart. "See you tomorrow," Rain said in response.

He turned around to walk to his room. Magnus was about to turn around when he remembered the bag on his back. "Rain, your clothes!" Rain whipped around, "Oh, right. Just toss them here." Magnus reached inside the bag, grabbed Rain's clothes and mask, and threw them. He caught them and started to walk back to his room again. As he did so, Magnus said, "Goodnight!" "Goodnight!" Rain yelled back. He turned and entered his father's room. Patri was still asleep, so he quietly slipped into his own room.

Magnus walked down the long hallway and quietly entered his room. They each took a quick, warm shower and put on their sleepwear. Both were also thinking about how lucky they were to have a brother and how they wouldn't trade it for the world. They had each grown up without a brother, and now, they both had their chance to finally have what the cruel city never gave them. This new sense of peace and security lured them to their beds, and within a matter of minutes of their heads hitting their pillows, they were fast asleep.

10

DRUNKEN MISPLACING

As Magnus and Rain left Higurn's, Cody went to clean off their table. He saw the massive sum of Ugurns on the table and nearly dropped to the ground. A tip like that was outrageous, so he gladly stuffed it into his pockets. He gathered himself and kept cleaning the rest of the table. He vigorously scrubbed the scraps they had left behind but saw something in the seat. *What is that?* He took the sheathed blade and gave it a spin in his hand. Immediately his curiosity took over, and he started to take it out. When he saw the golden glow, he quickly put it back. He knew if anyone saw it, they would want it. But he also saw a great opportunity for profit, so he planned on talking to the customers about a potential buyer during his shift. His shift wasn't based on time but on how many tables he served. So, he went to finish serving the three more tables he had left.

He approached the first table and asked, "Anyone want to buy something?" The customers gave him a strange look until a man at the end of the table spoke up, "What is it you have to sell?" "Here it is," Cody answered.

He pulled the first bit of the blade and showed it to the man across the table. He chuckled, "You're trying to sell me a sword? Cause if so, just take our plates and stop trying." Cody was disappointed but figured he had two more tables to speak to. But first, he did have to grab the plates from the table he just spoke with, so he did.

He walked to the following table, which he had already served and given the check to, and asked, "How was everything?" All the people at the table nodded happily. He took the bill with the Ugurns and asked, "Any of you interested in buying a sword? Someone left it here." The table's eyes poked up in interest. Then, Cody took the sword out and showed the first bit of the blade. The table looked in awe until a lady on the right side interjected, "If someone left it, maybe they'll come back." The rest of the table nodded in agreement as their awe turned to complacency. "Thank you for the offer, but we don't need it," the lady said. Cody was disappointed again but said, "Thank you anyway, and have a great night."

Only one more table was left for the night, and they had already paid, so their conversation would be quick. The group was standing to go, but Cody got there first, and he abruptly asked, "Did you all enjoy your time here?" The group turned around and seemed mildly annoyed. They wore rough clothing, but it was enough to get them by. The group and Cody stood awkwardly, looking at each other, until a cute boy looked up at Cody and said in a high-pitched squeal, "It was really good!" Cody smiled at the boy and then addressed the adults, "Any of you want to buy a sword?" The group looked very confused at the absurd question until he pulled it from his side. He took the beginning of the blade out, and they seemed awestruck by it, like the previous table. "So?" Cody asked hopefully. An older man responded with a melancholy voice, "Thanks for the offer, kid, but we don't have the money for something like that." "I understand," Cody said as he returned the sword to its sheath. The group walked out and left him ultimately disappointed. He put the sword back on his side and cleaned off the rest of his tables so he could leave. He figured he could bring the blade back the next day, and someone new would want to buy it from him.

As he walked back to finish his duties, a tall man with a brown cloak walked into the restaurant, past the hostess, and sat near the front. Cody had no idea and kept cleaning the last of his tables.

The last few groups left their tables clean and didn't give Cody much of a job. The first table left a 3Ʊ tip, the second a 7Ʊ tip and the third didn't leave any tip at all, but he figured it had something to do with the fact the man said they couldn't afford the sword. He pocketed the money and wiped the tables off. He finished and went to clock out in the kitchen. He walked with his head down, and his shoulders drooped in disappointment, but there was tomorrow.

All seemed normal as he walked towards the exit. He saw his co-worker, a shorter man with the same uniform and a faded name tag that read Andrew, and told him, "I'll see you tomorrow." Andrew nodded and waved him off.

He was near the exit and was preparing to tell the hostess goodnight when the lone man in a brown cloak stuck his hand up. It was dark and covered in calluses. "I'll take it," he said. Cody was started by the deepness of the voice but turned excitingly.

"How much will you pay for it?" he asked with greedy eyes. The man reached into his pocket, pulled out a bag of Ugurns, and dropped it onto the table. A few 500Ʉ coins fell out. "That should be more than enough," Cody said as he reached to grab the bag. He opened it and saw what he was hoping for. It was full of 500Ʉ coins. "Yeah, that'll, that'll do," he said in a shaky voice. He had never seen money like that, and it would be enough for him to finally leave this job. He put the sword on the table and walked away, counting his profits. *I'll never have to work again!* His fingers rummaged through the 500Ʉ coins. He left the restaurant without talking to the hostess, and he left the man with a sheathed sword on his table.

Shortly after, the man stood up, took the sword from the restaurant, and walked outside. He walked all the way to the platforms and hopped a descending one. He rode it all the way down to level 74, one of the last residential levels, and got off there. The lights in the houses were off, but most of the windows were boarded up anyway since no one cared to fix anything this far down. "Irresponsible," he whispered as he walked into the level. He looked around and found a small alley between two black houses roughly a ten-minute walk away from the platforms. *It'll do,* he thought, walking into the alley. He found a comfortable place and fell asleep with the sword in his lap.

* * *

At the same time, Magnus tossed and turned in his bed. It had only been a couple of hours since he fell asleep from the long night, but dreams take no account of the time. A dream rattled inside his head, causing his body to shift uncomfortably. He saw a blinding gold aura that made it hard to make out anything. Then, a faint symbol started to form in the distance. He started to walk towards it and found it hard to reach. Gold, alley-like walls started to form around him. He kept walking until he heard a man's voice echo unintelligibly through the alley it seemed he was in. Then, the voice said something clearly, "There you are."

He turned around and tried to see where the voice was coming from. It sounded familiar, but he couldn't quite remember where he had heard it before. He didn't see anything until he heard footsteps from behind him. He turned to face the sound and screamed. It was Helpar with golden blood oozing from the gash he left on his face over a year ago. His eyes glowed an ominous gold, and his teeth grit together through a layer of golden blood. Ever since he left, he was afraid Helpar would find him, and it seemed he had. The giant screamed, "Finally, I found you!" The scream echoed through Magnus's ears as Helpar brought Magnus's own sword to his side. Its golden edges flowed, and its hilt fit into his massive grip. Magnus frantically patted his side to find that his sword was gone. Helpar kept swinging, and Magnus tried to run, only to find the golden light returning in every direction, like a tunnel that only led to Helpar. Though he couldn't see anything, he tried to run away.

He sprinted into the light and heard Helpar's voice echo behind him, "Destiny always catches up." Magnus's eyes started to burn from the light, but he could not stop. He kept running until he ran right into a wall of light. It knocked him back, and he rolled over to face where Helpar would be, and he was there, following. It was like he had never moved, and now he stood facing Helpar again. "Running seems to be what you're good at," Helpar said as he swung the sword again. Magnus tried to throw what seemed like a basket from the alleyway, but it only shattered into golden dust over Helpar's face.

"You can't run, Magnus," Helpar said eerily.

Magnus's dream self froze in fear, and his real body was trashing in the bed. He tried to back up from the approaching giant, but he couldn't move. He tried to make a sound, but he couldn't. Helpar walked right in front of him, grabbed his head, pulled the sword back, and said, "Funny how one would gamble their life like this." He drove the blade through Magnus's chest, and gold blood oozed from his body. Magnus looked up one more time at Helpar and locked eyes. His golden gash dripped, and his eyes shone a vibrant, glistening gold. Then, in a strange voice that didn't belong to Helpar, he said, "seventy-four, seventy-four." He removed the sword, and Magnus's dream body fell to the floor. And right as his body landed, his eyes shot open.

His body was covered in sweat, and he sat up. He looked around the room frantically and realized what he had seen was only a nightmare. He thought nothing of it and simply believed it was a meaningless creation of his mind. So, he exhaled and laid his head back down to go to sleep. However, every time his eyes closed, he heard the voice in his head echo seventy-four. He kept turning, trying to go back to sleep because his head hurt and his body was tired, but the nagging repetition of seventy-four would not leave him alone. He was miserable and decided a trip to the bathroom to wash his face might help him calm down.

He got up and went to the bathroom. He washed his face and took his time feeling the water run down his chin. Eventually, he dried his face and walked out of the bathroom and saw his sword mount empty. *Where is it?* Panic set in as he realized it was gone. He started tearing apart his room, looking for anywhere he could have thrown it when he entered after his night out. *I brought it here. I know I did*, he thought as he lifted his bed sheets to look for it. After he looked everywhere, he gave up and sat on his bed with his head in his hands. He tried to remember the last night out and came to a realization. He remembered leaving his sword on the table and not grabbing it again. He was disappointed in himself and wasn't sure what he would do. *What will I do without my sword?*

He sat for a few minutes until the same number came to mind. When he first found his sword, it gave him a dream to find the Hand's compound. *Could it be doing the same now so I can find it?* He wondered if it was a possibility, but the truth he didn't want to be true hung in his mind. He had lost his sword, which was somewhere on level 74, and he had to get it back.

He sighed deeply, rubbed his eyes, and changed back into his battle clothes. He grabbed his mask and clipped it to his side. He grabbed a few spare daggers and put them on his waist. If he was going to get his sword back, he knew it wouldn't be simple. It was early morning, but that was irrelevant to levels as low as he would be traveling. He left his room and started walking down the hallway toward the doors.

He walked silently and reached the main chamber. It was usually quiet in the compound, and tonight was no different. He looked back at where Patri and Rain were sleeping, and he said, "I'll be back soon enough." He turned and slipped from the main doors. He walked toward the exit and saw the turn for the medical hallway. He put his head back down, walked toward the exit, opened the small door, and left the compound.

"Where are you going?" a voice asked.

Magnus jumped back and said, "Goodness, can you give me a warning or something." The guard laughed a bit but stopped when he recognized the voice.

"Magnus? What are you doing back out here?"

"I think I left my sword up on level seventy-four, so I'm going to get it back," Magnus answered.

"Alright, best of luck then," the guard said.

Magnus reached the elevator, and the doors opened up slowly. He stepped in, put his mask on, and the doors slowly closed behind him. He pressed the button for level 80, and the machine crawled up. It reached the top, and the doors opened. He nodded at the guard outside the door and grimaced after he passed him. He thought of how strange that man was, but that was nothing of his concern. He walked through the dark alley and eventually reached the other elevator. "Wait, what's the code?" he asked himself after popping out the keypad. He had never gotten it from Rain. "I guess I'm taking the platforms then," he said exasperatedly as he walked from the elevator and turned left.

He started walking, and it was pitch black after he passed a thin strip of strip clubs and bars. As he continued to walk, the air started to feel even colder. He brought his arms to his chest to try to get himself to warm up. While shivering, he continued and looked for where the platforms would be. It was dark enough that he couldn't tell where they were, and he watched every step so he wouldn't fall. He felt the ground change from the solid metal floor to the metal leading to the platforms that echoed when someone stepped on them. He took deep breaths and watched his step more carefully to ensure his safety.

Then, he saw the red and blue lights of one of the platforms coming toward him. The light was still faint and would've been hard to see if he wasn't looking. But with it, he was able to see just enough to make out the circular walkway's edge. He got to the edge and waited patiently for the platform to reach him. He started to take large puffs of air to entertain himself. It formed into warm clouds that diminished as they ventured from their source. Finally, the platform reached him, and he stepped on as it came to a complete stop. It soon started to crawl its way back up. No one was with him on the platform, and only one person would join him from levels 79 to 78. It was a hunched man who said no words and quietly walked away.

This is much slower and creepier than the elevator. He yawned into the cold night, and the air formed into more foamy clouds. His body was starting to feel the effects of his night out, but he had to get his sword back. He shook his head right and left to keep himself awake. "Stay awake, stay awake," he kept telling himself. He took his mask off to let the cold air smack his tired face. It wasn't easy, but he stayed awake.

Finally, the platform slowed on level 74, and he stepped onto the walkway. He wasn't sure how or where to start looking for his sword, so he closed his eyes, hoping it would talk to him again. He felt faint feelings like it was calling to him, and he kept thinking it was something. But it was only his tired mind making him believe random things. Then he felt something, a feeling stronger than the others that he couldn't quite explain. It was a drawing feeling, and it guided his steps. "There you are," he said to his sword that was now calling to him.

He continued to walk through the level and past residential houses whose lights were starting to flicker on, but only if their windows weren't boarded. He had been walking for a few minutes now, wondering where his gut was taking him. *Where am I?* he thought until the feeling inside of him halted. *Wait, where do I go now?* He hoped the feeling would return to him. Then, he thought, *Maybe I'm in the right place.*

He was standing next to two black houses with an alleyway on one side and more houses on the other. He kept looking around and thought that whoever lived in one of these houses must have stolen his sword. So, he was going to steal it back. He didn't want to simply barge in, so he looked for another way to get into the first house. He walked around the corner and into the alleyway to find a ladder or some other way in. It was lit dimly by a light hanging from the windowsill of a boarded window. It gave off just enough light to see but hardly enough to make out precise shapes.

He kept walking and didn't see a way into the house, but he saw a man in a brown cloak sleeping on the ground. He was holding something, but Magnus couldn't make it out in the dim light. *What a waste,* he thought as he saw the limp man sleeping. It wasn't uncommon to see something like a man or woman asleep on the cold ground, but Magnus always thought they were wasting themselves by just letting themselves sleep on the floor instead of trying to change things for themselves. Maybe they were just unfortunate and unable to care for themselves, but he still thought there was something they should be doing. Then, from behind him, the man said, "There you are." His voice was deep, and it startled Magnus.

He was still sitting on the ground as Magnus whipped around, drew one of his daggers, and said, "Who said that!?" The man stood up and held the sword across both hands. With his hood still drawn over his face, he answered, "I did. Now tell me, what brought you here?"

Magnus walked slowly and cautiously toward him and said defensively, "Why should I tell you anything?" The man smirked and let out a small laugh with his face still covered by his hood and removed the sword from its sheath. Then, he said, "Because I possess your very livelihood, and it would be a shame for it to be wasted." He dropped the sheath and held the sword down to his left. The gold shone into Magnus's eyes, and he felt a sense of fear staring at his own sword. It was the very thing that changed his life, and now, a random man was brandishing it.

He spoke with a mix of fear, but a wave of righteous anger bled into his voice, "Then, I will get it back." He pulled his dagger back and threw it as hard as he could. Without even thinking, the man stepped to the side, and the blade missed. It clattered somewhere in the dark, and Magnus's jaw dropped. He quickly threw another one, and without moving the sword, the man dodged flawlessly again. "You might want to stop trying," he said. He lowered his hood, and his golden eyes met Magnus's.

Magnus stepped back in shock, "Ghuri?" The man stood silent until he opened his mouth, "Yes, it is me, and be thankful I found this before anyone else did." Magnus tried to say something but was interrupted by Ghuri asking, "But, how did you know where to come to find me?" Magnus was still reserved, and his heart rate had just settled. But, he said, "It was a dream. I fought in a golden world and faced Helpar. He killed me, but he told me the number seventy-four as he did. I didn't want to move out of bed, but I figured washing off would help me fall back to sleep easier. That's when I noticed my sword was gone, and maybe my dream meant something. I came here on the platforms and started walking. I wasn't sure where to go, so I just walked around. After a minute, I closed my eyes and tried to focus because walking around wouldn't lead me anywhere. Once I did that, I felt weird feelings that led me here. Once I got here, the feeling stopped, and I assumed my sword was in a house, but you proved me wrong."

Ghuri bent down, picked up the sheath, and put the sword away. He raised his head and said, "Then you can have this back now. It still speaks to you, so it is still yours." He threw it to the ground, and it bounced toward Magnus. He looked at the sword and then back at Ghuri, who had turned around to leave.

He bent down and picked up the sword before hearing Ghuri say, "Next time, be more careful with your life." He turned from the alleyway and went somewhere else on level 74. Uncertainty flooded Magnus's mind as Ghuri walked away because he wasn't sure where he was going, and he wasn't sure he wanted to follow him anyway. He stood for a few minutes, pondering what Ghuri meant by his last foreboding line. *It's a sword. It isn't my life*, he thought, but he did know something was special about it. He wasn't sure what was so special besides its ability to give him dreams, but he was still proud to be the one who wielded it. Regardless, he put it back onto his belt and took a deep, reassuring breath. Then, he looked in both directions, left the alley, and began his walk back to the platforms.

As he was walking back, he realized he had no idea how he had gotten there. His sword had led him there, and now, he wasn't sure where to go. *I guess I'll go straight again since I came from there*, he thought before stepping forward. He walked past houses and saw dim lights shine in some of them; however, like most levels this far down, life and light were uncommon. On top of the already blanketing clouds on level 71, the dilapidated electricity system on the lower levels was to blame for many of the overhead lights' dysfunction.

Nevertheless, he walked on, hoping to hear the faint sound of the platforms passing by or a conversation he could interrupt to ask for directions. Unfortunately, it was silent, and no one was around. The level was massive, and one wrong turn could make his trip much longer. He knew it, and he was starting to panic over the thought that he could be lost.

He stopped to look around and look for any clues as to where the platforms would be, but he found none. Just dim houses and silence surrounded him. He stayed still to think of anything he could do to get out of level 74. *I guess I could just knock on one of these homes*, he thought, and that's what he did. He walked to a house with only one open window and dim light inside. Its outside looked brown from how dark it was, but the house was actually a comfortable beige. The stone steps to the front door looked like they were once grand stairs, but now, it was a simple stairway with cracked steps and uneven lines. So, he walked carefully up them and went to the door.

The light above the door was out, and the door itself was dark wood with triangle patterns adorning it. He raised his hand and calmly knocked on the door. He sat still and waited for someone to come, but no one did, so he backed up and started to walk away. The door cracked open as his foot hit the bottom of the steps, and an old woman's head popped out.

Looking around nervously, she ushered him to her, "What are you here for?" She looked around again like she was paranoid, mad, or a mix of the two. He walked back to the doorway and asked, "Why are you looking around like that?" The lady looked again and said, "I'm not looking around. I'm completely fine." He looked her up and down skeptically and mumbled, "Okay then. I'm just asking where the platforms are." She opened the door a little bit more to look at him deeper. She paused before pointing and telling him, "Just keep walking straight, and once the air gets cooler, follow that." He was still a few steps from the door because he didn't trust this interesting woman. He nodded, said, "Thank you," and walked back down the steps.

As the door shut, he exhaled and walked in the direction she had pointed. "That was different," he whispered. He kept walking past the absent homes and dim lights. All of them looked like an ugly brown or black, and most windows were still covered with boards. A couple even had bars on them. His pace continued to speed up, and the silence on the level was eerie. No one rummaged in the alleys or walked the streets with him. He started to wonder if that lady had lied to him and if she sent him somewhere dangerous. He looked around, paranoid-like, like the old lady did, and saw nothing. *You're just doing this to yourself*, he thought.

He continued walking alone on the dark street until he felt a cold gust of air come barreling through an alleyway. His eyes widened because he had found what the old lady had told him to look for. He picked up his speed and hastily moved toward the cooler air. The alleyway was as average as alleys in the city were. It was a dimly lit strip of metal with a few lights hanging from the side of buildings. He saw and heard nothing of interest, but he felt the cool winds that would mean his freedom. He started to jog and thought he saw the platforms' faint red and blue lights. His breath escalated in excitement, and his tired body craved to return home. He saw the lights now, and the alley was ending.

But before he could exit, two massive men jumped in front of him. They both brandished a pair of sickles with leather hanging from their hilts. They had brown, battle-worn leather jackets and some sort of black pants. They had no other shirt under their jackets, and their chests bore the weight of many scars. Additionally, they had scarring on their faces to the point it was almost impossible to make out what their faces used to look like.

Magnus leaped back and put his hand to his hilt. He looked straight at the two and waited for one to speak. "Where do you think you're off to," the one on the left said boisterously. Magnus, tired and frightened as he was, was annoyed that he would have to fight again. Then, he said to the two pleadingly, yet strongly, "I'm just trying to go back home, and I've had a lot happening today. Let me go for your own sake." Both laughed and looked at each other with broad smiles. The one on the right finished laughing and said, "For our sake? I'm glad to know you have a sense of humor. Dull people are boring to fight anyway." Magnus still held his sword in its hilt and tried again to talk himself out of a fight.

"I'm just trying to get home, and I don't feel like fighting anyone right now." The two men started to walk and push him back into the alley.

"Too bad you ran into us," the man on the right said.

"Who are you anyway?" Magnus asked with a tinge of intrigue.

"Us? You don't know us?" the man on the left said aggressively.

"Yeah, I have no idea who you are," Magnus smirked.

"Then you will soon know why they call us the brothers of the night," the man on the left said aggressively.

They jumped and swung at Magnus, who quickly stepped back and drew his sword. He had no time to put on his mask and had to fight with it dangling from his side. The two stood in awe for a split second at the sword he had pulled out. He took the chance and hurled himself at the left-hand brother. The man could block the first two swings and buy enough time for the other one to rush to his side. Magnus saw the second man start to swing and quickly hopped backward. The sickle missed and sparked against the ground.

"So, the boy can move? Not bad, not bad," the left-hand brother taunted as he wiped his brow. Magnus didn't reply, but a small smirk did cross his face. The man on the right jumped next and tried to bring his sickles downward. Magnus stepped to the side quickly and jabbed at the available target. Right before his sword would pierce the man's flesh, the other brother caught Magnus's sword and pushed it to the ground. He pulled his sword from under the man's sickles and moved back before the next round of swings neared his face.

By now, the two men had now pushed him back toward the center of the alleyway, and the dim lights above still shone on their deformed faces. Quickly following, the men swung in unison. Magnus parried and jumped over one swing and then another in one fluid movement. He landed, pointing his sword at one man and his hand at the other. The two looked at their opponent, shocked. Then, the man on the right contorted his face and said, "You can't run forever, kid. Death always catches up no matter how fast or far you run."

They both cracked their necks and rushed again. The man on the left arrived first and swung his sickles in a cross-motion at Magnus, who quickly intercepted. The man pushed into Magnus's blade in an attempt to break through his guard. The next man swung shortly after, and Magnus used his right leg to hit both the man's wrists in one kick. His wrists clashed together, and his right sickle fell with a clang.

Magnus's sword was still in between the other man's sickles, and after the kick, the man reared them back to strike again. The other scrambled to get his sickle back. The man swung low with his right sickle but was quickly blocked by the golden sword. Magnus pushed the sickle back to the ground as he leaped over it. The left sickle came dashing across, but he simply ducked, and the man missed. The swing was so powerful that the man threw himself off balance. So, it caused him to pull his right sickle from under Magnus's blade, and it caused Magnus to nearly lose his balance as well. It made him turn his back to the man, but he was still within striking range.

He saw the other was busy picking up his sickle and knew this was his last chance to give himself an advantage. As the man behind him rose, he jabbed his sword backward through the man's abdomen. A short cough left the man's mouth as he pulled the blade back out. The man's body fell to the ground, and Magnus looked directly into his brother's eyes, who looked up just in time to see the fatal blow.

The man screamed in utter fury as he bounded toward Magnus. He started swinging without control. His grunts and screams left his mouth in irregular intervals. Each blow was heavy and uncoordinated, but they knocked Magnus back bit by bit. Then, Magnus got an inkling of luck when the man's grip on his left sickle slipped and caused him to drop it at his feet.

Magnus reacted quickly and kicked the sickle away, and it scraped across the ground. The man grunted again and looked him dead in the eyes. Spit flew from his mouth as he said, "That was my brother you murdered, and you will meet him in hell!" Magnus looked up cockily and said with a snicker, "It's your family reunion." The man charged, engulfed in rage, and Magnus redirected his swing downwards. He used the man's wrist as a step to jump over and wrap his legs around his neck. As he stepped on his wrist, the man dropped his left sickle. He squeezed his legs around the man's neck and brought him to the ground. He couldn't breathe, and his body started to flail around. Weak coughs and grunts left the man's mouth, but they were fruitless. He tried to pull Magnus's legs apart, but this, too, was in vain.

Magnus knew he would be unable to hold him down for too much longer, so he had to end the fight. With his legs still locked, he grabbed his sword and pointed it at the man's chest. But before he could strike, the man knocked the sword away, and it fell to the ground. Magnus gasped in fear. The man tried punching Magnus to get him off his neck, so Magnus gritted his teeth together and squeezed even harder. At the same time, he pulled his face away from the hand that now assaulted his body. Each punch from the man was a desperate plea for salvation, but there was none. Slowly his punches became weaker and weaker, and finally, his body gave out.

Magnus felt it and gave one last squeeze before loosening his hold and sprawling on the ground. He took a few deep breaths before untangling himself from the dead body.

He stood up and walked to grab his sword from the ground. He bent down to pick it up and heard someone clapping above him. He quickly looked above and saw a young boy's head poking from a window. The boy kept clapping and, in a high-pitched tone, said, "You did it! You killed the brothers of the night!"

He quickly vanished, and Magnus was left dumbfounded. He put his blade away and started to walk toward the cold air. Then, he heard another sound from the window. It was faint, but he could hear the boy saying, "Mom! Mom! Someone killed the brothers of the night!"

Then, a young woman poked her head out and smiled before mouthing, "Thank you." The little boy's cheerfulness echoed through Magnus's heart, and he thought that maybe the city wasn't all that terrible. But, for a warrior like him, there was no time to think the city would be on his side, so he waved up at the two and turned to face the cold air of the platforms.

He still smiled at the little boy's joy, but his body was exhausted. He had to get back to the compound, so he quickly got onto a platform. The ride back down was longer than he remembered. Finally, the platform slowed on the 80th level, and he stepped into the darkness. He knew he only had to walk straight to get to the elevator down to level 87. His feet dragged behind him as he walked through the level. The hanging light marking the entrance to the elevator wasn't too far away, and he walked all the way toward it. He nodded at the guard, who reached out his arm to stop him. But he soon recognized Magnus and let him on the elevator without a problem.

It made its way down, and the doors opened into the dark of level 87. Magnus stepped out and heard the rustling of the guards outside the door. He didn't want them to play tricks or games with him.

"It's me, Magnus; I'm exhausted and don't want to hear it right now." The head guard changed his usual playful tone to a more caring one.

"Did you at least find your sword?" he asked. Magnus pulled the front part of the sword out, and the gold glistened.

"Yes, I found it," he said.

"Very good," the guard affirmed.

The rest of the walk was quiet, and Magnus opened the door. The hallway greeted him, and the massive doors sat in front of him. He walked through the main doors quietly and saw Patri getting ready at the table. He wanted to avoid talking to him but couldn't escape his eyes.

"Magnus!" he yelled across the room, "Where have you been?" Magnus rolled his eyes and told him, "I had to get my sword back from the last mission. I left it." Patri walked over, placing his hand on Magnus's shoulder, "You know better than that, but go get some rest. You look awful." Magnus nodded and turned toward his room. He walked in and didn't take the time to undress or wash off. He dropped his sword to the ground and went to the comfort of his own bed.

His body desperately needed the rest, so he slept through the entire next day and woke up the morning after. His eyes opened slowly, and he saw his sheets were blended together, and his body was lying diagonally across the bed. *I slept well then.* He saw his clothes still on and remembered the night before. He wanted to go check on Rain and tell him about the fun he got to have without him.

He quickly changed into another set of clothes and left for the main chamber because Rain would likely be there. He clipped his sword to his waist and left the room. He walked down the hallway, where he could hear the faint sound of others training in other rooms, and he nodded to a few people as they walked by. He continued until the end of the hallway, where he saw Patri and Rain discussing something. Rain was facing away from him because he was looking at his father's throne.

Patri was sitting on the throne and looking directly at Rain until he lifted his gaze and said, "Magnus, you finally woke up. I assume the sleep was much needed then." Magnus rubbed his eyes and nodded.

Rain whipped his body around when he heard Patri address his brother, and the faintest smile graced his face at the sight of him. Their last time together had strengthened his feelings, and it felt good for him to have someone he now genuinely cared for.

"You must be starving after sleeping through a whole day. Come and eat," Patri told Magnus.

"Wait, I slept through the entire day?" Magnus asked.

"Yes, you slept an entire day. But as I said, come and eat," Patri stated.

Magnus wiped the shocked expression off his face and went to eat what Patri had been brought for breakfast earlier that day. There were slices of bread with some blueish jam from the nurion fruit. It had a sweet, tangy flavor with even a bit of spice in the end. He gobbled down four slices with the jam on them and stood back up to face the others.

The two were heavily discussing something but soon stopped when he stood back up. Patri moved Rain from his path and went to put his hand on Magnus's shoulder. "Was everything good for you?" he asked. "What were you two talking about?" Magnus questioned. "Oh, it was nothing but some minuscule workings of the monetary side of this whole place. All boring things, really," Patri said. Magnus didn't believe him but nodded to agree anyway because he wanted the conversation to end. Patri took his hand off Magnus's shoulder and walked to clean the table off from the meal. As he walked away, the two brothers smiled at each other before hugging.

As they let go, Rain said, "Glad to know you got the rest you needed. But why did you sleep so long?" Magnus patted his sword and said, "I may or may not have left this in Higurn's and had to go find it." Rain gawked at his brother, "You left it at Higurn's? Stupid." He shoved Magnus and laughed at him. "Oh, shut up," Magnus hit back. Rain finished laughing and started to talk again.

"Well, did you find anything while you went back?"

"I got into and won a fight against some criminal brothers or something," Magnus answered nonchalantly.

"There you go. That's something. Did they have a name?" Rain asked, interested.

"Yeah, they called themselves the brothers of the night. It was kinda cool, but I'd think Night Brothers would be cooler," Magnus said.

"I like that a lot, Night Brothers; what if we called ourselves that?" Rain suggested.

"You want a nickname?" Magnus said sarcastically.

"Yes, I do want a nickname. Is there a problem with having a calling card? If we're going to do missions and such all the time, we might as well have a name," Rain said.

"I guess you're right. Night Brothers it is!" Magnus said proudly.

"If we're really going to have a name like that, we better start training like it," Rain said.

"Agreed," Magnus finished with a smile.

The two walked away from the throne and its obsidian steps toward the massive doors. Patri turned from cleaning the table and yelled, "Boys! Where are you two headed?" Rain turned his body around and said, "We're going to train." "Ah, well, train well, Night Brothers," Patri said through a thin smile. "You heard that?" Magnus asked. Patri's smirk stayed across his face, "You hear a lot of things when you have done as much as I have. Anyway, train well." He turned and wiped the last of the table off. He didn't have much of a job and finished rather quickly.

The two departed from the throne and walked to where the dummies stood at the opposite end of the chamber. They walked until Magnus remembered something and asked, "Rain, this is random, but what's the elevator code? When I got my sword back, I had to take the platforms up and down, which was annoying." Rain looked his brother up and down, "We only tell people that deserve that code. I'm not sure if you're ready for it." Magnus was slightly intimidated, "Oh, well, I hoped I would've earned it by now." Rain stopped walking and looked extremely serious, "I don't know. It took me years to get that code, and I'm not sure you're ready." Magnus looked disappointed and put his head down slightly, and said weakly, "Sorry, I'll get it another time then." He turned and started to saunter away. Rain laughed and grabbed his shoulder to turn him around, "You more than deserve the code. I was just messing with you."

Magnus's eyes opened again in excitement, "Well, what is it?" Rain checked over his shoulders and saw Patri retreating to his room. His guards followed him, and they could only wonder what was discussed behind the door. Once it closed, he looked back at Magnus.

"Don't tell Father about this, but the code is 338457."

"334857?" Magnus asked.

"No, it's 338457," Rain repeated.

"338457?" Magnus said.

"That's it, and remember, Father doesn't know about this yet." Rain said.

Magnus nodded quickly with a smile and turned away again. As they reached the dummies, Rain spoke in a soft, caring tone that was rare, "Magnus, you're special, you know." Magnus was confused by the sudden change in tone and in the emotion Rain was showing. "What do you mean special?" he asked through a sarcastic look. Rain looked very sincere, and the sarcastic look was wiped from Magnus's face. "Oh, you're serious," he said. Rain paused before saying, "Yes, I'm serious. You have changed my life in the time you have been here. You have turned Father back into a version closer to what I used to dream of. You gave me the ability to actually care about someone again. You are special, Magnus, and I don't know how else to say it. So, don't forget it" Taken aback by the sudden heartfelt speech, Magnus reeled himself back. He had no words in response and stood with a gaping look. "I mean that," Rain said to reinforce his point.

Magnus still couldn't speak, nor did he really know how. Displays like this were a new sensation for both, and neither knew what step was next. Finally, Magnus said, "Th-thank you, Rain. I don't really know what to say to you except that." He smiled a bit, and gloss started to form in his eyes. Rain followed suit and gave a little chuckle through his own glossed eyes. They simply went in for another hug and buried their faces into each other's shoulders. No tears were shed, and no words were said, but they had another moment that connected them even further. They embraced and stood for another moment before they broke off, looked at each other, and smiled. They faced the training area and walked to their first training session as the newly formed Night Brothers.

11

THE TRAP

After the mission in Higurn's that neither Rain nor Magnus could forget, they continued training and going on missions for three years. Every mission felt more like a playdate where they would laugh and feel accomplished by the end. Most times, they would arrive at the compound and give each other a hug before going to their rooms. It was truly special for both of them.

They had made a name for themselves within the compound, but they were a secret outside, except for the rare citizen that had heard of the Night Brothers. Most citizens brushed off anything that didn't really involve them, so it was easy for the two to remain secretive. But the Ugurian police force tried and failed to catch them on every occasion.

Magnus was weeks from turning 22, and Rain had turned 23 two months ago. They had accomplished over 500 successful missions for Patri, whose age was beginning to show, yet his hair remained a perfect blanket of gray. The missions were all pretty simple drug busts or weapon deals. It was nothing really important in nature, but it bonded them closer than they thought possible. And within the years, they had become very efficient and talented at their work. And when it came to killing, they were both frighteningly good at it. Magnus preferred non-lethal combat, but if the situation got hostile, so did he. Rain was similar but not identical. He was a trained killer, and it blended into his work. But all in all, they returned mission after mission with unrivaled success.

* * *

Magnus was in his room and grabbed his sword and some daggers to put in the folds of his newly tailored set of ninja armor. His old set was cut in a drug incident on level 67 not too long ago. They stopped the selling of some unknown drug and got the money, but his top got caught in the case with all the Ugurns, and he had to cut it off in the squabble. The new set was tight to the skin with gold embroidery around the shoulders and cuffs of the wrists on his right arm. He asked for the gold specifically on his right arm because it's the arm he liked to hold his sword with. Rain also had a similar design, except his outlines were red and went down both arms.

Magnus was looking in his mirror when Rain walked in and said, "Magnus looking good in his new robes!" He hugged him and said, "I have a new mission." "Well, what is it?" Magnus asked. Rain pulled out a piece of paper and said, "Father just gave me this. He says he has friends who keep him updated but are otherwise not to be trusted." "Who are they?" Magnus asked. Rain thought for a moment and answered, "I have no idea, but I don't really care as long as they give us information." Magnus nodded and said, "Well, let's open it."

Rain listened and opened it. His eyes widened when he saw that the Berserkers were involved. It was irregular because the Berserkers had been very quiet for the past two years, and no one for sure knew why. But he did know that if the Berserkers were involved, that meant a lot of money was involved too.

He smiled under the paper. Magnus saw him and needed to know what his brother was reading. "What is it?" he asked. Rain chuckled, "You're gonna like this. It's got some Berserkers, and I know both of us despise them." He hit Magnus jokingly, but Magnus's eyes gleamed at the new opportunity. "Rain, I want in on this one," he said in a serious tone. Rain matched the seriousness, "Then we leave tonight." They smiled at each other, and Rain went back to his room to gather his things. For him, it was a chance at a big prize; for Magnus, it was a chance at revenge. As Rain left, Magnus looked at himself in the mirror and saw the scared boy from all those nights ago. This was his chance to avenge that little boy.

As dusk began, Magnus walked to the king's chamber. He saw some familiar faces on the way, and his sense of belonging was becoming stronger with every day. He had known everyone in the Berserker compound, and yet, it felt like he was no one. Now, everyone knew his name, and he felt at home. He loved it so much and wished he could've found it sooner.

When Patri was sitting at his table with a couple others around him, and Rain walked out from his room and said, "Father, Magnus and I are going to head out." Patri moved the people aside and said, "Be careful. I cannot afford to lose either of you." "Yes, Father," they both responded as they bowed in front of him. They left the room via the double doors and went to the exit.

They walked out, put their masks on, and went towards the elevator. The floor right outside the compound was cold and dark. And from the dark, one of the guards spoke, "Fight well, you two." Magnus never liked the fact he couldn't see them and that they always spooked him. So, he said, "Please, can you guys announce yourself before you just say something?" The group from the dark chuckled as the two moved toward the elevator.

Rain hit a button, and the elevator came down to meet them. They stepped in and rode up to level 80. The doors opened, and they nodded at the guard outside. They still never spoke to him and always wondered who he was. They walked their way to the other elevator, and they rode up to level 63. They jumped out, where another dark alley met them. The night was crisp but provided all the cover they needed. They crept through the night with Magnus's new gold lining glistening in blinks of light from windows or even the lights above. They knew where this meeting was to take place, and it was in another alley not too far from the elevator.

They quietly walked towards the given location and saw two small men talking to the three monstrously sized Berserkers. The Berserker crest shone in the dim light from one singular streetlight. "Follow me," Rain whispered. He used the wall and climbed onto the rooftops, and Magnus followed behind him. They sat like cats, waiting to pounce.

Then, Rain said, "Magnus, on my cue, throw a dagger at that light and move in." He focused on the men beneath them without cease. Magnus kept looking at him, awaiting a signal until it happened. He moved his hands into the shape of devil horns, and Magnus took out his dagger, took a deep breath, and hurled it toward the light. It was true and shattered the bulb of the singular streetlight. The shattered glass sprayed all over the men, and panic set in on the smaller ones. "Get the money!" one of them yelled.

The Berserkers stayed calm and grabbed their weapons, one with a battle ax, another with a claymore, and the last with a war hammer. The cold metal shone in the night. "Who are you!" one yelled. Then the sound of swords and screams echoed through the alley. The two small men hit the ground and went quiet. Rain's masked eyes glistened as he said, "The devil." Magnus threw another dagger, hitting the largest of the three in the leg. "Ahhh!" the man screamed. Rain charged in with his blade and leaped at one of the Berserkers. The darkness was enough to disorient and send the Berserkers swinging in wild directions. The man with the hammer swung and hit the ground, and Rain jumped around and stabbed him in the back. He let out a small grunt, but when the blade left, his body fell dead.

Magnus leaped into the fight and rolled between swinging blades. And quiet as death itself, Rain killed another, the man with a claymore. He parried its devastating blow and swung upwards and sliced the man's arm. The stunned Berserker fell to the ground, and he put his blade through the Berserker crest. "That's two," he whispered.

While Rain fought the other man, Magnus threw another dagger and hit the last Berserker in the chest. "Damn you!" he yelled as he pulled the dagger out. He gripped his ax and swung. Magnus slid under the blade, cut through the inside of the man's leg, and he grunted in pain. He swung again in rage and slammed the ground. Magnus used the man's axe head as a step to spin through the air and kick through the Berserker's face. He heard a crunch, and the man fell down and landed with a thud. He saw Rain stand up from his second kill, and he ran over to help collect the bounty, forgetting to check if the Berserker was dead. In the darkness, he had misheard the crack. For what he thought was the sound of his foot breaking the man's neck was really the sound of the ax's handle snapping under the weight of his foot. It had cracked when the Berserker naturally tried to raise it up to block, and unknown to the brothers, he was still alive.

The two dug through a crate of Ugurns, and they both smiled. "Good work let's head home," Rain told Magnus. Magnus nodded. They carried the money back to the elevator and went back to the compound. And as the elevator slowly went down, the injured Berserker's eyes shot open. He slowly pushed himself to his feet through painful grunts and wheezes.

He lumbered his way back to the platforms with blood stains on his legs and chest. When he got there, he crawled onto a platform and went back to level 42, using the railings as his only way to stay upright. He got back into the door with his key and fell onto his face. Helpar happened to be lying awake in his bed. He shot up and saw the man's condition. He bounded down the hallway into the medical room and screamed at the doctor sitting in his chair, "Get up and follow me!" The doctor jolted up and followed him back to his room.

After they returned, Helpar helped lug the man's body into the medical room. The man was still unconscious, so Helpar went to change into more official clothes. As he did so, the man awoke in the medical room with the doctor next to him. The head doctor ran down the hallway and busted open Helpar's doors, "He's awake!" He threw on his shirt and ran out of the room.

The door to the medical bay opened, and Helpar walked in. His size was unmatched, his beard had touches of gray, and the scar from the golden blade stretched across his face. "Who did this to you, my friend?" he asked. The man was in a daze but gathered his thoughts, "They called themselves the devil." He coughed and winced from his pain. Helpar mind raced. The last time he heard any reference to the devil was when he fought Patri. He raised his tone.

"What were they wearing?" "They wore black, skin-tight armor with strange masks," the man said. "Black armor?! Strange masks?!" Helpar exclaimed.

The man nodded again. Helpar thought to himself. *They should be dead. I killed them.* His lips motioned the words he was thinking, and though the man was hurt, he was still aware of his surroundings. "What?" he asked. "Nothing, my friend. Get some rest." Helpar said. Deep in thought, he walked to the door. He left the room and shut the door. He also woke up Medya, Gret, and Darian to seek advice. Shortly after he woke them, they made their way to the council room and took their seats.

The room was usually filled with more Berserkers, but their status wasn't high enough to get them woken up for this meeting. He addressed the three, "My friends, a group we all thought was dead, has been reborn. The Devil's Hand is alive." A shocked silence went over the room. Both Gret and Darian had been there when Helpar threw his ax into Patri, and Medya had been around long enough to know who the Devil's Hand was. Gret finally broke the silence, "They cannot be strong if you're just now finding them." Helpar processed the idea and said, "Well thought, Gret, but I've seen them before, as have you, and they don't need numbers to be a threat." In a quiet but still powerful tone, Medya chimed in, "How did they know where our meeting was?" The room nodded and began to think.

"Could they have eyes and ears around the city?" Darian suggested.

"Darian, that's a good point. How else would they know?" Helpar said.

"What if we try to bait them out?" Darian proposed.

"How could you suggest we give up our plans like that?" Helpar asked.

"Helpar, we set up a trap and send our best to meet them and end them," Darian said enthusiastically.

"How do we know they will send their finest warriors?" Gret asked.

"Average men wouldn't be able to kill two and nearly kill three of our best soldiers. They have their best foot forward," Darian said.

"So, let me speak your ideas; we purposely give them information and set a trap for them? If so, who do we send?" Helpar asked.

"I want to finish what we started, Helpar," Darian said, offering himself.

"As would I," Gret added.

Helpar smiled at the camaraderie. Then he said, "Then it is decided. I will take you two to a planned trap on loading dock 15 to end this. I will contact an arms dealer and tell him to make sure the trade isn't secret. If the Devil's Hand is really back, then they will not miss this opportunity." They all nodded and broke into their separate rooms to get the rest of their needed sleep.

Rechnal had randomly woken in his sleep and heard mumbling from somewhere close. He went to investigate and saw that the council was in session. He knew not to disrupt, so he sat outside the doors to see if he could hear what was happening. Even though his ear was against the door, he couldn't hear anything, so he waited patiently.

Medya was the first to leave, followed by Darian and Gret. Rechnal saw them leave and entered behind them. Helpar was preparing to leave the room but stopped once Rechnal entered.

"What is it, son?"

"I wanted to know what the meeting was about. Meetings don't happen this late unless it's important," Rechnal said.

"It's nothing, son. It was just a simple meeting about an attack on one of our weapons trades. We lost some men, but we've figured it out now."

"Do you know who did it?" Rechnal asked.

"We think so, but I'll tell you later," Helpar said.

Rechnal, curious as he was, didn't really know when to stop. "I want to know," he said. Helpar slammed his war hammer on the table. It was a massive tool with a glowing blue liquid running through it. It moved through the engravings all over the hammer's head, and the sound of it hitting the table echoed through the room. Rechnal was silenced. He sat down in a chair angrily and complained to his father.

"Why can't I know? I've proved myself over and over again."

"Because you aren't ready for something like this. It is classified to the point that not even my own son knows. When it's done, I'll tell you about it," Helpar said definitively.

His tone told all Rechnal needed to hear, and his face dropped. "Understood," he said as he hunched his shoulders. He knew if he asked any further questions, he would be punished. So, he walked with his head down back to his room, where he would fall asleep again.

* * *

Rain and Magnus entered the king's chamber and dropped the loot they just killed for, and Patri walked to greet them. He said, "Well done, my sons; I'm proud." "Thanks, Father," both said. Magnus hugged Patri while Rain stood aside, and after, they went to their rooms.

Rain seemed reluctant to take the compliment because he thought Patri was only talking about Magnus, but something told him his father might have meant some of it. He went to his room, quickly showered, and put on the black boxers that he slept in. He was a hot sleeper and didn't sleep in much else.

Magnus walked back, took off his clothes, and went to shower and get ready for a night's sleep. Once his shower finished, he put on new clothes and laid his head down for the night.

* * *

The next week was normal, with training continuing as always. Then, one morning, Magnus went to the training room to practice swordsmanship, and Rain brought in another message from the upper levels. It was a weapons trade.

He walked into the room and said, "Hey, Magnus, the Berserkers still want their weapons. They have another trade on loading dock fifteen on level sixty-one. I say we can make quick work of it." All Magnus had to hear was Berserker, and he was ready. He asked, "When do we leave?" Rain looked at him, "Tonight." He playfully pushed him and went off to his room to prepare for the night. Magnus did the same. Thoughts of how well the last Berserker encounter went moved through his head, and he was excited that he had the chance to do it again.

Night fell, and rain fell as the two entered the main elevator. They could hear the faint pattering of the rain on the ground somewhere in the distance. The rain only ever went down the hollow center of the city where the levitating platforms went. It also doused the loading docks, including loading dock 15.

Magnus was silent, focused on getting the chance to kill more of the men who nearly killed him. But there was a bit of sorrow along with the thoughts of violence.

"Magnus, what's going on? You haven't spoken a word since I told you about this." Rain questioned.

"With fighting all these Berserkers, I don't wanna see someone I already know cause they hurt me, but some of them were my childhood. Some of

these people I trained with, and I don't know if I could kill them," Magnus said softly.

"These people aren't your home anymore; we are. We can't have split loyalties, so get your head straight," Rain ordered.

He slipped his mask over his face and stood valiantly. Magnus was surprised by the harshness, but he realized Rain was right. These people had hurt him, and there was no reason to pity them. He exhaled, put on his mask, and felt the elevator skid to a stop.

They stepped from their vertical chamber into the cold alley ahead of them. Their breath was visible with each exhale. They both climbed the level's ladder to see their destination. And not far ahead of them was the loading dock, a cold sheet of metal with blinking red and blue lights surrounding it. It was on the far side of the circular walkway, and they would have to go around via the roofs of level 61. And through loading dock 15's lights, three massive silhouettes stood. Unbeknownst to the two, it was Helpar, Darian, and Gret, patiently waiting.

They continued closer to the loading dock and heard the rain getting louder. Luckily for them, a roof on level 61 stretched above the edge of the loading dock. They crawled across the roof and felt the cold rain patter their skulls.

They sat on the roof, rain-wetted, ready to pounce on the men beneath them. Their breaths steamed into the cold air, and Rain gave the signal to jump down. They landed on the edge of the loading dock in elegant style, with the three men facing them.

Helpar instantly recognized the crest on Magnus's armor and said, "Ah, my old friends, good to see you again. Happy you got my invitation cause tonight I will finish what I started." He drew his war hammer with the blue ether running through it, and it reflected beautifully with the red and blue lights. Magnus's blood ran more frigid than the rain falling on his head. That voice. That voice was Helpar. Fear crossed his hidden eyes. Helpar continued to speak, "We have you outnumbered yet again, and this time, we will finish what we couldn't before." Gret and Darian drew their weapons, both battle axes that glistened in the light. They stood on either side, and they weren't much smaller than Helpar. Magnus was frozen in fear and couldn't speak, and Rain stayed silent for other reasons. He was preparing for something.

Then, suddenly, a dagger flew from his hand. Whistling as it flew, it hit Gret's forehead and immediately toppled the ax-wielding giant with a loud thud. He spoke from the dark red and blue flashing, "If I'm to fight, I want the numbers to be equal." Helpar grunted, rolled his shoulders, and said, "I still favor my odds."

He charged at the brothers, and they dashed apart as fast as lightning. Darian went after Magnus and, Helpar, Rain. Helpar swung, and Rain parried, but each blow of his hammer felt like tons. The rain poured and flew from their bodies as they attacked and evaded in a sinister dance. Darian swung his sharpened blade, and Magnus rolled to the side. The ax slammed into the cold metal, and he swung again with more rage. Magnus kept evading and shifting from the blows, his blade glowing faintly through the crisp night. The quick nature of attacks made it almost impossible to counterattack; never had he learned to fight an opponent like Darian.

As Magnus struggled, Rain couldn't keep up with Helpar's violent slams, and his stamina was running dry. Helpar's screaming tore into the dark. He kept swinging and swinging with no sign of ever stopping, and Rain's breath left his lips with increasing speed. The two kept banging weapons together, and Rain barely escaped a deathly blow. Unlike most, Helpar frightened Rain, but he still had faith in himself. He tried to swing, but Helpar spun his hammer and smacked his blade down. It nearly fell from his hand, but he managed to catch its hilt. But as he lifted his head, Helpar's knee came to meet him. He moved as fast as he could, but the leg still hit him back. He stuttered his way to the edge and saw the vicious beast of a man standing in front of him. Helpar looked at his foe and taunted, "You were close" The monster smiled through the cold rain as he walked toward Rain.

Rain saw Magnus struggling with Darian but couldn't do anything to help. Helpar had pinned him, and in desperation, he leaped to the side. Helpar swung his hammer down where he had been standing. He dodged it, but his blade did not. It struck his blade down, and it fell near the edge of the loading dock. Helpar walked in front and cut him off from his sword. His eyes filled with terror as a mountain of a man stood between him and his weapon. Helpar looked at Rain, who was holding his fists up to fight, "You won't be needing this." He kicked the sword toward the loading dock's edge, and it skidded across the metal before it fell into the city's darkness. Rain shuddered. He knew his odds were slim, but he couldn't stop now.

The skidding echoed through the night, and Magnus looked over, terrified, "Rain!" He lunged at Darian in an attempt to get to his brother, who was now running for his life. He caught Darian's arm with his sword and drew the Berserker's blood. He reeled in pain and swung even harder at Magnus's elusive frame. Magnus ducked under the vicious swing and quickly jabbed up. Through his rage, Darian had let his guard down and gave way to the jab. The blade pierced through his chest, and he fell back onto the cold metal. His eyes shot briefly in pain and shock, but their pain halted as his blood mixed with the puddles on the loading dock. His body turned as cold as the metal he laid on.

As Magnus jabbed, Helpar's hammer swung, and Rain was able to evade the swing, but Helpar quickly raised his hammer in front of him and jammed it through Rain's chest. It knocked him flat on his back, and his head bashed into the floor, knocking him out. His limp body slid across the water and metal. Helpar stood prideful and began to stomp towards his body. And as Magnus looked up from Darian, he saw him standing over his brother and raising his hammer with a triumphant cackle.

"Rain!!" he screamed. He quickly threw his last dagger, and it landed in Helpar's right leg. He roared, and his scream echoed through the cold rainy night. He then turned to face Magnus, who cowered in fear as he saw the scar he cut lie across his adversary's face blinking between red and blue. Helpar ripped the dagger from his leg and threw it to the ground. As it clattered, he said, "You think a measly dagger can hurt a king!"

He beat his chest and spun his hammer to point directly at Magnus. Water ran from his hair and beard, leaving nothing but his terrifying blue eyes. He spoke into the night, "I am not sure who you are, but that blade was stolen from me before, and I will have it again." His breaths turned into white clouds. Magnus began to back away slowly and approach the edge of the loading dock, where the lights made the gray hair in Helpar's beard shine. Rain still lay limp on the other side of the loading dock, lifeless.

"You can't run forever, boy," Helpar taunted. The taunting echoed through Magnus's head as he remembered all the scolding he received as a child. His blood began to curdle with a rage, a rage not to kill Helpar but to humiliate him as he had been humiliated. With courage, he lunged toward Helpar. Helpar countered his blade easily and almost disarmed him in one swing. The counterattack impacted Magnus himself, and he knew he wasn't going to defeat Helpar as he did Darian.

Helpar continued to taunt, "I have defeated hundreds; what chance does a boy like you stand?!" Magnus tried again to rush and put the giant on defense. His attack failed when Helpar swung from left to right with one hand on the hammer. Magnus jumped away, only for his face to be caught by the giant's left hand. Magnus pulled away, and the rain allowed him to slip out of Heplar's grip. However, his mask was ripped from his face. Helpar held it and looked down at Magnus's exposed face. He snapped the mask into pieces with only one hand as he saw him. He yelled, "You, You, You! You tore that sword from me! You left this gash on my face! You left me beaten by a child! My pride will never be diminished by the children of the dust! Your mother was nothing! I saved you! How did you repay me? You ran away! There will be no running for the little coward this time!" He spun the hammer and held it to his right.

Then, with an act of newfound courage, Magnus spoke, "I ran because I knew I could be better, stronger, and more powerful than you could ever teach me! I saw a flawed system that beat its children and starved the ones who couldn't win a fistfight! I saw a tyrant sitting on his throne, waiting for more people to fall to his reign! And it ends today!" He stood and held his blade in a ready position. Then, he pointed his sword directly at Helpar's chest.

Helpar banged his chest again and charged. His first blow crashed against the floor and knocked Magnus back. But he quickly recovered and jabbed back. With luck, he broke the skin of the beast. Helpar wailed and swung again. Magnus slid under the blow, but Helpar quickly swung his paw of a hand and hit him across the face. He skidded across the wet ground but quickly rose to his feet again. He felt a warmness on his face, so he felt his nose, and when he brought his hand in front of his eyes, he saw crimson blood.

The rain mixed with it to form drops that fell from his face, and they stained the puddles beneath him. Helpar saw the blood and said, "How does it feel to bleed?" he paused, "Magnus." He charged again and swung upwards. This show of pure rage allowed Magnus to slip his blade into his left leg. Not a deep wound but a hindrance. Now stumbling with a lesser grace, Helpar swung again. Determination crossed his scarred face, "I will not lose to the Devil's Hand! And especially to you!"

His hammer swung and missed yet again. The blow was close enough to the edge to shatter one of the lights. Magnus continued to move with quickness as each cloudy breath left his lungs. He then took a step towards Helpar and brought his blade into the hammer. Leaping from the swing, he jumped into the air and landed a fist on Helpar's face. Helpar stood back and smiled, "You really think your fists can damage me?! That you have some power here?! Your end is tonight; you are only delaying it!" Magnus twirled his sword and braced for another swing of the hammer.

Helpar's next swing was clumsy. The pain from his leg caused him to misstep and leave an opening in his guard. Magnus slashed the inside of his other leg, swung upwards, and cut through his right forearm. He roared again, dropped his hammer, and it slammed to the ground. His left hand came from the darkness, but Magnus's blade was waiting for it. It was cut clean off, and it hit the ground with a thud. He stumbled back and tried to maintain his balance but couldn't, and he fell to his knees. He was holding his newly severed arm and looked up in helpless rage. His legs were weak, his right arm throbbed from the gash, and his left hand was gone. He didn't want to admit it, but he had been bested.

By this point, the fight had taken up the entire loading dock. They had done their dance around the platform, and now they sat not too far from where Rain still lay. But now, Magnus stood with aggressive pride and yelled, "After all this time, I finally see your eyes defeated! I can see you fall!" The golden edge of his sword shone in the night as he raised it into the air. "Then finish it," Helpar winced. His voice still had a touch of arrogance to it, but its confidence was diminished. Magnus pointed the sword at Helpar's chest, ready to impale. His hand quaked, and his breaths became shorter.

Helpar noticed, and a last fiber of pride emerged. He taunted, "You can't do it. I've seen you. You're no killer. You're just a kid." Magnus began to shake more because he knew Helpar was right. His claims were what he feared to be true his whole life; that he was no warrior. His gaze was focused on Helpar's eyes, and he didn't see Helpar reaching for the dagger he had thrown into his leg initially. Helpar hoped to make one final thrust and bring Magnus with him.

The rain fell through Magnus's eyes and mixed with the blood from his nose as he held the blade in the air. His arm was quaking. He knew he had to kill Helpar, yet he couldn't. Helpar's fingers wrapped around the dagger and twisted it to face Magnus. He yelled, "I knew it! You are nothing more than a coward! A boy paralyzed in his own fear! A failure to his family and to himself!" The taunt echoed and rattled through Magnus's skull, and his confidence was stolen from him. His drive was devastated, and he began to lower his sword unconsciously.

This was Helpar's cue. He drove his better leg into the ground to push himself off the ground. "Hraaaaah!" he screamed as he raised the knife. Then the sound of punctured flesh rang in Magnus's ears. His eyes were stunned at what he saw in front of him. The dagger clattered on the ground, and he lost his breath as blood fell from Helpar's mouth. A blade was barely poking through his chest, and he coughed and fell forward. From behind, Rain pulled the blade out and fell onto his face. "Rain!" Magnus yelled.

The stab had ended Helpar's attack, but he was clinging to life. He couldn't move or muster the strength to speak or even hardly breathe, but he was still alive.

"Rain, Rain, are you okay? How did you get here?" Magnus asked. He flipped Rain over onto his back through much wincing and many cries. He took off Rain's mask and allowed his brother to speak freely. Coughing, he said, "I-I came over to help when I saw you fighting, and." He coughed roughly, "And I had one dagger left, so I started to crawl towards you. Then, when you put him down, I saw him reach for the knife. So, before he could do anything, I stabbed him."

Magnus joked back, "I asked if you were okay, not how you killed him." Rain winced again, "Well, that hammer hit me pretty hard, didn't it?" Magnus answered, "Yeah, yeah it did." He sat silently for a moment to ponder what losing Rain would've been like.

But he hadn't, so he dismissed the thought. The rain continued to pour, and Rain winced again. "Okay, so how am I helping you get back to the elevator and back home?" Magnus asked, concerned. "Just help me up and let me lean on you. I should be fine." Magnus gave him a doubtful look. "Just get me up," Rain repeated. Magnus nodded and scooped Rain up from the ground, and he winced as he got to his feet. The two kept walking, got off the loading dock, and headed down the empty alleys. Rain spoke through his pain, "Why didn't you kill him, Magnus?" Magnus replayed the image of Helpar staring up at him in his head.

"I don't know. The stuff he said. It got to me, and I don't wanna hear any more about it tonight," he said.

"I understand, but you have to be able to kill someone who's gonna kill you," Rain said seriously.

"I know, Rain. Don't try to scold me right now. Let's just get home," Magnus said, exasperated.

"Fine," Rain winced.

They limped their way back to the elevator and got inside. It shot down and arrived at level 80 yet again. Magnus guided Rain back to the smaller elevator, and the guard let them in instantly. Once it hit the ground, they wandered back to the door but were quickly surrounded by the guards. "Who dares show their faces here?" the head guard asked. Magnus quickly responded, "It's Magnus and Rain, we're coming back from loading dock fifteen, and my brother needs medical help. If you try to stop me, I will do anything to get him help." The guards quickly realized their mistake and went to help. He looked at the head guard and said, "Take my brother to the medical room and have him evaluated and tell me what his results are." The guards took Rain as Magnus went to see his father.

He rushed to Patri's room and burst in. Patri slowly woke up and exclaimed, "Magnus!" He got up from his bed in a flash and walked toward him. But before he got to him, Magnus said, "Father, I have finished what you and I started. The head of the Berserker clan is dead." Patri's eyes were shocked and proud as he embraced his son. But as he let go, he noticed that Rain wasn't there.

"Well done, but where is your brother? We didn't lose him, right?" he asked.

"No, Father, he's just in the medical room, but a hammer doesn't land lightly on the chest," Magnus answered.

"Oh, thank god, I'm going to see him again. Get some much-needed rest," Patri said, rushing out of the room.

"Thank you," Magnus bowed.

He entered his room and walked past the mirror, where his reflection stood to face him. Helpar's words ran again through his blood, and he wondered if they meant anything at all. A tear ran down his right cheek and glistened in the room's gentle light. He knew his childhood was gone, any tie to who he once was was gone, and now, he was the one who remained. He wiped the tear and, along with it, any remorse he had for killing Darian and his once-beheld king. But Helpar's words haunted him and would rattle through his skull for a long time to come. His confidence was wounded, but he wouldn't let a dead man's words control him.

He hoped this was the last time he would encounter his childhood demons, but he knew it most likely wasn't. He also knew he had to rest to prepare to fight again because the Berserkers wouldn't give up easily. He was now the first line of defense and the hope of his aging father's compound. He couldn't let them down, and the weight of his world rested on his shoulders as he finally collapsed on the bed.

12

A PLOT AGAINST HELL

The Berserker camp was silent while they awaited Helpar to return that night, but Rechnal couldn't sit in the compound any longer. He heard the rain pouring down on the city's center and began to wonder and worry for his father. He wasn't worried for Helpar's life, but he wondered why he wasn't back yet. He left his room and grabbed his two double-bladed war axes from the wall beside him. One was like his father's because it flowed with a red liquid, but the other was a simple one from his childhood. He strapped them to his back and walked silently through the halls. He also grabbed his battle mask and strapped it to his waist.

He went straight through Helpar's room and descended to loading dock 15. The rain met his dirty blonde hair, his messy beard and ran down his determined face. As he stepped onto a platform, he heard a guttural yell from below and knew the sound. He couldn't tell if his father was screaming in triumph or pain, but he needed to know.

He could see the lights of the loading dock below him and two more miniature figures leaving. The descending platform he was on moved too slowly for him to get close enough for a view. He tried to remain patient, but he was slowly losing it. He saw three prominent figures strewn across the platform, and panic started to set in. He wouldn't believe anything could happen to his father, so he ignored what he saw. As he got closer, he was alarmed by the eerie silence he heard from below and hoped the rain was just beating away any noise. His breath formed in clouds as he got close enough to see that the bodies on the ground were indeed his fellow Berserkers. He was only one level away, so he took out one of his axes to prepare for anything. The platform slowed on level 61, and Rechnal ran to loading dock 15.

He stepped onto it and looked around, hoping to see the bodies get back up. Then, with the flash of the lights, he saw his father's face. Scrunched in pain, he wasn't yet dead but soon would be. "Father!" Rechnal yelled as his ax clanged to the floor. Through bloody coughs, Helpar weakly said, "My son, kill the ones who did this. His mask-it-it's on the floor." His lungs expelled more harsh air that formed into peaceful clouds. He fought to speak, "Use the hounds."

(The Berserkers had bred hounds since the construction of Uguria, and they were the only people in the city to still have animals from the old world.)

"Track them. Do it," he said. Rechnal had no care for finding them because he thought he could still save his father. He scooped under Helpar's body, and he winced greatly. He looked into his father's eyes, "I won't have to because you are not leaving me. We have fought for too much for you to give up now." He cradled his father's limp shoulders. Helpar's eyes started to go between a life and a lifeless glaze, "My time, it's out, but I have always loved you. Now let me see my son's face one more time." Rechnal started to feel the weight of his father's words and reassured both Helpar and himself, "This won't be the last time. I won't let it be." Helpar raised a weak finger and put it in front of his lips to silence him. His hand weakly tried to remove Rechnal's mask, but it fell without moving it. Rechnal stripped the mask off and threw it down while still holding his father. His face couldn't feel the cold as his entire being was focused on saving his doomed father. His eyes were watering, and his right leg quivered.

"Dad, you can't go," he said through bit lips.

"Death is part of all of us. It is your time to be what I could not," Helpar said. He gasped in a desperate cling to life.

"So, fin-f-f-finish this fo-o-r us."

The light dyed from his eyes, his lips fell silent, his head dropped, and his last breath formed into a blissful cloud.

"Dad, Dad?!" Rechnal screamed. He shook the corpse, but his shaking was in vain. There was nothing he could do, and it finally hit him. It had finally happened, and he was now the head of the Berserkers.

A tear of his combined agonies fell from his cheek as the harsh realization set in, and it mixed in with the cold rain that beat on his head. His head hung low, with his body curled towards his father. His breath paused as chills rushed through his robust frame. He had seen death before but never had it hurt him like this. He could do nothing except sit with his father, so that's what he did.

Then his mourning began to stop, and his tears ran dry. He sat up on his knees and looked at the city around him. He was in charge of a clan that meant something in the city. The realization slapped him, and stoically, he looked up through strained eyes at the mask across the ground. He looked back into his father's eyes and said, "Your will be done. I will avenge you." His blue eyes pierced the night with anger and lamentation as he stood to take the shards of Magnus's mask.

He picked up the largest piece and clipped it to his belt. He looked at Gret and Darian, and he didn't really care. He only cared about his father, so with his robust strength and shaky breath, he hoisted the body onto his shoulders and began the short walk to the platforms. Luckily, no one was out that night, and they were empty. He boarded a platform as the last tear from his father's death ran down his exposed cheek.

* * *

Patri made his way into the medical room and saw Rain on one of the beds. His hair was damp, and he was wincing in pain. "Rain, my son," he said. His tone was low and caring. Rain turned his head to see who was talking to him. He saw his father and felt he only came to pity him. "Don't flatter me," he said back. Patri heard the indifference in his voice and said, "I'm here for you." Rain grimaced and said sarcastically, "Funny since you've always been here when I needed you." His voice felt jagged. Patri knew Rain wanted no part in having him around, so he prepared to leave. "So be it then," he said. He left with a frown and walked back to his room.

Rain watched his father leave and knew what he said had hurt him. He was pleased that he had affected him, but he was still upset. His relationship with Patri was ruined, but what else could he do now? The damage had already been done. He brushed off the encounter and rolled his head over, and through great pain, he was the last person to fall asleep in the compound.

* * *

It was early morning as Rechnal unlocked the Berserker doors. His father's body was draped over his shoulder and coated in blood. He barged down the large open hallway, screaming incoherently to wake everyone up, and went toward the council room. The remaining council members bumbled down the hallway as they slowly woke up. He kicked open the council room door and waited for the members to enter. Once they all did, he slammed the massive body onto the wooden table. The room silenced itself in grave shock as the remaining jaws dropped to the floor.

"How is this possible?" muttered a man who walked into the light above the table. He was slightly hunched and wore a ragged coat with holes in the sleeves and down the back, but a hood kept his face well hidden. He rarely spoke, and Rechnal had only heard of him. However, he knew his name, Jasper. He was rumored to have been a great warrior until age overcame his body. His body was still large and strong but couldn't move as easily as it once did. Many thought he could fight well, but no one dared test him to find out. His face was scarred, and what seemed to be a small brand poked from underneath his sleeve. He slowly walked over to look at the lifeless and bloody body on the table. He felt the wound in Helpar's chest and nodded to himself before he hobbled back. Rechnal watched and was offended at the gesture. "What was that old man?! You asked what it was, and you seemed to know, so what was it?!" he screamed.

Jasper calmly sat down and raised his head to look at Rechnal, his hood providing shadow over his eyes. He said, "Patient, Rechnal. No need to attack an old soul. I was simply looking at your father." Rechnal was surprised he knew his name, so he would use Jasper's name. With a more raspy and desperate tone, he responded, "You have seen a lot, Jasper, and maybe your opinion could help find the people behind this. But all you do is sit in your little corner and watch, so maybe this time you can do something!" He slammed his fists onto the table, and the body shook lifelessly. Jaspar sat unfazed by the eruption of anger and adjusted his posture. After exhaling, he said, "I have seen a lot of dead bodies, but this is something I thought died years ago at the hands of the man lying here."

"Who are they?" Rechnal asked.

"What is truly more intriguing is the wound on his leg. Not a lethal blow, but it's even cleaner than the lethal one. And if that lethal blow was done by the ones I'm thinking of, then this strike is terrifying. Because the warriors who use those blades have terrorized lower Uguria for my life and lives before that. If it is true, then it spells doom for us all if they have it again," Jasper said. Rechnal waited for him to say something else, but nothing followed.

"Who! Who! Old man, tell me who it is!" he yelled.

He approached Jasper with untamed veracity and almost put his hands on him before Medya smacked his hand. She scorned, "No one attacks another member of the council. Just because you're a king now does not allow you to break these rules." He pushed her hand away and backed away reluctantly.

"Well, old man, who did this to my father?" he said, quieter.

"If I have anything in this age-logged mind, there is only one possible answer. They have killed before, and it seems that your father's suspicion was well placed. Your father was right. The Devil's Hand has returned," Jasper said ominously.

The room fell silent. And with three vacant seats, they had to decide their next action. Rechnal broke the silence, "We fight them back." Cheers from others erupted after him. Medya hit the table, "We have seen their strength, Rechnal; even your father, Darian, and Gret couldn't stand up to them. If we were to attack, any failure would lead to a retaliation we could not handle, and I have lived too many years to see this clan fall because of the actions of an angry boy!" The chamber burst into squabbles between the members on whether an attack should be mounted. The little arguments echoed throughout until Rechnal yelled, "My father is dead! Our king is dead!"

All the eyes focused on him, and he continued, "We sit here and argue over whether or not to fight! Helpar is dead! Our best warriors are dead! How can we not be called to avenge them?!" Mumbling rumbled across the room. He continued, "His last words were to do just that, and as your new king, I want to remember my father." The room fell silent again until another raised his voice. Rechnal's closest friend and someone he even considered a brother, Frory, took the lead. He sat on Rechnal's right side and said to the group, "He has lost his father, and taking away his ability to fight would be nothing short of a disgrace. He is our king, and we will follow his reign!" The people nodded in agreement, and it seemed everyone was thinking the same thing.

Rechnal raised out his hand, "Thank you, Frory. We will fight back! We will avenge my father, and we will destroy the Devil's Hand!" Again, the room nodded and whispered in agreement, all except Medya. She was not impressed and countered, "How are you, the new king, going to find this extinct clan?" Members also agreed with this question, and even a bit of doubt befell Frory's eyes.

"How are you going to do that?" he whispered into Rechnal's ear. He hated that his own people wouldn't trust him. The frustration was building, and he finally erupted, "Quiet!" The chamber silenced itself. He looked around the room and said, "I have a way to find them." He held up Magnus's broken mask. "This belonged to one of those murderers; our hounds will track them." The room seemed to agree, but no one voiced their approval until Frory stood and said, "All hail the new king!" The room stood, cheered, and clapped for Rechnal—all except for Medya, who wasn't happy with his first decree.

He held up his hands to quiet the room, "We will track them starting at dusk tomorrow, and once the location is found, we will attack. But tonight, we remember the greatest king this clan ever had." He gestured toward Helpar's body, and a somber wave hit the room. They all looked as Rechnal and Frory stood to move the body.

They picked him up and moved him to the funeral room. It was an open space with a stone altar at the center. Rough around the edges, it was engraved with runes of protection and had a hollow strip down the middle for starting a fire underneath bodies. A relightable torch was on the side with a small bucket to extinguish it after a ceremony. The rest of the people followed them and stood around the altar. Frory let the body go and walked across the room to a cabinet. He opened it and grabbed a vase from inside.

It was plain white and was made of a porcelain-like material. The cabinet it was in had a small rock-like plant on the ceiling. None of the Berserkers knew what it was. However, it was the last piece of natural ragupt in the entire city. It hung from the top of the cabinet and grew its roots into a plot of dirt put there by the original Berserkers. The modern Berserkers weren't aware it was ragupt, but they knew the liquid dripping from it was highly flammable. It was poured to burn a body on the altar, and a small hole in the side allowed for the torch to be inserted and light the liquid underneath.

He poured the clear liquid into the altar and put the vase back into its cabinet. It would only take the torch, and then it would alight. He made his way back to the body and raised it back again. He and Rechnal laid the body face up on the center of the altar. Rechnal grabbed the torch and held it in the air, "In the memory of a king and my father! To Helpar!" He struck the torch on the ground, and it erupted. He stared into its flames and lowered it to the altar. The liquid burst into flames, and Helpar's body began to glow from underneath. He quickly dunked the torch into the water and set it back in its place. He watched in silence as the fire started to engulf his father. Helpar's hair curled from the fire, and his clothes burnt rapidly, but everyone could still see his face, an orangly-lit, stoic man's face with a scar across it.

The group circled around the altar and began to chant a Berserker cry of battle and suffering but also of hope and reassurance. It sounded as eerie as it was consoling. The body burned smoothly, and tears were shed for the king, but it was a rallying cry for the clan. They all unified over the death and silently agreed that something needed to be done.

His face finally disappeared in the fire, and Rechnal's final tear glistened from his cheek. Frory saw the tear and put his hand around him, "It's gonna be alright." Rechnal shook his head and bit his lower lip. He tried to collect his thoughts but shook his head again. Frory tightened his hold, "It will be okay. It will be." Rechnal put his head down and looked at the floor. He took a deep breath and raised his head back to look at Frory. They locked eyes, and Frory's eyes offered a sense of comfort. He sniffled, "It will be." He collected himself and continued, "It will be hard, but death is natural. I never wanted to see him go, but I will finish his work and lead this clan to heights it never dreamed of." Frory pulled his arm to bring him closer, "Glad to hear it, brother."

The body had burned, but a few shards of bones were left. So, one of the others gathered them to be discarded. The group started the file out of the room, but Rechnal stayed. He blankly stared at the altar, but Frory never left his side. He kept his arm wrapped around him until he turned to face the door. When, finally, he was ready to leave, Rechnal took another look at the altar and said, "It's time to go." Frory agreed, and they walked out of the room together.

Rechnal watched the door shut and whispered angrily, "We need to find them." Frory could hear the anger in his tone. He also knew that Rechnal would exhaust himself before giving up.

"I would recover before starting anything. It'll give you and us time to think about what we need to do. This won't be easy either. I doubt the devil plays fair, so you must be rested," he said.

"You're right. But I'll only be able to fully rest once his will is complete," Rechnal said confidently.

Frory paused a moment, "Then we get ready."

"Get your wife and a couple others and meet me in my room. I'm going to etch my father's name into the training room," Rechnal said quickly.

Frory nodded and took off down the hallway. Rechnal turned and walked into the training room. It was vacant and quiet, so he drew his ax and approached the wall. He carefully carved Helpar Caddel into it and let another tear slowly roll down his cheek. At that moment, he sniffled his sadness away and replaced it with anger. With this anger, he turned away and stormed out of the room.

He walked the hallway until he reached his father's old room, and it hit him, yet again, that he was the new king, and what was once his father's chamber was now his. He opened the door and saw the bed, perfectly made, and he was hit with another violent wave of grief and sadness. All the memories in this room flooded in, but it was over now, and he wanted to come to terms with it. But he couldn't until he avenged his father. He would find his revenge, and it would start tonight.

* * *

Magnus woke up, recovered from his fight with Helpar, and checked on Rain. He opened the door and saw him lying awake.

"Rain, how's the morning?" he asked.

"I've been better, but the doctor says my sternum is broken. It'll take weeks for me to be better," Rain said, disappointed.

"I'm sorry. Keep resting, and I'll be back to check in all the time," Magnus assured.

"I'll look forward to seeing you, but you don't have to worry about me. I'll be back before you know I'm gone." Rain smirked a bit, "And what would you do without me?"

"I don't have anything for a bit, but I'll be fine when I get back out there," Magnus smiled.

"You know you're gonna miss me," Rain joked.

"I'll be just fine," Magnus quipped.

He sat quietly until he remembered, "Oh, I also have a new mask being made." Rain laughed but stopped because of the throbbing pain in his chest. He put his hand over his chest and said, "Glad to hear it." He turned his head the other way to stop himself from showing how much pain he was in. He wasn't sure if he could keep talking, so he kept his head facing away. Magnus thought Rain was done with the conversation, so he started backing to the door. His hand reached it, and he said, "It was good to see you, but you look like you need rest." Rain had to force his head back in Magnus's direction. He saw him leaving and said, "You're right. But thanks for coming in." Magnus pushed the door open, and Rain jeered, "Don't get yourself killed when you don't have me to save you." Magnus laughed and joked back, "I never needed you anyway." Rain smiled before turning his head back to where it was comfortable. He tried to fall back asleep but to no avail. So, he just sat restlessly in his bed.

Magnus walked by the main chamber and saw his father exiting his room. He felt the need to say something.

"Father! Is there anything you need from me tonight?" he asked.

"Well, I'd love for you to go check loading dock 15 to see if there's anything left or any investigation going on around it. I want us to stay as low profile as possible, and we can't if they find something on the platform," Patri said.

"Seems fair. I'll check it out tomorrow night. Anything else you need?" Magnus asked.

"Not right now," Patri finished.

He walked into his room, and Magnus went to walk back out. He looked up and studied the tapestry on the roof. As old as the entire building, it hung from strings in the corners and had supporting strings along the edges. It depicted epic battles but also serene scenes of beauty. It told of the glories and terrors of life, and it all hung from the ceiling.

He stared for a couple of minutes until he noticed something new. He had looked at this tapestry for a while but never saw one of the war depictions. He saw his sword glisten in the fabric. The same golden sword he was using had been used by members of the hand that he never knew of. This blade was truly powerful, and it struck him how much it meant to brandish it. He had more power than he even realized. With his fingers wrapped around the glistening blade's hilt, he left the main chamber. For the rest of the day, he spent his time stretching or just resting. He was still feeling sore from the fight and figured a day off wouldn't hurt.

* * *

That evening, Frory, his wife, and the others formed a group at Rechnal's door. He knocked, "Rechnal?" Rechnal opened the door,

"Let's go." He told the group, "We have to go get the dogs, so let's go." He stomped off down the hallway. Frory followed. Rechnal opened a door and saw two crates on the ground. "There they are," he whispered. He picked one up in each arm and walked out. He didn't say a word and walked past Frory and his wife. They both pivoted and walked back. When he got there, Rechnal opened the door to the city and turned, "We're going to loading dock 15." He stepped onto the walkway and started to walk. The group looked at each other and followed.

* * *

At the same time, Magnus returned to his room and felt a wave of tiredness. He yawned and figured it was time to sleep. He took a shower and put on comfortable clothes. And after a while, he fell asleep.

* * *

The group arranged themselves on loading dock 15 and waited patiently for Rechnal to open the crates. The massive dogs were the last two left. They were aggressive bloodhounds. Their fur was a motley of brown, black, and scars, and their eyes broke through the evening light. They also had their mouths muzzled to prevent barking. There was a male and a female, and they were more than likely going to breed when they returned. They were the last of their kind, but they had been bred for a moment like this.

Rechnal put the cages down and saw Darian and Gret's bodies still on the floor. He turned toward the group, "Grab their bodies to be taken care of. Don't forget their weapons. We can put them in the forge." Frory and his wife moved out of the way as the rest of the group went to handle the corpses. Rechnal, Frory, and his wife all paid their respects by putting their right hands to their chests. All the others hoisted the bodies up and began to walk back to the platforms, leaving only Rechnal, Frory, and his wife. It was a somber moment for them as they watched the platform carry their fellow Berserkers into the night. But it soon ended.

As they disappeared, Rechnal turned and opened the crates. The two dogs walked out and sniffed the cold air. He held the piece of the mask to the bloodhound's noses. They took deep breaths to get the scent. Once they found it, their black, muzzled noses pinned themselves to the metal floor, and they began to walk towards the Hand's hidden elevator. He held the hounds on leather leashes, and the two behind him followed. They walked into the level and quietly waited for the dogs to find something. Then, they turned sharply and went to a dead end. It was one of the city's support beams. They butted against the wall, and the three looked at the dogs, confused. The dogs kept bashing their heads and sniffing the wall, so Rechnal figured something was there. He took an ax from his back and smashed it into the wall. With a pop, doors opened, revealing a shaft leading straight down. The dogs peered over the edge, looked down, growled at the hollow shaft, and their breaths created little white clouds around their smooth noses.

The group looked in shock at the shaft before them, and they all took peeks over the edge. Rechnal pulled on the dog's leashes, "Wherever this goes is where we find them." It was still silent, but he looked back, "Frory, time to have fun."

He examined the shaft, and Frory turned to his wife, "You ready, Treni?" Treni may have been Frory's wife, but she was also a fine warrior. She helped train all the Berserker children in combat and was highly respected in the clan. She was soft-spoken and quiet, but her fists could do much more than her mouth ever could.

Frory looked at the shaft and back to Rechnal, "So, how are we going down?" Rechnal held up three grappling guns with winches and shot one into the far wall of the elevator shaft, "We climb." He tossed each Frory and Treni their guns, and they fired to the left and right of him.

"And the dogs?" Treni muttered.

Rechnal answered, "Frory and I will put them over our shoulders as we descend. Grab one, whichever you think you can carry."

"I could carry either, thank you, we're not that different strength-wise, you know," Frory snipped.

Rechnal smiled, "I've always been stronger than you, and you know it."

"Oh, shut up," Frory jokingly pushed him, and they smiled.

"Boys, we got something to do," Treni said.

Frory put his hand up, "Alright, Treni, let us get the dogs."

They hoisted the dogs onto their shoulders and grabbed their guns from the ground. "Attach the hook from the gun to your belts," Rechnal said as he clipped his hook to his belt. Frory and Treni followed suit. They all walked up to the edge and pulled on their hook. Rechnal looked down and said, "These guns have plenty of cable length, so just keep going down until we hit bottom, and once we get there, the dogs will do the rest." Frory looked down and smiled, "I'll beat you down there." He jumped first, and Rechnal smiled and followed with Treni hopping in last.

"Kinda tight in here, isn't it, Rechnal," Frory joked. Rechnal made his tone more serious, "Stay focused, Frory. We actually have something important to do this time." Frory went quiet as he continued to lower himself down. The dogs were still pointing their noses down, so the group knew they had to go lower. The sound of running metal cables filled the shaft as they dropped into the dark. Treni lit her torch against the wall, and she saw an actual elevator not much further down. Rechnal saw it and whispered, "Be ready for anything at this point." They nodded in agreement. Frory reached the bottom first and unclipped the clasp from his belt. He also struck his torch on the wall. He looked around, "Well, now what?" The other two touched down shortly after, and Treni hit a hollower spot than the others.

"There could be a hatch or something right here," she said. Then she turned, and her torch lit up a dainty handle. She looked down at it, "Well, we have our way in." She pulled on it, and the hinges screamed, but the hatch opened. Frory looked into the elevator, "Rechnal, you first." Rechnal looked at him and said sarcastically, "Says the one that made getting down here a race, but sure I'll go."

He took the dog from his shoulders and lowered it down, and said, "Dogs first, actually." Frory lowered his dog down after. With both the dogs down and their noses pointed at the door, Rechnal hopped down. The elevator shook, but there was nothing to be afraid of yet. Frory gestured toward the hatch, "Ladies first, right?" Treni looked annoyed at him, but she leaped down into the elevator, and Rechnal caught her.

Frory exhaled and whispered to himself, "Well, here we go." He jumped down, and Rechnal purposely let him fall. He looked up from the floor, "Really, you're gonna do that?" Rechnal smiled and lowered his hand to help him up, "Yeah, now get up." Frory pushed it away, "No, I'll be okay." Once he stood up, they all faced the door, and the dogs jumped against it, ready to continue their search. Rechnal stood in front, and with his massive arms, he ripped the doors apart and held them for the dogs and his party to get out.

As Rechnal slipped through the doorway, he quietly pushed the doors together. The alleyway before them was dark, so they all drew their weapons. The dog's noses led the group in their torchlight. They turned a corner, and a dim light far off hung above what looked like a prominent figure on their right. They pulled back from the corner, and Rechnal ordered, "Put out your torches. The hounds are pointed straight through that thing, so we need to have the surprise, at least." They put out their torches and faced the corner that was now much darker. Frory felt the tension in the air and tried to lighten it, "Well, it's light, so that's still a good thing, right?" Treni whipped around, "Shut up, Frory. Your blabbering is gonna get us killed one of these days." Rechnal tightened his hold on the leashes as the dogs pulled tighter toward the figure. They moved silently until they got close enough to release the dogs. "Go," he whispered into the dogs' ears as he removed their muzzles.

They sprinted at the figure, who stood up and turned towards the sounds of barking and cold paws on the ground. He pulled two daggers from underneath his seat and pointed them toward the dogs. The hilts were silver engraved with ornate designs of vines. The end of each vine held a red gemstone, with three on each dagger. He could see the Berserkers by now, but he stood unfazed and focused on the hounds headed for him. They barked louder and, in a sprint, closed closer and closer. They both jumped toward the figure, but their motion was cut short. With nothing but a grunt, the man stabbed them with utmost precision. And with the slightest of whimpers, the dogs fell from the blades.

He looked directly at the Berserkers, "Who are you? This is no place for cowards who send their dogs to do their fighting. I suggest you head back before you join your hounds." His voice echoed through the dark but didn't faze the three. They walked into the edges of the light where both Rechnal and Frory stood massive. Treni walked behind and walked around the left side of the two men. Rechnal had his ax, which flowed with a similar ether to his father's, but his flowed with scarlet red. He also had another ax from his childhood, which he used when he needed it, strapped to his back. Frory wielded a polished claymore with runes of good fortune and protection running down it. Treni held two elegant swords in each hand. Their blades were corkscrewed, making recovering from a wound nearly impossible. They were light enough for agility, and their hilts were wrapped in fine leather. They had been a gift from her grandmother, who died shortly after she was born, but the swords were said to have been used by the most powerful Berserker women from generations before.

Rechnal heard the man's voice and responded in a deeper tone, "We are Berserkers. There is no more you need to know. Now tell us what you know about the Devil's Hand before we give you the same treatment as you gave our dogs." The man stood tall, "No knowledge of mine is relevant to the minds of your type. Now, before you join your dogs, turn around." Rechnal smiled evilly, "The suggestion is a nice gesture, but not the information I thought you would give. We can get what we need out of you, though."

The three brandished their weapons and charged. The man fought all three well, with his swings being calculated and precise. The Berserkers had never seen anything like his use of daggers, but the advantage was still theirs. He was even able to disarm one of Treni's swords, a feat no Berserker had ever dreamed of. But his strength only lasted so long, and his guard began to falter with each tiring counter. His ability couldn't compete with three Berserkers.

With a grunt, Frory's blade landed under the right rib and left a gash on the man's side. His body curled from the blow. His dagger fell from his left hand as he went to cover the wound, and he staggered back to guard the elevator. Rechnal smiled confidently, "So that's what you're protecting." The man looked up from his wound and realized his mistake and that the fight was lost. For the first time, the guard felt true terror, a terror that bled into his eyes and gave the Berserkers pride. He had failed, and he knew it. With nothing left to lose, he leaped at Rechnal, who dodged him and swung down with his ax. The ax hit his airborne body, and life was stolen from him as he, and the ax, hit the ground.

The three breathed heavily, recovering from a brief yet surprisingly challenging encounter. Treni went to pick up her sword with a scowl. For even after winning, she was disappointed in herself for getting disarmed. Frory perked up, "Well, we won, guys." She looked at him with an annoyed grimace.

"Frory, I get it, but can you not make a joke out of things for once? I want to be serious, and you're over here joking with your friend about the fact we just killed a man," she said.

"Woah, okay, I'm sorry. I thought my wife would be used to my joking by now," he said, throwing his hands up.

"I am. It just needs to be in the right place," she retorted.

She always seemed to disagree with him nowadays, or maybe she was more outspoken now. Regardless, the two were having more squabbles, and they seemed to argue over nearly everything. Rechnal overheard and ordered, "Can we save the useless banter for later and find out what's behind this door?" She glared at Frory, "You're right, Rechnal. Let's see what's behind the door, and maybe there won't be any dumb jokes this time, right?" Frory answered, "Yes, of course, no jokes this time."

Rechnal used his robust strength to pry open another set of doors. He looked down and saw a shorter elevator shaft, but he could see the bottom this time. He was surprised that anyone would live further down.

"People live down here?" he questioned.

"I guess so. But if that's where a secret clan is, I bet they have some sort of security beyond one man," Frory said.

"You're right, but how are we gonna get down there to see where it is? They probably have this elevator guarded at the bottom. And personally,

I don't feel like fighting a bunch of guards like that last one. We would get slaughtered," Rechnal stated.

He gestured at the man's dead body and shut the doors. As he did, he saw a button with a faint 87 on it. It was just outside the elevator doors and was used before the Devil's Hand put its own machinery in the elevator. He pushed it, and nothing happened. Disappointed, he turned around. But then, he had an idea. *If there's a guard in front of a button labeled 87, then the Devil's Hand is there.*

"We know where they are," he whispered.

"What?" Frory asked.

"Frory, we found them. Look at the button." Frory walked over and studied it. He turned around with a small smile.

"So, we have," he said proudly. "But we still have to find another way down there." Rechnal still had his stoic tone.

"So, let's find another way down there. Grab one of the dogs, and I'll get the other one."

Frory picked up the limp dog, and Rechnal picked up the other. Their torches were all reusable, and the three lit them again before heading into the dark. They knew where the elevator was, but they continued straight to find anything else useful to them.

They continued walking silently until they felt a cold gust from ahead. Frory was surprised and said, "You guys felt that right, or am I just stupid." Through the dark, Treni responded, "We all felt it, and stop trying to make this a pity show cause I got onto you once." Rechnal was upset with the banter and raised his tone, "Will you two just keep it to yourselves until we get back because this is more important than your little argument." The two got quiet and walked behind him. Their torchlight began to fall off, and less light hit the ground. The wind got cooler and stronger. They saw an alley with lights on the left, but they didn't plan to go to a strip club or a bar. They kept on walking until it became dark again. Rechnal walked slowly to prevent stepping on something he couldn't see, and he was worried about why the gusts were getting stronger.

Then, his step was answered with a hollow bang. He stuck out his arms to block the other two walking close behind him. They both stepped back quickly and realized what he stepped on, the path to the platforms. They all carefully continued forward, with their footsteps echoing through the hollow city. Then, Rechnal saw the edge of the circular walkway and the city's hollow center. "There it is," he said as he slowed. As they stopped, Frory looked up and down the dark center and saw a platform approaching them. It hit in front of them, stopped, and changed direction. He stated, "This is where it stops." Treni stayed quiet, looked around, and saw the light coming from way up. Neon signs and the slightest glimpse of flower pod light shone down at her eyes. Still not enough to light this dark shaft, but proof of life above. Rechnal stayed quiet, and Frory said, "How about we put these dogs down for a minute?" Rechnal gave him a look and said, "Fine. Seeing as you're the one who needs the break, we can put the dogs down for a minute." They set the dogs down and kept looking around.

Rechnal looked down and saw platforms still locked into their docks on the other levels. They had been locked in place when the city stopped using them. Since no one lived this far down, they were basically useless. He kept looking down and pointed to the platform close to them, "Do you think we could get these going again?" Treni heard him and asked, "Get what going?" He pointed again, "These platforms." Frory was still looking up and basically clueless about what the others were talking about. Treni and Rechnal continued to talk about the possibility of rerunning the platforms. He thought out loud, "If I can get our people down here this way, it would be way more efficient than that elevator." He turned back, and Frory was still looking up. He got his attention, "Hey, Frory! Get over here and help us."

"What? Oh, right; what are we working on?" Frory asked cluelessly. Treni put her hand to her forehead and whispered, "How did I marry an idiot?" Frory whipped his head around, "I heard that, and I was just looking at all the stuff up there." Rechnal had to play the middleman again and said, "Just focus, both of you. There's a platform still docked at level 81 and a panel next to it. Could we get down there, and if so, would that panel even do anything?" Frory quickly answered, "Well, if that's level eighty-one, then that panel is the master panel located on every ninth floor. So if we can start it again, then these levels should be accessible by the platforms. That would be easier to get all of us down here." Rechnal was taken aback.

"How did you? How did you know that?" he asked.

"Oh, I studied the history of the platforms and their operations not too long ago," Frory said proudly.

"You, you studied something?" Rechnal joked.

"Yeah, I did, actually, so get me down there, and I'll get that thing going," Frory said confidently.

"Can that old platform even hold you? You have been eating a little more lately."

Rechnal laughed at his joke, but it made a valid point. Then, Treni suggested, "What if you boys toss the dogs onto it and see if the platform can hold them?" Rechnal turned to face her, "That's a good idea. Frory, grab one of them." The two each picked up a dog and walked to the edge. Rechnal looked at his target and back to Frory, "On three. One, two, three!" The two grunted and threw the dogs down towards the platform. With a thud, the bodies landed on the platform. Rechnal's had landed near the edge and Frory's toward the center. Frory held his arm out, "How about that, Rechnal? Someone is more accurate than you." Rechnal looked unhappy, but Frory was always a better thrower than he was, so he accepted it.

He looked down, "Well, it'll hold you, so how do we get you down there?" "Anyone got a rope?" Treni asked from behind the two as a joke. "Well, actually, I do," Frory said. He took a rope from under his shirt and handed it to her. Rechnal was confused, "Wait, why do you have a rope just on you?" "Don't question the ways of your advisors, my king," Frory smiled.

Treni then found a metal rod that was used to ground something into place a long time ago and tied a tight knot onto it. She tugged four times to make sure it was secure. Once she figured it was safe, she ran the rope over the edge, and it was just long enough to reach the platform. She turned back, "Your turn, Frory." He tilted his head back and forth and took a deep breath. As he looked over the edge and faced the dark, he said, "No wishing of luck or anything; I am about to climb a rope into the dark?" Treni looked at him and gave him a soft kiss, "Fine, good luck." "Thank you," he said with a blushed smile. It was time for the climb down to start.

He put his torch into his mouth and squatted to pick up the rope. Rechnal playfully said, "Don't die now. The king still needs his advisor." Frory made a muffled noise and nodded. He shook off the nerves and sat down on the edge of the walkway. He gave the rope a good tug and then scooted off the edge. His body hung as his legs wrapped around the rope. He then started descending. After about three minutes of silence, his feet touched down. He pushed down on the platform, and it seemed in good condition. He let go of the rope and took the torch from his mouth. "We're good!" he yelled back up. He hit one of the dogs with his feet, "Oh yeah, the dogs." He bent his neck up and yelled, "Hey! Should I just push the dogs off?!" "Just go ahead!" Rechnal yelled back. He worked to push the dogs into the black beneath him. It was a struggle, but he managed to push them off. Then, he looked over to the control panel and walked over.

* * *

Magnus woke up in the middle of the night to two loud thumps but thought nothing of it, as members would usually have late-night training sessions anyway. He rolled back over and began to doze off again until he felt a strange feeling. This feeling usually occurred before a fight but also before training or any time he used his sword. It felt like it would call him to action, but he couldn't describe it. His best attempts are usually described as if the sword was part of his mind somehow. He had never known what it was, but he assumed it was part of the legacy of the weapon he carried. There was definitely some magic or something supernatural about it, but he wasn't sure what it meant. Every time he used it, he felt stronger and more in control. His movements felt natural, and he almost didn't have to think about them. It felt as if it guided him, yet at the same time; he also guided it. He was connected to it, but this time the feeling wasn't enough to keep his exhausted body from falling back to sleep.

* * *

Frory had been laboring at opening the panel control box to see if the electronics inside were even salvageable, but he finally popped it open and saw the wires inside. "That's actually not too bad," he whispered to himself. "How's it going down there?!" Rechnal asked. He kept his eyes on the panel before him and yelled back, "Actually, not that bad! These wires are still pretty much perfect! I just have to hot-wire them to get the platforms to rotate! And once I turn it on, all the platforms will circulate down to these levels!" Rechnal and Treni nodded and watched his torch flicker in the dark.

He held his torch in one hand and began messing with wires. He was looking for the two red wires marked with the symbol ⊕. He had learned that those wires were used to hotwire anything in the city. He eventually put the torch back to his lips and worked with both hands. He found one deep in the box but couldn't see the other. Finally, after another five minutes, he found the other red wire. He took out his pocketknife and cut through them. He dropped the torch out of his mouth and yelled, "I got it! Now I just have to hotwire the power, and if it comes on, we're good!" Rechnal got excited, "Okay, let's see it then!"

Frory put the two wires together, and they sparked twice. And after a few tries, the system turned on. The lights of the platform ignited, and the dark of the levels revealed four more platforms still docked at lower levels. The eerie darkness from the other levels overwhelmed the platform lights, but the way for the Berserkers was paved. "Yes!" he yelled. Rechnal quickly wiped the smile off his face and ordered, "Frory, turn it off before someone sees it!" He hurriedly pulled the wires apart, and the lights turned back off.

The platforms would start running again once someone pushed the green start button on the console. Frory looked up, "Alright, guys, help me up!" He put the torch in his mouth and grabbed onto the rope again. Rechnal and Treni began pulling the rope up as he climbed. Rechnal chuckled, "You really are getting heavy." Frory couldn't say anything, but his muffled sound sounded like, "Shut up." They kept pulling until he got back to level 80. Rechnal asked him, "So you can get it to work again, right?" He took the torch out of his mouth, "Of course." "Our whole army now depends on you," Rechnal said as he touched Frory's shoulder. Frory stood up straight as he realized how important his role was. He had always been in Rechnal's shadow, and this was his time to finally shine.

Rechnal moved his hand, "Let's go back to the council and make our plan of attack." Frory was brushing himself off, "Sounds good to me." Treni nodded, and they began to head back to the elevator. She grabbed the rope and rolled it up, and Rechnal and Frory followed close behind. They held their torches and looked at the markings and drawings on the walls and the boarded-up windows. Rechnal said, "This is what happens when you let people like the Devil's Hand control you. Just look at this place, a disgrace." He kept looking around to see all the dilapidated things around them.

Finally, they all approached the turn on their right and walked towards the elevator when they saw the light. Treni had a sudden realization, "Rechnal! We forgot about the guard's body." Rechnal looked at the dim light across the alley, "You're right. I'll open the doors to the elevator back up, and you can head back. We'll take care of the body. Go tell the others we will be right behind." "Will do," she nodded. He pried the doors open again, and she went inside. "Frory, help her get to the roof," Rechnal said. Frory dashed over and lifted her up. She popped open the hatch and climbed to the top. She clipped the grapple rope to her belt and said, "See you later." She kicked the hatch shut and began to go up.

Rechnal looked back to Frory, "Let's dump the body." Frory got out of the elevator, and Rechnal shut the doors. The two sprinted toward the light and saw the body right where they had left it. The ground was already stained from blood and other things, so the dried blood matched. "I'll get the left, and you get the right," Rechnal said. He grabbed the left arm and began pulling. Frory joined, and they dragged the body face down across the nasty floor. "You remember where the edge is, right?" Frory asked. Rechnal looked confident, "Of course, I remember. We're almost there." The wind started to pick up, and the torchlight lit less and less.

"Here we are. I told you I remembered," Rechnal said.

"Are we just throwing the body off?" Frory asked.

"Yep, it should be easy for a man of your size, considering you're getting big," Rechnal joked with a smile. Frory gave him a quick glare.

"Just drop it. I had a big dinner," he said.

But when he saw Rechnal smiling, he couldn't help but smile with him. Rechnal tightened his grip, "On three, one, two, three." The two heaved the body into the dark, and when they heard the thud, they knew the work was done.

They turned around and began to jog back to the elevator. Then Frory asked the question even Rechnal himself couldn't answer, "So, how sure are you that we can beat these devils?" Rechnal slowed to a walk and tried to answer.

"Honestly, I have no idea, but I know they killed my father, and I will gladly die if that's what it takes to avenge him. They might be more powerful than we know, but I'm not gonna let fear stop me from doing my father's dying wish."

"Respectable, and know I will be here until the end, my friend. You know my father died before I ever knew him. But I know he fought beside your father, so for him; I will also avenge your father. We're in this together, you and me, so let's fight until we can't," Frory said.

The two shook hands and hugged in the darkness of level 80. Rechnal pulled away, "Let's go back to the council and tell them our plan." Frory nodded, and the two ran to the elevator.

* * *

Treni had just returned to the Berserker compound, where she ran into her mother, Medya. "I was worried about you going down there. Are you okay? And where are the others?" she asked worriedly. Treni answered nonchalantly, "I'm fine, and they're close behind me. We found a way to attack, and when they get back, a meeting will be held to make it official." Medya shook her head and responded with, "You know I don't like this idea because I was around when we beat them the first time, and the only reason we won that fight is that we outnumbered them 2 to 1." Treni looked puzzled, "That can't be true. I was always told that we easily defeated their entire army." Medya looked around to ensure no one could hear her and whispered, "That's just something we tell the children to install pride. We lost a great number of men that day, and we had the advantage. Helpar made up large portions of the story. All he knew was that he killed the king and blew that fact out of proportion. I'm not afraid of what our attack will do because I'm sure we can hurt them with surprise, but if any of them survive, their retaliation could be devastating." Treni reassured, "Don't worry, Mother; we will take care of them. Now let's both prepare for the meeting Rechnal will call when he gets here."

They hugged quickly, and each went their separate ways alerting the council to the next meeting. Treni was stunned by this information, and a small part of her doubted the power and worth of her entire Berserker clan and life. However, she shook it off and went to tell the rest of the compound about the news. After the two finished, the compound was on edge and waited for the men to return.

* * *

Rechnal opened the doors again and helped Frory to the hatch. He shut the doors and jumped up where Frory could catch and help him up the hatch. They closed the hatch and buckled their belts to the grapple ropes. They both tugged on them, and the winch pulled them back up. They returned to level 42 as the light began to pour in from the sky. The great city was waking up, and the men were heading home. Frory asked another question, "You think the council will approve of your plan?" Rechnal said in all seriousness, "They will have to because, as I said earlier, I will avenge my father, and no one is stopping me." Frory shrugged, "Fair enough then." After a while of nonsensical conversation, the two arrived at the door.

* * *

Magnus was waking up again and wanted to check on Rain, so he got dressed and headed toward the medical room. When he opened the door, he saw Rain reading some old book.

"What are you reading?" he asked.

Rain looked up, "Oh, not much, just some old book I found back here. It was all covered in dust, so I picked it up. It also talks about your sword a lot. I'm not sure why, but it does. But your sword has some pretty cool abilities, you know. This sounds random, but have you ever been saved by it?" Magnus thought for a moment, but then he remembered.

"Helpar did tell me that he cut my umbilical cord with the sword to save me."

Rain's eyes lit up, "Really?! Cause this book says that, in your case, the sword creates a soul bond. It's not clear what that means, but I know it means there is a special connection between you and that sword."

Magnus tilted his head to the right and asked, "What else is in there?"

Rain slowly flipped the book in his hands, "I'm not sure. I've just started reading it, but I'll tell you more later."

"Well, tell me more as soon as you can, and keep resting. I'm gonna miss you out there tonight," Magnus said.

"Of course you will," Rain poked.

The two chuckled as Magnus left to discuss his missions with Patri.

* * *

Rechnal and Frory walked into a welcoming party demanding more about their plan. Rechnal held both his hands up, "Wait, my people. You will all know once we start the meeting. But I promise you one thing; we will attack and avenge the fallen." He walked into the council room and walked towards the front. He called for all the members of the council to take their seats. It had slowly turned into basically all the Berserkers as their numbers were starting to wear thin, and the majority were men. He waited for all the members to sit before addressing them. He set his hands on the table and said, "Today was a big day for me and for the future. We have found a way to attack the people who killed our king. They live all the way to the bottom of the city, level eighty-seven.

But Frory has found a way to access them in a way we can bring mass numbers and the element of surprise." The council started nodding and mumbling in approval.

He continued, "On the eightieth level, there was an elevator guarded by a man to which the hounds led us straight to. We killed him in search of answers, but he didn't give any. But when I opened the doors he was guarding, I saw the elevator that led to what looked like the lowest floor." The council all looked intrigued, so he continued on, "But how were we supposed to use an elevator without knowing how it works or the knowledge of other security?"

He let all the members sit on the rhetorical question before giving the answer, "We weren't sure, so we turned around and continued to investigate level eighty. We found the platforms that used to run down to those levels, but they haven't been used for as long as I know. But we saw the control panel on the level beneath us, so we sent Frory, who knows how the control panel worked, to see if the platforms were still usable. Once down there, he hotwired the power, and the system turned on for the first time in who knows how long." The council still followed in approval. He looked around the room and back to Frory. He saw his best friend staring back at him and said in a grandiose tone, "Please applaud Frory's efforts."

He never thought he would say those words, but the room applauded. After a moment, he raised his hands for silence. Then, he boldly yelled, "We have found a way to exact revenge on the ones who killed my father and our king!" The room started to shift in excitement and anticipation as his voice grew. Even louder, he said, "We will avenge them! We will leave here tomorrow at dusk, and under cover of night, we will kill anything that moves in our way! We will be victorious and bring glory to the Berserker name! We will unleash hell on the devil!!"

The room burst into cheers and screams as his voice called everyone to action. Frory came up next to him in all the commotion. "You did it, Rechnal. You got us ready for war." "Thank you," Rechnal said. They embraced again, and Frory yelled, "To the new king! To Rechnal!" He raised his claymore into the air as the rest of the room erupted again into cheers and revelry. Rechnal looked upon his people and felt nothing but pride for himself and what he could do. A new era of the Berserkers had begun, and he was at the head of it.

13

REVENGE OF A SON

Rechnal and Frory left the room to the sounds of cheering and war cries. Rechnal looked proudly at his friend, "Rest up. We need all the strength we have." Frory reached out his hand to grab Rechnal's and said, "I agree. See you in the morning, brother." Then, they each pulled toward each other and hugged once again. Once they let go, they went to their separate rooms to rest.

* * *

Magnus walked into the main chamber and saw Patri training. But before he could say anything, Patri said, "Hello, Magnus." Then, he jumped through the air and impaled a training dummy. Though he was aging, Patri was still proficient with a blade.

He used a spear that he crafted when he was a boy. It was beautiful and had an ornate metal hilt. Marked with signs of wear, it was wrapped with beautiful black leather that made the weapon feel natural to the hand. It was painted royal red near the blade with a gold string intertwined into the hilt. This gold ran up into the spearhead made of the finest jade. Its green hue gleamed with the rest of the blade. It was sharp enough to cut someone with a simple poke and rested strongly in the king's hands. "Father, I see you still have it," Magnus said proudly. "Did you ever think I didn't?" Patri said sarcastically. He smiled as he took the spear out of the dummy. He tossed the spear and caught it, "What can I do for you, my son?" While walking closer, Magnus said, "Well, I was just coming in to make sure you knew where I was gonna go tonight.

You said you wanted loading dock fifteen checked, so I'm going to do that tonight after a few things."

"What things?" Patri asked.

"I'm going to get the money from a drug deal and a weapons deal, then I'll check out loading dock fifteen," Magnus said.

"Good, I'll be here getting a little work in if you need me. I suggest you do the same," Patri stated.

"Maybe I will. Have fun with your dummy," Magnus said as he turned to leave.

He walked out of the chamber to go train himself in the main training area. He rarely ever trained here, but with Patri occupying his usual space, he didn't have much of a choice. He took out his sword and started training against dummies. He watched all the younglings and others learn new moves and felt a sense of pride for his home. He loved it here and wanted to bring peace so that no one would have to die because of irrelevant fighting again. He continued to train into the afternoon until he ate and returned to his room to meditate. He had started meditating recently as a way to focus his mind on a fight or challenge he was facing. This time was for the missions he had later that night. He sat in silence for over two hours, this time reliving his fight with Helpar and how he could have done better or maybe stopped Rain from being hurt.

After the mediation, he changed into his battle clothes and went to eat a light supper. He also collected his new mask, which was almost identical to his first one. But because he killed Helpar in battle, he was given a mask with a golden slash from the left cheek to the right temple. The dinner consisted mainly of fruits and a bit of trug. He ate in silence again, trying to focus his mind on the night ahead.

As the afternoon faded, he went into Patri's chamber again. He was enjoying his meal and ushered Magnus in. "You headed off?" he asked. Magnus walked to the table, "Yeah, I just wanted to let you know." Patri put his food down, "Well, good luck, and I'll see you later. If I'm asleep when you return, we can talk in the morning." "Sounds good. I'll see you later,"

Magnus bowed and walked out of the room. He wanted to stop by Rain again in the medical center on the way out. Since the medical center was close to the entrance, it worked out. He walked in and saw Rain lying on his back.

"Rain, how are you feeling?" he asked.

Rain faced him, "Not too bad, actually. I assume you're headed off for the night?"

"Yes, I am. I'm gonna miss having you out there." Rain patted the book on the shelf next to him.

"Well, I wanted to tell you more about what I read, but it can wait until tomorrow. Good luck."

"Thanks. See you tomorrow," Magnus said as he shut the door and walked out the front doors.

Patri watched him leave and felt a sense of remorse. It wasn't for him but for Rain. He had never cleared things up with his son, and he figured that once he was done with his training, he would finally tell Rain about his mother. It was his right to know, and the guilt of holding the truth back finally won Patri over.

As Magnus walked outside, he heard a guard yell, "Magnus!" By now, he had gotten used to their banter, but it still startled him. "Can you please give me a warning next time?" he asked playfully. The guards chuckled as he stepped into the first elevator. When he got to the top, he didn't notice that the guard at the top was missing, as he figured he was handling business somewhere else. He took a deep breath and put on his mask. He went to the main elevator and rode it to level 39 for his first mission.

When he got there, the elevator locked into place, and he climbed to the rooftops. He bounded toward the given location, looking for signs of his target. He leaped from building to building and finally saw the drug deal underneath. It was a one-on-one affair, so it would be easy work. He took a deep breath and leaped down.

He landed with a thud and quickly took down one with a slash of his sword. "What are you?" the other man said fearfully. Magnus raised his sword to him, "I only want the money. You give it to me, I walk away, and you live." The man did the foolish thing and started to run. He was surprisingly quick and could evade Magnus well. But after some chasing, Magnus hopped on an alleyway wall and pinned him down, "I told you not to run, but I'll give you another chance. Give me the money, and you walk away." The man glared up and said in a deep tone, "No." He threw a perfect punch. It knocked Magnus off him, and he tried to get up before Magnus could recover.

But Magnus was quicker and slashed his sword through his leg. He fell forward and rolled in pain. Magnus looked down at the wincing man with a cold stare, "I wish it didn't have to end this way, but you chose this." He brought his sword down. He still didn't enjoy killing, but in some cases, it was the only answer. He collected the money and put it in the elevator. The rest of his tasks were above this level except for loading dock 15, but that was the last thing he planned on doing. But the Berserker army went down as he went up to do business for the rest of the night.

* * *

Patri didn't end up training for much longer and instead decided to visit Rain. He opened the door to see Rain still reading the old book. Rain rolled his eyes when he walked in.

"What do you want, Father?" he asked.

"I just want to talk," Patri said calmly.

"Sure, like all the other times you wanted to talk to me," Rain said in a dull tone. Patri pulled up a stool and sat. Rain looked annoyed, but he didn't have anywhere to go.

"That's fair, but will you please let me talk this time?" Patri asked.

"Seeing as I can't really move, sure," Rain pouted.

"I wanted to say I'm sorry. I've failed you, Rain, and I want to fix it before I can't anymore," Patri said sorrowfully.

"Why now? After all this time, why try to fix it now?" Rain asked with a tint of pain echoing in his tone.

"I've realized everything I did wrong and want to fix it. Can an old man not do that?" Patri begged.

"You can try. You have done lots of wrongs, and I'm ready for an apology."

His tone was very harsh, and it felt like the grudge was still fresh. Patri bit his tongue and said, "I guess I deserve that. I just wanted to confess to you and finally ask for your forgiveness." Rain seemed impatient but was willing to listen. He shut the book and set it down on his nightstand. Patri waited for him to turn back and said, "I want to start with your mother. She didn't run away with you. I forced her away." Rain's eyes opened in shock, "So you lied to me about my entire life?" Patri knew what he was preparing to say would hurt, but it had to be said.

"To be completely honest with you, Rain, yes, I have. Your mother was a beautiful woman, and I took advantage of that. I was stupid and didn't look into the future. I let the night take me over, and I gave her you. And when I found out, I went ballistic. I left her. She didn't run or hide. I left." Rain was listening intensely, soaking up every word, yet Patri wasn't finished.

"Then, after that, she was going to give you up to the Berserkers, but I got greedy. I wanted you back so I could raise you to fight for me. I took you before you could get handed over to the Berserkers. It was all me. I'm the reason you're here. I'm sorry."

Rain had no words and was lost in his own mind. Patri felt the tension and broke it by saying, "I just wanted to get that off of me, so now, you can really make your choice." He sniffled, and his eyes started to turn red, but he held back the tears.

Rain finally spoke, and it was rash and aggressive, "You, you did all of this. You turned me into a monster, and now I just kill for you! That's all you wanted me for, to do your killing?!" Patri said nothing in return. Rain struggled but was able to stand up with the help of the bed. He angrily continued, "All this time, I just thought you were a terrible father," he scoffed, "It's worse than I thought." He stood weakly, but his tone was stronger than Patri had ever heard, "So what actually became of my mother? Tell me."

His eyes were watering, and he put his hand on Patri's chest, "What happened to her?!" Patri wrapped his hand around his wrist, "I don't know what became of your mother, but I wish I did." He pushed harder into Patri's chest and screamed, "So you took me and disposed of her! Makes sense seeing as you never even cared!"

His emotions overcame him, and he started to cry. Patri tried to push his hand off him, but he wouldn't be moved. He said in a caring and almost frightened tone, "But I did, Rain; every day, I fought with myself over what I did to her and what I did to you. I am in the wrong, and I don't need your forgiveness. I just wanted to tell you while I had the courage." Rain collected himself just enough to say, "Well, I'm glad you did. But get away from me and let me think."

His tears were drying now, but he was deeply hurt. The memory of the day when Patri scorned him flooded his mind. He heard the same line repeatedly until he finally said, "Something you said those years ago still hurts me, and I want to know if you meant it." Patri looked confused, and Rain asked through choppy breaths, "Would you disown me?! Would you?!" Patri immediately knew what he was referring to. He started to say, "My son-" But Rain cut him off and yelled, "Would you?!"

He was grabbing at Patri's clothes in desperation. Patri tightened his grip to assure him.

"No, Rain, I couldn't have then and can't now. You are special to me. I just never knew how to show it."

"Well, maybe having a dad that's more than just a king would have!" Rain cried.

"It was how I was treated, but it is no excuse for what I did to you," Patri said in a hurt tone. Rain had taken some breaths and was beginning to calm himself. He looked Patri straight in the eyes.

"I don't think I can forgive you, not now. Give me time to process, and maybe we can build up from here, but it will take time." It was the response Patri was expecting, resentment. He hoped he wouldn't hear it, but he had to accept it.

"I'm sorry, Rain, I really am. But I've sworn to myself that I'll be better from now on. Then, if you choose to forgive me, we can start over," he said sorrowfully.

Rain had sat back on his bed and gestured his hand toward the door, "Get out. I don't want to hear anything else from you right now." He started to lie back down, and he felt a bit of remorse for lashing out at his father. It was only a small string that played in his harp of a heart, yet it was enough to make music, or in this case, emotion. In a more caring and gentle tone, he said, "Thank you for the openness, but I cannot take anything else today." Patri nodded slowly, "I understand. Thank you for listening."

He left the medical room, fighting tears. His past had caught up, and his son was against him. He sat on his throne to process the magnitude of what had just happened. His emotions raged. Finally, one last tear left his aged face, and his green eyes cried no more. He still sat on the throne and called his guards to discuss something to get his mind off Rain.

* * *

During this time, Rechnal had taken his army and assembled it on loading dock 15. He turned and gave Frory two grappling guns. He told him, "Your turn." Frory nodded and sprinted to the secret elevator shaft. He pulled the doors apart and grappled down. The elevator was somewhere above him, but Magnus was still going up. He hit the bottom, pried those doors open, and lit his torch. He slipped into the cold night and went to the walkway's edge. He looked over and saw the platform docked on level 81. He shot the grappling gun into the ground and attached it to his belt. He tugged it to make sure it was secure. Once he was convinced, he walked off and dangled down into the night. He got to the platform and unhooked the grapple gun from his belt. He quickly ran to the console and turned it on. It buzzed to life, and he smiled, "I'm so good." The platforms were loud but not loud enough to wake anyone. The Hand's guards did notice the buzzing but assumed it was something the city was doing, so they paid no attention to it.

He quickly latched himself back to the grapple gun, and the winch pulled him back up. He meandered his way onto the walkway and unlocked the grappling gun. He put it under his shirt and sprinted to the elevator shaft. He attached the other grappling gun to his belt, and it dragged him back to level 61. He detached the second gun from the wall and began to run to loading dock 15.

Rechnal's army was gathered on the walkway facing the platforms. The group was divided into two groups, with Rechnal leading the first and Frory leading the second. He spoke to everyone, a mix of older men and women from Helpar's time and the young men of his, "Once Frory returns; we will descend. There are no second thoughts, no remorse. We avenge our fallen. Treni and Medya will stay with the youths and make sure they are safe. If none of us return, they are prepared to defend them." As he spoke, a figure appeared. It was Frory. Rechnal saw him and yelled, "He has returned! Now we will fight!" He raised his ax to the air, and the first group prepared to board the first platform.

The first platform slowed in front of them, and Rechnal gave Frory a nod. After everyone in his group was ready, he said, "You know what to do. All of you do. I believe in my people." All the heads nodded. The group stayed silent for the remainder of the ride in preparation for the fight.

A few Berserkers lit their torches as the platform descended beneath the cloud level. Rechnal stood stoic and quiet as the platform descended. Among the mass of bodies, he uttered a small prayer, "Father, I know you can hear me, and I want to avenge you. I pray for your blessing to do so." As he finished, he put his mask over his eyes and shook off his nerves.

His platform was nearing the bottom, and Frory's group wasn't far behind. He could smell the air getting thicker and the light leaving faster. Only the torches lit the platforms.

The platform reached the bottom, and the first group leaped onto the ground. "Who are you?" a voice from the dark said. It was followed by shuffling. "We are your end," Rechnal said confidently as he brandished his ax.

The Berserkers all unloaded and tried to look around. It was pitch black, and the torchlight was all they had. They stayed close together and put whoever held the torches on the outside to give off light. The mysterious voice spoke again. It said, "We will end you before you ever see it happen." It went completely silent, and a cool breeze was all the Berserkers felt aside from their own heartbeats. Then slowly, screams of agony came as torches clattered to the floor. One by one, the torches fell. There was no telling how many enemies were in front of the Berserkers, so they stayed compact. Fear ran through the group until one caught the blade of the Hand's guards and grabbed his outer garment. He pulled the guard in, impaled him onto his sword, and let out a battle scream that all the others joined in.

The torches stopped disappearing, and the screaming grew louder. Then from above, Frory's group joined the noise, and it echoed through the darkness. Then, they chanted in a tongue unknown to the Hand's fighters. And at the crescendo of noise, Frory arrived, and with his crew's torches, the area was light enough to reveal four more black-clad guards. The guards staggered back and realized this fight would not end in their favor. They looked at each, nodded, and sprung at the Berserkers. They all dueled ferociously, but three were slain in mere seconds. One lasted nearly a full minute against an army, but his fight ended with an ax to his neck. The deaths were quick and quiet, so no one inside the compound knew what was outside their own door.

The Berserkers gathered their dead and put them at the edge to address when the attack was finished. In total, eight had died. Rechnal then walked to the front. He turned towards his army and said, "We have no idea what's behind these doors, but nothing will stand in our way." He turned to face the doorway and smashed his ax into it, and it popped open. They all tossed their torches to the ground and stepped on them to extinguish them. The army was met with a giant set of double doors in front of them. "There," Rechnal said as he ran to the ornate doors and slammed against them with his ax. It echoed through the hallway, and after three vicious swings, it popped open. The rest of the army ripped it open, and they poured into the main chamber.

The king's guards were present and shuffled into position, and Patri was on his throne, recovering from his conversation with Rain. The threat before him made him forget everything he had discussed, and he shot up to grab his spear from beside him. He ushered Shew, who happened to be in the room, over, "Take Ghuri and protect the young." He nodded and disappeared into a side door that led into the main hallway. The guards all yelled a cry that alerted all of the Devil's Hand to come to the main chamber. However, some were still sleeping and couldn't hear the cry for help.

The guards met in fierce combat with the first wave of Berserkers. Rechnal sat behind, raised his mask from his face, and spoke directly to Patri. He saw the leader of the people that murdered his father, and something switched inside of him. Aggression and hatred drove him, and he yelled, "My people and I will not rest until this hell is taken care of! So why fight?!" "Because we are stronger than you'll ever be!" Patri yelled in response. Their voices echoed over the sound of clashing metal. Rechnal laughed back ominously. Patri grimaced as he watched him burst into laughter and put his mask on.

He ran at one of the guards with both axes flying through the air. In moments, he killed the guard and faced a young boy whose eyes were a mix of fear and hope. He sinisterly grinned, "So this is what I am faced with. The great Rechnal left to fight a boy!" He swung his ax, and it cracked the ground beneath him. He laughed the whole time as his blade came dangerously close to even his own men. He kept swinging manically until he hit the boy's sword from his hands. The boy's body paralyzed itself in fear. Rechnal smiled at the sight and swung his ax. It connected with the boy's head and killed him instantly.

Rechnal went from person to person, slaughtering anyone in his path. Other members of the Hand were coming into the room only to be greeted with blades. The Berserkers were taking losses, but not nearly as bad as the Hand was. Twenty-four Berserkers remained. The Hand had similar numbers remaining but had lost nearly double the number of people. The guards had fallen back to the throne where Patri stood fighting.

He was fighting for his life. Constantly charged by Berserkers, he flipped, dodged, and slayed four. His prowess was unmatched by the lesser-trained Berserkers. But as he drove his spear into another, Rechnal's eyes met his. They gleamed with passion and anger as he rushed at him with his axes glistening. Patri quickly backstepped and parried the first of his swings. With the throne behind them, the two fought with power as Rechnal stayed on the attack, and Patri defended himself. He leaped through the air to dodge Rechnal's swings. "Is that really all you know how to do, run?!" Rechnal taunted. He fought with a wide smile and crazy eyes. He laughed again and threw himself at Patri, who quickly sidestepped. However, Rechnal made one error as his foot landed on the edge of the first step, and his balance was thrown off. And in a matter of seconds, the tide of the fight changed.

Patri stabbed his spear into the floor and jumped through the air. He spun around his spear and double-foot kicked Rechnal in the chest. The kick threw Rechnal from the throne and down the stairs. He pulled his spear from the ground and held it at the ready. He looked down at Rechnal and said, "I still have a few things to be proud of."

At this point, the numbers on both sides grew thin, but another wave of Hand members entered the room and distracted the rest of the Berserkers. This left two guards unmanned. So, they stepped in front of Rechnal to block him from Patri and pointed their glaives at him. He crawled back quickly and got his footing. He faced the two guards and wiped a drop of sweat from his brow. "Hrahh!" he yelled as he jumped through the air, but the guards met his attack well. Their guards were nearly impenetrable, but this didn't slow him. He relentlessly attacked in hopes of getting another chance at Patri.

As he dueled with the guards, Frory knocked a guard's glaive into the ground, kneed his face, and jammed his claymore through his chest. There was no one in front of him, and he saw the king standing on his raised platform. He charged.

His first hits were dodged, but his claymore's speed was much different than an axe. This allowed Patri to counter him much easier and for the fight to be almost perfectly balanced. The two grunted and pushed each other to the limit. Then Patri pushed him back, and the two stood and rested for only a second. Then, they both charged again, and their blades clashed before the throne. The sound echoed through the room as Patri backed up, spun his weapon over his back, and jabbed it. Frory quickly blocked, and the fight continued.

As they dueled, Rechnal was losing his fight. He had been pushed away from the throne, lost his main ax, and was getting tired. He had also lost his mask when one of the guards hit his face with the blunt of a blade. He tried to get glimpses of Frory fighting but was blocked by the guards in front of him.

But the guards relented for a moment, and it was long enough for him to see Frory raise his sword in the air, swinging down at Patri. Then, the guards collapsed onto him and blocked his vision for what came next.

As Frory swung down, Patri used the hilt of his spear to push the blade back into the air. Frory was stunned for a split second, and that's all Patri needed. He moved his spear down and stabbed it through Frory's chest. The claymore fell to the ground, and Frory fell back as he pulled his spear out. His body tumbled down the stairs and landed behind the guards Rechnal was fighting.

He had just gotten his only ax pinned when he saw Frory roll down the stairs. He started to shake in fury and screamed a demonic howl. His energy was replenished, and he was fueled by pure anger.

Patri turned to face him and saw that he had a chance to attack, so he prepared to jump down the stairs and land on his foe. At that exact moment, Rechnal took his left hand and threw a dagger from his waist into the left-hand guard's forehead.

Patri's knees bent to jump, and he raised his spear into the air.

Rechnal dropped his ax and caught the guard's glaive after the dagger made him drop it. The other guard had no time to react before Rechnal charged with another dagger in his left hand.

Patri's feet left the obsidian floor, and he began to fly.

Rechnal stabbed the other guard while he jumped over him. The dagger landed in the guard's neck, and he bent over in pain and shock. Rechnal rolled over his back, screamed, and released the glaive. It was a perfect throw with incredible power. Patri's eyes shot open with fear.

His body was suspended in the air with a glaive flying toward him, and there was nothing he could do. Before his feet ever reached the ground, the spear shot through his body and impaled into the obsidian stairs. The perfect black stairs, shattered.

Rechnal's face was shaking with fury. He went to visit his kill and saw Patri's mouth leaking blood. The king had fallen. He uttered another guttural scream before seeing Frory, who lay cold on the floor. He stopped in front of the body and said, "No, Frory, not you. You weren't supposed to go like this." His eyes started to water, and he cradled Frory's shoulders. He sat for a moment before remembering he was fighting a battle. He looked back down and wiped his eyes, "I'll finish this for us." He used two fingers to close Frory's frozen eyes. "May you rest well, brother," he said as he looked back across the chamber.

* * *

Magnus was handling an arms deal that went wrong. It was on loading dock 10. He had killed the others there, but in the heat of the fight, someone pushed the weapons crate over. This spilled weapons across the entire loading dock, and some fell onto the walkways of the levels beneath. And now, he had to clean up his mess.

As he was gathering weapons, the silence bored him, so he told himself, "Of course, this happens to me. Nearly had them all, and now I'm finding lost weapons for the rest of the night." The platforms went up and down, and he hopped from platform to platform, collecting any loose weapons he could see that fell onto the circular walkways. He knew he wouldn't collect all of them, but he figured he could find most of them. He spent a good portion of the night cleaning up, and he still had one more drug deal to bust before the night was done. But now he had to pick up several loose weapons like swords, cutlasses, nun chucks, and even bows. What would usually take him an hour was now going to take long enough for the Berserkers to finish their attack.

* * *

The fight was over, and bodies were strewn across the floor. Only seven other Berserkers remained now, and Rechnal turned to face them with a tear running down his cheek. He got up from holding Frory, his face shaking with fury and sadness. He saw the men he had left, and his voice thundered, "We do not leave this building until every single one of them is dead! I don't care if they're women, children, or animals! Anything that breathes under this roof dies!" Spit flew from his mouth, and he lost all control of his emotions. He didn't know how to feel anything but pure rage and hatred. The chamber went silent. "Do you understand?!" he screamed. "Yes, my king," replied the others in fearful unison. He stormed past the bloody bodies to pick up his two axes and mask while ordering his men, "You three with me! The rest of you go that way!" He slipped the mask into his pocket when he saw it was cracked from the blow.

They all nodded and ran down the hallways looking for any sign of life. Any closed door was kicked in, and any sound was traced. Multiple were killed in their sleep; others woke up just in time to see furious, Berserker eyes above them. As Rechnal and his crew reached the end of their side, they saw one more doorway. It was tightly shut, and he pounded with his ax on the door. He screamed viciously with each hit. Finally, it broke open, and inside were the young, protected by Shew and Ghuri. Rechnal and his men walked in and blocked the doorway. All their weapons shone in the dim light. Shew's voice was shaky, uncertain, and terrified, "You cannot kill them I-I won't let you." Rechnal spoke to his men without breaking his gaze with the doctor, "Block the doors." They all nodded and stood in front of the doorway.

He replied to Shew in sheer confidence and bitterness, "Good thing you won't be alive to see it." He dragged his axes along the ground and started swinging. And, in just three quick swings, Shew was overpowered and killed by the ax Rechnal drove into his chest.

Ghuri drew his curved sword but couldn't react in time to save Shew. He stepped in front of the children, "I have seen warriors much finer than you, and today I will fight until your end, not mine." He spun his sword in the air and held it to his side. Rechnal smiled at him and pulled the blood-stained ax from Shew, "My end will follow yours and your people." The children were terrified and couldn't do anything but sit and watch.

He swung his axe down to Ghuri, who stepped back and blocked it into the ground. The children behind him shrieked in fear. But as he pinned the first ax, Rechnal brought his other ax through his shoulder. "Argh!" he screamed as he stepped back. He turned his wounded side toward the children, and their eyes opened to the sight of blood.

Bloodstained, Ghuri and his sword hung low to the floor. Rechnal quickly gestured toward his men, and they started walking toward the children. They were backing Ghuri and the children into the corner of the room. Ghuri raised his sword and waved it at the men in front of him. His golden eyes felt the chill of death approaching. He swung desperately, hoping to land one hit, at Rechnal, who blocked his blade and dislodged it from his hand. The curved sword flew across the room and clattered against the wall. Ghuri backed the children into the corner with both arms outstretched, protecting them. His eyes filled with hopeless rage because he knew Rechnal wouldn't stop, and he could do nothing. He let out another scream and jumped into the air in a last attempt to hit Rechnal.

But his body was stopped in midair. Rechnal's massive hand caught his neck. He held him in the air, smiled, and tilted his neck to the right. He looked directly into Ghuri's golden eyes and said, "Look at them behind you. They're afraid, and you failed them. Pathetic." He tightened his grip. Ghuri flailed, and his eyes became bloodshot. The children were all frozen in horror at Ghuri's flailing body. His legs slowly stopped moving, and all his energy went into one final insult, "May death find you." He tried to say something else, but his airways closed, and his eyes rolled back into his head. His head fell forward, lifeless. Rechnal dropped him to the ground, and it landed with a quiet thud.

"Finish this," he uttered to his men. One of the men looked at him with a concerned look, and he dared to speak, "They're only children. We could bring them back with us." Rechnal turned back around and drew his ax. He jammed the man's neck on the top curve of the blade and pinned him to a wall. He started to choke on the metal, and Rechnal said to him, "Do as I say." The man nodded in terror, and Rechnal released him from the ax. He gasped for air and held his neck.

Rechnal faced his men again, "Like I said, finish this." The rest of the men looked concerned but feared for their own lives. Rechnal walked from the room, and the other Berserkers stepped toward the cowering children. They weren't sure they wanted to do this, but they had no other choice. In the end, they killed every single child.

Rechnal was still thirsty for more blood. He screamed through the hallway, "If any more of you live, come out and face me like the warriors you claim to be!" The cry hit no ears except one last man, Rain. But he heard nothing and kept walking to the main chamber. He and the other Berserkers met at the main doorway.

"All of them?" he asked.

A man addressed him, "Yes, my king. There weren't too many left, to begin with. I think we only dispensed four in total." Rechnal looked at the group.

"Well done, men. When we arrive back at the compound, I will reward you for your valiant efforts."

"Thank you, my king," they all said in unison.

* * *

Rain had heard the battle and spent his time trying to dress for combat or just merely stay standing. The information about his mother still haunted him, but at this point, he was ready to accept what came through the doors. His body fought any movement, but he pushed through until he was finally ready to open his door. But as he did, his wounded chest shot in pain, and he let go of a sword he found in the room to put his hand to his chest. It clattered to the ground loudly, and he knew what he had done. He scrambled to pick it up, but it was too late. He had ushered in death.

* * *

From the silence, the Berserkers heard the clang. "Did you hear that?" Rechnal asked intuitively. All the others nodded, and one said, "Yes, my lord." "With me!" Rechnal screamed. He tore off towards the sound, and the others followed behind him. He looked around until he saw a small doorway outside the massive double doors. "There!" he yelled as he pointed to the medical door Rain sat behind. The other men gathered behind him until he spoke, "This is my kill. I want to finish this, so you men stay out of it." The group nodded in agreement as he walked to the door and clipped one ax to his back.

Rain sat inside, and he was petrified for once in his life. He knew he stood no chance and prayed whoever was outside didn't come in. But he knew his wish wouldn't come true and that he wouldn't survive what would happen next. *You've done all you can. Just fight one last time.* He tried to calm himself, but he was shaking, and his heart rate was fast. He had faced death, but never this close. He took his sword and pointed it at the door, ready for his last fight.

Rechnal burst through the door and looked at him. He saw a wounded man and smiled villainously.

"You're the last one in my way, and you're already in pain. What's the worst that can happen if you feel more?" Rain held his sword as straight as possible.

"I will fight until there is nothing left in me, and if I die, I die," he said.

"You're a noble warrior. But nobility isn't enough to save you," Rechnal threatened. Rain adjusted his stance through a wince.

"So be it."

He tightened his grip on his sword, and Rechnal brandished his ax. He swung first, and Rain blocked the swing well. However, the block caused extreme pain, and Rain doubted he could do it again. He knew he had to kill Rechnal now, or it was over. So, he lunged, but Rechnal casually blocked his blade and nearly knocked him down. He doubled over in pain, and Rechnal smiled at the crippled warrior. "You really thought that you stood any chance?" he mocked. Rain coughed and looked back with passion in his eyes. He looked at him and said, "No, as you said, I'm fighting for nobility. That means I will fight until I cannot anymore."

He lunged again. Rechnal quickly stepped back and spun his ax to hit the sword from below. The blade flew from Rain's hand and landed beside him. "Pathetic," Rechnal muttered. He saw Rain bending down to pick up the sword, and he threw a punch. It connected with Rain's face, and he flew back. His back smashed into the bed, and pain shot from his chest. He fell to the ground, nearly unconscious, and knew his fate was sealed by now. He prayed internally that his death would be quick. Rechnal looked down and said, "You did well for a man fighting from a hospital bed, but now you die."

He stomped over to Rain and picked him up by the shirt. Blood ran from his nose, and his eyes fought to stay open. The pain was excruciating, and he couldn't move. Rechnal raised his ax with his right hand to strike his face and end the battle. He sat for a few seconds, taking the moment in, and saw the pain in Rain's eyes. But then he smiled an evil grin, "I have an idea. If you're already in so much pain, why can't you die with even more?"

He laughed and punched Rain again. Not as hard as the first, but enough to knock him out. He dragged him across the floor and to the front of his men. One of them asked, "What are you doing with him?" Rechnal snapped back, "None of your concern. Grab any of the bodies you want to bring home. I'll grab Frory when we're finished. Anybody you don't want to bring back, throw them over the edge." The men nodded affirmingly and returned to the chamber to collect the bodies. They decided to throw all the Berserker casualties off the side of the levitation platform, which wasn't that far of a drop.

Rechnal looked at Rain. He mocked the unconscious warrior, "Your face is at peace. Enjoy it, for it will be the last time it ever is." He dragged him all the way across the main chamber, over fallen warriors, and next to his dead father. He pulled him up to the throne and sat him on it. He paused momentarily until he saw Patri's spear on the ground. He picked it up and slammed it across Rain's body and into the left armrest of the throne. It went deep enough that he even struggled to move it. So, it acted as an unmovable restraint for Rain. Rechnal turned to his men, who had just finished their job, and ordered, "When he wakes, we leave." His order echoed over the empty chamber. He stood in pride over the room and looked at the whole place until he saw Frory again. His eyes almost started to water before he contained himself. He walked over and picked up his friend's body. He said to it, "I will give you a king's funeral, my friend. You deserve it more than any of us." He walked silently through the room and separated Frory from the others.

He went back inside and saw Rain shifting on the throne. "Are you awake, friend?" he said mockingly. Rain moved and spoke weakly, "I am not your friend." He tried to move the spear but couldn't, and it pinned him to the seat. The pain in his chest was brutal, and his head pounded from Rechnal's punches. He started to panic and tried to find a way to escape, but it was all pointless. Rechnal saw the struggle and said, "Save yourself the pain and stop moving. You're going to be squirming soon enough." He gave Rain one last look and walked back to the double doors. The others were gathered outside and were waiting for orders. Rechnal looked over his shoulder and told them, "I'm almost done. You all can head back and get some rest." "Yes, sir," they said. They all took a platform and slowly returned to level 42. And when they returned, they went inside and got the rest that they needed.

Rain sat and began to recognize the bodies on the floor. But soon, he focused on the body not too far from him. Patri's body lay pinned to the stairs. "Father?" he whispered. He was hoping that Patri was alive by some miracle, but no light was left in his father's eyes. Rain's lips were sealed with remorse. He had never corrected things with his father, and now the last thing Patri heard from him was his anger. It ate at him. He couldn't redeem himself and prove that he wanted to fix things. Deep down, he understood and loved his father, and seeing him dead brought out a new sadness he had not yet experienced. He had already accepted his fate, but seeing his dead father reminded him of everything he never got to achieve. A single tear ran down his cheek for the things he never got to say and for the anger he showed before his father left him.

Rechnal stood as his men left and turned to face the chamber again. On either side of the massive doors, mounted on the wall, were torches. He took one from the left side and walked into the room. He started directly at Rain and squatted down. He lit the wooden floor on fire, and it began to spread around the chamber. "No!" Rain yelled. He struggled in his imprisonment. Rechnal stood in the massive doorway and said, "This is how this ends. I drown hell in its own fire!" He squatted down and threw the torch up to the ceiling, hitting the tapestry and catching it on fire. The torch hit the ground, and it burned more of the floor. He was pleased and turned to leave the chamber. He walked out with the fire lighting his back.

The fire spread rapidly, and the smoke was beginning to block Rain. "You bastard!" he yelled from the smoke. He thrashed against the spear to no avail. Rechnal smiled as he heard this, and he grabbed Frory's body and got on the levitating platform. "Just in case someone wants to know who did this," he said. He took his mask from his pocket and tossed it onto the floor next to the platforms. The platform he rode crawled upwards. His face was tired, and he had to address Frory before he could do anything else.

* * *

At this same time, Magnus was finishing up the last of his nightly activities, another drug deal that he needed to steal the money from. At this point, he was on level 61 and waited on the roof to pounce on the people below. It was a four-man ordeal. He jumped from the building and quickly killed two of them. "Who are you?" one of them asked as they cowered together. Magnus was exhausted and said, "Honestly, I'm just tired of doing all this, and I really don't want to kill either of you. So if you can just give me my money, I'll be on my way. Did I mention both of you stay alive?" The men dared to strike a deal. One said, "We'll give you half." Magnus held his sword out and threatened, "Are you really trying to barter right now? You saw what I did to them, and I'll do it to you if I have to." The two drug dealers looked at each other and agreed to hand over the money. They tossed the bag of Ugurns to the ground and ran into the alleyway. "See, that wasn't too hard!" Magnus yelled as they disappeared.

He was glad this one ended quickly and happily collected the money. He still had to investigate loading dock 15, and since he was on level 61, it was a short walk away. He eventually got there and looked around. It was eerily quiet. He wondered where the bodies were, but he figured it wasn't important. He did one pass across the area and concluded that all was normal. "Well, that was a night," he whispered with a sigh to himself. He quickly returned to the rooftops and hopped until he reached the elevator. He opened it and headed back to level 80.

* * *

Rechnal reached the Berserker compound as Magnus reached the elevator. He carried Frory's body through the quiet halls and to the altar room. He grabbed the vase and poured the liquid in before setting his body down. He crossed Frory's arms over his claymore and stuck the torch into its place. The altar caught fire, and his body began to burn. Rechnal was distraught and let out more tears. "I finished it for you, and my throw wasn't even that bad," he chuckled through his tears. He watched it burn and had to say something else.

"It's over now, Frory, and maybe you can meet your father and my father wherever you are. I'm proud that you stayed next to me all these years. I never thought this day would come, and I never thought it would be so soon. But I will continue and rebuild this place to the glory it deserves. I'm disheartened you cannot be here to see it, but I will do this for my father and for you."

He lowered his head as the fire engulfed the body. He dropped to a knee in silence, looking at the flames. His eyes wanted to cry, but the heat of the fire dried them up. He finally curled his head towards himself in pure exhaustion and sadness. The fire started to slow as Frory turned into ashes at the bottom of the altar. Rechnal eventually stood back up, sniffled, and said, "Rest peacefully, my brother." He turned and walked out of the room and headed for his chamber.

He felt no remorse for what he did, but he was plagued by losing his close friend. The night was ending, and he knew he needed to rest. His body was aching, and his head was spinning. So much had happened to him, but if he had to kill again, he would do it gladly.

* * *

The elevator touched down, and Magnus stepped out. He sniffed the air and caught the whiff of smoke. He thought it was nothing because things always smelled off on level 80. This changed when he got to the elevator and saw the smoke seeping through the gaps. *Wait, no. It can't be.* He hoped and assumed it was from another one of the levels.

But as the elevator went down, the smell got stronger and stronger. *Please don't let me see what I think I'm going to do.*

Finally, the elevator screeched to a stop, and the doors opened. The smoke was everywhere but still thin enough for him to see through. It was coming from the doors of the compound. He ran from the elevator and saw the first of many woes ahead of him. He saw the guard's bodies laid out on the floor. "It can't be," he said. Smoke and an orange glow were pouring out of the doorway. He ran to the door and lowered his head to push it open. He froze as he couldn't believe what he saw. The main chamber doors were broken open, and fire engulfed the entire room. And as he stood in the doorway, he saw the tapestry break and fall. Its embers spread across the room, and the fire continued to grow. He stepped back with a gaping jaw. He couldn't believe it. His entire life was up in flames.

14

NEW ROLES

Magnus stood for a few more seconds before rushing into the fire to look for anyone left. There had to be someone. It was hotter than anything he had ever felt, and it dried his eyes. He put his head down as he ran and dodged body after body. Some had already caught fire, and others were about to be emblazoned. He started to cough and yelled, "Is anyone here?" No response. His voice was straining, "Patri, Rain, Anyone?!" No response.

The smoke had become so thick that his vision was limited to only an arm's length away. He was blindly moving through the room, finding nothing but more bodies. He wished he could've saved them, but they were already dead. Then, he fell over next to a body on the stairs and saw Patri's face. A muffled scream came from his lips as he realized who he had stumbled over, "Father, Father?" He jumped next to his body and put his hands on its face. His hands were shaking, "It can't be. Not you." His hand drifted towards the glaive, and he tried pulling it out. It was stuck in the king's chest. "No, no!" he yelled. He pushed on Patri's body in an attempt to free the glaive. It wouldn't move, and he wasn't sure he could get it out. But he needed to free his father. He had to.

He pulled with everything he had, and it finally dislodged itself from the obsidian stairs and Patri's body. Magnus threw the glaive into the nearby flames and tried to lift his father's body, but he couldn't. The smoke was too thick, and his strength was fading. He knew he had to get out before he died with his father. He tried to escape the building, but the smoke was a massive hazard. He stumbled his way back towards the front doors. He was beginning to cough more violently, but he remembered a filter mask in the medical room. It was a glass mask with a filter under the chin. Rain had used one when Helpar first hurt him. If he could find it, then he could rescue Patri. He finally found the massive doors and saw the orange glow of fire overtaking their frame. It was humbling and scary. His home was nearly gone.

He passed through the doors and took a quick left. He burst into the medical bay, which was still calm compared to the rest of the compound. The smoke thinned out, and he saw the mask hanging on a hook in the corner. He grabbed it and sealed it to his face. He gasped for air as it filtered his breathing. But as he left the medical room, he realized Rain was gone. It hit him that the door was broken open, and something must have happened to his brother. While leaving, he whispered, "Where are you, Rain? Maybe you made it out of here, and if not, I'll find you."

He caught his breath and sprinted back into the room to get his father's body. The smoke was even thicker now, and his vision was even worse, but he remembered how to reach Patri. "Come on, come on," he whispered to himself as he got closer. He got his hands under Patri and lifted him into the air with desperate determination. The dead weight was staggering, but he would not give up. He plowed through the smoke with his right hand under Patri's back and the left supporting his legs. "Come one, come on," he told himself quietly.

The doors never seemed so far away, and the extra weight wasn't helping. He was close to the door when a wooden plank fell from the ceiling. It landed next to him, and the embers shot at his clothes. Some burned onto his skin, and he felt the searing pain. Tiny grunts and groans of pain followed as he dragged himself through the front door. He carefully put Patri down far enough away to keep his body safe and patted the embers off himself.

Then, he heard rumbling from inside and saw parts collapsing. The firelight smacked his face, and fear overcame his eyes. He didn't want to go back, but he couldn't leave without finding Rain or at least what was left of him. There was something left inside for him to find. He felt a feeling inside of dread at what he was going to discover, but he charged headlong into the flames again.

* * *

It was the middle of the night when Rechnal finally laid his head down. He couldn't fall asleep and was growing increasingly restless. The fight had left his heart racing, and he was still too excited to calm back down. Frory also kept his eyes from shutting. He relived watching his friend die repeatedly and loathed himself for letting it happen. However, he didn't know what else he could have done. He had already murdered everyone.

So, he left his room and headed toward the training area to use his nervous energy and channel his anger. He snuck down the halls as his people slept. The fear of waking people was less than before, as there weren't too many people left after the fight except for Treni and Medya. The clan already had little numbers due to Helpar's law, and now, after the battle, all the generation's women, except Treni, were gone. She was the last one able to bear children. Medya was beyond her years. So, in all, he and seven other men were left to protect Treni and Medya.

He got to the training room and took his ax from its strap on his back. He only carried his personal ax this time. He had left his secondary ax in his room. He twirled it in his right arm and thought about everything that had just occurred. Pride swelled in his chest from the victory, but anger and remorse for Frory caused him to lose control. "I killed them all! And I'm repaid with Frory's death!" he yelled. He threw his ax across the room and split a wooden target into two pieces. He stood upright and allowed himself to catch his breath. He could do nothing to save Frory now, but he could keep training to become purely unstoppable. He went to the wall and pulled his ax from it. He kicked the two pieces of the target aside and walked back toward the other training dummies.

As he did, the door cracked open. Treni had been woken up by his training.

"What do you want?!" he bellowed. He thought it was one of his men, and he wasn't in the mood to talk to them. But it was Treni.

"I just wanted to see what all this noise was," she said. He was surprised and lightened his tone.

"Treni, how are the children? With all the other women dead, I and the rest depend on you."

"Did you say all the other women are dead?" she asked worriedly. He held his ax by his side.

"Have none of the others told you about the fight?" he asked.

"No, no, they haven't," she said hastily.

He clipped his ax back into place on his back and said, "Well, it was our victory, but we took heavy losses. Only seven men are left standing, but we killed every single person in that compound, Treni, every single one." He ended with a string of pride for his actions. Her jaw dropped, and she raised her tone.

"You killed everyone in that entire compound?!"

"Yes, Treni, that's what I said," he said calmly. She took a step back and processed what that meant.

"Even the kids?"

"Even the kids. We killed all of them," Rechnal said nonchalantly. She was at a loss.

"Then how are we any better than them?"

"We fight for honor. They fight for the thrill and for the killing." He kept a straight face with no emotion about what he did.

"Still doesn't justify murdering children," she snapped. His tone was still monotonous, like nothing he had done bothered him.

"I did what I must do, and if it involves killing children, so be it."

She was stunned and nearly began to tear up. She kept her calm in front of him, but she knew she couldn't support a man, or a king, who would do such things.

He noticed her distress and said, "I don't know how you feel about that, but I'm sorry it had to be done." She still looked distraught. He tried again to get her to support his actions and raised his voice slightly, "Don't sympathize with them; they murdered Frory!"

She stood silent. The news shocked her, and she fell to the floor. He saw it as an opportunity to drive his point home. He continued yelling,

"They stabbed him through the chest! He's dead! And now we must feel the pain of surviving when he could not!"

She started to cry on the floor. He stood over her and knew he had driven a point into her. Then, he calmly tried to help her to her feet. She pushed him away and said, "He was my husband, and sure, he didn't treat me the best. He would yell and argue, but he was still something. He would protect me, and I know that." She was still distressed.

"Where is his body?"

"I already cremated it," he answered. She looked at him through watery eyes, offended.

"You did it without me?!"

"I'm sorry, I didn't really think about you when I got back," he answered.

She didn't respond, but instead, she gave him a glare. It would have impacted him, but he didn't care enough to even look back at her. When he finally did, she looked away and loathed his actions. But she couldn't do anything about it, so she sniffled and collected herself.

She stood and turned to leave when he grabbed her shoulder. She jumped a little because of how massive his hand was. He said, "Treni, you need to think about your future role in this clan. You're the only woman left capable of having children. And you know that I'm the new king, so do with that as you will." She shook herself free from his paw-sized hands. Her anger had reached its peak, and she pushed him and screamed, "Can you wait just one day before saying something like that?! I know what I'll have to do! It sickens me to know that I have to have an evil man's children! It started when you made Magnus leave." She mumbled the last line, but he heard parts of it. It wasn't enough for him to understand the name she said.

"Who?" he asked. She was still fuming, and her hands were shaking.

"Magnus, the boy that you bullied into running away. Who knows where he is now? You probably killed him by sending him out there. You know nothing but violence and harm. Look at your own people and see what has become of them! You got them all killed because of your own desire for blood!"

She pushed him again, and he stood stunned at her. She was usually quiet, but now, she was yelling at him. He stretched his hand out and said, "Treni, take a breath and calm down." She burst into another fury, "Calm down! You got everyone killed, and you killed everyone you saw!" He tried to say something, but she continued yelling, "Take any hopes you have of me continuing your line! You might as well take a girl from the street and steal her whole life from her!"

She stormed out and went back to her room. He stood in shock for only a moment before shrugging it off. "Well, someone had a rough night," he whispered. He knew he would get his way, so he went and grabbed his ax to continue training.

She went back to Medya's room and shut herself in with her mother. She sat on the bed and started to cry, and it showed no signs of relenting. Medya, who was also awake, was caught off guard by the sudden outburst and went to comfort her daughter. "What's this about?" she asked. She couldn't stop herself from crying, so Medya went and held her. She tightened her grip and tried to wipe some of the tears away. She shushed Treni calmly, but her eyes still poured. She finally caught enough breath to say, "Rechnal, he k-killed them, all of them." She burst into tears again. "I can't, I can't," she continued to whimper in her mother's arms. She repeated herself, "Every last one of them." She still could not stop her tears. Medya tried to comfort her, "It's okay, my child. It is what needed to be done." Treni raised her face from her mother's arms and raised her tone

"How-how is killing children needed? Tell me that."

"This is war, Treni. It pains me, too. I don't want to see all this killing, but it needs to be done." Treni pushed a little gap between her and Medya.

"What if I'm not like you? What if I can't handle all this violence?" she said exasperatedly. Medya looked her daughter in the eyes.

"As the married Berserker woman you are, yes, you should. It has been a part of this clan for generations," she lowered her tone, "I wanted the same as you for a time, but I had to realize that I couldn't have one or the other. I chose my people, my blood. I would suggest you do the same. There's nothing I can do to change anything. As much as I want to, I can't, not with all the people that have seen me live this life." Treni pushed herself away.

"Frory is dead! What husband am I supposed to have, Rechnal?! I will not stoop so low as to marry a murderer!"

"Everyone here is a murderer," Medya replied.

Treni wiped her left eye and said, "Not like that. Everyone here hasn't ordered to have children slaughtered." Medya stayed calm enough to speak.

"That is true, but you must do what your people require of you. That is what you must do."

"I can't, Mom, I can't," Treni pleaded. Medya noticed her efforts to calm her were fruitless.

"Let's go get something to eat. It might help," she suggested.

"Are you trying to distract me?" Treni asked with an angry undertone. Medya put her hand on her thigh.

"Treni, I'm trying to get your mind off something obviously hurting you. You must choose your people, and you will do what's best for this clan."

Treni had no immediate response and stared at her mother with a mix of sorrow and numbness. Medya stood up from the bed and pulled her up. She wiped her last tear and said, "I'm sorry, but this is what you must do." She didn't feel like fighting Medya anymore, so she went along. But, deep down, she knew she would fight in every way she could.

Her anger had overflowed briefly, but she was calming down. However, her resolve was never stronger. She would not let what other people said dictate what she would do for herself and the future of the Berserkers.

It was just a couple hours past midnight, and nothing was available except porridge which both sat down to eat. Since the new day had started, it was available as the breakfast option. The meals were randomly made, and no one changed whatever the machine decided to make.

As the two sat and ate, Jasper sat next to them. He had been relatively quiet in the affairs of the attack, but now, he wanted to know more. "So, do you know what happened last night?" he asked. Treni was visibly annoyed, but that didn't affect him. He nagged, "Well, what happened?" She dropped her spoon into the porridge and said coldly, "We won. They killed all of them. We took heavy losses, and now we have to rebuild." He seemed pleased with the information but wanted more.

"How many losses?" he asked, concerned.

"Well, Rechnal said there are only seven men left besides him and you, no women," she answered.

"Then you must be the lucky one to still be able to help us," he said as he smiled and ate his porridge.

"I guess I am," she said with a scoff.

She put on a fake smile and walked away without her food, leaving Medya and Jasper at the table. Medya watched her walk away but didn't bother to stop her. She had seen how bothered Treni looked and figured she was just getting away. He swallowed another bite and turned to Medya.

"So, Medya, how do you feel about this whole thing?"

"Honestly, Jasper, I don't know. I've been around it my whole life, but I'm not sure if killing all of them was the right thing to do. What if Rechnal missed someone? Are they really as powerful as you said in that meeting?" she said.

He answered the flood of questions, "They were. I wasn't there when Helpar fought them that day, but I saw what they did to us. We easily overtook them, but no one except Helpar came back without some form of injury. They knew how to fight and could stand a chance with a numerical disadvantage."

"I doubt they would have an advantage if any survived, right?" Medya asked.

"Let's hope not," Jasper muttered. His voice trailed off as he took another bite of his porridge. He finished his bowl and saw Treni's half-eaten bowl across the table.

"You think your daughter would mind if I took hers?" he asked.

She shrugged, "With the state she's in, I highly doubt it."

He poured Treni's porridge into his bowl and kept eating. "Thanks," he said as he finished. She nodded at him and stood up to leave. She wanted to check on Treni, who, at this point, was crying in her room. She walked into the room and saw her on her bed, crying.

"Are you still on this, Treni? I've told you that you need to accept it and do what's right." Treni's answer was muffled.

"Mom, I don't think I can; I really don't." Medya sat on the bed and cleared her throat.

"I don't have any advice. I was forced into marrying your father, you know."

"You what?" Treni asked, bewildered.

Medya lowered her tone and became very serious. She said, "I married to continue the clan, not for some perfect man. I did what I had to, and I won't let my daughter back out from the same. And yes, it will hurt, but it is part of serving your people." She took another deep breath and continued, "My husband needed to marry to earn his father's respect, and I needed to marry to earn respect in this clan. It may not be fair, but it is how it operates. So, I'm sorry it turned out this way, but this is what you need to do."

She talked with a passion that Treni had never heard before. Her mother was pushing her, and she didn't want to let her down. She never knew her mother's history to this degree, and it inspired her to at least endure. After a moment's silence, she uttered, "For you, I can change, but I will never give up on what I want to be. I won't be happy." Medya patted her shoulder, "If that's what it means for you to do the right thing, then let it be." She tried to say something else, but nothing came to mind. So, she said, "I'll leave you to think about it some more."

She stood up and smirked a bit. She hoped her advice had helped to relieve Treni. Regardless, she left the room to deal with the rest of the day's affairs. Treni sat in the room for a long time before deciding to try to sleep the rest of the night.

* * *

Magnus went back through the first door and saw the double doors covered in orange fire. The flames ran through the entire structure, and it wouldn't be much longer before they fell. He double-checked his mask and ran inside. The heat was nearly unbearable, and the sweat from his face already drenched his hair. Embers burned at his side, and some burnt holes into his clothes. The smoke had nearly doubled, and the firelight was the only way to see vague shapes. But its light was only a blinding, molten array of orange and red. He didn't know what he would find, but he hoped it would be his brother.

The room wasn't far from caving in completely, and he knew it. If he was to find what he was looking for, time was running out. "Rain!" he yelled into the fire. There was no one he really wanted to find except his brother. He hastily checked all the bodies spread across the floor, hoping one would be alive, but Rain was nowhere to be found. "Rain, where are you!" he yelled. His heart pulled on him as he realized what the silence could mean. *He must have died along with all the others. If all these people died, how could he have survived?*

He panted as he went around the room. Then he heard a crash from behind him. The right-side hallway had caved in. The sound echoed, reassuring his fear of the building collapsing. Sparks flew through the air, and he dropped to the ground to avoid them. The hot gust of air made his skin feel like it was peeling off, but he had to keep going. He staggered to his feet and continued to walk. His vision was nearly gone, and he was reaching the end of the main chamber. He looked back to see the massive double doors with a wall of fire forming in front. It was another reminder that his time was almost up.

The fire was closing in on the throne, and he was moving toward it. "Let me find him," he said to anyone or anything that could hear him. He climbed the obsidian stairs looking for anything he could find. His head was drenched in sweat now, and the smoke was so thick he could taste it through the filter. The embers had burned his skin in places, and the pricks of pain were annoying but not enough to stop his determination. *I'm going to find him.* His legs were sore from constant movement, but he pushed on. He saw another body on the stairs and rushed to it. "Please, please, please," he prayed while running over. He looked at it and immediately knew it wasn't his brother. "Ahhh!" he screamed. He pushed the body in frustration and went up the last two stairs which were engulfed in smoke. His vision was basically gone, so he felt his way to the throne with his hands.

He felt someone's legs sitting in it. He got as close as possible to see the face. "Rain, Rain! Please tell me it's you!" he yelled. He wiped his mask off and saw it was his brother. He gasped, "Rain!" He reached his hand to feel Rain's heart and was blocked by the spear. He tried to move it, but it was stuck. "Are you alive?!" he asked. He put his hand past the spear and onto his chest to feel his heartbeat. He felt a light *thump thump, thump thump*. He yelled, "Yes! Rain, Thank you!" He tried to pull him by his legs, but the spear was placed perfectly so that it had to be moved for him to be freed.

With a groan, Magnus put his hands on the spear and tried to pull it loose, but it wouldn't budge. The slightest bit of panic crept into his nerves as he pulled harder to no avail. "I did not come in here to let a spear get in my way!" He pulled on the spear again, even harder than the last, but it was still lodged into the throne. Then, instead of pulling, he tried to push it through the armrest and felt the slightest movement. This was his last chance. The smoke was getting too thick, and his face was pouring sweat. "Please work," he whispered. He screamed and pushed with everything he had left. His scream echoed through the engulfed room. The left hallway caved, and a large crash boomed over his cry. He relieved the pressure on the spear to look back and see the hallway gone. He was panicking and screamed, "Not like this!!" He pushed with every ounce of strength, and the spear broke through the throne.

The left armrest crumbled, and he nearly fell with it. He quickly let go of the spear. He had no time to feel anything as he pulled Rain onto his shoulders and turned to face the room ahead. Holes in the floor, ceiling pieces, bodies, and collapsed hallways blocked the way. "Hold on," he said to his unconscious brother. He took off across the room, weaving his way through the debris. The door felt even further away than it was when he was carrying Patri. The roof was starting to cave in, and pieces fell and nearly hit them.

Finally, he made it to the hallways, which were collapsed and blocked by debris. The debris had also poured in front of the double doors, blocking the exit. He stopped and panicked briefly before his last idea came to him. Embers burned his skin as he took his right hand from Rain and drew his sword. The fire had made the hilt blisteringly hot, but he gripped it with great strength. He slashed at the wooden debris until it was weak enough to run through. He took a deep breath, paused, and ran through with an intense scream. The pieces shattered as he burst to the other side. His clothes nearly caught on fire, but he didn't stop. He had to survive.

He saw the double doors still smoldering, and as he ran under them, the ceiling behind him collapsed. The impact caused one of the door's hinges to fail. They had melted, allowing for the collapse to break them, and it started falling toward them. The ceiling's crash had discombobulated him, but he knew he needed to move. He used all his strength to sprint to the exit. The door was growing closer and closer, and he knew he wouldn't make it, so he dove. It hit the ground while he was in midair, knocking Rain off his shoulders, and his body rolled outside. Magnus landed close to the door and pushed himself back up. His legs were on fire from the embers flung into the air by the door. "Ah!" he yelled, taking his hand and slapping the fire out. The smoke billowed, and he had to get Rain away.

He looked at Rain and saw his clothes starting to catch on fire. He quickly slapped the fire out and dragged him to safety on the ground outside the compound. The light of the fire illuminated the usually dark floor, and he saw Rain's face clearly for the first time. It was covered in soot, and his nose had dried blood caked on it. He felt his chest again to check that he was still alive. Rain's breathing was weak, and his heart rate was slowed. "Come on, Rain, fight!" he yelled down at him. Rain's breathing was getting raspier and raspier. Magnus looked for anything that could help until he remembered his mask. He stripped it off and felt cold air slap his face. He couldn't appreciate the relief until Rain was dealt with. "Here, here," he said as he placed the mask on him. He locked it into place and waited, hoping that Rain would wake up. The fire raged behind them, and he could still feel the heat. But it was irrelevant now, and Rain's survival was the only thing that mattered.

He clutched him in his arms, waiting for his breathing to stabilize. "Wake up. Please," he begged. He shook him lightly, hoping something would happen, then something did. He stopped breathing. "No, No, No!" Magnus yelled. He clutched onto his body and buried his head into his chest. "Please, Rain, not you too," he cried. His head stayed there until he felt something grab his arm. He lifted his head and said, "What?" He looked to see what held him. It was Rain's hand, and with a heavy gasp, his eyes shot open. He coughed, and his breath was still raspy. His eyes darted back and forth, trying to make sense of where he was. He failed and started panicking. He tried to open his mouth to speak, and no words came out. It scared him, and the fear and shock in his eyes were visible. He started trying to move to escape Magnus's grip, but Magnus held firm. He said, "Rain! It's okay! You're safe!" He stopped thrashing and collapsed into his arms once he recognized the voice. Magnus hugged him and held him in the firelight. He began to cry tears from every emotion he could process, sadness, joy, anger. He held Rain tighter and buried his head further. So much had happened, and there was so much loss. However, he knew one thing. Rain had survived.

15

RECOVERY

After a few minutes of tears, Magnus lifted his head from Rain's chest and looked into his eyes. He saw the pain and asked, "What happened?" Rain tried to speak, but his throat was damaged from the ashes and smoke. Magnus saw him struggling and held him tighter, "It's okay; you don't need to say anything now. I should let you rest, not bug you with questions." Rain just acknowledged and tried gasping another breath to speak. Magnus tried to understand what he was trying to say. "What?" he asked. Rain pointed to his mouth. Magnus's eyes lit up, "Water! I think I have some left in my canteen."

He reached through the folds of his clothes and pulled out a small canteen. There wasn't much left, and the water was warm, but it was something. He shook it, and the water sloshed around, "It's not much, but it's all I have." He lifted Rain up and held his back so he could sit upright and drink. Rain popped off the mask for a moment and let the water flow into his mouth. Even though it was warm, it was still refreshing.

When all the water finished, he clipped the mask back on and took a large gasp of air. Magnus laid him back down and asked, "Better?" He nodded, but then his eyes opened in shock again. "What? What is it?" Magnus asked in a panic. He lifted his finger weakly and pointed at Patri's body. His hand wobbled in the air as he did. Magnus bit his lip, "I couldn't do anything. He was already dead." He sniffled but was able to hold back tears this time. He looked again at his father's body, lit from behind by the ongoing fire.

As they sat there, another large crash came from inside the burning mess. The second giant door had fallen, and with it, the last recognizable standing piece of the compound. The small doorway frame that used to lead to the massive doors still stood, but it was just a charred remnant. A hot blast of air exited with the crash, and Magnus covered Rain's body. The heat washed over both of them, but it didn't do anything harmful.

Rain winced as Magnus climbed off of him. He was bruised and beaten beyond belief, but Magnus had been lucky enough to have gotten to him just in time to save him from any real burns. Magnus scooped his hands under Rain and held him there.

Both their clothes had holes burnt into them, and soot covered their already black clothing. As the crash disappeared into the dark, he again pointed at Patri's body. "What do you want me to do? He's already dead," Magnus said dryly. Rain mouthed the word funeral, but Magnus couldn't make it out. "What?" he asked. Rain mouthed it again. "What? I can't read your lips," Magnus said with light frustration. Rain mouthed funeral with more emphasis on each mouth movement. Magnus was trying to interpret him and stuttered, "F-u-ner-al, Funeral?" Rain nodded weakly. Magnus looked at him, "How am I supposed to do that?" Rain was puzzled until he had an idea. He pointed at a plank not too far away that was burning slowly. "I should burn him?" Magnus asked. Rain nodded. So, Magnus sighed and said, "Well, let me start gathering things then."

He carefully set Rain down on the ground and went to collect any scraps that hadn't been completely burnt. It took him longer than he thought, but he found enough to make a pile large enough for Patri. It was close enough to the building so that the ashes would sink into the rest once the compound stopped burning.

He dragged Patri across the floor and hoisted him onto his shoulders. He looked at the pile of debris, which already had embers burning, "I'm sorry, Father." He slowly put his body onto the pile of debris, and it came to rest. The embers weren't enough to catch it on fire, so he ripped a piece of Patri's clothing off and wrapped it around another plank.

He walked towards a burning piece near the doorway and caught the clothes on fire. He walked back to the pile and put the makeshift torch in its center. It quickly caught fire, and he dropped the makeshift torch in with the rest. He stood solemnly as the fire began to catch the bottom of Patri's body. Then, there was a light shuffling sound from behind, so he turned around. He saw Rain shifting in his direction and rushed over to help. He scooped his hands back under and said, "Rain, stop moving. You're already hurt as it is. You need rest. I'll get you over there." He tried to pick him up, but Rain's face scrunched in pain. "Can I pick you up," Magnus asked. Rain shook his head. Magnus responded, "Then how are you going to get over there?"

Rain looked offended at the question and decided he would prove himself. He looked back with determination in his eyes and rolled onto his chest. Pain shot through him, but he didn't care. He brought his right leg up to his stomach and propped himself up with it. His left arm pushed against the ground, and soon his left leg was also holding him up. He was on all fours now, and the pain wouldn't subside. He pushed off his right leg and got his left foot to the ground. Magnus looked concerned and gave a warning, "Rain, you shouldn't be doing this." He didn't say a word, but his glare told Magnus all he could have heard. So, he let him be.

He pushed with his leg and, with a tremendous huff, pushed himself to his feet. Magnus extended his arms and asked, "You want me to help you walk?" He looked at him with the same glare and started to limp toward the fire. The distance felt eternal, but he put one foot after another, holding his pounding chest the whole way. The resilience kept him going, and with time he got to the fire. "Can I at least help you stand at least?" Magnus asked. He finally nodded, and Magnus put his right arm around him.

The fire lit their faces, and they shared tears for their father. The silence was eerie, with the only sound coming from the mask filtering and the fire crackling. Patri's hair caught alight, and his face started to cover itself in flame. Magnus looked away, but Rain stared longingly into the face that never got the peace it wanted. The memories of his father, the beatings, and the scorns echoed in his brain like the inside of a cathedral. But, deep down, he loathed that he never fixed things. But in the end, he watched the body burn without a word.

It was now covered in flames, and Magnus said, "May you rest well, Patri. You were the father I never had and the support I always needed." As Rain heard this, he broke down completely. He nearly fell down, but Magnus caught him. "What is it?" he asked. Rain tried speaking again, and nothing came out. Frustrated, he started taking the mask off. "What are you doing?!" Magnus asked. He tried to put the mask back on, but Rain pushed him away. It had been supporting his lungs since he got to safety, and he struggled to breathe otherwise. Regardless, he took it off and shoved it into Magnus's arms. His breathing became raspy again, and Magnus was immediately concerned. "Here, here, put it on," he urged. Rain held up a finger and faced his father.

In a voice that Magnus could barely make out, he said, "I'm sorry. I-" He paused to get enough air to speak his next line, "I-I failed you." He was gasping and running out of air. Magnus heard his breaths getting weaker and weaker. He urged again, "Rain, put the mask on." He reached to give it back, but Rain pushed it away. He turned back to Patri and said weakly, "I loved you, Father." He coughed and took a raspy breath, "I wish I could've told you."

He dropped his head as he finished, and tears started to stain his cheek. The emotion of ending the relationship on bad terms broke him.

Magnus was so caught up in what Rain said that he didn't see him signaling for the mask. He was trying to yell for the mask, but he was silent. He started waving his arms, and it snapped Magnus out of his trace. He rushed over and started putting the mask on, but he was a bit too late. And as he tightened the mask, Rain passed out. He caught him and yelled, "Rain!" He started feeling his chest for a pulse or any sign of life. He felt the slightest breath rise and fall. So he carefully set him down, took a sigh of relief, and pulled him back to a safe distance. It was still close enough for the light and warmth of the fire to reach them. As he watched, he was concerned Rain would never wake up, but the slow chest movements reassured him.

It had been a long night, and he started to lie down in exhaustion. Then, Rain's eyes opened, and he shot up. He crawled over to hold him. "Rain, you're back! You alright?" he said excitedly. Rain nodded weakly. Magnus dropped his tone and spoke in all seriousness, "Don't take that mask off again. I need you to stay with me now more than ever. You're all I have left." Rain smiled, but his face quickly turned as he remembered what had happened before passing out. The tears on his face left stained lines where the soot used to be, and new ones were running down his cheek. Magnus saw and asked, "Rain, can you tell me what it is?" Rain shook his head. "Maybe later you can," he whispered. Rain nodded.

Both their eyes felt heavy and tired, and they couldn't fight sleep anymore. It was quiet, and each blink felt like lifting bricks. Magnus yawned, saying, "As much as I hate to stop now, I can't go without some rest." Rain nodded in agreement. Magnus made sure Rain was comfortable enough and went to lay next to him. He turned his head away and said, "Rest well. We will find who did this tomorrow." Rain knew who it was but didn't have the energy to try to sound it out, so he nodded meekly.

Now that his brother was safe and his father was taken care of, Magnus wanted to continue looking for evidence and figure out who did this, but he was too tired to even begin. The night was ending, and the morning rose over the city, but for him, only the light of the fire was burning. *Tomorrow*, he thought as his eyes began to shut. He had been up all night and the day before and couldn't handle being awake any longer. "Tomorrow, we can solve this," he reassured. He rolled onto his side and went quiet as his body gave in to the sleep he desperately needed.

After he turned away, Rain turned his head and tried to sleep. But the pain was horrible. He tried shifting for what felt like forever until, finally, his body gave in to exhaustion.

* * *

Rechnal trained for hours after Treni left. He had taken his shirt off to cool himself. He was sweating and panting from swinging his ax through the air over and over. His skin was shining in the morning light coming from the window, and his figure was as magnificent as it was terrifying. He threw his ax again and hit the target just to the left. The training had distracted him enough, but he was tiring again. He put his hands on his knees to catch his breath. Through heavy inhales, he said, "Okay, I'm done." He walked over to the ax and plucked it from the wall. His pace was sluggish, and he went back to his room to wash off.

When he got there, he hung his ax on its hook and undressed for a shower. It was luxurious, with two heads and perfect water pressure. The inside was a sleek black with calming white lights. He stepped in, and the sweat washed away. The warm water moved through his hair and beard, and he took a deep breath.

He hadn't calmed down since his father died, but now, he felt his revenge was complete. This whole time he had been fueled by anger, and now it was starting to subside. However, Frory's death haunted him. As the water ran down his body, he saw Frory fall again and again. He had always been there for him, but he was gone. The same was true of his father, and no matter the effort, the deaths would always stain him. There was nothing he could do. The fight was over, he had won, but it didn't truly feel like it.

The last day was only anger and motivation to get revenge, but now there was nothing. So he continued sitting in the shower, trying to find a new motivation, and only his thoughts kept him company. And after what turned into nearly an hour of thought, he finally came to terms with his new role. He was a king, and the people that were left needed him. He was the future, and he was not going to let the death of his father and his friend stop him from getting what he desired. He was the Berserker king, and he would be the most powerful one there ever was.

He quickly turned the water off and stepped out. He reached for his towel and began to dry himself. Once dry, he put on what used to be his father's silk pajamas and went to his room. The bed was on the opposite side with a sword mount where Helpar had kept the golden blade. On his right was a hallway that led to the door where Magnus had escaped. He shut the metal door his father used to leave open. It shut with a metallic clang, and he walked to his bed. The night was over, morning rose over the city, but he was just now lying in bed. It wasn't long before his eyes closed, and beautiful sleep overcame him.

* * *

Treni was just waking up from her rest, which was less fulfilling than she had hoped. The episode in the middle of the night messed with her mentally and now physically. She was so tired that she could barely move. She was also still upset, and the fact her mother wasn't there to support her bothered her. She wanted to keep talking, but every response was the same. So she continued to sit alone in her room, and it felt like her entire life was against her.

Her room was smaller, with a blue twin bed in the corner. A nightstand sat on the right side of the bed with a lamp. A small doorway led to a quaint bathroom on the right side of the room. It had a mirror with a sink beneath, and the shower was a modest one that did the job.

After finally moving, she sat on the edge of the bed with her head in her hands. The emotions of sadness and pain were becoming all too much, and her body was giving out due to stress. She collapsed backward on her bed and began to sniffle again. Her eyes were out of tears to cry, and her body was out of energy to give. She had to get ready to attend to the children, but she didn't know if she could. *There are people besides you*, she thought to herself, *for the kids*.

She heaved herself upright and sat on the edge of the bed again before standing up. She wiped her face, went to the mirror, tied her hair into a bun, and took one last look into her own eyes. She pointed at herself in the mirror before leaving, "Nothing they do is going to get to you." When she reached the door, she took one last deep breath and left her room.

She walked down the hallway and into the training room. It was quiet. And with all the others gone, it was going to stay that way. The large window overlooked the platforms that constantly moved and carried citizens around. She wondered what life out there was like, but there was no time for her to think. She had duties with the children. Their training room branched from the main area behind a stone door.

It was a massive slab of rock, the only one in the room, and it was nearly impossible for light and sound to get in. It was still early in the morning, and most of them were still sleeping, so she worked quietly to begin setting up for the day.

First, they would learn how to perfect their blocking. She dragged dummies across the room and moved them into place. The children's dummies were cushioned with weights at the bottom to prevent them from moving. The task helped her distract herself from her own mind's swirling.

She moved the last one into place. And as she did, the first child walked out. There were only six of them, but they were enough to keep her busy. The first child was named Qutir, and he was days from turning sixteen years old. He was a taller boy with blonde hair and the son of one of the remaining men. He looked at her with wide eyes.

"Treni, why are you awake so early?"

"I couldn't get any real sleep, so I came to get a head start on the day," she said tiredly. He looked at her for a quick moment.

"No one else is awake yet, so should I wake them or let them sleep some more?" he asked. She kept moving a dummy across the room.

"Let them be for now. I'll finish out here and come get you. So, go back in and wait," she answered.

"Okay," he said as he sulked back to his bed to lie down.

The door shut, and her mind began to race again. She still couldn't come to terms with the idea that she was the only one left and that the man she would be stuck with was insane. Rechnal was the last person she would consider loving. He was obnoxious and violent; to her, he was a man-child. But what could she do? She was stuck, and she knew it. Every ounce of her wanted to fight, but she had nothing to fight with. She felt tears building up in her eyes again. "No, you can't cry, not again," she commanded herself. She turned to one of the dummies and, in sorrowful anger, punched it. A swirl of attacks followed. "Why! Is! It! Always! Me?!" she yelled.

For minutes she pounded her fists into the dummy through teary breaths. Then, finally, she screamed, "It's been like this forever! Why won't it go away?!" She slammed her weight down onto the dummy. Her face was covered by her hair, tears, and sweat. She was on all fours, trying to catch her breath, when Qutir walked back in.

"Um, Treni, are you okay?" he asked with a confused face. She shot him a glare.

"I'm fine now. But how much of that did you see?"

"I walked out when I heard you scream a moment ago. I was waiting like you said," he answered. But he was interrupted.

"Good, good, go wake the others. We can start now," she ordered.

He nodded and woke the others. She stood back up and wiped the tears as she put her hair back into a bun. *No more; you're a grown woman,* she thought. She sniffled one more time and quickly changed to a happy expression when the children walked in.

She addressed them, "Time for training, all of you. I have had a rough morning already and would love to have you all listen today." They all nodded in agreement. "Okay, everyone, start with some stretches," she ordered. They all touched their toes and did arm circles, amongst other stretches.

"What are we learning today?" one asked eagerly. She looked at them and responded, "Today, we are learning about blocking. I know we have done some blocking in the past, but this is more complex blocking." The kids all smiled in excitement. "All of you grab your swords," she said. They all went to a barrel on the side of the room that held wooden training swords. They were made perfectly to practice without any real threat of injury. They all grabbed one and walked back to the center of the room where Treni was waiting. She yelled, "Formation!" They all lined up in two rows with three in each. The oldest was in the back left corner of the group, and the youngest was in the top right.

Once they were all ready, Treni said, "When blocking a strong attack, not only do you want to block it, but you also want to put energy into their attack. Almost as if you're swinging into their weapon. Understand?" The children looked confused but nodded along. She could sense that they didn't quite understand, so she said, "Here, I'll show you. Qutir, come here and draw your sword." Qutir took the wooden sword from its cover and pointed it at her. She also took a wooden sword from a bin beside her and instructed, "Okay, watch. Qutir, swing lightly at me." She held her sword, and he swung into it. His sword bounced back and barely moved her. She turned to face the children, "You see how my blade could block him because he didn't swing hard?" The class nodded in agreement. She continued, "Now, watch if he swings harder, and I just hold my sword in the same way."

She looked at him and whispered, "Swing as hard as you can into my sword." He nodded and stepped back. He reeled his sword back and swung as hard as he could into her. Her sword was knocked back and nearly fell from her hands.

With a bit of shock from his power, she said, "Well done. Now see how I didn't try to stop him and how it led to my sword being hit back." The group nodded again. "So, what could happen if someone stronger were to hit your sword?" she asked. They were silent for a moment before a small girl raised her hand. "Yes, Holta?" Treni asked.

Holta was the youngest of the group, being only eight years old, but she was also one of the smartest. Her voice was quiet, but she said, "It would get knocked out of your hand." Treni smiled, "Very good. Now all of you watch what happens when I swing into his swing." The others' eyes opened wide in anticipation of what she would do. "Qutir, swing," she commanded. He drew his wooden sword back and swung at her. This time she swung into his blade with a graceful motion, and the two wooden swords clattered in the air. His blade fell from his hand, flew through the air, and smacked to the ground behind him. She brought her sword back and put it into a fighting position. Soon, she put it down and picked up Qutir's. She handed it back and said, "Great job. You can go into your place now."

She then turned to the whole group and asked, "So why was that so much better?" Again, Holta raised her hand. Treni saw her hand and called on her.

"Holta again, wow, I'm impressed. So, what is it?"

"Is it because you parried his swing?" she said shyly. Treni looked surprised and excited.

"Yes, yes, it is a parry. How did you know that?"

"I did some reading on combat the last few days," Holta said with the faintest of smiles.

"I'm very impressed. That is the student I'm looking for," Treni responded proudly.

She then turned her gaze back upon the whole group before speaking again, "Now that Holta has spoiled my surprise, this move is called a parry. A more complex block allows you to protect yourself more effectively. You simply put energy into your opponent's swing, and it will knock off their balance and give you a chance to hit them back." All the children nodded at each other. She continued, "Now face your partner and get ready to learn in real life."

They all turned around to face their combat partners. "Ready your weapons!" she yelled across the room. They all readied their wooden swords. She waited until all their hands were steady and said, "The side closest to me will be parrying first, so the other side will do slower attacks at first. This will help your partner learn how it feels to parry and when to time their swing. Understood?" The children all nodded, with some replying with a faint yes. "Begin!" Treni yelled.

The kids started to spar slowly. Some picked it up much easier than others. While they trained, she paced around the group to correct form and applaud good work. "Switch!" she yelled. Now the blockers were the attackers. The children stopped and took a moment's breath before continuing. It was now Qutir's turn to parry, and he did perfectly. She saw his performance and complimented him, "Well done, Qutir. You have great form here but remember to keep your shoulders level." "Thank you," he responded, as he kept sparring with his partner.

They continued until the morning was coming to a close. Treni was also responsible for taking them to lunch. She had skipped a true breakfast because she let the children sleep, but lunch and dinner were usually heavy meals anyway.

She heard her stomach growl and yelled, "Stop!" They all stopped immediately and turned to face her. "Put your weapons away. It is time for lunch," she said. They put their swords away and walked towards the door. She let them line up and went to open the door. As she opened it, she told them, "Stay together, and don't make too much noise in case someone is still asleep." They all filed out of the room and began walking to the dining room.

She sighed as she walked behind the children. It had already been a long day, and she felt the exhaustion beginning to take hold of her. Unfortunately, the day was far from over, and she had to teach another lesson to the children.

She opened the door to the cafeteria-like room and saw that a trug sandwich was available. It was artificial trug meat in between two pieces of crispy bread. It had cheese and some type of savory sauce to bring out the flavor of the trug. She stepped to the front of the line and announced, "Qutir and Holta, to the front of the line for this morning's performance." Qutir smiled and walked to the front of the line. Holta was a bit shyer, but she took her place in the line.

The kids all mumbled and giggled to each other as they walked to get their food. They could also choose a fruit option as a side or no side at all. They walked over and pressed the buttons before the machine printed out their food. Treni was the last to get her food, and as she did, all the others sat down to eat. Everyone talked and mumbled about their day so far and what they thought they were going to learn next.

However, she ate in silence due to her tiredness. She bit into the sandwich and found it was delicious. The artificial taste was good enough, and she quickly finished.

The rest were still finishing their meal when she told them, "Five minutes, and we head back." A groan went across the table from all the kids except for Holta, who wasn't with the others. She had just sat with Treni and was talking about the lesson. Then, she asked a question Treni wasn't hoping to hear.

"Where is everybody?" she asked.

Treni froze up and stuttered for a response. She didn't want to tell a young girl that almost all the Berserkers had died in a massive fight. She stumbled over her words, "Um-uh, they're out doing real-world training." Holta was a curious little girl and continued to question.

"What type of real-world training?"

Treni was partially annoyed with her for the questioning due to tiredness, but she also appreciated the little girl taking action. She tried to think of a quick response and said, "They are making a weapons trade to get more supplies for the main training room." Holta was still unsatisfied.

"What type of weapons?"

This question started to push Treni over the edge, and she snapped back quickly, "I don't know, honestly, and no more questions. It's time to go back." Holta looked disappointed but went to join her friends. Treni stood up from the table, "Time to head back!" The kids were a bit sluggish, but they all returned to their training area.

When they got back, Treni announced, "Since we just learned how to parry, I want to teach you all how to recover from being parried." The children's eyes lit up in excitement, and, at the same time, the door opened. It was Medya. She had just woken up and wanted to check on Treni. She motioned Treni to step outside. Treni looked a bit annoyed but talked with her anyway. She turned to the class and said, "Give me just a moment." As the door shut behind her, she looked at Medya.

"Took you long enough to get here."

Medya sighed, "When you're as old as I am, sleep is more important. I just came in to check on you since I know you were having a rough time." Treni's tiredness got to her as she raised her tone.

"So now you come to check on me just when you're done sleeping? It makes sense seeing as I'm no one's priority around here, and what I think doesn't matter." Medya lowered her tone to calm her.

"Treni, you do matter. There's just a lot going on right now, and you are being called into a new role."

"Mom, I don't want to talk about it right now. Leave me alone, and I'll keep teaching the kids."

Medya went to speak, but Treni turned her back and walked into the children's room to finish training.

The heavy door slammed behind her, leaving Medya in the main training room. She stood outside momentarily before sighing and turning back. *I guess I can just go get some lunch then*, she thought. She walked to the exit and went to the cafeteria. She got her sandwich and sat down to eat. Nowadays, she was doing less and less due to her old age. She usually just ate and returned to her room to sleep or reminded herself of old memories.

Over her lunch, she had a moment just like this. She remembered the power she used to have but also all the suffering she had caused and endured. Her whole life had been fighting for this clan and her own name, but now, her clan was in shambles under a new king. It had lost the power she once knew. Her faith in the Berserkers was fading, but she had nowhere else to turn.

The rest of her meal struggled to go down as her brain continued to whirl. Never had peace been a real idea to her; however, with the new king and massive losses, it could be possible. *What if I could manage to convince Rechnal to make peace and let the clan rebuild?* But she knew it would never happen with him on the throne, so she gave up on the idea. The Berserkers had lived with violence her whole life, and there was no sign of it ceasing any time soon. She complacently finished her last bite and moved on.

It had nearly been two hours, and she was completely full. As she went to leave, Jasper walked in. "Ah, Medya, how's the food today?!" he shouted. She lightly sighed, "It's nothing special, but it's pretty good." He walked over, grabbed his food, and sat next to her. She wasn't in the mood for a full conversation but entertained him anyway. He was louder than usual and started the conversation with a question. "You like how Rechnal is handling everything?" he asked. She paused momentarily to consider whether she should tell her opinion or just let it be. She decided that lying would be the better option.

"I'm happy with it. I think he's doing a great job for being so young."

"I agree. I loved that he went to our enemies and actually did something. This clan has gone passive, and I am thrilled to see Rechnal bring us back to our former prestige," he said with a smile. He ripped through his first bite and talked again.

"I am becoming proud to call myself a Berserker again."

Through a faked confidence, Medya replied, "As am I. It's great to see this place come back."

She nodded her head and forced a fake smile. She didn't want to drag on a fake conversation, so she made an excuse to leave.

"I was planning on leaving the room to go help Treni with training, so good talking with you." His mouth was still half-full of food.

"Of course, always good talking to you," he blabbered.

She waved, left, and returned to the training room, hoping Treni would allow her to help.

* * *

After walking away from Medya, Treni saw the kids staring back at her. "Formation!" she yelled. They all scrambled to their places while she said, "Back to what I was saying, we need to focus on recovering from getting parried." She paced around before speaking again, "When you get parried, you must recover quickly and not let it phase you. A good parry will knock you back, but a good fighter won't let it phase them. Make sense?"

The children all nodded in agreement. "Face each other and draw your swords!" she yelled. They all turned and pointed their weapons at each other. She paced, "Like always, the side closest to me will be learning first. Those facing me will parry the original swing and continue to attack slowly. I will walk around and instruct each of you." Again, they all nodded and braced for combat. "Begin!" she yelled.

They started swinging and parrying. They were all doing well, and it impressed her. She spoke to all of them, "Good, good. Well done, all of you. You all are picking this up faster than I thought." Then, she saw Qutir in the corner of her eye bullying Sid, his training partner, and hitting him harder than he should have. She walked over to the left side and spoke to him, "Remember you're not trying to actually hit them, Qutir. You are helping them learn how to recover, not attacking him. You are moving too quickly for him to respond." He nodded sternly and began to slow his movements. She returned to her normal position.

Then, the door cracked open, and Medya walked into the room. Before Treni could respond, she said, "Treni, I'm here to help you out. We don't have to talk about anything else." She was annoyed but allowed Medya to help her anyway.

The two continued to monitor the children and instruct them on their abilities. After a few minutes of this, Treni yelled, "Stop! You all are moving too quickly for your partner to respond and understand the recovery process. Start this over and, this time, slow it all down. Ready?" They all took their battle stance and waited for her to send them into the fight. "Go!" she yelled. The clatter of wooden swords echoed and pleased her tired eyes. Her day was rough but seeing these children do well brought some good to the day. They continued on until dinner.

As they were working, Medya had gone to dinner early and talked with another Berserker about monetary issues.

After a while, Treni told the group to stop and line up for dinner. None of the children complained since they were all exhausted from a day's work. They all walked from the training room and got in line. Again, Qutir and Holta had performed the best and would get food first. The machine created a stew from any leftover artificial trug and some broth. Not the most appetizing, but their training-worn bodies would gladly take the food.

They walked through the line and grabbed their bowls. Training had also run a bit later than usual, so the dinner time would be cut short. Treni addressed the short time, "Eat quickly. We must head back and begin nightly recovery and everything else that entails." The children groaned but ate anyway. The stew was quite good, and they all finished their entire portions. As they ate, Treni craved sleep, but the children still had to rest before she could escape to her room.

She finished her last bite and instructed the children to return to the training room to recover. Once they arrived, she commanded, "Formation!" She yawned as she did, and the bags under her eyes carried the weight of her life. She finished another yawn, "I want everyone to stretch their legs and do arm circles. Afterward, I want you to all head to the showers to wash up." They got into place and began to touch their toes. They also swung their arms around until she motioned for them to be finished after a few minutes. "Time for showers, all of you," she commanded.

They entered their room which had twelve beds and a bathroom on each side. The beds were paired with ornate wooden nightstands with dark green lamps on them. Many more used to come through here, but after Helpar's law, the numbers had dropped drastically. There were six showers in each bathroom. The two girls went to the left side and the four boys to the right. "Make sure to actually clean yourself," she told the boys. She had to remind them that being clean was good and having sweat in your hair wasn't.

They all showered and changed into their pajamas. They all wore maroon robes with the Berserker crest on them. "All of you cleaned up?" she asked the group. They all respond with a yes. Then, she quickly said, "Very good. Now get into your beds and get the rest you need. We trained hard today, and I would hate to see you not get the rest you need for tomorrow." She turned off the light and left the room. Usually, she would help put them to sleep, but she was utterly exhausted.

She groaned as she saw the training room still needed to be cleaned. Her exhaustion was getting to her, and her mother had already gone to bed. She dragged herself across the room to start cleaning. She picked up one wooden sword, put it back in the container, and started to drag the dummies around. Her body was getting weaker. *Just a little longer*, she told herself.

She continued dragging the dummies fighting off yawn after yawn. "Just one more." Her mouth opened, and another yawn snuck out. She dragged the last dummy back into its place for what felt like hours and immediately had to sit on it to catch her breath. She breathed heavily and realized how truly exhausted she was. Her head was pounding, and her body was weak. She fell forward. The dummy wasn't the most comfortable, but it was perfect for her tired body. Her eyes began to shut, and she whispered, "We didn't even use these today. I could've just left them here." She smiled at her own comment, but the smile faded as she succumbed to exhaustion. She fell into a deep sleep that would be hard for anyone to wake her up from. And with her, the rest of the compound fell asleep.

16

THE PASSION OF SONS

The air was cold, and the fire the brothers had gotten close to had calmed. Magnus opened his eyes to the darkness that beheld him on level 87. He had slept through the entire day and was waking up as the rest of the city, like Treni, slept. The firelight still dimly lit Rain's frame, and the platform lights shone dimly in the distance. The guards' bodies also became silhouettes with the light from the platforms. He sat up and tried to make out anything from the remains. Dim light from the embers shone on different collapsed pieces of the compound. Only the throne, obsidian stairs, and a charred door frame ominously stood above the rest.

He stood up to bring more wood toward the fire. Once the wood caught, it blazed again, and the heat was enough to wake Rain. He shifted before opening his eyes and groaning. It was all he could really get out of his damaged lungs. Magnus saw him shuffling and asked, "Rain, you're awake. Can you talk?" He went and sat next to him. He had woken up energized and full of questions. The original threat of his brother's death was gone for the moment, and his mind was racing. "Do you remember who did this?" he asked. Rain nodded, but the night had not been good for his declining speaking ability. He tried to talk but couldn't even effectively mouth Berserker. Magnus looked around for anything since he knew he couldn't speak. "Well, is there anything they left that could point them out?" He had only just started the questioning, but his voice seemed desperate. Rain tried to look for anything he could point at until the platform's blue light revealed his answer. He pointed at a vague shape on the ground, and Magnus turned to face it. "That weird shape?" he asked.

Rain nodded again. Magnus immediately stood to go see what his brother was pointing at. He turned to grab a piece of wood from the fire to act as a torch. He walked over and picked up the object on the ground. His eyes widened, and his grip tightened as he realized he was holding Rechnal's mask. *It can't be.* He hadn't seen it in ages, and now, its empty eye holes stared back into his. The memories of being beaten by this one man flooded back. All the curses he yelled at him for missing a simple block and all the hell this man caused shook him to his core. His hand began to quake in anger as he neared Rain. "It was them," he said with no tone but pure rage. Rain nodded only once.

Silence followed the affirmation until Magnus unleashed a burst of rage. His breaths were heavy and furious as he squeezed the mask as hard as he could hurled it into the fire. The eye sockets glowed back until the fire consumed them. His breaths were heavy as he yelled, "Bastard!"

Rain was shocked as he watched his brother erupt. Magnus stood and watched it burn into ashes until he finally turned to Rain, "I'm going to end this now. I've ran away my whole life, but not now." He grabbed his sword from the ground, only to find it covered in soot. He shook it off and quickly went to feel his own face. His hand came back with a light coating of black. This concerned him because he didn't know how the mask was holding up, so he asked, "Rain, you're breathing fine, right?" Another nod was the response.

Magnus carefully checked the mask and found it was still working perfectly. He nodded and told Rain again, "I'm going to finish this now." Rain grabbed onto his burnt shirt and pulled him back. He was bothered and asked, "What are you doing? Let me go!" He shook free from Rain's hand, but the pull dragged him with it. He was now face down on the floor and struggled to get himself back up. Magnus rushed to flip him over, and he groaned in pain. Once he flipped him over, he said, "I'm leaving, Rain, and you can't stop me."

Rain's face strained, and he was able to speak just one word, "Wait." Magnus was stunned by the voice he heard and turned back, so he asked, "Did you just talk?" Rain nodded weakly, but Magnus was still focused on his boiling anger. He said, "That's great. We can celebrate when I come back." Before he could look away, Rain grunted again. This time he couldn't get the words to escape his mouth. "What?" Magnus said harshly. He was obviously annoyed with being held up. Rain looked around frantically for a way to get his idea across. He then looked down and saw his hand had left marks in the thin layer of soot, so he pointed at it. Magnus was still annoyed and wanted to go to find Rechnal, "What is it, Rain?" His hand traced in the ash, and Magnus walked over once he realized his brother was writing on the ground. He walked the torch over and held it to the ground. In faint writing, it read: *Can't lose you. I go?*

Magnus responded, "You are in no condition to fight. It is also night, and the whole camp will be sleeping. Rechnal should be in his room right by the entrance. I'll be in and out. Stay here and wait for me to come back, please." Rain shook his head and tried to reach for him. Magnus backed up, "I can't lose you either; if you joined me, you would die. I will not put you in more danger, Rain. Please just rest, and I'll be back." Rain again turned to the ground. It took him some time, but he wrote, *Scared.* Magnus looked back and Rain wiped the word away. Then, he wrote, *You're family. Come back.* He wiped the ash again and wrote, *Need you.* Magnus almost felt a tear come from his eye, but he stopped and said, "I will come back, and we will be the brothers we are meant to be." He leaned down and hugged him, "Stay here, Rain. I will come back. I promise you."

He put more fuel into the fire and walked towards the platforms. He stepped onto an ascending one and slowly disappeared. Seeing him leave didn't sit right with Rain, but there was nothing he could do. So, he tried just to put his head down and rest, but his mind began to think of all the ways he would never see Magnus again.

* * *

Shortly after Magnus had woken up, Rechnal opened his eyes. The night mission had messed up his sleep cycle, and he tried to fall back asleep. However, he tossed and turned and couldn't get rest to overtake his body again. He figured he could go to the cafeteria to see if anyone was awake, and if not, he could train more. So he got up from the bed and took off the silk he was wearing in exchange for a tunic and pants. He put on the straps that held his axes and put them in place. He crept down the hallway, found the compound silent, and walked until he entered the cafeteria.

He realized how famished he was, so he went to get whatever food the machine had ready. The stew the children had eaten was still available since it was still early in the night. He grabbed a bowl and began feasting. He had finished three bowls in nearly ten minutes and felt content with himself. He stood up and knew he still wasn't tired, so he spoke to himself and said, "I'll get some more work in then."

He walked into the lonely training room and looked out the window. When he looked left, he saw the platforms all running up and down and wondered what every other person thought about. There were so many people, and he wanted to be in charge of them all. He sat with his hands behind his back, watching the city move, and took a deep breath. It fogged up the glass, and his stare focused on the reflection staring back at him. He looked into his soul, and he saw the passion within his own eyes.

A moment of self-reflection came to him as he stared. His reason for fighting and his motivation to keep going wasn't just for a father or a friend. It was for himself. He wanted to become the most powerful, feared, and respected man in all of Uguria. He wouldn't stop for anyone, and his fight would never end. His breathing kept fogging up the glass until, finally, it covered up the fiery eyes that stared out the window.

He shook himself out of the trance he put himself in. "Time to go," he said as he turned back to the training room. He took the ax from his back and began to practice swinging and all sorts of turns that could annihilate any enemy. After a few minutes of practice, he took out his second ax. He stood momentarily to catch his breath with an ax on either side. One was his standard ax, and the second glowed with the red liquid that flowed through it. He jumped through the air and spun with a violent grace. He landed softly for a man his size and quickly combined a swing with the two brutish blades. He stood back up, smiled at his move, and told himself, "There you go, someone is good."

As he finished speaking, another Berserker walked in. He was caught off guard by the man and quickly put his axes away.

"Why are you up at this hour?" he asked.

The other man responded, "Struggled to sleep. Figured I could come in and see if anyone else was here, but you seem busy."

"I'm trying to have a moment with myself, but I'll train with all of you another day. So, if you would leave me," Rechnal said.

"As you wish," the man said disappointedly.

He bowed and started to walk back to his room which was close to Rechnal's and the entrance. As he left, Rechnal took both his axes back out and continued practicing fiercely.

* * *

Magnus was starting to near the Berserker compound. He saw the lights of signs and flower pods on his way up. The city was the peaceful dark he had always known from his time fighting under its cover, but something felt different. The dim lights usually comforted him, but tonight, they were the signs of the fight he was planning to have. He had spent his whole life going level by level, but he never returned to what he once called home. Memories of his escape flooded his mind as the wooden door appeared. The abuse he faced at the hands of this place stirred his anger even more. His hands began to shake with rage and nerves as the platform was seconds away from letting him step off onto the metal walkway. But this time, he wouldn't have to jump across a descending one and could just step off.

Finally, he stepped off and froze for a moment to look at the rest of the level. It was dark, with nothing else except for a few stores. He looked down, took a deep breath, and turned to face the doorway. The walk felt eternal. Each step was like a memory that flashed back into his head. Each memory was another piece of anger. Each piece of anger built the motivation to end the Berserker clan. He finally reached the doorway and looked at its engraving.

TO DEATH.

He knew what that meant now. He had never understood or felt the passion this engraving entailed, but this time, he would do it to death.

He stared into the doorway again, and though it was made of wood, it carried the weight of his entire life. His breath became shaky with nerves and passion as he took his golden blade from its place. He raised it in the air and whispered, "To death." He pulled his mask over his face and jabbed the sword into the handle. It popped open. The sound of cracked wood and the cling of metal rang into his ears. His sword gave the slightest amount of light into the dark doorway, so he stepped in. He opened it expecting to see Rechnal stirring in his bed but found the metal door locked instead.

He inspected it and tried to find a weakness to plunge his sword into. Opening it would be louder than he wanted it to be, but he had to break through somehow. He continued to search. *Come on. There's got to be some lock or something.* He kept looking and feeling around. There wasn't a lot of light to work with, but he finally found a slit on the side of the door. *There it is.* He smiled as he pointed his sword at the weakness. The lock ran through the slit in the door, and his blade would easily cut through it. He poked the sword through until it poked out the other side. Once he felt it was through, he breathed in and, on the exhale, drove the blade down.

It cut through the metal, and the door was unlocked. The same room he had run from was now his only destination. He was still anticipating Rechnal to be turning in his bed, but when he opened the door, he saw the room was vacant. *Where is he?*

He entered and saw the mount where his blade used to be. Nothing in the room had changed since he left, leaving an eerie feeling in his gut. The wooden door quietly shut behind him while the metal one hung open. He kept quietly creeping through the room, hoping to find something.

Finally, he went towards the bathroom and saw nothing. Confused, he went to open the door to the hallway. This is where all the other Berserkers and Treni were sleeping. As he did, he found it empty too. *Where is everyone?* He crept further down and heard footsteps. He quickly hid against the wall. The curve was enough to hide him, but not well. The owner of the footsteps was mumbling to himself and was getting louder. Magnus wasn't sure if an attack was the right plan of action, but he didn't seem to have a choice.

He exhaled sharply and turned from his hiding spot with his blade drawn. The man shot back, drew his weapon, a longsword, and asked, "Who are you? Why are your clothes burnt like that?" Any pity fled Magnus's body as he saw him. This was the incarnation of his anger in front of him. With fierce eyes, he said, "I am Magnus Aureum, and I will be the last person you lay your eyes on. You know why I have been burnt, and you will not be forgiven."

Fear entered the man's eyes before he found himself under attack. Magnus charged with his sword and bashed it into the man's sword. He attacked with precision but also with an aggression he didn't know he had. The fight moved backward, with Magnus taking the main tide. The Berserker was simply trying not to get his life taken. His blade twirled to meet Magnus's over and over, and the fight continued.

Magnus leaped, trying to land a blow. But the blades clashed perfectly. One would attack, and one would block in a cruel tango. The gold sword glistened in the light and was amazingly elegant. He tried to swing overhead but was effectively blocked again. It caused him to stutter back. "I have no idea who you are or what happened," the man said through heavy breaths. Magnus had no empathy and responded bleakly, "I will kill you, and there's nothing you can do to stop me." He charged again so that the man couldn't catch his breath. The two grunted and clashed until Magnus finally struck his target.

The longsword swung from the right side, and he blocked it perfectly. It shocked the Berserker and allowed Magnus to plunge his sword into his chest. He grunted in pain, and Magnus pushed the blade further. He pushed the sword until it caused the man to slam into the wall with a crash. He tore the sword from the man's body, which hit the ground with a thud. He watched it fall through heavy breaths and wiped his forehead with a bent posture. "Rest well," he said over the corpse; six remained.

He stood straight and turned towards the rest of the hallway. The bash had stirred the rest of the compound, and other doors started to creak open. He knew he had alerted everyone and had to prepare for the worst. He took a deep breath and spun his sword to his side. He saw four Berserkers, three were dressed, and one didn't have a shirt. "I'll do the same to every one of you!" he screamed. The idea of stealth was gone, and he charged straight at the group.

He let out a quick yell and jumped through the air. His feet landed in front of the men, who had a mix of swords and axes. The first swung, and Magnus jumped again. This time he jumped towards the wall and pushed off. He dragged his sword behind him, cutting through the first's neck. The man made a choking sound and grabbed his neck to try to stop the bleeding. But he fell to his knees and fell forward, dead; five remained.

Magnus landed on two feet, raising his head to lock eyes with the next. A Berserker looked behind him and waved his hand before yelling, "Charge!" The other two ran at him, and the two other doors began opening. He had to act fast to keep any sort of advantage. He blocked and blocked, but the number of Berserkers pushed him back toward Rechnal's room. He backed into the doorway and looked for anything he could use to his advantage. The other two had left their rooms and joined the remaining three. "Where are you gonna go?" one of them said.

Magnus's eyes still frantically looked for a way out that wasn't running through that same door he left years ago. Then he saw it. The ivory handles of the doorway poked out. "I'm going to end every single one of you," he taunted. The men laughed obnoxiously at his seemingly ill-placed confidence. As they laughed, Magnus ran over to the door and sliced an ivory handle off. It had a sharp tip, and he pointed it in his hand. The laughter quickly turned to silence as the white spike impaled one of their numbers; four remained.

Magnus quickly ran to the other handle and cut it from the wall. "Ahh!" He threw this one harder, and it also hit his mark; three remained.

He dragged his sword against the ground towards the fear-struck men and sliced through the lights on the wall. Each went black as he passed it. Finally, after six lights, the hallway became black enough for him to hide in. He held his sword behind him so none of the gold shone through the darkness. The Berserkers stood outside where he had backed into, quivering in fear. "Where did he go?" one asked. It was quiet as they shook, looking for the devil of darkness Magnus had become. And in a swift, sudden movement, he leaped out to the screams of the Berserker men. He jabbed the closest man and disappeared back into the dark; two remained.

The men's jaws fell in fear and shock. Then, in a shaky voice, one said, "What are you?" The darkness answered with silence until the gold blade reflected. "There!" the other man yelled while pointing. The other said, "Where?" Magnus again used the wall to leap onto the Berserker. "Right here," he said as his sword drove through the other man's skull. He fell back into the darkness; one remained.

The last man knew what would become of him, yet, he pleaded, "What are you? At least let me know before you kill me." From the darkness, Magnus answered, "I am the end of the Berserkers."

The last man stepped back fearfully and tried to retreat into a part of the hallway where maybe Medya or Jasper could hear him. But before he could move, Magnus spun through the air, disarmed him in one easy swing, and drove his sword into him; none remained. "Got you," he said as he removed the sword.

He looked up toward the rest of the hallway and started to walk toward the end. He wiped the blood from his sword onto his clothes which were too dark to show the crimson taint. He wasn't satisfied. He still needed to find Rechnal. Once he was dead, maybe the fighting could end, and his need for revenge would be satisfied.

With his sword drawn, he walked the hallway to find nothing. He passed Jasper's and Medya's rooms. He was full of impatience and anger from not finding Rechnal. He opened the door to the cafeteria and saw no one but the machine humming.

Then, he thought a sip of water would be a good idea. He hadn't been able to drink in a while, and the place was tranquil, so he walked to the machine and quickly grabbed a glass. It was the same glasses he had drunk out of as a boy. Once he finished, he set the cup back down and walked back into the hallway. Only one room was left that Rechnal could be in, the training room.

The doors sat before him; he knew Rechnal had to be in this room. His whole life seemed to amount to this very moment. All the pain, all the suffering, all the destruction, it could all end now. His hands shook ever so slightly as he went to rest them on the door. A deep exhale followed, and he shoved them open.

Rechnal stood on the far side and faced the wall. He had been preparing to go back to his room to get more sleep, so his axes were clipped to his back, and four daggers hung from his belt. "Rechnal!" Magnus screamed into the room as the doors shut behind him. He ripped his mask from his face and threw it to the ground so Rechnal could look into his eyes and feel every bit of rage that flowed through him.

Rechnal turned around, expecting another one of his men, "Yes?" Then, his eyes met Magnus's, and he instantly recognized him. He went to say something, but then, he glanced at the same mask his father handed him on loading dock 15. His eyes widened and his tone gradually rose, "It can't be. You're the one that killed my father. You will die, Magnus." Magnus was standing across the room with his sword in his right hand, unfazed by the threat. He shook in anger as he stared at the man who had ruined his whole life, "You will be dead at my feet so that I can avenge everyone you killed." He pulled his sword closer to him and squatted lower to the ground. His body shook angrily, and his fingers twitched on the blade's hilt.

Rechnal looked and chuckled, "So you really are one of them?" "Yes, I am, and I'm proud to be," Magnus said in a quick, angry response. Rechnal laughed again and said, "Pride might not be the best thing since not a single one of your people gave me a good fight, and your king was a disgrace. I have killed your people, and if they would've allowed children to use real weapons when we were kids, I could've killed you then! So, what is stopping me from doing it now?! I have beaten you over and over, and I will not lose today!" Magnus stood silent in a mix of fear from his past and unfiltered hatred.

Rechnal reached for his axes but paused when he studied Magnus's weapon. He recognized the golden aura that used to belong to his father. They were still circling the room when he asked, "Is that what used to belong to my father and your savior?" Magnus pointed the blade directly at him, so he took it as a yes. Magnus also looked confused. Rechnal saw the look and chuckled, "Don't think my father didn't tell me how he saved you as an infant and regretted his choice every time you failed. You stole that from him just as you stole his life. I will end this tonight, and I'm glad it will end with you." Magnus still shook in anger and kept his lips sealed. Rechnal saw the frustration brewing and smiled, "You have come all this way to avenge your people, your king, for what? Just so you can die at my feet."

Magnus was furious about everything, even this speech, and through hate-filled lips, he finally said, "That king was my father." Rechnal let out another slight smile and said, "Your father? Then you know how it feels to have it taken from you! But don't worry. You will see him soon enough."

As he said this, he drew a dagger into each hand and threw them straight at Magnus with a loud grunt. The blades cut through the air, and their aim was true. But right before the edges could hit him, Magnus flipped backward through the air. His body soared over the two blades, whose power was enough to puncture the wall behind him. He landed gracefully and looked back up at Rechnal, who laughed again, "Looks like someone picked up a couple of things. It'll make killing you all the more fun."

He unclipped his axes and brought them into his massive hands. He held them down and waist length. Magnus scowled at the giant in front of him and brought his sword to the ready. He had no words, just pure fury. Rechnal smashed the axes together, and the sound rang into Magnus's ears. He did it again, taunting Magnus to make the first move.

Their eyes locked in an impasse. He kept bashing the axes together until Magnus finally charged.

He squatted down, spun his axes around, and said, "Finally." He ran to meet Magnus, and the two clashed their weapons in the air. His strength was his greatest asset, and with one clash, Magnus knew his foe's power was more immense than he imagined. The first impact had knocked him back a few steps, and Rechnal locked haughty eyes with him again. Magnus grunted and charged. He tried to undercut Rechnal, who swiftly deflected the blow. He was moving slower than most Berserkers would just to taunt. He watched Magnus barely keep his footing after the block, "Still the same. Just trying to land quick, cheap shots with no real power and pride. A shame really."

The comments were breaking Magnus's mental wall, and he charged again. He tried to swing only to find it perfectly blocked. He stumbled away, and Rechnal taunted, "Pathetic as always." There was no point in prolonging the fight anymore, so he stepped toward Magnus and swung both axes in perfect unison. Magnus tried to block the blades, but there was no possibility. He had to just evade and run. Rechnal watched him back away from every swing, "Look at you, running as always. Nothing has changed in you, Magnus. Nothing!" He jumped through the air, and if his blades had been any closer, Magnus's head would've been across the room. Instead, the swoosh of the ax rang in his ears, and he backed away in circles across the room.

His eyes had switched from rage to fear as Rechnal kept swinging at him. Rechnal paused for only a moment to appreciate the fear entering his eyes, "Ah, the sight of fear. Your father looked just the same." He slammed his axes into the ground and narrowly missed again. Magnus felt his anger boiling but still couldn't find any chance to fit his sword through the axes. Rechnal swung with his right hand, then his left, then his right, then his left, and by the time Magnus had dodged it, the right hand was swinging again.

Magnus's breath was getting heavier as all the running and evading was catching up to him. The fight had moved closer to the window, and both could see the quiet city. Rechnal paused again for only a quick moment to taunt with a faint grin, "All those people out there, and not a single one will know who you were."

His left side faced the window, and he swung first with his red-axed, right hand. The swing was low, and Magnus jumped over it. The left hand followed with a diagonal swing down from his standard ax. But Magnus caught it with his sword that went across his right shoulder. Rechnal pushed his ax down and nearly caused Magnus's own blade to dig into his own shoulder. He smiled as he pushed it harder and harder down. Magnus's knees were bent and strained, trying to keep himself from getting crushed. "Ahhh!" he yelled as he pushed up. He was able to move the axe, much to Rechnal's surprise. But he pushed even harder and nearly flattened Magnus. He watched a bead of sweat trickle down his opponent's head, "You cannot match me, Magnus. You never could."

These words gave Magnus the last bit of inspiration he needed, so he screamed and gave everything he had. He pushed up and jumped into the air, twisting his body and taking the ax with it. Rechnal swung the other ax and missed. As Magnus landed, he finished the flip motion and pushed his blade and the ax outwards. The force was enough to fling it from Rechnal's grasp, and it flew through the glass. A loud crash followed, and it disappeared into the night.

A cold wind entered the room and slapped the faces of both men. Rechnal stepped back after the impressive maneuver, and Magnus landed and stood with a valiant posture. The fight was nowhere near over, but Magnus felt he had a chance. Rechnal pulled the other ax back to his side and stared directly at Magnus. "Impressive," he said before leaping back toward his foe. Metallic bashing echoed through the room as they swung. They let out grunts and screams as they clashed with each other. Rechnal had taken a step back only to charge again, so Magnus did a backflip to get himself into the clear.

Rechnal's ax landed right where Magnus would have been. "You're hard to catch. I'll give you that," he said in an increasingly tired breath. He used his other hand to grab another one of the daggers. Magnus's eyes opened wide as his hand released the dagger directly at him. In only a blink of his eye, Magnus moved his sword in front of it and cut it down. Sparks flew as it was hit and bounced across the training room floor. "You're just full of surprises, aren't you?" Rechnal said with a touch of anger in his voice. People could never evade him this long, and it was bothering him. "You have impressed me, but that will not matter when your blood is spread across this room!" he screamed.

He charged again and swung, with both hands on the ax, directly to Magnus's right side. He was able to block the swing, but Rechnal kept pushing. The force from his ax alone started to move Magnus across the floor. He brought his left hand to push against the ax. Rechnal laughed as he saw him struggle to resist. The two were in front of the youth-training door, where silence and slumber ruled. Magnus struggled and knew pushing back wouldn't work much longer. He grunted and jumped into the air to try to get over the ax. He was successful but forgot to account for Rechnal using his other hand. So while he was in the air, Rechnal's right hand came free and hit him across the face.

The blow was hard enough to make him bounce on the ground and land face down on the other end of the room. His sword fell from his hands and landed on the ground to his right. He struggled to get up and felt blood dripping from his nose. He flipped himself onto his back and saw Rechnal walking towards him with no intent except to finish him off.

Rechnal's stomps boomed in his ringing ears until his thunderous voice brought him back to reality, "Now that's the Magnus, I remember. The poor helpless boy who couldn't win a fight! It feels so good to see you like this!" Magnus tried to get back up, but he couldn't. Fear struck his eyes as Rechnal raised his ax into the air. It came hurling toward the ground and slammed where he had been.

But right before it could deal its blow, Magnus had rolled away to get his sword back. He crawled and slid back to his sword. He grabbed it and quickly pushed himself up to stare at Rechnal, who was removing the ax from the ground. Magnus wiped the blood from his nose and stood shaken but not defeated. His breath wavered, and every nerve in his body was on edge. His ears still rang, but he had to fight.

Rechnal plucked the ax from the ground and saw a little pool of blood left from Magnus's nose. He reached down and put his finger into it. He raised it, looked at the blood, and said, "Only the beginning, Magnus, only the beginning." He rubbed it under each eye and stained his face with blood-red streaks.

Magnus was still frozen in fear. Never had he faced an enemy as brutal, not even Helpar. Rechnal's voice boomed again, "That look, that look of terror. I saw it in your father's eyes, and I see it in you! I love it!" He charged, and Magnus could barely block his ax. The screaming also resonated with Magnus, but he didn't have time to think. He had to play more defense and was constantly pushed according to how Rechnal moved. Finally, he was able to roll away just far enough for Rechnal to slow himself down. And as he caught his breath and slowly walked towards him, Magnus's fear gradually switched to anger. The image of his father's dead body burned in his mind, driving him into aggression. He started to fight with more veracity, and his strikes started to push Rechnal back ever so little.

He swung over his right shoulder, and Rechnal barely managed to catch it with his ax. Rechnal's face was still confident, but Magnus could see the tiniest glimpse of self-doubt entering his mind. He looked into Rechnal's eyes again and said, "I won't be afraid of you, not anymore." He took his sword and jabbed it into Rechnal's lower left leg. He winced and stepped back. A single drop of blood fell, and Magnus uttered, "Only the beginning, Rechnal. Only the beginning." The tide of the fight had shifted. He was pushing Rechnal on defense and making him feel that he was in actual danger.

The wind from the window blew into the room, chilling every part. Magnus kept swinging until his blade bounced from the ax, allowing him to quickly slice into Rechnal's left arm. This cut was deeper than the leg wound and caused him to yell in agony. The blood was dripping from his arm and staining the floor beneath. He looked back at Magnus in pain and genuine fear for the first time in his life. Magnus looked back in pride and said, "That look, it was just like your father's that night."

Rechnal's eyes shot again with rage. He couldn't tolerate defeat, and his agony only amplified his aggression. His eyes glowed in a fury, "You, you killed him! You killed him!" He roared and swung his ax through the air with more power than he had ever known he was capable of, "You were there!" He swung in a blind rage, and Magnus smiled because he knew he had done precisely what he intended. He wanted to make Rechnal fight in anger and lose his composure.

So, he backed away and taunted, "Yes, I was. I saw him die. I killed him." The lie enraged Rechnal even more. "You bastard!" he screamed as he swung overhand and hit the ground with a thunderous slam. The floor beneath the ax splintered. "You killed him!" he yelled with a wave of untamed anger. He went to pull his ax from the ground, but he found it was stuck. He tugged at it, but it stayed in the floor.

Magnus leaped at the opportunity. As Rechnal finally plucked the ax from the ground, Magnus jumped over, and sliced through his back from the neck down. Rechnal flopped forward and dropped his ax. Magnus kicked it across the room, far out of their reach. Blood stained through Rechnal's shirt as he hobbled back. His hands went to hold the gash on his back, and shock and fear ruled the domain of his eyes. Magnus stood with his sword by his side and said, "Kneel, Rechnal. I want your final moments to be humiliation. You spent my entire life humiliating me, and now it's finally my turn."

Rechnal was in tremendous pain but still resisted, "I will die a thousand times before I would kneel to you." Blood started to stain his teeth as his body was fading. Magnus pointed his sword at him as he said, "That wasn't a choice. So, if you resist, I will make you kneel." Rechnal smiled, "As I said, I would die one thousand times before I ever kneel to you." Magnus responded with more anger in his voice, "As you wish." He reeled back and jabbed the sword through the wound already in Rechnal's leg. The blade cut cleanly through, and he drew it back to his side. Rechnal roared in pain and dropped to one knee.

* * *

Rechnal's screaming was enough to stir Jasper in his bed. His room was close enough to the training room to hear a yell of that magnitude. But the children's room, where Treni rested, remained silent.

He opened his eyes and was confused by the sound, so he slowly rose from his bed and went to take care of his morning needs. He wasn't rushed, so it would take quite some time.

* * *

Rechnal sat on his knee, looking up at Magnus. He was standing over his foe and said, "Look at me. All that time, you stood above me. Now I have won. You have failed, Rechnal. You have failed!" Rechnal grunted and tried to swing his left hand. Magnus promptly met it with his sword and cut it next to the old wound. Rechnal reeled his arm back with a shallow scream. He looked up at Magnus in utter hatred, but he knew he was right. He had lost.

He looked up while holding his freshly cut arm and spat blood at Magnus's feet. Magnus smiled, "Good to know you have nothing left. You murdered my people, and I will do the same to you." Rechnal smiled maniacally. The threat of death didn't faze him, and he taunted again, "Do it, coward. You were never a killer, and you won't be able to do it now." It was similar to Helpar's final words, but this time, Magnus would finish the job.

He confidently pointed his sword directly at Rechnal, "Before I do it, do you have any last plea or anything you want to get off your chest?" Rechnal saw the determination in his eyes and knew he meant what he was saying. There was nothing meaningful for him to say, so he said coldly, "Nothing that you are meant to hear." Magnus stepped back, "So be it. May your soul be tormented in hell."

He reared his sword back and began to jab it toward Rechnal's chest. As he did so, Rechnal stepped on his good leg into the blade, impaling himself on its golden edges. It dug through his chest and vital organs. He was silent and looked into Magnus's eyes with a smile. His teeth were blood-stained, and his eyes were going dim. Magnus looked at the smiling face in front of him. "Why are you smiling?" he asked faintly.

Rechnal laughed weakly, "I'll get to see you there." His eyes rolled into his head, and his body fell backward.

Magnus was confused until he felt a warm feeling from his chest. He looked down and saw the last of Rechnal's daggers embedded perfectly in the center of his chest. "No, no, no," he whispered. His sword fell to the ground as he staggered back. "No, no!" he yelled. His hands went to the dagger, and he pulled it out. Blood started gushing from the wound. "Not like this. Please, not like this," he begged. He started to feel his eyes water, and his breath was weakening. Tears began to slowly fall from his cheek. He fell to his knees, and his vision became blurry. He looked to the roof in a silent prayer that he could somehow survive. His voice was weak, and he felt his energy draining like his blood. "After all this?" he muttered through his helpless tears.

His muscles gave out, and he fell onto his back, looking for a miracle. There was none to be found. He breathed one more time, his eyes closed, and his head fell. Magnus of the Devil's hand was dead.

17

A BROTHER'S DEATH

Rain sat after Magnus left, wondering if he would really make it back. He had seen him fight before and had confidence in him, but he wasn't quite sure what to do now. His body was slowly recovering, but it was nowhere near ready to help against a foe like Rechnal or any other healthy Berserker. So, he continued to weigh leaving or staying by the fireside. He eventually concluded that his fighting wouldn't help, so he tried to pass the time by sleeping again.

His eyes closed as he was close to giving in to sleep until he heard a metallic clank followed by others until it ended with a bang. Something had fallen onto the level's darkness next to him. He turned his head and saw the slightest shimmer from where the sound came. He squinted to see what it was, but he couldn't make it out from the distance he was at. He knew standing would be challenging, but his curiosity begged and motivated him. He turned to his stomach and brought his knees back to his chest. The physical pain was still digging into his core, but what he endured already seemed to take away from it. So, he pushed himself onto his knees and slowly rose. His mouth still burned, but he could feel it was slowly recovering; however, he wasn't sure about his lungs. Each breath still pained him and felt like heavy weights, even with the mask on.

He dragged himself over toward the object and saw it was what looked like an double-bladed ax. It was too dark for him to make out anything other than the shape. He looked up at where it could have fallen from and saw nothing, so he took it back towards the fire to get a better look.

He got back and slowly sat back down. He had to go onto one knee and slip his weight to the other side to get down as softly as possible. Once on the ground, he brought the ax into his lap. It looked as normal as any other with a strong blade and leather-wrapped handle, and it had engravings on the side that seemed to be only for decoration. But then, he recognized them. They were the same marks he saw when Rechnal burst into his medical room.

He started to flip it around, looking for more proof of his thinking. Then, he saw the bottom side of the handle. It had the infamous Berserker crest on it, and he gasped for air. It was what he thought it was. His mind started racing with questions. *Why would a Berserker ax have fallen all the way down if something big wasn't happening on level fourty-two?* He could only think of a massive battle Magnus was having where an ax would have fallen. *Could he be fighting outside and wasn't able to get in? Could he have gotten a lucky blow and was now surrounded?* These were the only thoughts that raced across his mind. The stress and worry finally made him realize he had to go up to help.

He didn't care that he wouldn't do much and would probably die if any half-witted warrior crossed his path. He stood himself back up and looked into the fire. He looked down at the ax and saw an image of Rechnal's face glaring into him. That man represented the entirety of the people that burned his home and killed his father.

But he also saw his own reflection staring back at him. The man he used to be was covered in a mask. It physically represented what he could no longer hide from. He had always tried to forget his problems and ignore them. He had tried to disappear and become a mysterious warrior to appease his father. His problems were real; living in denial would only push him further off the edge. He couldn't take it off, at least for now, but it clung to him as his problems clung to his heart. His life had been a cover-up to hide the issues of neglect that hung onto him. He never felt truly loved, so he had always tried to earn it. Everything had been a mask for him to hide behind the fact he never felt like he belonged. But with Magnus, something was different. His brother treated him fair and made him feel like he was beyond the worth of his work. That boy had brought out a positive side of Rain he had never seen before. His life had turned for the better since Magnus entered the picture, and he knew now he had to go help the brother that helped him.

After his moment of reflection, he stared back at the ax and back at the fire. He knew he needed a weapon but would not use the one that burned everything he knew. So, he tossed it into the fire and watched the leather around the handle curl in flames. The new light gave him enough to see if there was anything else he could use to defend himself. Then he saw it. A glimmer in the corner next to one of the guard's bodies.

He walked to pick it up and found it was the head guard's weapon. It was similar to his old sword in length and weight. Its handle was a sleek black, and the blade was a curved, classic silver. He turned it up and down to make sure it was fit for combat if need be, and after careful examination, he figured it would suffice. He took it in his right hand, and it fit nearly perfectly. Then, he saw one of the platforms lowering itself to him.

He turned to look at the compound's remains and saw the crumbled throne and the charred and mangled wood around the obsidian stairs. Then, in a raspy voice, with little sound, he said, "For all of them." He stepped on the platform, tightened his mask, and he began his ascent.

* * *

Jasper was in the restroom doing morning activities. He was dressed in a longer, torn tunic and rugged pants that looked to have seen their days. Once he finished, he walked out and stood in the doorway for a bit. It all seemed normal until a foreboding feeling overtook him as he stood there. He felt like something wasn't right. He wasn't sure why, but he was a man that had always trusted his gut. So he walked to his nightstand and opened the first drawer. He looked inside and saw his weapon, a collapsible spear divided into four parts.

Each part folded in on itself and was held together by a string. And if it were to be untied, it would unfold and extend into a full-length spear. It was made of fine mahogany with white and gray marble built into its staff. The spearhead was perfectly sharpened with eloquent carvings on it. The carvings were like branches of a tree that ran up the spearhead, rooting it to the staff portion. He reached down, ensured the string was secure, and picked it up. He pushed it into his pocket, closed the drawer, and turned for the door.

He opened it and looked into the long hallway. Things seemed normal, except the right side seemed darker than usual. "Hello?" he asked. His voice trailed through the hallway, but no response was given. He walked and turned to the right. The light seemed to disappear somewhere down the curve. He looked with intrigue and walked towards it. The darkness was getting closer, so he took out his spear. His eyes frantically scanned the area, and he was about to untie the string when he saw a dead man on the floor.

His eyes shot open, and he was speechless. He looked around to see if there was any evidence or threat. He saw and heard nothing, so he stuffed his spear into his pocket in order to tend to the body on the floor. He got down to a knee and felt where a pulse would have been on the man's neck. But soon, he saw the pool of blood that had collected. He took his hand back and looked up at the other bodies. He walked to the next one that caught his eye. It was impaled by a blood-stained spike. He pulled the spike out and examined it, and he noticed it looked similar to the handle that was on Rechnal's door. He put the spike back down to the ground. *Who? Who could've done this?* he thought as he stood back to his feet.

He saw the even darker part of the hallway and hoped it would give him answers. He took out his spear again and untied it. However, he clutched onto it to keep it from unfolding. The tension in his hand felt like the spear was begging to be used.

He was a cold-nerved man, but the darkness still unsettled him. He walked through until a bit of light from Rechnal's room shone through. He saw the doors were cracked open and went to reach for where the handle would be. Then, he remembered the spike he saw embedded in the man's forehead. So, he reached into the doors and opened them to see a normal room except for the open metal door. He saw no threat, so he re-tied his spear. *What happened?* His hands ran up the door until he saw the lock was cut through. He moved it back and forth to see if any more marks were visible, and the metal hinges squeaked.

He found nothing and moved his gaze to the wooden door. It seemed broken as well, so he went to push it. It easily opened, and the city unfolded in front of him. He looked up and down outside the doorway to see the platforms moving routinely and the flower pods of the level above. If whatever killed these men left, it was long gone, so he turned back into the room.

The door slowly squeaked closed behind him. His mind swarmed with questions. *Who did this? Why? Are they still here?* He left the room and took his spear out again, holding it without letting it fully spring into its potential. He walked out from the dark and figured he would start looking in each room to see if the intruder was still around.

He cracked open each of the doors only to be met with darkness from the vacant rooms that Berserkers used to occupy. He worked his way down the hallway and found nothing until he opened one of the dead Berserker's rooms. It had scratches on the floor that he didn't recognize, so he went inside to look. The marks were only from the Berserker constantly dropping his sword to the ground in that one spot, but he didn't know. So, he spent his time carefully inspecting the spot. He got on his knees and ran his fingers across the floor, feeling every crevice. He didn't know what they were, so he got up to look around. He spent a while inspecting the entire room for anything else that could help him.

* * *

Rain was still on the platform, and his body was fighting his mind. He could barely keep up with only standing on the platform, but he pushed through. He was nearing the doorway to the compound that he had only passed before.

Finally, the platform slowed for his stop, and his foot met the cool metal of the walkway as he stepped off. He made his way to the door and saw the inscription on it. He had no clue what it said, and he simply went to open it. It opened easily, and he was happy that the open door at least meant Magnus had made it inside.

He stepped into Rechnal's room, and the door quietly shut behind him. He looked around the room and saw nothing. *Where are you, Magnus?* he thought while approaching the double doors out of the room. Since he had never been inside the Berserker compound, he had no idea where to go. So, he put his hand to his sword and peeked out of the door. He saw the darkness that enveloped it, and a seed of fear was planted in his heart. *Why was it dark? Would it stay that way? Why was it silent? Did Magnus do this? Was he even here?*

He wasn't sure, but he raised his new sword in front of him to protect himself. He knew what he could find on the other side of the darkness could be precisely what he feared, and he knew that if another Berserker was in the compound, they could easily defeat him. But none of that mattered now. He was too close to give in to fear. "For Magnus," he whispered before he walked into the dark.

He blindly moved, taking all the time he needed to make sure he didn't hit or trip over a random object. After meandering his way through the dark portion, he came into the light where a few Berserker bodies rested. At first, he only saw one body resembling his brother in the dim light. Weakly he said, "No, it can't be." He moved as fast as he could, only to see more bodies in front of him. His face was scrunched up in worry and stress as he reached the first one and used his sword to turn the head toward him. He hoped that when he turned the man's face at him, it wouldn't be Magnus.

When the head turned, he saw that it wasn't him. He breathed deeply and, through the pain in his chest, "Okay, he could still be alive." The silence started to eat at his mind. *Why would it be this quiet? Was there some other room I didn't know about?* He still wasn't sure, but he kept walking. He saw the other slaughtered men and noticed all were Berserkers. Hope for Magnus's success was building, but he still couldn't find his brother. The hallway ahead of him was long and filled with rooms, but he would not let the vastness of the building stop him from seeing his brother.

He kept walking past many already-opened doors, and his heart beat faster as he felt an eerie sense that someone else was still there. He held his sword higher, but no one was to be found. He passed a shut door and wondered if anything was inside. *Surely not. You are letting your mind play tricks on you.* He walked past and continued to look down the hallway. Then he heard the sound of a door swinging open from behind him.

He turned his head to see an older man exit the room. His head was down, and his clothes were worn. Rain couldn't speak loud enough for him to hear, but he wanted to get his attention. The man was walking toward him, and he slowly backed up to keep his distance. But then he had an idea. He swung his sword and struck the ground near his feet.

The man looked startled and screamed, "You! You're the one responsible for all of this! Finally, I found you!" He tossed something into the air, and it unfolded with a snap. Next thing Rain knew, the man had a full-length spear in his right hand. "You will not get away!" he yelled as he started to walk toward Rain. His movement wasn't the fastest, but any opponent was formidable. "Who are you? Speak!" he yelled as he grew closer. Rain was still backing up, but he was not moving fast enough to outpace the old man. His face remained emotionless, and he took one last deep breath before the man could reach him. "Speak!" the man yelled before thrusting his spear. Rain was able to deflect the attack with perfect form, but the pain in his chest had already stung from deep inside.

The man took a moment's pause after noticing Rain's prowess and asked, "Why won't you speak?" Rain gave no response, and the man was bothered by his silence. He said menacingly, "I'll make you talk then." He swung, and Rain barely deflected the spear. The man was still strong through his aged appearance, and Rain knew it wouldn't be easy to beat him, especially in his state. He jabbed his spear, and Rain was able to deflect it toward the ground and take a step back to create more space. He looked him directly in the eyes and said as loud as he could through his strained lungs, "Rain." The man stood back and said, "Rain? What about it?" Rain pointed to himself. "That's what you call yourself?" the man asked. Rain nodded and gestured his hand at the man to ask him the same question. He took a moment to understand the gesture, but he responded, "I am Jasper of the Berserker clan, and your acts will not go unforgiven." He tightened his grip on his spear and started to walk again.

Rain was confused. *What acts? Who is he talking about?* Then, he understood. The accusation wouldn't make sense unless Jasper was actively searching for someone. Which meant Magnus could still be alive.

He had only a moment to process this hope before Jasper lunged at him again. He quickly brought his sword to the spear and tried to push it toward the ground. Unfortunately, he was weak and couldn't fully hold it. Jasper smiled a cruel smirk and taunted, "For the man that killed all these people, I would expect you to have more strength." He could feel how weak Rain was and felt confident in his old ability.

Rain said nothing in response but held his sword at the ready. He couldn't move quick enough to charge, so he sat back to stay on defense. He knew getting close to the spear would make it easier to win, but his body wouldn't permit him to move that quickly.

Jasper's spear pushed him down the hallway and past other closed doors. He wondered if more Berserkers sat behind them, and he prayed not. Jasper's spear could barely stay in range since he was just backing up. "Fight me, boy!" Jasper yelled as he kept pushing his spear. But Rain kept blocking it away from his body. Each block was a shot of pain, and his defense wouldn't sustain itself for much longer. Jasper himself was beginning to tire, but his resolve was not so.

The two continued to march their way down the hallway, clashing blades. As they passed Medya's room, Jasper pulled his spear back and spun it in his hands. "You can't keep this up forever, Rain," he said in a foreboding tone. Rain's own name echoed through the hallway and his skull.

He continued to walk slowly at Rain, who kept walking back and constantly checking his shoulder to see if another Berserker was coming out to attack. He knew what Jasper said was right and was scared for what would become of him if he kept fighting like this. Nevertheless, he was trying to gather his thoughts and body in an attempt to keep fighting.

The two backed all the way to the training room doors without any fighting. They just stared at each other, and though no words were spoken, Jasper's eyes shot fear into Rain's heart. Though his old body didn't have the ability or stature it once did, he still stood tall in Rain's mind space. He could see the fear and doubt in Rain's eyes and smiled, "You know it, don't you?" Rain felt terror travel his veins, and his grip on his sword tightened.

Jasper was slowly cornering him to the training room doors where no sound came from inside, but a cold draft infiltrated the end of the hallway. The cold added to Rain's already strained nerves, and chills ran up his spine. His back hit the door, and his breath left him sharply. His nerves heightened, and his hands started to quiver. He had no way out except to keep fighting. He knew if it wasn't for his chest, Jasper would have been an easy victory, but now, he was fighting through unbearable pain. He wanted to open the doors behind him, but he wasn't sure if more Berserkers were waiting.

While spinning his spear, Jasper said, "I have you now. Fight." He brought his blade and struck the ground with the blunt end. He ran it along the ground before he took it and pointed it at Rain. His hand and weapon were steady, and Rain looked down the length of it, afraid.

But he had to fight. He took a deep breath, looked Jasper directly in the eyes, and weakly said, "I will." He took all of his strength and brought the fight to Jasper. He was caught off guard by the sudden aggression, so he spun his spear down into Rain's charging blade and pushed it away. Now he had his back to the door, and Rain pointed his sword at him. The thrill of the fight numbed the pain in his chest slightly, but his breath was still getting heavier.

He charged again and knocked into Jasper's spear. The force pushed him back, and his hand made the door open. The one open door was enough for both to fit into. Rain charged again and met Jasper in the doorway. His spear caught the sword, and he turned the blade towards the inside of the room. He flung Rain across the room with a strong push, and his body tumbled to the ground. His eyes shut tight from the pain that shot through his chest, and his head turned away from Jasper.

Then, he opened his eyes. Sheer panic overcame him as his eyes met the closed eyelids of Magnus's body. He shifted back in shock, and anger brewed inside his broken body. He was unsure what even to think to expect for one emotion, desperation. Desperation to avenge his brother and desperation to survive. He turned his head back around and saw Jasper staring at something else across the room.

"No! My king!" he yelled as he went and put his hand on Rechnal's chest. He felt the wounds and stood back up, furious. He put it together that Magnus was the one who killed Rechnal and was enraged. He saw Rain next to Magnus, "You know him, don't you? I saw it when you looked at him." Rain, who was up to one knee now, shook his head no. Jasper looked at him again and said, "Liar! I see it in your eyes. You knew him. You are one of them!"

He took his spear, held it above his head, and broke it over his knee into two even pieces at the middle joint. He could put it back together if he chose to. The side with the spearhead went to his right hand, and the staff went to his left. He screamed, "And now you will die!" He started to rush at Rain, who was just getting to his feet.

He picked up his sword and brought it in front of him. Jasper jabbed his blade at him, and he shifted to the side to dodge. The staff came swinging in, and he barely brought his sword into it. His mouth opened in pain, and a faint scream squealed. He quickly moved from the staff and found the spear nearly missing his face. Jasper kept grunting and throwing his blade and staff. Rain slowly fought, trying to evade any strike from his onslaught. "Come here!" Jasper yelled as his strikes couldn't hit their target. The fight ran its course around the room and made its way to the doors again.

Both were starting to feel the effects of the fight, and their breaths were heavy. Jasper was frustrated at Rain's ability to simply dodge and not strike back. He said, between labored breaths, "Are you a man of cowardice? If not, fight me face to face." This command sat with Rain. *I am no coward, and I can't run away from him forever, so I'll fight.*

He made no sound but planted his foot on the ground and held his sword up again. He ensured his mask was on correctly and gestured for Jasper to attack. "There it is," Jasper said as he lunged. Rain used his sword to pop the spear in the air, and for the first time in the entire fight, he jabbed at Jasper. The staff blocked the attack, but he had made his first advancements.

"Finally, you did something," Jasper taunted as Rain put his other hand to his chest and felt the pain radiating from it. Jasper unleashed another fury of attacks that Rain could only dodge. The fight was still in his hands, and Rain was genuinely beginning to worry about his fate. The two moved past the window where Rechnal's ax had smashed through. Rain kept moving around just enough to escape. Jasper grunted with every attack hoping it would find its mark, but none did.

Finally, they made their way away from the window and were beginning to near the children's training door. "I know you're tiring, Rain," Jasper said. He charged again and swung overhead with both hands. Rain met his weapons with his sword, but the pain in his chest was near unbearable. He had to get out of the situation, so he quickly stepped back, removing his sword from under Jasper. The weapons fell to the floor, and in a moment of quickness, he pinned the spearhead to the ground. He had enough strength to hold down one of Jasper's limbs, unlike when he had both hands on his spear earlier in the fight. He went to bring his foot to Jasper's face but was interrupted. Jasper's left hand brought the staff from the ground, uppercut him across the left side of his jaw, and knocked him into the wall behind him. His sword flew from his hand but still landed close to him.

The blow was shattering, and it rang through his skull. His body hit the front side first into the wall, and he felt his chest scream from inside. Something had moved, and the pain escalated to levels worse than when

Helpar first slammed him with his hammer. He slowly turned his body back around to face Jasper. Jasper stood with the weapons extended at each hand. "Time's up, Rain," he said as he raised the spearhead and jumped toward him.

He flew through the air, and the spear was aimed perfectly at Rain's head. Rain saw death staring back at him, but he wouldn't let Jasper be the one who dealt it. He dropped to his knees at the last second and grabbed his sword. Fortunately, Jasper's spear missed and lodged itself into the wall he had been leaning on. So, Rain stabbed the sword through Jasper's stomach as he stood over him. He groaned and immediately dropped the spear and the staff. His face was overcome by pain and shock.

Rain pushed the blade in further, forcing Jasper's body back to the wall. Rain stood through the pain, looking at his face, and mouthed, "No, yours is, Jasper." He pulled out the sword, and the body fell to the ground. Finally, the room was silent except for the faint sound of a cold draft from the shattered window.

He stood proud of his accomplishment until his own eyes terrorized him at the sight of a single drop of blood falling from his nose and onto the floor.

His mask was shattered.

He immediately felt the struggle to breathe and dropped to his knees. Each breath felt like lifting the weight of the death that surrounded him. He raised his head and saw Magnus's body across the room. If he were going to die, he would be by his brother's side.

He stood back up and walked back. He saw Magnus lying there and still felt grief until he saw the golden sword on the ground. His face, though struggling to breathe, lit with excitement as he remembered something he had read in his hospital bed before the attack. *Could it actually work?* He had to try.

He lumbered his way to it and picked it up from the ground. Its edges still ran gold, and its center reflected the light through distorted blood stains. As he went to stand back up, his lungs couldn't get the air in. He dropped back to the ground, and with all his power, he whispered, "No." He lifted his head and began to crawl to his brother. His resilience would not die, so he pushed himself onto his knees. The pain was worse than he could imagine, but none of it mattered. He finally got to Magnus and started feeling his body for any signs of what had happened.

He felt until his fingers touched the still-warm blood from the dagger's wound. Finally, he had found what he was looking for. He raised the sword into the air and pointed it at the wound. He pushed it in, and the gold around the blade hummed. It glowed brighter than usual, and the gold started to move faster. Magnus's body twitched as it hummed louder and shined even brighter. Rain used every bit of his will and strength to keep the sword in place.

Magnus's eyes were still shut, but his body twitched even more. Then, the gold from the sword started to run into him. His veins began to show the faintest hint of gold, and his body shifted even more. As the gold ran into him, something else took its place on the edge of the blade. The dead blood took the areas where the gold used to run and turned them crimson red. It continued to flow, and he was twitching violently now. Rain struggled to hold the blade in place due to his pain and lack of proper breaths. Magnus's veins were popping with gold, and the blade was almost entirely crimson. And finally, the last bit of gold ran into him, and his wound began to close itself.

Gold stitching came from his own skin and healed it from top to bottom. It continued to shine gold as the stitching sealed itself, and as it fully sealed, the sword shone bright red before turning again to solid crimson. Rain threw it down and looked back at his brother, whose body lay still. The sword hit the ground and started to beat like a heart going from crimson to scarlet and back again. Through his raspy breaths, he begged, "Please, please."

Then the sword stopped beating and settled to a crimson red. For a matter of seconds, the room sat quietly until Magnus's eyes shot open.

His breath was extremely heavy, and his hand immediately grabbed at Rain's clothes. He looked around, but his eyes were unfocused, and they swarmed across the room. His inhale was sharp, and his exhale was weighted as he grabbed tighter and asked harshly, "How?" Rain looked at him and smiled through the pain of the hand slamming into his chest, and whispered, "Told you that sword is special." Magnus looked and saw his sword, whose edges now ran crimson, and looked back at Rain. He was still unaware of what was happening and asked, "I'm alive?" Rain nodded, and he smiled as he felt where his cut used to be, "It's gone. I'm alive!" Rain smiled again and looked into his brother's eyes.

Then, in a sudden burst of panic, Magnus said, "Rain, your mask!" He let go of Rain's clothes and grabbed at the mask. Rain gasped for a breath and said, "I know, Magnus, I know."

His body suddenly gave out, and he fell to the ground. Magnus shot to his knees and cradled his now gasping brother, "Rain! Rain, it's okay. Look at me. Rain, look at me!" Rain weakly turned back and gasped again. His face showed pain but also a sense of satisfaction. He has saved his brother, something he deemed a noble accomplishment. "I told you to stay down there," Magnus said, shifting his weight into his arms. Rain responded, "I-I know." The harsh tone told Magnus his brother was in trouble. He looked around and remembered where the medical bay was. He said, "Rain, I can get you to the medical bay; come on!" He stood and tried to pick up Rain, whose weak voice screamed in pain, "Stop, stop!" He set him back down and stared at him, "I can save you, but we have to get there! Come on!" He tried pulling Rain up, only for him to grimace and yell in pain.

He realized he couldn't move his brother, and a sense of doom befell his heart. It pained him to his core to see Rain like this, and a tear began to form in his eye. He sniffled it back and said, "It's going to be okay." Rain paused for a moment and then shook his head. Magnus looked back at him and told him, "That wasn't a question. You are going to be okay." Rain's body was starting to give out completely, and he forced the air from his lungs.

"No. No, Magnus, it won't be, not this time," he said slowly. Magnus let go of the tear in his eyes.

"It will be okay," he told Rain and himself.

"N-not this t-time Magnus," Rain struggled.

"No, Rain, no," Magnus said through teary eyes. He was on the brink of crying but held his composure.

"We can get you out of here, Rain. I can," he said with an increasingly desperate tone.

Rain contorted in pain, "I'm t-tired, Magnus." He inhaled a shaky gasp of air and continued, "I don't want to f-fight anymore."

"You have to fight Rain. You have to," Magnus urged desperately.

Rain took another painful gasp, "I've fought my whole life. It's finally time I don't."

He grabbed at Magnus, and a tear ran down his cheek. He couldn't get the words out, but Magnus understood he was barely hanging on. He started to feel tears running down his face, "I'm here, Rain. I'm here." Rain's body shook and started to feel even weaker. However, he had enough strength to say, "Thank you, Magnus." Magnus looked back and said, "For what?" Rain gritted his teeth together and forced another breath. He raised his hand and wiped the tear from Magnus's face. "I've been fighting and killing my whole life," he struggled. His body contorted again, and he forced in one more breath, "B-but now I can finally say I sav-ved someone." He smiled weakly as a tear ran from his cheek. Magnus sat silently until Rain's neck bent back, and he struggled to get his next breath out. He clutched onto his brother to bring him even closer, and Rain let out one last breath. He struggled, but he pointed at Magnus and whispered, "Brother." He struggled again, and with all his power, he let one last word, "Love." He smiled and grabbed one last time. Magnus grabbed back and barely said, "I love you too, brother." Rain's eyes rolled back, and his head dropped.

Then he went limp, and Magnus's arm gave with it. His body lay down, his head turned to Magnus, and a dead tear ran down his face. His body lowered to the floor, and Magnus's own tears began to wet its clothes. "Rain! Rain! Please!" he yelled to the empty room. He shook his brother's body, and no response came. He put his head to Rain's chest and heard no heartbeat. His tears began to stream from his cheek as he looked at Rain. "I told you to stay, Rain! I told you to stay!" he yelled as he slammed himself into the ground in pain-filled anger. It was followed by more sobbing, and he grabbed at Rain even more, "I need you. I can't do this by myself, Rain. I need you! Come back!" He pounded at the ground with his fist, "Come back!" His vision was blurry from the tears, and his heart felt nothing but anguish. He stopped banging the ground and let out another plea, "Rain, please. Please come back." He couldn't get any more words from his mouth. He tried to pull himself together and move Rain's body, but he couldn't.

He saw his brother's face lifeless, and he couldn't help but put the blame on himself. If he hadn't left the Berserkers in the first place, this never would have happened. He could have stopped all of this if he had been there when Rechnal attacked. He could've saved his brother if he didn't lose to Rechnal. He raised his head and leaned back on his knees. He looked through the shattered window that mirrored the mask on Rain's face. The cold wind slapped his face and chilled his soul. He pulled Rain's body onto his knees and sat for a moment.

Then, he unleashed a bellow that encompassed his entire life. All his pain, all his turmoil, and all his anger fueled his roar into the night. It echoed through the whole Berserker compound, and every remaining ear could hear it.

Finally, his air ran out, and he collapsed his head onto Rain's chest. He gasped for another breath before sobbing uncontrollably again. His body and mind couldn't handle all his emotions, so he dug his head further and cried harder. He didn't want to accept the harsh truth; Rain of the Devil's hand was dead.

18

A WAR FOR PEACE

An echoing scream bounced around the room, and Treni's eyes slowly opened. Her face was compressed against the dummy, and her body was sore from the awkward position she slept in. But as her eyes fully opened, she understood what had woken her. She was still in a groggy trance but quickly attached her swords to either hip. She made sure her clothes were on correctly and went to push open the door to the main training room. As she did so, another door behind her opened. Qutir's head poked from behind it, "What was that?" he asked. She was startled and jumped back slightly. "I'm not sure what it is, but I'll find out," she said as she reached for the door again. His eyes widened, "Can I–?" "No," she interrupted. He frowned but listened, and he went back into his room. He walked into the other waking children.

"Treni said not to join her, so we're gonna sit here and wait." Sid perked up.

"Why can't we just go in?" he asked.

"What Treni says goes, and I don't feel like finding that sound alone," Qutir answered. The others agreed, and they sat in their room waiting for news of what it was that woke them.

Treni pushed her way through the massive stone door and saw the unthinkable. Rechnal's body was on the floor, followed by Jasper's, and on the other side, a man sat on his knees. He was curled into a ball around another body while cradling his face. His sobs echoed throughout the room and caused him to be deaf to her entrance. His sword was close to him but not close enough that he could grab it if she attacked.

However, she did not charge or attack him but drew her swords and addressed him, "Weaper! Show who you are!"

His sniffling halted, and he wiped his eyes. They were a tender red, and his cheeks were flush. He raised his head and, through blurry eyes, saw the figure of a woman standing across the room. He had no idea who it was or what she would do, but he yelled, "Go away!" He buried his head back into the body, and light tears again began to flow. She paused to process the face she was seeing. She wondered if it could really be who she thought it was. It had been years since she had seen him, yet she was looking directly at him. As much as she couldn't believe it, she had to accept that Magnus was in front of her again.

She lowered her blades slightly, but they were still ready for a fight. She walked a bit closer and asked, "Magnus?" Again, his crying halted, and he raised his head. His eyes were still watery, and his mouth was dry from heavy breaths. He yelled, "Go away!" He lowered his head back down, and she knew for sure that it was him. She probed him again, "Magnus, what happened here?" This time he realized she called him by name and was curious. "Who are you?" he simply asked. She waited a moment but said, "It's me, Treni." He felt a rush of emotion that quickly died after remembering what she had done and who she stood for. But his heart still longed to call her more than a Berserker.

He raised his head back up and wiped the water from his eyes. He saw her standing there, and her beauty stunned him for a moment. He then responded, "What are you here to do?" She hesitated momentarily while trying to think of what she was actually there for. *I don't really want to kill him, but what other choice is there?* She continued contemplating until she gave a generic response, "I'm here finish this."

He chuckled a bit and leaned all the way back on his knees. He didn't reach for his sword but just looked at her, "If you want to kill me, go ahead. You have taken everything from me anyway, so you might as well take my life. You killed my father, my people, and my-my brother." Finally, his tone became distressed and angry, "You burned my home to the ground! I lost everything! I have nowhere to rest, and nothing to care about!" He raised a knee, put his foot to the ground, and reached for his sword. She quickly reacted and pointed her sword at him. But he stopped and stepped back down before she had to do anything. For a split second, he thought of rising, grabbing his sword, and raising it for combat again, but the thought did nothing but die in his grief-exhausted mind.

He sat there on his knee before he yelled, much quieter than his first scream, "Arhh!" He slammed his fist into the ground and broke into more tears. "So if you're going to kill me, do it. You killed everything else," he said exasperatedly through sniffling and blurry vision. She lowered her sword back to her side and stood in shock at his state. This was the same person that she knew as a kid, and it hurt, deep down, to see him like this.

Lost for words, she sat with her sword dangling by her side. She couldn't speak before he finally inhaled deeply and calmed his tone down, "This war we fought has led us here, and I've lost everything. I have nothing left to fight for, so do it if you want. I don't want to fight anymore, and I know it will all end if you kill me. So have your way. I am done." No more tears could reach his red, swollen eyes. She stood, taken aback and frozen in her place. Then, he continued, "Please, I ask for you to let me join him," while he grabbed onto Rain, "I have nothing to gain from fighting again." He continued to rest on his knees and stare at Treni, who was still shocked by the plea for death.

She raised her sword and stared at him without saying a word. She walked over and stood just a sword's reach away from him. He looked at her and said, "Are you gonna do it?" She paused once more and looked at her hands. She knew what she had to do, so she raised her right sword and jabbed it. He closed his eyes in anticipation of a quick death, but none was found. She held the sword a finger length from his neck and pointed it directly at him. She stared into his teary eyes, "I have seen so much violence in this place. There are dead bodies here as we speak." She gestured to the corpses spread across the room, "I have hated every bit of this war waged between us, and I have wanted peace forever. There doesn't have to be any fighting to continue. We can end it here and move on like I have dreamed of since I grew up and saw the atrocities my own people committed." She inhaled deeply and lowered her sword a bit, "It was these men like Rechnal and Jasper who drove this war machine that killed everything you loved. I am not like them, and I never wanted to be. I stand here glad they are dead."

He watched and could hear the passion in her voice. She didn't sound like she was lying as she continued, "I would've had to marry that man and saw no honor in that, just as I see no honor in continuing this useless fight. This war had taken away ideas of what peace is. This whole place has. But I have wanted to bring peace as long as I have seen the effects of hate and violence, so when it comes to your request, no, I will not be your killer. Instead, I offer you peace. You can take it or run away with it. I would even let you remain here for the time being. I want peace Magnus, and killing you is not on that path. I will not kill you."

She brought her swords back to her side and sheathed both blades simultaneously. He sat and wondered if death would've been better, but he was still alive. He knew his life would be abysmal for some time, but yet something inside of him hung onto the will to live. He wasn't truly ready to give up yet.

He needed somewhere to stay, and she had offered the Berserker compound. *She's serious if she's offering this place for me to stay in.* Ultimately, he concluded she wasn't lying, and her reason for peace was actually believable.

"How can I know you, of all people, want peace? We have been fighting our whole lives, and we're supposed to just turn around? There is so much to fix, which doesn't even count what happened between us." He went to keep speaking, but she interrupted.

"What happened between us doesn't have to affect what happens now," she said. He smiled a bit to cover the pain from his childhood, and he bit his tongue.

"I'm not sure it fully can, after what you did, but maybe time could fix it." She looked offended.

"I'm sorry for what I did. I should've treated you better, but I was stupid like all kids. I don't know if you can forgive me, but can I ask you to try?" she asked. Magnus nodded his head and looked away at the window. His lips puckered.

"I can try, but it will take some time. Everything will take some time."

She nodded sadly because what she did in the past bothered her, but she couldn't fully express that pain. It was one of her greatest regrets, but she understood why he couldn't forgive her. He was still on his bent knees and looked at his brother again. The face he loved now stared back at him without any expression or life. It hurt, but now if he could finally bring peace, Rain's death would mean something other than sadness.

His body was still weak from the battle, resurrection, and sobbing, but he started to stand up. She watched in silence as he slowly lifted himself from his knees. He whispered under his breath as he turned away from Rain's face, "I'm sorry this didn't happen sooner."

He finally lifted his head and stared into her eyes. Their gray hue was like storm clouds that brought terror but also like benevolent rain clouds in the spring that promised a new blossom. He stood up straight and said, "I'll try your peace. I won't forgive you, but I will try to start the peace you're offering." He extended his hand to do a traditional Berserker sign of friendship. It was a customary handshake until the end portion, when both would loosen their grip and slip their arm together until their hands were at the other's elbow. She met his hand, and they interlocked. Their arms slid into one another, and though it was usually a sign of strong camaraderie, it was a mere formality.

Their hands parted, and they looked back at each other. "Well, what now?" he asked in a monotone voice. She went to speak, but the door behind her cracked open. She turned her head around and saw Qutir beginning to poke his head through the door. "Go inside!" she yelled as she ran to the door to shut it again. He had slipped his head out for a moment and saw nothing but Treni running toward him and Rechnal's body dead on the floor. Questions flooded his mind but were silenced by her scolding, "I told you to stay there! I didn't know what was out here, and now you know more than you should! I don't know what happened to Rechnal, but I don't think it was anyone's fault but his own!" He had no words, and the rest of the children who sat patiently in their training room also quieted down. "Now, all of you, stay here!" she yelled, shutting them back into the training room.

Magnus saw her run to the door, and he turned back to look at Rain. His dead body showed the cost paid for peace, and it nearly broke him. He looked away in pain and saw his sword on the ground. A new red liquid flowed around and through it. He hadn't had time to really see what it was like, and he was curious. So, with Treni's back still turned, he bent down to pick it back up again.

His cold hand touched the hilt, and the red liquid in and around the sword pulsed like a heartbeat. Shocked, he threw it back to the ground, and it clattered on the floorboards. He looked at Rain as if he would receive some advice, but there was none to hear.

Finally, curiosity overcame him, and he reached his hand back toward the sword. As his hand was about to grasp the hilt again, Treni turned around, "What are you doing?!" Her voice was tense, and her hand went to her waist. "It's not what you think! My sword has changed," he said defensively. She looked at him in confusion, "Changed?" He raised his hands into the air and said, "Watch." Her hand stayed glued to her sword, but it was still sheathed. "I'm watching," she said sternly.

He lowered his right arm to the sword and picked it back up. The blade pulsed again, and he backed away from it; however, he didn't drop it. Instead, he moved it around, "See, see, it glows." Her jaw dropped in shock, "Yeah, yeah. It does." As he held it, the pulsing began to slow, and it eventually stopped. It settled to its original crimson hue and rested perfectly in his hand. He felt comfortable with it like he could never be harmed while using it. It was a spectacular feeling, but now wasn't the time to ponder what it meant. He didn't want to put it away, so he held it by his side.

"Where were we?" he asked as he straightened himself. She looked a bit threatened by the blade, but she moved her hand from her waist.

"Peace, that's where," she responded.

"So how are you gonna make peace again? Seeing as the last time we tried, it didn't work," he said with a tinge of pain in his voice.

Her face contorted in offense, "I already apologized, so let's just move past it."

He snickered a bit and said, "First, I'm gonna need a place to sleep since, you know, my home was burned to the ground." She was quick in her response.

"You can stay here. It's only me, the kids, and Medya. I can give you one of the empty rooms."

He shivered at Medya's name since it had been so long since he'd heard it. She had never done anything of significant harm, but she was still a memory of his childhood. Treni saw this in his face and wanted to bolster her mother.

"She's not who she used to be. She told me she wanted peace, so maybe she meant it."

He shook his head, "I'm not believing that."

She cut in as he finished, "Give it a try, please." He bit his lip and thought quietly. Then, he realized he was still holding his sword. He accidently locked eyes with her as he went to put it away. Her beauty stunned him, and he missed the sheath entirely. The sword clattered to the ground, and he blushed. He went to pick it up until the doors burst open.

* * *

Magnus's scream echoed through the hallway and into Medya's room. It resembled the others, with a small twin bed and a modest nightstand on the side. A small bathroom was on the right side of the room, and it served its purpose. Her groggy eyes slowly opened, and she realized what she had heard. Her body was old, but she could still get out of bed.

She moved her covers off and swung her legs off the bed. The scream had piqued her interest, and she had to get into the hallway to find whatever made it. She hurriedly moved to the bathroom, where she tied her long gray hair into a bun. She left and went to grab her weapon, an elegant dagger with a jagged blade and an engraving on the hilt that had been worn away from years of constant use. She opened the drawer in her nightstand where she kept it, but it wasn't there. Her eyes opened in panic, and she frantically looked around her room. *Where is it?*

She started tearing apart the room, looking for it, and, by the end, all her nightstand drawers were ripped open. She hopped to the floor and looked under the bed, and her hand ran under the dark underside. There was nothing but a pair of old pants that she had no idea when she last wore. Defeated, she stood back up and wondered where she could have left it. *Could it be in the bathroom?* She had figured she hadn't left it there, but it wouldn't hurt to look.

So, she walked back in and started opening the drawers and cupboards. Going from left to right of her bathroom dresser, she eventually opened the top right drawer. The dagger hit the front, and she smiled. She didn't remember when she had put it there but shrugged it off.

She grabbed and held it in preparation for what she would find outside her door. But when she walked and opened it, it was eerily quiet, and it felt colder than usual. She turned her head both ways, and on one end, she saw the doors to the training room and, on the other, scratch marks on the walls.

"What is-?" she whispered as she walked to them and reached her old hand out. She felt around and became increasingly nervous. There were more scratches down the hallway, so, in a streak of bravery, she paced down it. With her dagger by her side, she took deep, cautious breaths. Her eyes moved from side to side like quicksilver. Each breath was heavier than the last, followed by heavier nerves.

Then, after walking for only a few moments, she saw the first of the bodies. She gasped, her jaw dropped, and she hurried as she went to see it. She went to her knees and placed her hands on the man's face; it was cold and dead. A gasp of fear and sorrow was all she could mutter. She saw the blood pooling, and immediately, her mind wandered as to who could have committed such an act. Then, she saw the rest of the bodies spread across the floor, and a wave of terror crashed over her.

She stood back up slowly and looked further into the hallway, where the lights were extinguished. *Should I? What if whoever did this is in there?* She pondered for even longer until she concluded that her people were her responsibility, and if she left without exploring everything, she would be a disgrace and a coward. So, she stepped toward the darker end and began to walk. Each body she saw caused her to let out a short exhale. Sorrow began to accumulate within her, but also, fear kept festering as she was nearly encompassed by darkness. Her hand shook as she held her dagger by her side, hoping nothing would spring out and make her meet the same fate. She was old, but she wasn't ready to die.

Her pace remained slow, unlike her heart, and she reached the end of the hallway. Rechnal's chamber was vacant, with ruffled sheets left on the bed. "Rechnal?" she asked as she poked her head further into the room. No response followed, and she cautiously walked in.

She still gripped her dagger and walked toward the bathroom. It was silent as she turned the corner, and she lowered her dagger as she saw there was nothing or no one there. She turned back around to face the room and sighed in minor relief. But it was short-lived. She wasted no time and began to walk back down the hallway.

It wasn't long before she was in the dark again, and her dagger was gripped tightly by her side. Her pace was much faster now, and she bolted to leave the darkness as quickly as possible. She bounded down the rest of the hallway and past her room. She continued walking until she reached the training room. The massive doors were shut and felt much cooler from underneath, like a draft. She was confused by the chill but figured it wasn't important.

When her heart finally stopped pounding, she stood and listened. She heard what sounded like muffled talking, so she held her ears to the door to listen for anything before just barging in. She couldn't make out any sounds, so she listened even closer. Her ear was pressed against the door, yet she still couldn't understand what was happening inside. Then, she stepped back and wondered if just running in would be the best idea.

Whatever is happening inside isn't loud or cantankerous, so maybe the scream I heard was nothing at all. She thought this until she heard a clear sound, a sword hitting the ground. She immediately panicked at the sound of weaponry and what it could entail. She held her dagger even tighter and burst through the two doors to see Treni and another figure in the room. She saw Rechnal's and Jasper's bodies on the ground and became overcome with dumbfounded rage.

However, the slightest inkling of relief fell over her, looking at Rechnal's body. She was never a supporter of his ideas, but soon after, guilt ran over her for feeling anything good about her king's death.

Treni and Magnus looked over at the now-open doors and were surprised. For her, it was a simple surprise from her mother without any formal warning. For him, it was another glance into his past that had caused this future. Medya stood in the doorway until she squinted at him, "Is that?" "Yes, that's Magnus," Treni interrupted. Medya's eyes filled with revenge and hatred, and she said, "You, the coward who ran. You're the one who did this." She started to shake with rage and gripped the dagger with strength like she didn't know she possessed. Then, she charged.

"Ahhh!" she yelled as she brandished her dagger. Magnus started bending down to pick up his sword to defend himself. At the same time, Treni yelled, "Stop!" She withheld her blade and instead chose to try to tackle her mother. She bolted to intercept Medya before she could reach Magnus.

Medya looked at her daughter. She knew she wouldn't make it to him before she intercepted her, so she went to throw the dagger. As her hand released, Treni wrapped her arms around and brought her to the ground. The two tumbled and broke apart during the fall, but Treni quickly climbed on top and pinned her down. Unfortunately, it was too late, and the dagger was already flying, but the impact knocked the blade off course just enough.

Magnus was lifting his head when the dagger pierced his left leg. He screamed in pain, dropped his blade, and fell to the floor. His hands started shaking as he touched the embedded dagger, and Treni looked over in horror as he fell. Medya tried to free herself to no success.

"Let. Me. Go," she demanded. Treni struggled but maintained her position over her mother.

"No, we have a chance," she said. Medya still squirmed under her arm.

"A chance for what?" she asked impatiently.

Treni, still in control of her mother, replied, "A chance for the peace we want."

Medya looked confused, "Peace? With him?" She continued to speak before Treni silenced her.

"Yes, peace with him."

"How could you be so foolish?" Medya gawked.

Offended, Treni replied, "Foolish? I'm the one trying to solve our problem."

"What problem? We're at war, Treni!" Medya yelled as she desperately tried to squirm her way out. Treni pushed her shoulders even harder into the floor.

"We don't have to be! Rechnal is dead!" Medya opened her mouth to say something but was pushed into the floor again.

"He said he wanted peace! And now you put a dagger in his leg!" Treni yelled through another push. Her desperate tone shook something inside Medya, and she realized that her daughter was right.

She turned to Magnus and saw him struggling on the floor. She didn't speak but instead gave a sorrowful gasp. If Treni was truthful, which she always had been, Medya knew she could have ruined whatever peace she spoke of. The same peace she had always wanted deep down that she had ignored for years. It could now be a reality, and she may have foiled it. A wave of guilt overran her, and she gave up fighting. She wanted peace as much as her daughter, and seeing it so close only for it to be possibly stripped away by a throw was devastating. Treni slowly moved and started to move toward Magnus.

He scooted on the floor with his good leg. "Back up! Back up!" he yelled. "I'm trying to help," Treni said reassuringly, but she was silenced by his screaming. "Get away!" he cried as he held a hand toward her. She froze as she looked at his leg, which, somehow, wasn't bleeding. She struggled to get any words out and, in the end, stood with a gaping mouth.

As she stood gawking, Medya moved. She pushed past her and went to the ground to help Magnus. "Get away!" he yelled again, but she had no care to listen. If there was any chance of fixing the problem, she had to help him now. He tried to push her away, but there was no stopping her. He winced in pain as he tried to evade. "Stay still," she commanded. He tried to keep scooting away, but the pain eventually stopped him.

Finally, he let her hands examine the wound. "There's no blood, but once I move it, there will be," she said to him. He winced again as she lightly pressed around the wound. He felt the blade move within his leg, but it was more than side to side. He tried to take deep breaths to calm himself but merely caused himself only to breathe faster and heavier. "Treni, grab a piece of Rechnal's clothes!" Medya yelled. Treni was still frozen and didn't respond. "Treni!" she yelled again. This shook her from her shocked state, and she stared directly at her mother. "Get a piece of Rechnal's clothes! I need to make a tourniquet!" Medya yelled.

Magnus leaned his head back and gritted his teeth in pain. Treni ran across the room and ripped some of Rechnal's pants off the calf. "This enough?!" she asked while holding up the fabric. "Yes, bring it here," Medya replied.

"We need to get this thing out now," Medya told him. He nodded and braced for a rush of pain. Treni dropped the fabric next to his leg and watched anxiously. "Thank you," Medya said to her.

"Ready?" she asked. He nodded again and leaned his head back to look away. She wrapped her hands around the dagger and yelled, "Now!" She started pulling it from his leg, and it moved relatively easy. His body shook in pain, and his breath left through grinding teeth. It squelched as it exited the wound, and Medya and Treni looked on in shock. She tossed it to the side, but she couldn't speak through a gaping jaw. "What, what is it?" he said as he looked back at his leg. His own voice was stolen by what he saw. The blood coming from the wound was rich gold.

The three remained in pure shock as the sword behind them started to pulse again. No one could speak, but as they turned their heads back to his leg, the wound was stitching itself back together with golden threads. "How?" Medya whispered. Finally, it fully closed, the scar shone gold before fading back into his tan skin tone, and the sword's pulsing stopped. The three sat stunned and started where a dagger used to be planted.

He slowly flexed the muscles in his legs, and no pain greeted him. He bent and straightened it to no pain at all. Pure ecstasy ran through him as he started scoffing through smiles. "That's impossible," Treni said from behind. He said nothing back and kept moving his leg back and forth with a smile. He stood to his feet and went to grab his sword again. As he grabbed it from the ground, it pulsed in his hand momentarily. He observed it until the pulsing faded away. "Thank you," he whispered to it as he sheathed it.

Medya stopped staring like a child and turned to Treni. "Help me up," she demanded. Treni looked down and extended her hand. She pulled Medya to her feet and dusted her off. The two stood looking at a miracle that they couldn't possibly comprehend.

Magnus turned back to face them, and the only evidence of the dagger was a cut in his already-damaged clothes. "Thank you," he told Medya. She immediately said, "I'm sorry. I didn't know that you wanted peace. I have always fought, but it could be time to change." He looked at the same woman who had meant so little to him as a boy and felt a bit of pity for her. "I can forgive you for that, but as I told Treni, the past will take time," he responded in a monotone voice. She nodded just like Treni had when he had said the same to her. The room sat silent again until Treni spoke, "What do we do now?" He had no response, but Medya did. She said, "We handle the dead." He turned to look at Rain's dead body, and all the emotion started to flood back into him. He quickly suppressed it and looked up normally. Treni looked and saw Rechnal and Jasper, two she was never fond of, but their bodies had to be handled, nonetheless.

She turned to Medya and commanded, "Go take care of the children, and don't let them out until we finish." "Smart," Medya said as she turned for the children's room. Once she entered, she was bombarded with questions about what had happened. She ignored them all and began to teach a lesson on honor and dignity while in combat. As the door shut, Treni and Magnus remained.

"What will you do with your brother? I know we will burn our bodies as always, but I don't want to assume you want the same fate for him?" she asked. The concept of dealing with Rain's death still hadn't set in for him, so the question mentally stunned him.

"I-uh, I want to take him back home," he answered after a moment's pause.

"Then do that. The doors will be open when you come back, and as you know, there's plenty of space for you," she said kindly.

He nodded, "I know we're not on the best of terms, but I appreciate the hospitality."

She smiled and nodded in acknowledgment. She turned to face the first of the bodies she would clean up, Rechnal. She started to walk toward it as he went toward Rain.

"Finally, you're gone," she whispered under her breath.

"What?" he asked after hearing her. Her face flushed red.

"Nothing. I didn't say anything," she answered hastily.

He saw through her blushing and asked again curiously, "What did you say?"

"I'm happy to get rid of Rechnal. That's all I said," she replied.

He was surprised and questioned, "Why would you be happy to dispose of a king?"

"He was a monster, not a king," she said with an angry undertone.

The sudden switch in tone threw him off, and he stayed quiet. "Now, go handle your dead," she directed. She stormed away to Rechnal, and he, to Rain. They each grabbed their bodies, and he cradled Rain as she went to drag a lifeless Rechnal across the floor.

19

HANDLING THE DEAD

Treni struggled to move Rechnal's body out of the room, and she grunted and heaved over the body. Yet, it hardly moved. Magnus still cradled Rain in his arms and would have started to cry again if it was for her letting out a massive grunt. He looked away from his brother and saw her barely moving the dead behemoth.

She dropped to the ground after her latest pull and began to think of other ways to move the body. He stood up and walked over to her, "You need help?" She looked up at him with determination, "No, I got it." She stood back up as she finished and wrapped her hands around Rechnal's wrist. "Go ahead then," he said sarcastically. She braced herself and pulled at his wrist again. She groaned, and, again, the body barely moved. He didn't have to say anything for her to turn around and say, "Yeah, help would be great."

He smirked a bit and grabbed Rechnal's other arm. Seeing him with dead eyes on the ground, he felt a sense of relief. He had tried to avenge his own death, but he had failed. He had "killed" Magnus, but now, he was dead at his feet. This fact made him a bit joyful, but he still realized how fortunate he was to be alive. "You gonna pull?" she asked, annoyed. His eyes opened wide, "Sorry, yeah. Pulling." They both strained and pulled on his massive arms. Their mouths clamped together in grit, but it finally started moving.

"Yeah, yes, keep pulling," she said with a strained smile. After it had started moving, it became easier to drag. "Where are we going?" he managed to get out through his heavy breaths. "Just follow me," she reassured him. He didn't respond verbally, but he did give a quick nod. They both lowered their bodies to pull with all their strength.

The two eventually got the body out of the training room and into the hallway. "Left!" she exclaimed as they exited the doorway. They moved down the hallway until a faint bit of darkness crept across the walls. Then, she opened her eyes from the straining and saw the figure of the man on the ground.

"You killed them too?" she asked in an aggressive tone.

"They were trying to kill me. I only really wanted-," he defended.

"So, you killed them?" she interrupted a bit more aggressively. At this point, they had stopped moving the body and stood facing each other.

"Yes, but listen. I only wanted to kill Rechnal. They stepped in my way," he said.

She wasn't pleased with the answer, "You still killed them." He still had to defend himself.

"Yes, I did. I can't talk my way around that. But it had to be done for peace." She sat quietly with a blank face and thought, *Peace does take sacrifice.*

"If it had to be done, then the act is already done. All we can do is move forward. Peace takes sacrifice, and as painful as death is, it may have been essential," she said decisively. He sighed a breath of relief after extinguishing the situation, and she looked at the fallen.

"We will give them a proper burial, for their death is actually something to be mourned," she said seriously.

"What will we do with him?" He gestured his open hand toward Rechnal.

"We treat him like the worthless hunk he really is," she said coldly.

Her tone gave no room for remorse for her once king. He liked the way she spoke and realized she was serious about what she said about Rechnal. He was lost in thought until she snapped him out of it. "Grab the arm," she demanded. He quickly shook himself out and listened. He bent over and grabbed the dead wrist yet again.

They had to strain to get it moving again, but their journey wasn't much further. Finally, she turned her head and opened the door to her right. It opened to reveal the massive stone altar where Helpar was cremated not too long ago. It sat with the unlit torch on its side and a water bucket on the ground.

He stood in awe for a moment because he had never seen this room in his time living in the Berserker camp. "Move; let's go!" she yelled to snap him out of his glazed trance. He quickly grabbed Rechnal's arm and used his and Treni's collective strength to move the body to the foot of the altar. Once they got there, they dropped their arms and breathed a breath of relief. She put her hands on her hips, and he put his hands on his knees.

"How are we gonna move him on to that?" he asked through a fast-paced breath. She looked from Rechnal to the altar and back.

"We could start with the shoulders and work his body onto it."

"Yeah, that might work," he replied.

"What do I need to do?" he asked. He lifted his head, and she gestured to Rechnal's shoulder.

"Get under his back and pick him up as high as possible," she said.

He nodded and put his hands under the shoulder. He could already feel how heavy and difficult lifting it would be, but it wouldn't stop him. Before they lifted, she stopped, "Wait, flip him onto his stomach." He looked at her, confused and asked, "Why?"

She responded coldly, "Because I will not give this monster of man a proper funeral. It's a disgrace for anyone to be burned face down, and now we will do just that to him." He was taken aback. She finished and started to lift her side up, "Are you gonna help me?" she asked. He didn't respond but came to her aid and started lifting the side he was on. They labored over it, flipping it until they finally pushed it over. Their hands let go, and it flipped onto its stomach with a loud thud.

"Grab his arms again," she commanded. He followed suit. They spread the arms out wide, and each grabbed under the shoulder/chest area. "Ready?" she asked as she looked over. He gave an affirmative nod, and the two started to lift. They both lifted to the point where the head hung just below the altar's edge. "Just a little more," she struggled. They raised it all the way until Rechnal's face finally caught the edge of the altar. They moved their way down his body, slowly pushing it onto the altar. It took much longer than they thought, but eventually, they reached his legs and pivoted his body to line up straight with where the flame would erupt.

Finally, they got the body to rest perfectly. They let go, and she said, "Now we burn him." She started to walk away towards a cabinet on the other side of the room. "Where are you-?" he asked. But before he could finish his thought, she said, "To get the fluid to light his corpse." She opened the cabinet and took out the vase. She walked to the front of the altar and looked down at Rechnal's body. "For a king," she said mockingly.

While tilting the vase, the clear liquid poured over his body and into the hollow portion underneath. Once she figured there was enough fluid, she returned the vase to its cabinet and started to approach the altar. She said nothing, and her face was stern as she walked over to the side with the torch, grabbed it, and raised it above her head. "Your life will not be remembered as one of greatness but horror. You were a vile monster who craved violence like that of a true beast," she said, striking the ground and igniting the torch. "And may your soul take the most treacherous and vile path to the very place you belong, the pits of hell," she ended. She reached the torch to the liquid, which burst into flames that took no time to envelop his face.

Magnus was captivated by how much she hated him, and their views may not be as different as he thought. She said the words in such a way that expressed hate and suffering. It wasn't something anyone could feign.

She quickly dipped the torch into the water bucket, and a loud sizzle echoed under the blazing fire. She attached the torch to the side of the altar where the fire would dry it for its next use. The fire was quick and violent. It spread across Rechnal's entire body and melted the clothes from his skin. The smoke and stench caused both to start coughing. She quickly dashed over to the left side of the room and pulled a lever that opened a vent in the ceiling. The smoke quickly bellowed through it, and the two could breathe again.

The fire grew brighter and lit the whole room as the rest of Rechnal's clothes burned to ash and dust. The flame caused them to step back and cover their faces. They both stood watching the body burn, and a shared sense of resolve and relief entered. Then, she finally spoke in a mimicking way while holding an imaginary cup, "A toast! To the Berserker king! The man who couldn't avenge his father and the same man who killed his entire clan because of his thirst for blood. Well done, Rechnal, well done." She raised the cup toward Magnus, who conjured his own imaginary cup and toasted Rechnal's death.

They both drank from their cups, and she stomped her foot to the ground. "May hell treat you well," she said before settling back down. Like her, the fire was calming down as the last of Rechnal turned to ash. The fluid under him was running out, and his body was almost nothing but charred skin and bones. Her attitude returned, and she made one more mockery of the charred bones. She stepped towards the altar and said, "Here lies the king, the title that meant nothing for a beast." She bowed sarcastically and stood back up as the last of the fluid burnt away. No part of him except the ashes and bones that used to carry his massive frame remained.

Magnus was still stunned by how much she truly hated Rechnal but knew he agreed regardless. She turned to walk out the door and brushed past him. "What are you doing? Don't we have to clean up the bones?" he asked while turning around. She didn't even turn and said, "Move his bones to the center of the altar so they can fuel the next burning. Then, come grab these other bodies." He stood for a moment before shrugging and doing as she asked.

He carefully pushed what was left of Rechnal's bones into the area where more fluid would be. They clattered hollowly on the stone and came to rest.

Afterward, he quickly left the room and looked down the hallway to where she was already making progress on dragging one of the bodies. She looked at him and nodded toward the man's other arm. He went and grabbed it. They dragged it much quicker than Rechnal's and entered the altar room again. "Lift him up," she said. They both lifted and placed the body face-up on the altar. "Let me get the vase," she said after they got the body to rest. She stayed silent and grabbed the vase again. It only had about half its contents remaining, but it would be more than enough to burn the remaining Berserkers.

She walked back to the altar and poured it into the center space. Once she finished, she returned it to the cabinet and walked back out the door. "Aren't we going to burn him?" Magnus questioned. "Once we get all the others," she replied. She walked into the hallway, and he followed. They grabbed body after body and placed it onto the altar. It was massive enough to hold all of them, and eventually, they were stacked on each other. Limbs of some hung down from the pile, but, in the end, every man Magnus killed was there. It was somber for him to see the consequences of his actions. He wished killing all these men wasn't the only way he could've won, but it was.

She went to grab the torch and plucked it from its stand where it had dried out. She went to strike the ground to light it but suddenly stopped and turned. "Would you like to do the honors?" she asked, extending the torch to him. He looked at her extended arm and said, "Sure." He grabbed it from her hand and raised it above his head, "May your souls travel with haste, peace, and glory to eternal rest. Your death was my doing. For that, I offer a plea for forgiveness. A plea that will allow for peace inside of me, inside of this compound, and inside this decrepit city. Your death was my doing, as I said. So, rest, weary souls, and may you find the rest you deserve." He struck the ground, and the torch lit. He inserted it into the altar, and the fluid erupted under the bodies.

He quickly dunked the torch in the water and put it back on the altar's side before the flames overtook the pile of men. The bodies on the bottom caught alight, and the funeral had started. She sat in silence, mourning her fellow Berserkers that she was sad had to go. But she never knew these men well, so it was mostly a formality.

Magnus knew he had meant to slay these men, but now, a sense of remorse and regret washed over him. He wasn't sure why he felt pity and guilt for his actions, but he hoped giving them proper treatment would ease his mind. So, he sat with a restless but easing posture as the bodies roared into a flame, nearly reaching the room's roof.

She uttered her first word towards the pile of men, "Rest well." It was a quick and quiet moment of tribute. Then, she took her hand, placed it on her chest, and reached out. He looked confused but assumed it was a traditional gesture he had never learned. She put her hand back down without saying a word and calmly stood watching the fire. The light flashed on both their faces; it lit his left side while also lighting her right. The cracking overshadowed the silence from their mouths.

After some time, the clothes on the bodies were gone, and most of the actual skin was gone. It was a disturbing sight, so she took to one knee and rested her head on it. Confused, he did the same. "It's a final sign of reverence," she said in response to his confused look. "Oh," he mouthed. He also put his head down and sat there until she finally moved. She put her hand to her chest and rose without a word.

Then, she turned to him. "We're finished here; go handle your dead," she muttered as she walked from the room and down the hallway toward the training room. As she turned away, he asked, "The bones?" She stopped and stepped back into the room, "Leave them. They can remind us of what it takes to have peace." He sat with the comment and took another look at the remains of the men he had killed.

She was gone, and he was left with only himself and bones. Anything of Rechnal was entirely gone, and whatever was left on the altar was only the men from the hallway. He walked, and though the altar was still hot, he placed his left hand on it. It sizzled, and the pain shot toward his brain. His hand started to burn, and his arm was shaking. Then, through the heavy pain, he said to the bones, "Now I have felt a pain like yours." Even though he had died alongside them, he still felt guilty for being the only one who was given another chance.

He took his hand off and saw the burns. His hand was shaking from the searing pain, and blisters were already forming. But then, his sword started pulsing again, and the burns slowly disappeared. He turned his hand over to look at all sides, and his jaw hung open. "So, I, I just heal?" he said to himself. He turned and put his hand back on the altar. He gritted his teeth and watched it get burned worse than before. Finally, he couldn't bear the pain and yanked it away. It stung worse than he could imagine, but again, the sword began to pulse, and the burns went away. He made excited gasps since he couldn't really understand what was happening. He thought the healing was a one-time thing, but now he had some superpower. Any of the guilt he was feeling washed away as the excitement screamed through his body. He quickly calmed himself down and remembered the somber place he was in. He didn't have the time to explore his new ability fully, so he turned back to the remains, gave a bow, and walked back to the training room.

Once he entered, he found it empty except for Rain and Jasper's bodies. They had forgotten to get Jasper's body, so he looked for any sign of her but couldn't find Treni. "Treni!" he yelled into the room and down the hallway. It was quiet momentarily, but she yelled back, "What?!" She had left to ensure there were no leftover bodies from his killing spree. She started walking back toward Magnus, who was now in the doorway of the training room. Once she got there, he said, "We forgot him." He pointed to Jasper's body. She groaned as she saw it, "Come grab it." She walked past him and toward Jasper.

He followed as they went to pick up the old body. They each grabbed an underarm and started to drag him. He began to pull the body to the hallway when she stopped him.

"We're not burning him," she said plainly.

He was confused and asked, "What do you mean? We're not gonna burn him?"

She looked over toward the shattered window, "We're tossing him."

"Wow, that seems a bit worse than we treated Rechnal, so why are we tossing his guy and not him?" he asked. She pulled the body toward the window, and he followed. She grunted.

"Couple reasons. First, I'm not sure we could have thrown Rechnal, and second, I didn't want there to be a single piece of him. Even his corpse could remind people of him. Jasper, I never really cared about him."

He had no critiques and nodded in agreement. The two lugged it across the room and got to the window. The air rushing through the hole was warming up as the day's light was entirely on the city.

She dropped the body and said, "I'll get the legs. You stay with the arms." He quickly picked up the arm she had dropped and stood ready to throw. Then, she hoisted up the legs and said, "On three." "On three," he repeated back. "One, two, three," she counted, and on three, they let the body go. It broke more of the glass, but nothing much worse than Rechnal's ax had done. Magnus backed away, and she looked down to see the body fall out of sight.

Once it was gone, she said, "Now you can handle your dead." He turned and saw Rain lying lifeless and said solemnly, "I will. I'm gonna take him back to what's left of my home and burn his body there." She nodded in reverence, "Send him off well. I will check what my mother is up to with the children." She turned to the children's area, and he turned to a dead body.

* * *

She pushed the children's training door open and saw Medya talking with all the children sitting around her. Medya turned her head around.

"Treni, there you are. I was just telling them funny stories from when you were their age."

"Hopefully, nothing too embarrassing," Treni said with a masking smile.

Medya chuckled back, "Oh, it's just the story of you stuffing your face with trug when you were this tiny." She held her hand just above her waistline and turned toward the kids, "You should have seen her little cheeks."

They all laughed except for Qutir, who only gave a small chuckle. Seeing Rechnal's body had impacted him, and he had no answers for what happened outside of Treni's burst when he opened the door. She saw this and whispered into her mother's ear, "Let me talk with Qutir." She had assumed that seeing Rechnal had bothered him and wanted to discuss it with him. Medya nodded and said, "Qutir, go with Treni into your room."

He stood up quickly and looked from Medya to Treni and back again. He didn't say anything but turned and dashed into his room for her to follow. She looked at her mother with a look that seemed to ask for luck, and she left to follow him. Medya continued telling her stories that Treni was pretty sure she was exaggerating, but she didn't care as long as the kids laughed. She opened the door and saw Qutir already sitting on his bed with a tiny glare in his eyes.

She wasn't sure where to start with him, so she calmly sat down next to him. At first, he didn't say anything, so she started the conversation, "What's wrong, Qutir?" He wouldn't answer, and he turned his head away from her. She leaned across the bed and asked again, "What's wrong? Something is bothering you, and I'm trying to help you." He still didn't want to say anything and tried turning away even further. She then grabbed his shoulders and made him face her. He still tried moving his head away, but she grabbed it and turned it to her. "What's wrong?" she asked again with a hint of impatience.

He couldn't squirm his way out and finally decided to answer her, "Why was he dead?" His tone was as hurt as it was interrogative. She was ready for him to say something like this, but she wasn't quite sure what to say. She sat still and looked into his questioning eyes. She finally moved a bit closer and said, "Qutir, war leads to things that no one wants to see but that man-" "Rechnal?" he interrupted. She continued, "Yes, Rechnal. The war led us to this point, and people were lost that didn't have to be. But Rechnal, he was worse than you know. He took us further into the fighting than we ever had to be, and if I'm honest, he more than likely earned his fate. I hate to say it, but that's what I believe."

He got defensive, "He was our king!" She put her hands on his shoulders to calm him down and said, "I know, I know. But he was a monster, Qutir, a monster. He killed so many people, and now his reign is over." She took a deep breath and continued, "He was the reason for our fighting, and for that, he deserved his death." Still, he was unsettled. "But, but, he was a king," he stuttered. Then, she snapped back, "He was a king that had no real power. He killed people that had no business being killed." She silenced him with her little burst, and he failed to make a rebuttal. She saw his state, removed her hand from his shoulders, and said, "There you go. He was a bad person, and we can move on." He was still in a state of shock, but he lowered his head into her chest. He didn't cry or anything of the sort but let go of his resentment and fell into her arms.

She wrapped her arms around him and rocked him. She comforted, "It's okay. Death is never easy to bear, even for the ones who have seen it most." He still didn't cry or even whimper. He simply let out heavy exhales and sat in her arms. It was only for a moment because he lifted his head again and looked right at her. She asked him another question, "Does this all make sense?" He quietly nodded, and she put her arm on his back. "Let's go back with the others now," she told him positively. He nodded again and slid off the bed. She followed, and they walked to the door.

They walked back into the training room where Medya was still entertaining the kids, and their laughter rang across the room. He went and sat with the rest of them. He was still quiet but had a bit more clarity and agreement with what had happened that night.

"What story were you telling them now?" Treni asked with her feigned smile. Medya was in a happy mood that Treni couldn't interpret if it were real or fake. She assumed it was faked because her mother was already a bit more of a curmudgeon anyway, but she played along with a happy face.

"I was telling them about myself, actually," Medya said through her smile.

"Oh, which one?" Treni asked back.

"That time I was raising you and got so tired, I fell asleep on top of you!" Medya said while bursting into laughter.

All the kids laughed, and even Qutir let out a smirk. Holta shot her hand up and asked, "Was she okay?" Medya stopped laughing and pointed her thumb at Treni, "Her, okay? I think that's up to all of you to decide." She laughed at her own joke. Even though Treni was slightly offended by the joke, she had to admit it was funny.

She stepped back and said to Medya, "I'm starving, so I'm gonna go eat something. You take the kids until I get back and ensure Magnus is gone." Medya nodded and turned to tell another story. "Another one! Another one!" all the kids chanted as she took her first inhale. She started telling the story, and the room filled with more laughter. It was soon drowned out by the door to the room that blocked the noise from Treni's ears as she left to eat.

20

THE FINAL FUNERAL

As Treni went into the children's training room, Magnus went to stoop down to Rain's body. He knew he would need light when he got to level 87, so he went to the part of the training room where torches were stored. It was a small closet in the very back corner. He reached in, grabbed one, and shoved it into the folds of his clothes.

All the emotions tried to rush through his tired body, but he knew he had to take care of his brother. Rain was much lighter than all the Berserkers he had lugged through the hallways, so he was able to hoist him onto his shoulders and walk to the exit. He tried to keep himself collected and not break down from feeling the dead weight hanging from his shoulders, but it was near impossible. Tears started forming in his eyes, but he wiped them away every time and pushed on.

Finally, he made it out of the dark part of the hallway and walked into the king's chamber. It now had no owner, and its doors were breached. *What would past me think if I saw all this?* His mind raced with the idea as he stood in the exit's doorway for some time. It was the same doorway where he stood to start his whole journey, and it was where he stood near the end of it. It was poetic to him. Everything he fought for, his life, his family, his power, it all came back to this place. But unlike the last time, he would come back through these doors again under terms of peace.

Since the locks he had shattered were still broken, he almost opened the door too far. It bounced back from him opening it, and he caught it from slamming shut with his right foot. He looked outside at the city and the metal walkway before him. The daylight's reflection from the ground glared into his eyes, and he squinted to block it off. Once his eyes adjusted, he looked left and right and saw the alleys on either side.

He never saw people go there, but he did know people lived outside the compound's walls, and a moment of insignificance crashed over him. All his losses and all his pains were a speck within this city. It was so massive that he rarely saw anyone else outside their levels, and his whole life was built on only two compounds. It was a harsh realization, but he moved on.

Regardless of how small he felt, he had some purpose somewhere, and being brought back from the dead wasn't for the weak-minded. He took a deep exhale, and the feeling of insignificance left with it. He had to press on, so he did.

He stepped out onto the walkway in front of him, and he could see the shine of the metal on the platforms shimmering in the daylight. He walked closer and closer and closer and saw a few people on the platforms. He had always seen the city at night, so the idea of seeing it in the daylight was a bit different. He also wanted to keep as many people as possible from seeing Rain's body, but that would be nearly impossible. He was too tired to care anyway. So he walked normally and approached the walkway's end. As he was doing so, he saw people looking confusedly at Rain's body, but, in the end, they all seemed indifferent.

He continued standing with pairs of eyes glaring at him until he finally saw a platform slowing toward him. And once it reached him, he stepped on. Luckily for him, it was empty, and it slowly started to descend. After a moment, it sped up and started its journey back to level 87. It slowed at each level on the way down, and no one got on until a drunk man hobbled on at level 76. It was dark under the cloud layer, and the red and blue lights of the platform were the only light source.

The man stumbled on and started blabbering in an attempt to make a sentence. He closed in on Magnus and got touchy with him. Magnus quickly rejected this and pushed him to the rail.

"Woah, Woah!" he said as he held a weak hand to Magnus's face. "You think you can push me away!"

Magnus wasn't in the mood, so he quickly said, "I can, and I will so shut up." The man waddled over and tried to put another hand on him.

He blabbered, "My friend, it's not that personal."

His hand touched Magnus's chest, and Magnus snapped. He set Rain down and punched him square in the nose. The man's body violently folded and fell to the platform floor. He shook his fist off and wiped it on his clothes. He went to pick up Rain but realized it would be much easier if he waited until they reached level 87.

Once he passed what looked to be level 85, he bent down and hoisted Rain back onto his shoulders. The stench seemed worse than he remembered. It smelled like rot and decay, and that's precisely what it was. Unknown to him, all the bodies the Berserkers had disposed of were left on the ground to decompose. They had already started to rot in the time they had been resting, and it wouldn't get any better.

Finally, the platform came to a halt, and he looked into the dark. There was nothing for him to see, not even the teasing from the guards to comfort him.

He toughed out the smell, walked onto the floor, and saw what remained of his compound. He set Rain down, reached into the folds of his robes, and took out the torch. He struck it to the ground, and it burst into flames. The fire's crackle was the only sound, minus the dull sound of the platform's humming. There were other faint outlines of where old buildings used to be, but they had been destroyed by time. It was sobering, and he stood wondering what would have happened if he was in the compound that night. *I could have stopped all of this. I could have.*

He almost cried again until he pulled himself together and remembered he had a job to do. He carefully set the torch down and picked Rain up again. After another solemn breath, he walked toward where the old door used to stand. Only the frame was left, and the rest of the shambles cast shadows from the torchlight. It was ironic that the same

Berserker fire that burned the compound to the ground was now the thing illuminating its remains. It was still faintly smoking, and he had to watch his step not to step on hot embers.

He went to the leftover frame and put his hand on it. Its charred wood was flimsy, and he pushed it to the ground. He walked through where the doorway would have been and saw the remains of the giant door that had nearly fallen on him. It felt like ages ago when that had happened, but time moves differently when one is fighting for their life. He knew that fact and had to accept how quickly his world had changed. All he knew now was that he wanted to take care of Rain by giving him a proper cremation on the very throne his father used to sit in.

He cautiously stepped over planks and crumpled pieces of metal, all smoldering with remnants of fire. The path to the throne was long, and he wasn't even sure if it would still be there. But he hoped it was. He held the torch up, hoping to see a rough outline, but there wasn't anything for him to see yet. He kept treading through the rubble until he did see a faint outline. The left armrest was missing, and the back of the seat was barely visible. But now, he had an actual path to walk to instead of just guessing.

His next steps were very cautious. The floor under him creaked and groaned with each step, and holes/weak spots were everywhere. One misstep and his foot would be in a hole, Rain's body would probably fall from his shoulders, and his torch could relight the entire area. With every step, he placed his foot and pressed down to ensure the floor wouldn't crumple underneath him. He finally made his way to the center, where the throne's remains stood tall and eerily. The cracked obsidian stairs, broken from Rechnal's lethal throw, lead to the throne Rain had been placed into to die on. He looked over the edge of where the left armrest would've been and saw the jade spearhead. It was stuck in a pile of rubble, but he could just make it out. It was deformed since a piece of stone landed on it when he broke it through the throne. That stone saved a part of the blade from being completely incinerated. But otherwise, it was out of reach, so he figured he would leave it there as a memory. He took a moment's pause to mourn his father again, but he moved on quickly.

He went up the stairs and turned back to look at the rest of the rubble. Despair ran over his tired frame yet again. His life was different now, and he had to start accepting it. His time with the Devil's Hand, though shorter compared to his time as a Berserker, felt genuine. But now, it was over. *It really is gone, isn't it? What am I going to do now? It's all gone.*

After a moment of thought, he took a deep breath and turned back to the throne to finish his task. He carefully set the torch down so that he could have both hands on Rain. After he made sure the flame wouldn't burn anything else, he gently put Rain onto the throne. And after an awkward motion, his body was finally sitting upright. After moving his arms out from under him, Magnus picked up the torch, lifted his head back up, and looked into Rain's perished eyes. Immediately, flashbacks to the fire dashed through his mind, and all the memories he had made flashed before him. It was all in front of him now—all his struggle and fighting were represented in his brother's body. Tears formed in his eyes, and he put his left hand to his mouth to try to wipe away the imminent wave of sadness.

But it was in vain. His legs failed to support him, and he dropped to his knees. The cool air around him didn't help as he began to sniffle. He bit his tongue and shut his eyes in an attempt to stop his crying. *But why should I stop? There is no one around.* He lifted his head back up and saw Rain looking down at him. "I'm forever sorry," he said before tears and crying choked him up. He found a portion of rubble to stand the torch in so that it didn't burn anything else.

He was sobbing, but his voice broke through, and he said through ugly tears, "I'm sorry." He put his face to the foot of the throne and placed his left hand on it. He sniffled and gagged on his own sadness. Each breath was shakier than the last, and they all became shorter. This was pure emotion. This was like when Rain had first died in his arms. He managed to suppress it around Treni, but now it was emerging again. He couldn't control his own body, and his head seemed stuck to the floor as he flooded it with tears. His back and shoulders raised and lowered with breaths that left his lips in the form of agonizing sobbing, sobbing that would continue without words or relief.

His throat was aching, and his stomach churned, but he kept sobbing. He was unable to stop himself. Hours passed as he saw memories of Rain, his smile, his voice, all of him. But it was gone. All of it was gone. More time passed, and he couldn't even cry anymore, but he still sat, curled up, heaving every breath out. There were moments when the pain would stop, but as soon as he looked back up, it would come back worse. For the last portions of the day, he just sat with his back at the foot of the throne and felt numb. His closest friend, his brother, was gone, and he had no idea how to move on. His head leaned on Rain's leg, and he could smell the smokey scent from his clothing. He saw the fire again and the suffering it caused. *I could have saved them.* He couldn't overcome this thought. He blamed himself. He had nothing left to cry, but the numbness didn't leave. It wasn't much longer until he realized how long he had been sitting. He wasn't sure he wanted to stand up, but he knew he had to. It was the only thing he knew he had to do.

So, he raised his head again and locked eyes with Rain's closed eyelids. He had to turn his head away to prevent him from collapsing again. The dark outlines of the mangled building greeted his sorrowful eyes, and it almost caused him to break down. Everything overwhelmed him with sadness and grief, but he knew he had to finish what he had started.

He mustered all his strength, rose to his feet, and took another deep exhale to calm himself before facing his brother's corpse. He turned and stared at the body in front of him, but he stood tall. His resolve to finish the task was strong enough to keep him on his feet. He reached down, picked up the torch, and looked from it to its target and back again. He turned his eyes away and held the torch on Rain's stomach. "So, this is it. You fought well, brother," he said weakly. The torch caught Rain's clothes, and the fire slowly spread. He held it until the fire was sufficient on its own. He moved the torch away and held it by his side. A stoic look crossed his face but not for reasons of emotional conclusion. It was because he had no emotion left to show. He was truly and utterly devastated.

He stepped back and watched his brother's body burn away. The light flickered across the room and offered warmth in an otherwise cold moment. He didn't know how to express his feelings, but he tried, "I only knew you for a few years." His voice shook, and he was one breath away from falling again. But he continued, "But you were my brother. You, you were special. You were." He looked up and bit his lip again to hold back. His legs started to shake, and his stomach felt full of rocks. He dropped again to his knees, but this time, he still looked at that body in front of him. His lips were already shaking, "It should've been me! Why wasn't it me?!"

He pushed his hands into the ground and started crying again. This cry wasn't as fierce as the last, but the emotion still controlled him. There weren't many tears either, for his eyes had run dry. So, he sat heaving gasps of air with the occasional drop from his face. Small tears rolled down and fell to the ground. The body burned brighter, the skin was starting to burn away, and he just sat there, powerless to stop his emotion. The fire kept crackling, and he sat helplessly under its light.

He stayed there and cried until the body was nearly gone. And by the end, he was simply holding himself in a small ball to comfort himself. He hadn't wished to take the position again, but it was all he could do. Rain's skin was burnt and unrecognizable, and the clothes were incinerated. The stone beneath the body was even a bit charred, but it was still relatively unmarked.

He sat with his head buried in his chest, all while the same realization crashed over him. He'd lost his family, his home, and now, he was alone. He had to survive independently, which frightened him a bit. However, he had a moment of resolve that cleared his mind. *I am the boy who ran away from the Berserkers and survived in the city. I've defeated Helpar and Rechnal. Some sort of magic resurrected me. I'm alive, and there is something special about that.*

Afterward, he raised his head again because he knew he had to keep going. He couldn't just sit in a crippled ball. He had to keep moving. The fire lit a single tear that ran down his face. It would be the last tear he would shed, and as it fell to the ground, he used all his strength to stand back up again.

Even though Rain's body was unrecognizable and nearly gone, he still spoke to it, "Thank you, Rain. What you did changed me. My gratitude is something I can't fully express." He paused and let in another deep breath. He sat and watched the last bits of the body turn to ashes and marks that faintly stained the throne. "May you find the rest you deserve. I loved you, brother," he said. He watched the last of the flame die out, and the room became lit solely by his torch. He took one last look at the throne, "Goodbye, Rain." He paused again and took another deep, full breath before finally turning his back to the throne and walking down the obsidian stairs one last time.

21

DISCOVERY AND RECONCILIATION

He carefully walked, torch in hand, down the stairs and faced the dangerous floor ahead. It wouldn't be as hard to traverse now that Rain wasn't on his shoulders, but he still had to be very careful. He watched each step and prodded the ground to prevent him from falling. The floor creaked and groaned under his weight, but each step was safe enough. He crept his way back, and luckily, the distraction of watching his feet kept him from looking back.

He made his way to where the old dining table had been, and it seemed no different from the rest of the destruction. He walked on until he tapped the ground to ensure his next step was safe and heard a hollow sound from below. He tapped again, and another hollow sound echoed into his ear. He tilted his head inquisitively and whispered, "What?" He tapped and tapped, and the same echo bounded to his ears. He had never noticed this before, nor did Patri mention anything about something under the compound.

His curiosity took over, and he seemed to forget everything that he just went through. His body was exasperated, but his mind was firing. He wasn't sure how long his body would allow him, but he wanted to see at least what was under his foot. He started to pound into the floor, and the sound came back louder. "Come on," he whispered with a grunt. The floor seemed stronger as if it was reinforced by something; or protecting something. But finally, his foot cracked it.

He gasped in excitement, but suddenly, a wave of exhaustion caught up to him. His head rushed, his eyes felt heavy, his legs turned to rods, and he nearly fell back over; however, he was able to catch himself. He wobbled before shaking it off and letting his curiosity reign once more. He still needed to know what was under him.

He gave the ground all his force, and it cracked more and more. Excitement filled his weary, tear-stained eyes. And finally, after four more kicks, the floor gave in, and his leg went through. He didn't have time to react, so he closed his eyes, and a quick grunt left his mouth as his foot hit what he assumed to be ground. And when he opened his eyes again, he saw that the hole had engulfed most of his leg. The shattered wood around it scraped him a bit, but he was already so beaten and bruised it felt like nothing. He lifted himself out and went down to his knees to get a closer look. He couldn't see anything right away, so he reached the torch toward the hole. It wasn't big enough for him to put his head in, so he slowly stuck his hand in.

"Impossible," he whispered as he felt what he never thought he would, the ground of Carenth. The brown dirt was an amazing sight for a man who had seen only cold metal and lights his whole life. He stuck his arm further in, felt the soil, and ran it between his fingers. He smiled wide. The dirt got in between his hands and under his fingernails. It was such a raw feeling, and he loved every second of it.

He had to have more, so he took his hands and started breaking off more pieces of the reinforced flooring. His attempts were unsuccessful, so he stood back up and started kicking again. The wood splintered under his feet, and after a while, the hole was large enough for him to squeeze his head through. He dropped to his knees and peered in.

He couldn't make anything out from the torch's dim light outside the hole, so he held it closer. He still couldn't see quite enough, so he took his head out and put the torch in. After, he slowly lowered his head in for a better look. It finally illuminated the area of the ground underneath the hole, which was larger than he initially thought. He looked around again, and something caught his eye.

He had to know what he was seeing, so he got onto his stomach and reached his head as far as he could. He walked the torch along the ground, careful not to catch the floor above it on fire. He was looking back to make sure his stomach was sliding in without breaking the floor when the torch ran into something. It made the faintest of echoes. He jolted his head back to see whatever it was he had hit.

His jaw dropped, and he nearly let go of the torch as his eyes saw what he couldn't believe. There was a metal handle that was attached to a rusted metal hatch. His mind started to race. *What is it? How long has it been here? Who built it?* He moved the torch around to see how large the hatch was. It was about four times his size. He always knew he wasn't the biggest, but an underground hatch that size felt a bit unnecessary.

It had remnants to paint or marks, but nothing he could make out or understand. The hinges were rusted, but the handle was in decent shape. After looking around a bit more, he reached for it. It was an awkward stretch to get his hand to it, but he managed. His arm was fully extended as his fingers wrapped around it. He pulled, and nothing happened. A faint echo rattled the door, but it was stuck in place. He tilted his head at the sound but figured it wasn't important.

He wasn't sure if it was locked or just rusted shut, so he pulled again. It still didn't budge, so he yanked again and again. It must've been locked. *Why would it be locked from the inside?* He kept giving pulls, hoping it would just pop open, but there was no result. *What if I cut through it? I did it to the Berserker door, and that was much stronger. So, this should work.* He stuck the torch into the ground and got it to stand straight up. He started to back out of the hole to reach for his sword.

As he did, he heard something from inside. It was like the sound of breathing, almost guttural. He stopped and lowered himself back down to hear whatever it was. But, it had stopped, and he assumed he had heard things. So, he continued to reach for his sword so he could try to open the door. It was quiet until, suddenly, whatever was inside rammed against the door. Dust flew into the air. "Ahhh!" he screamed. The bash startled him, and he smacked his head on the floor above him. "Gah!" he yelled as he pulled himself out. His head started pounding with pain. But at the same time, he was wondering what was behind that door. He thought he could still hear the heavy breathing from underneath, so he scooted back.

But before he could get back to the hole, it pounded again, and he shot back further. His curiosity became stained with fear, yet he was still captivated by what he had found. He tried to lean himself back forward but felt pain from where he had hit his head. He put his hand up to it and felt the warm feeling of blood he was all too familiar with. "Damn it," he said. But as he brought his hand back, he saw his blood was shimmering gold in the dim torchlight. And not much after, the sword started to pulse in its sheath again. The wound sealed itself back, and the pain started to subside. But the impact still ratted him. He realized how tired he was and that trying to start another adventure that evening wasn't the right thing to do. He was reluctant to give up, and he was a bit disappointed; however, he didn't want to put himself in any more danger.

So, carefully, he stuck his hand back down into the hole and grabbed the torch from its place in the ground. The sound from inside the hatch had quieted down, but he knew something else was there. He also knew he would come back to find out more, but today wasn't that day.

He stood up, and his head rushed. Then, he balanced himself out with his hands and started carefully making his way back toward the outside of the compound. Once he could feel the air from outside, he noticed it was much cooler than when he first came down, and because of this, he knew that night was upon Uguria.

He was faster leaving than he entered, and his steps were harsher, but he was still careful. The floor creaked underneath him, but nothing broke. He made his way back to where he knocked over the door frame and kept walking back onto the metal outside. The idea of what was behind that door ate at him, almost making him forget about the entire time he had been balling at the foot of the throne. But Rain's death would always sting, and he wasn't sure if he would ever recover.

Then, he saw the platform's light starting to blink in front of him and knew it was finally time to leave. He looked back and sighed deeply, "I will miss you." He wasn't sure if he was speaking to Rain, the compound, or both. Regardless, he meant it. Finally, he turned around and stepped onto the platform, and it began its long journey back up.

* * *

Treni left the children's room and saw that Magnus had left. She quickly went back inside and whispered to Medya, "He's gone, but give me a minute by myself to just relax." Medya nodded and turned back to the kids, "Okay, it's time to start some training. Today will just be a short exercise day. How does that sound?" They all groaned a bit, but they stood up and got ready. She turned back to Treni, "I've got them. Go have your time." "Thank you," Treni whispered as she went for the door again.

She left quickly and went right to the dining area. She noticed the machine had made a yogurt parfait topped with beautiful fruit. She got excited and grabbed two before sitting alone at one of the tables. The parfaits disappeared as she devoured both of them with ease. She wiped her face with her shirt and went back to grab another. Something about the delicate nature of the parfait was very appealing to her, so after the third, she grabbed a fourth. She didn't bother to sit back down because it only took a few large bites to get it down.

After the fourth vanished, she put all the dishes back and almost returned for a fifth before stopping. "You've had enough," she told herself. It was difficult for her to resist the urge, but she did. She then went to sit down at one of the tables and just unwind from the stressful day. She sighed as she sat and rested her face in her hands.

Her mind was still processing everything that had happened to her and what it meant for her future. Peace was now on the table. Her new life had unlimited potential, yet she felt lost. She didn't know where to go or what to do, and it was slowly creeping through her mind. The old plan for her life that she despised was gone, but deep down, she wished that sense of security was still there. She wouldn't have to worry if her entire life was planned, but now, her life was all she could worry about.

On top of that, trusting Magnus was risky, and she wasn't sure how much he meant anything he said. But there weren't any other real options. There was one good way all this ended; peace would win over everything else. She knew she wanted it and hoped he wanted the same. It was a grim future ahead, but she knew that if she could maintain peace, it would be better than any future of war. That much was a fact. She had been sitting longer than she had planned before she remembered that Medya and the children were waiting on her. The daze she put herself in made her completely forget about anything else.

"The kids," she whispered. She popped up from her seat and started for the door. It didn't take her long to get back to the children's room but walking across the eerily quiet main training room with a shattered window was still unsettling. It caused her to pause again and realize her monumental morning. It was over now, but the sight of the bodies strewn across the floor still burned in her head. She didn't sit on it too long before shaking it off and turning for the children's door.

She carefully opened it, hoping not to disturb anything Medya was doing. And when she did, she saw all the children doing jumping jacks that Medya was counting off. They were on their own exercise mats made of a furry yet bouncy surface. "89, 90, 91," Medya and all the children counted as their breaths grew heavier. She kept counting as she turned around to look at Treni. Her face lit up. "Qutir, continue until all of you reach 150," she told the group. He immediately raised his voice and started counting, "102, 103, 104." She turned to Treni and started in a whisper.

"Has he come back yet?"

"Not yet," Treni responded.

She changed the conversation quickly so the kids wouldn't get suspicious, "On a more important note, what's the food like today?"

"Oh, it was delicious. It's parfaits with fruit," Treni said lightly.

"That sounds pretty good, actually. I'll take the kids when they're done," Medya smiled.

She turned around as Qutir gasped, "150!" The kids all stopped and put their hands on their hips or knees to catch their breaths. She looked around the room and saw that the children really were tired, "Everyone! To the dining hall!"

They all perked up and got themselves ready to leave. As they cleaned their things, Treni went to talk again. "What exactly did you make them do?" she asked. Medya smiled proudly, "100 push-ups, 100 sit-ups, 50 squat jumps, and those 150 jumping jacks." Treni stood shocked for a second because she never made them do that much. Then, she said, "Wow, that's, that's something." Medya smiled and nodded. She then turned back to the children.

"Alright, let's go!" she yelled. They all finished and gathered by the door. "Everyone here?" she asked while looking over all the little heads. She counted all six kids and opened the door. They all funneled out, and Treni made sure to block their view of the window. She wasn't ready for them to figure out what had happened just yet. She planned to tell them all once they got back from their late lunch.

In the end, she did enough, and the children went into the dining hall unfazed. They all lined up and grabbed their parfaits. She considered grabbing another, but the previous four kept her satisfied. So she went to her table and waited for Medya to grab her food and sit beside her. All the kids sat at their seats and started enjoying their food. "No more than two parfaits!" Medya yelled across the room as she watched Qutir leave the machine with one in each hand. She finally got her food and sat next to Treni. She took her first bite and said, "Hmmm, that's not bad at all." She picked up the cup it was in and admired it.

"I wonder what's in this."

"It's just a parfait. It's not that special," Treni said back.

Defensively, Medya retorted, "It just tastes good, that's all. No need to get all critical."

"Fine, fine," Treni said as she put her hands up playfully.

Medya kept eating the food, and all the children talked with full mouths. They all enjoyed their meals, and their empty, clear cups started to litter the tables. They all ate two of the parfaits, and they were satisfied after a good workout and a meal.

"How long are we staying here?" Medya asked Treni.

"Just a bit longer. I want to give them time to recover after you killed them," Treni answered sarcastically.

Medya scoffed, "If you think that's killing them, you clearly don't remember what we did with you."

"Well, I do, and that's why I'm trying not to make them do the same," Treni quipped.

Medya smirked, "It all worked out for you. Didn't it?"

Treni crooked her head, "I mean, sure. If you say so." Afterward, she got up and went to talk to the kids, but more importantly, Qutir.

He felt a tap on his shoulder and turned his neck to see which one of his friends was messing with him. He was surprised to find Treni looking down at him. She signaled him to follow, so he stood up and did as he was asked. "You okay?" she asked him. He checked over his shoulders, "Yeah, I'm okay. Are you gonna tell everyone else about what happened?" She looked over her shoulders and answered, "I'm telling them when we return to your rooms." He looked at her as if he was waiting to hear more. She saw the look and patted him on the shoulder while saying, "Alright, you can head back now if you want. I was just checking in." He nodded and turned back to the table where he could rejoin his friends. She smirked and went to sit with Medya.

"What was that about?" Medya asked. "I was just checking in on him," Treni answered. Medya shrugged it off as she finished the last spoonful of her parfait. Then, she suggested, "Let's get them back to finish their training for the day." "Good idea, and let's get them to sleep early cause I'm exhausted," Treni agreed.

They both nodded, and Medya went to put her dishes away. She put her dishes into the space next to the machine which got ready to wash them. Then, she turned back to the group and commanded, "Finish up; we leave soon." The kids scrambled to get the last of their food down and hopped up to put their dishes away. Treni got up slowly and walked to the door to lead everyone out. She was thinking about how she could hide the window, but she was about to tell them about it anyway, so she figured it was okay if they saw it. They all lined up behind her, with Medya behind all of them. "Let's go!" she yelled. Treni opened the door. Finally, they all filed out and quickly walked back to the children's room.

As they were walking, most of the kids were watching their feet take the next step, except for Sid. He was at the back of the line and stopped when he saw the broken window. Medya bumped into him and nearly fell over. "Keep walking, Sid," she told him. He didn't move. Then, he raised his hand to point at the window and asked, "What happened?" All the kids lifted their heads and saw the shattered glass. They started to whisper among themselves about what they thought had happened.

"Quiet!" Treni yelled over all of them. They all immediately shut up and looked at her. "I'll tell you what happened when we get into the room, so keep moving," she said. They followed her order and made their way back into their training area.

Once they all arrived, Medya shut the door, and Treni said, "Everyone sit down. I'll tell you what happened." They all sat quickly and turned their attentive eyes to her. Medya went and sat behind all of them and also looked at her with a similar look. She began, "Okay, a lot happened while you were sleeping. Qutir and I already talked about some of it because he saw it before the rest of you. But, in short, war killed everyone. Rechnal, our old king, was killed fighting Magnus Aureum. That's also why the window you all saw was shattered. They had a brutal fight, which Magnus won. I'll get back to this, but I have given him a chance to come and stay with us because his home was destroyed in this war."

All the kids were confused by the fact that the man who killed their king could be coming to live with them. She saw their confusion and went to address it quicker than she thought she would've had to, "Rechnal was an evil man. He led this clan to do evil things. He killed all of Magnus's family and burned his home to the ground. He was avenging his family, and that's something all of you know to be worthy. We are built on ideas of loyalty, and if someone came and killed all the people sitting next to you out of nowhere, you would probably fight back, right?" All the kids slowly nodded in agreement. She nodded along with them and continued, "I know it's a lot to hear, but everything is going to be okay. I have made peace with Magnus, and the fighting that brought him here in the first place is over. I'm sorry I had to tell all of you like this, but this is super important for me and for all of you."

They all stared blankly at her until Holta's hand went up. "Yes, Holta?" Treni asked. "So, he killed our people? And we're letting him live with us?" Holta asked with concern. The kids all seemed to be asking the same question, and most of them nodded along. Treni held her hand out and answered, "I know, I know it sounds crazy, but he didn't just come to kill us. He was distraught and wanted to avenge his people. It will take time, but we have a chance to create a new peace our people haven't seen in ages." Holta was still skeptical, but she went along with the answer.

Then, Sid raised his hand. "Sid?" Treni answered. "Where is he gonna stay?" he asked. She went to respond but realized she didn't have an answer. She paused to think and finally said, "Um, uh, we will give one of the old rooms in the main hallway. I'm not sure which one yet, but we'll get him one." He had another question and didn't bother to raise his hand before asking, "Where is Magnus anyway?" She paused to think before answering, "He's tending to his brother, who got killed in this mess. We weren't the only people that lost someone."

The last line resonated with the kids, and their questioning stopped. They sat still, looking at her, waiting for her to say something else. Then, Medya stood from the back and broke the silence by saying, "Let's get back to work. We have a bit more training to do, and then we're going to get ready to sleep." The kids all groaned, but they got to their feet. "Line up," she told them. They all listened and got in line. She commanded, "We're going to focus on throwing today. I know we did this not too long ago, but it still needs some work. Go grab your weapons."

They all went to grab their daggers, and she leaned over to Treni, "Can you help move the dummies?" "Of course," Treni said before moving to get the dummies into place. They had three dummies and two children in front of each. Once Treni had finished putting them in place, Medya said, "Make sure the path is clear when you throw." She continued, "Treni and I will be behind you correcting your form and such. Once we move, you start." The three in the front of their lines got ready for the throw, and Medya, with Treni, moved out of the way.

"Begin!" Medya yelled across the room. They all threw the first wave of daggers, and Qutir was the only one who hit the target. He hit the dummy in the lower right abdomen. Medya walked behind the first thrower, a girl named Wink, and reached for her arms. She instructed, "You need to stabilize your arms. You see how your arm finished all the way to your side?" She nodded, and Medya started talking again, "If you throw it a bit earlier, it will fly much smoother." "Okay, okay," Wink responded.

Next was Holta, whose dagger fell short of the target. Medya told her, "I know you're the youngest here, so keep working on your strength because otherwise, your throw was accurate." Holta nodded and walked behind her partner.

Next, Medya addressed Qutir, "Qutir, you're the oldest, so I expect you to hit the target, but I'm going to say the same thing I said to Wink. You let go of the dagger a bit too late, and it brought the dagger to the side and low." He nodded as he plucked his dagger from the dummy and walked behind Sid.

The next of the kids threw, and the results were similar. Sid was the only one who hit the dummy in the leg, while the others simply missed. They repeated the process over and over again until it was time to get another meal and get ready to sleep.

The kids were worn out from all the throwing when Medya raised her hand, "Stop!" The last dagger landed on the dummy, and all the children looked to her for instruction. She yelled, "Dinner time! Line up!" They all listened quickly and got ready to leave. "We're not going anywhere until we all clean up the mess you made," she told them. They all ran across the room, cleaning and moving dummies back to their places until the room looked like no one had ever been in it.

"Much better," Medya said as she looked at the children's work. Then she looked toward Treni and told her, "Grab the door for us." She listened and opened the door for all the children to walk out. All the kids murmured about what could be for dinner tonight. Qutir hoped it was either trug or yut, while most of the others wanted something like the parfaits they had for lunch. They also hoped that dessert would be an option because the machine would rarely make a dessert. But when it did, they would always devour it.

They got to the dining hall and eagerly ran to the machine. Qutir pumped his arm in celebration because that night's menu was freshly made yut with a side of kipply beans, a stringy bean with a curvy stalk and purple hue. The others groaned but still filled their plates to ease their hungry stomachs. Once they all got their food, Treni and Medya got their plates and stacked them up.

Yut was a very hefty food, yet Treni was ready to eat mounds of it. Something about everything that had happened still starved her, so she indulged. They all ate quietly, with Qutir and Treni digging through their portions. Medya didn't complain, but she was a slow eater.

The other kids ate light or played with the kipply beans to avoid eating them. Medya saw their empty forks and corrected them, "Eat the kipplys. They are great for you and will fill you up. No one goes back until they have at least three bites of them." The kids wanted to refuse, but also, they wanted to sleep. So, they forced the beans down and washed the taste away with tall glasses of water. "Very good," Medya said as she watched them go ahead and clear their plates of the kipply beans, except for Holta, who had taken her three bites and wanted nothing to do with taking another. Medya didn't feel like pestering her about it, so she let her leave her plate a bit full.

They all sat and ate until Medya finished her meal. Since she was usually the slowest eater in the group, it was always annoying for everyone to wait for her. "You almost done?" Treni asked impatiently. She slowly swallowed and wiped her face from her last bite, "I am now." She stood up and walked her plate back to the machine for it to be washed. "Let's go!" she yelled. The kids all turned their attention and registered what she said. They were all ready to leave, so it took them no time to all line up at the door. "The door," Medya told Treni. She propped it open, and all the children walked out. She carefully shut it behind them and walked to the back of the line. They all made the short walk back, and Treni paused when she saw the window. It was getting darker out, and it would be night by the time the children were cared for. Then, she could finally get the rest she needed.

After they headed inside their room, she said, "Showers, and make sure to clean yourselves." With the sound of light footsteps, they all shuffled to the showers, splitting girls and boys. The sound of running water echoed through the room, and she returned to the training area, where she found Medya sitting on a dummy she had tilted over. "Come sit," Medya told her. She hesitated, "Why?" "No reason," Medya responded. She was still hesitant, but she listened.

The two sat together until the sound of running water started to slow. Medya heard it and figured it was time to speak. She asked, "Are you okay?" Treni looked at her mother longingly. She knew she wasn't the definition of okay, but she didn't know how to explain it. She had witnessed lots of death and made peace within the same day. She had more uncertainty now than she ever really had, and a part of her still wondered if she was making the right choice in any of it. She didn't realize it, but the question had put her into a trance where she just stared. "Treni? Treni?" Medya snapped. Her name woke her, and she said, "I'm fine, really. It's just been a long day." Medya nodded, "If you say so. I'm gonna go make sure they're all dressed and ready to sleep." She stood up from the dummy and walked into the bedroom. Treni quickly followed to feel useful. The more she sat around, the more she remembered the day.

Sid and Wink were the first to come out from their respective sides, and Medya guided them to their beds. She tucked them in and wished them a good night's sleep before turning off their lamp and returning to Treni.

"That was really fast," Treni said, surprised.

Medya looked at her, confused, "You do more?"

Treni quickly responded, "Of course I do. I always tuck them in and talk with them about their days."

"Goodness, you really do treat them soft," Medya teased.

As they finished, Holta walked out, and Treni went to get to her before Medya could. "I got her," she said while rushing past Medya. "Fine, fine," Medya said as she threw her hands up. After she walked off with Holta, all the other boys, except Qutir, came out and were escorted to bed by Medya.

Treni slowly walked Holta to her bed and tucked her into the sheets. She hopped onto the end of the bed and asked, "You okay after everything today?" Holta was a bit thrown off by the question, but she answered the best she could, "I'm okay. It's still confusing; we're letting him stay here?" She rolled deeper into the sheets, and only her little hands stuck out from under the covers. Treni calmly said, "I know it is, but I think it could really help us over time. And there's no reason to fear him. He's a good person, and we're gonna figure everything out. Okay?" Holta quietly nodded and rolled to her side. Treni felt the conversation was over and said, "Sleep well, Holta. I'll see you in the morning."

She slipped off the edge of the bed and turned the lamp off. She walked back to the doorway where Medya was already standing with her hands on her hips.

"Took you a minute, didn't it," she teased.

Treni rolled her eyes, "Sure, but she actually feels cared for."

Medya just shrugged it off, "I still haven't seen Qutir, and to be honest, I'm getting tired. So, could you wait for and take care of him in because I think I need to go to bed."

"Of course, go get some sleep," Treni said back.

"Thanks," Medya answered as she walked off to her room.

Treni stood and waited for a while before Qutir finally rounded the corner. "There he is," she whispered to herself. She walked over to talk to him, but he seemed uninterested. He walked to his bed, turned off the light, and rolled into his covers. Perplexed, she walked to sit on his bed and talk with him. She hopped on and felt him shift away from her. "It's okay, Qutir. You don't have to run from me," she said, trying to comfort him. He just shifted again, and she concluded they wouldn't have a meaningful conversation that night. So, she got off the bed, and as she walked away, she said, "It will all work out. I promise. Sleep well. We will talk in the morning because I'm not letting you ignore me forever." He just shifted again and drifted off to sleep not too long after.

She walked out of the bedroom, quietly shut the door, and made sure to straighten any of the mess the kids left behind, but there wasn't much to clean up except a few daggers someone had kicked out of the way while trying to get in line for dinner. She put them away and went to leave the room. Her bed sounded so comfortable, and she was more than ready to shower and sleep. But she still had to wait for Magnus to return. She figured she could shower and then return to the training room to wait on him. So, she walked to her room, which wasn't too far down the hall.

She went into her bathroom and started to undress. The same clothes she had collapsed in the day before felt nasty and taking them off was a major relief. She turned on the shower to a scorching temperature. She had always loved scalding showers since she was little and figured there wasn't a time as good as then to have a relaxing time. When she felt that the water was as hot as she loved it, she knew that it was about to be perfect.

She stepped in, and the water running down her body felt amazing. The drops falling from her hair felt rejuvenating. She was still exhausted, but the shower did give her a breath of life. There was no rush to get out, so she washed everything twice and spent time just sitting under the water pondering what she had done. She had made peace, and for that, she was proud. *But was it worth it?*

That question nagged at her, and she knew there wasn't a clear answer yet. Time would unravel her decisions and judge whether it was the right or wrong thing to do. That was the pain of her choice. What she did that day would reap its consequences much later than she wished. But the time would move on its own, and her power to stop it was minimal. She could only really go with her choices and see what path they led her to. So, after the moment of deep thought, she tried to ignore what had happened that day and take the relaxing shower she needed.

22

THE GILDED BOY

Magnus was alone on the platform for many levels and stood with a surprisingly empty mind. The pure and raw devastation he experienced left him completely void, even after his short discovery. He didn't know what exactly to think, so he didn't. He sat, growing increasingly tired. What he found had excited him, but the feeling was wearing off.

The ride was long and slow, but it was making its way. He passed level 71 and its black clouds and could tell it was still early in the evening. He kept riding alone until the platform slowed on level 54. An older lady walked on and stood next to him. She was quiet for a few levels until she got a good look at his clothes under the light of one of the flower pods. They were covered in gashes and burn marks and stained with blood and ash. "Oh my, what happened to you?" she prodded at him. He wasn't in the mind space to have an entire conversation, so he tried to make it as short and dry as possible.

"Had a work incident. I work down on the metal processing floor on sixty-seven. We had someone put a piece in the furnace wrong, and the sparks went everywhere. The roof caught on fire, and we all ran for our lives." She put her hand to her mouth but quickly removed it.

"That's some story, but why is there blood?" He scrambled to think of an answer.

"My friend, he was a great person, but I couldn't save him. A piece from the roof fell and hit his head, and he bled out in front of me."

He tried to make it look like he was crying, but it was an abysmal effort. The dim evening light must have been enough for her to believe him because she bought on and nearly started to cry with him.

"I'm so sorry," she said. "No, no, it's alright. It'll take time to adjust, but I'll recover," he sniffled. He stopped his forced sniffling, and it became real as he realized he was talking about Rain. Questions about whether he could move on and recover flew through his mind. Doubt ran rampant through his head until he felt the lady's warm touch. "It'll be okay. I lost my husband a while ago in a devastating way. It will be okay. I promise," she said in the most reassuring tone he had ever heard. Somehow her words and touch calmed him, and his sniffling faded. He wasn't quite sure how she did it, but it was a marvelous feeling. "Thank you," he said while he wiped his face.

She kept her hand on his shoulder until he finally asked, "What's your name?" She still held her hand on his shoulder.

"It's Elia."

"That's a beautiful name," he said.

"Thank you, young man," she answered. Then, she quicky asked, "Where are you headed?" He had to think of a reason to go back to level 42.

"I have some other friends that live on level forty-two that said they would help me if something happened, so I'm holding them to their word."

She chuckled, "Well, if they don't hold their word, you have a place with me up on level thirty-three. I was just visiting my son, so that's why I was down on fifty-four, in case you were wondering."

"Thank you, Elia. This means more than you know," he said.

She looked into his devastated eyes and reached into her pocket. She extended her hand and said, "Here, take this. It was my husband's, and he told me to give it to someone who deserved it. Something tells me he was talking about you."

She opened her hand and inside was a pendant. It hung from a gold string and had a chiseled piece of wood on it. It was small, and the carvings were something like a face. It had sunken-in sides and little markings and scratches all over. Whatever it was, it had been worn over time. Even the little dents made for the eyes of the face looked more pronounced. It was like it had seen everything he had. He flipped it in his hands and looked back at her, "Thank you, but you don't need to do this." She smiled, "Take it, I insist. I have no use for it, and it will fulfill my husband's last wish." He couldn't deny a man's final wish, so he put the pendant around his neck and tucked it into his shirt. "Thank you, really," he said. He reached out and gave her a light hug. "It's my pleasure," she said.

They were nearing level 42, so he ensured his sword was strapped to his waist and looked upward to the metal ring he would get off on. "Good luck," she said as he stepped off the platform. "It was great to meet you," he yelled as the platform started to speed off. "And you as well," she responded.

The platform went off into the night, and he hoped he'd see her again. But for now, he wanted to get back inside, shower, and rest. He walked into the compound and through the broken front doors. He walked back through the hallway, which was still creepily dark, and toward the main training room.

* * *

Prior to him entering the compound, Treni had finished her long, much-needed shower and got herself into comfortable clothes. She still had to wait on him, but that didn't stop her from being ready to sleep as soon as he returned.

She entered the training room and looked out at the window overlooking the city. It was chaotic out there, but it was her home. She had lived, fought, and worked to live here, and now she could leave her mark on it. She didn't want to overpower or overthrow; instead, she wanted to help the city and try to fix the problems she had the power to fix. She stared and watched the platforms go up and down, with a couple of people on one of them every once in a while, until she heard the door open behind her.

She quickly turned around and saw Magnus walkthrough, "There you are," she said. "Where do I go?" he said directly. He didn't want any small talk except that which related to him finding a place to wash off and sleep. She read his mood and said, "Follow me."

She walked back out to the hallway until she got to a room on the left and opened the door. She walked in and clicked on the lamp, which sat next to a massive bed with navy bedding. She turned around and said, "The room used to belong to Frory, but he's not around anymore, so it's all yours. There should be some clothes in the drawers in the dresser, and if they're too big, I'll get you more tomorrow. And the shower is in there." She gestured to the bathroom and reassured him, "Just make yourself at home. It probably feels wrong to be back here, but it's all we have, so hopefully, it's enough." He looked around the room, and the bed, though it wasn't his own, it called for him to lay in it. He said, "It's all great. It really is. Thank you, Treni." She smirked lightly and said, "You're welcome. Now, I'm tired, so I'll leave you to your business."

She went to walk out of the room when he remembered what he had found on level 87. "Treni, I want to tell you about something I found," he told her. She turned in the doorway and asked, "Can it wait for tomorrow?" He thought about it for a moment and knew he was just as tired as she was, and starting a conversation like that would be significant. And an important conversation wasn't what he thought was best to have right then. "It can. I'll tell you tomorrow," he finally said. "Okay, I'll see you then," she said as she shut the door behind her.

She walked down to her room and went inside. She sighed as the door shut behind her. The day had been long and slow, and now, she finally got to rest. Her mind was still flooded with questions and ideas about what this new peace would entail and whatever he wanted to talk to her about. But the drowsiness had turned to exhaustion, and she couldn't stay on her feet too much longer.

She hobbled over to the bathroom and shut the door without turning off the light; she had always left the light on in the bathroom since she was a girl. She turned and made it to her bed, where she threw back the covers and collapsed onto it. She tucked herself in, and the feeling of the pillow on her head was heavenly. Quickly, she turned off her lamp, rolled over, and pulled the covers to her neck and ears. It took her no time for her to feel her body start to fade. Then, in just a matter of moments, her eyes shut.

Her last thoughts of the day were about sleep and nothing that had happened. Nothing about peace or death scrambled across her mind. She was free for a moment, but those thoughts would return in the morning. But for the night, she carelessly drifted into a deep sleep.

After she left, Magnus unclipped his sword from his side and carefully propped it up against the wall next to the bed. He was by himself and knew that sleep was calling him, but he couldn't sleep in his battered clothes or with his soot-covered skin. The first thing he thought of was a new outfit to sleep in, so he went to the dresser and grabbed something that used to belong to Frory. It was a bit big, but he didn't really care. He took it with him as he walked over to the bathroom. Then, he looked at his face for the first time in a while. It was covered in soot, with clean lines drawn by tears that had run down the sides. He tried to wipe it off, but it was stained on his skin.

He sighed and went to the shower, and he turned the water on. He let it run for a while until it got to the perfect mix of warm and cool, enough to refresh but also to feel clean. As he stepped in, the dirt of the last few days circled to the drain beneath him, and with it came a sense of acceptance. There were still countless images of Rain that flashed through his head. Countless memories of tears streaking down his face plagued him, yet there was acceptance. He wasn't entirely sure where it had come from, but it felt like what happened was the beginning of something new. Through all the suffering, he had made peace between groups that could have never imagined it. Yet, Rain was still there.

The water ran from his hair down his back and to his feet, and every drop felt perfect. He carefully washed his hair and tried to avoid thinking, but the images of Rain replayed through his mind. He couldn't forget him now, and he doubted he would ever be able to. The water kept running down his body as he replayed every second over and over in his head. The feeling of acceptance was fading, but he knew there wasn't another plan besides it. He knew moving on was what it would come to if he wanted to live a proper life.

But this logic led him to feel guilty for even being alive. He placed his head carefully on the shower wall and whispered, "It wasn't your fault." He couldn't believe himself, and, in frustration, he quietly hit the side of his fists on the wall. There wasn't anything he could do now, but the guilt and sadness still dug at him. Moving on felt impossible, but he had to. This stoic notion allowed him to stand himself up. "You're not gonna stop," he whispered as he stood. Finally, he reached down and turned the water off.

The new silence echoed through his ears, and a wave of loneliness came over him. He stood, in the shower, with no one but himself to keep him company. It wasn't for long as he grabbed his towel and dried himself from the head down. He shook his head dry and started to put the clothes on. The soft, unused fabric was pleasing to his battle-beaten body. It didn't take long for him to put the clothes on, and he was quickly in front of the mirror again.

His exasperated eyes greeted him. They were the same shade of green he had always seen, but something felt different. They had seen much more than the old pair he was used to looking into. They were hurt, but they were alive.

He stared at himself a bit more until he nodded and shut the door. He always left the light on when he slept. The reason he nodded was a reconciliation with himself. He had no other plan but to keep moving regardless of what came at him. There was so much pain inside, but he wasn't going to let it dominate him. So, the nod was one of acceptance for what had happened but also a nod of self-agreement. The sadness still pulsed through his golden blood, but it he wouldn't let it be the only thing he focused on. That's what that nod meant; it meant moving on. He could never move on in one day, but this was the first step to him finding what it really meant.

Only the vacant bed sat in front of him, and he yearned for it. He hoped that the exhaustion would make him collapse before any thoughts could cross his mind. Then, he fell into the bed and stared at the ceiling. He took a deep exhale and rolled to turn off the light. The lamp clicked, he pulled the covers to his chest, and he rolled over. The pillow greeted his head with the comfort he had nearly forgotten. His eyelids got heavy, and his mind started to go numb. His last blink shut off any thoughts, and the last thing that crossed his mind before drifting away was Rain's face, a memory that would be with him for the rest of his life. Then his body shut off, and he succumbed to exhaustion and fell into a deep sleep.

So, both Magnus and Treni slept in shallow tranquility, for their pain and hardships would not be easily forgotten. But they were the remains of the Berserkers and the Devil's Hand, and their pain was only a catalyst for what could happen next: peace. That is what the city and the clan's remains had won through their pain, peace.

ABOUT THE AUTHOR

Connor MacHarg is a rising freshman in college. He has always been fascinated by storytelling and the power it has over the imagination. Over the course of his final year of high school, he played goalkeeper for the soccer team, spent time forming lasting friendships, some being characters in the story, and decided to embark on a writing journey he never thought would happen. Sure, he had written a small book in the sixth grade, but the quality was questionable. He currently lives in Georgia with his loving family and adorable dog named Finn. He also plans on writing two more novels following the story of *The Gilded Boy*. He is looking forward to whomever reads his story to be as captivated and immersed as he was while writing it. Thank you for the support, and he hopes you enjoy.

www.ingramcontent.com/pod-product-compliance
Lightning Source LLC
LaVergne TN
LVHW041747060526
838201LV00046B/930